FOR THE PEOPLE OF KENYA

WHAT THE CROCODILES DON'T EAT...

WILL BE WASHED INTO THE SEA

GUY HALLOWES

National Library of Australia Cataloguing-in-Publication entry

Creator: Hallowes, Guy, 1941- author.

Title: What the crocodiles don't eat... will be washed into the sea / Guy Hallowes.

ISBN: 978-0-6484790-8-6 (paperback)

Series: Hallowes, Guy, 1941- author. Winds of change ; bk. 2.

Subjects: Corruption--Fiction.

 Kenya--Fiction.

Dewey Number: A823.4

Cover design by Designerbility www.designerbility.com.au
Layout by OMNE www.omne.com.au

Published by OMNE www.omne.com.au

Contents

Chapter 1 7

Chapter 2 13

Chapter 3 33

Chapter 4 39

Chapter 5 49

Chapter 6 64

Chapter 7 69

Chapter 8 73

Chapter 9 77

Chapter 10 91

Chapter 11 103

Chapter 12 111

Chapter 13 117

Chapter 14 127

Chapter 15 133

Chapter 16 137

Chapter 17 144

Chapter 18 168

Chapter 19 172

Chapter 20 180

Chapter 21 185

Chapter 22 190

Chapter 23 200

Chapter 24 214

Chapter 25 227

Chapter 26 231

Chapter 27 235

Chapter 28 249

Chapter 29 273

Chapter 30 284

Chapter 31 292

CHAPTER 1

After a Mau-Mau raid on a farm in the so-called White Highlands and the subsequent long chase by the Kenya security forces, Kinua had, with two colleagues, stayed behind in a desperate rearguard action to allow his friend and leader Kahinga and the rest of the gang to escape into the dense forests of the Aberdares where they thought they would be safe from further pursuit. Kinua's two colleagues were killed and he was captured.

Militarily, in this, the later stages of the Mau-Mau emergency in Kenya, the insurgents had been all but defeated by the massive British military machine now in place in the Colony. Kahinga led one of the few gangs remaining at large in the forests.

Kinua was tall for a Kikuyu, at almost six foot; normally he was slim and athletic. He had high cheekbones and an aquiline look to his face, indicating some Masai blood in his background. The girls generally found him very handsome. Now he was thin and undernourished, and slightly stooped and worn out from his long sojourn in the forests of the Aberdares being constantly harried by the security forces; his hair was long and unkempt and full of lice. He stank since he had not had a wash for at least two years; partly this was from necessity and lack of facilities but this helped the Mau-Mau in their need to remain undetected: like any wild animal they could smell a security force patrol from a mile away especially if the wind was favourable.

After his capture he was immediately taken to the major interrogation base in Nairobi and there despite the very harsh interrogations he had to endure was at least allowed to wash and his head was shaved and for the first time for some years he had three meals a day. The authorities in the interrogation base, whatever their inclinations, were obliged to treat prisoners with some appearance of decency, being in the eye of the high command. The interrogators wished to know where Kahinga was headed. Kinua had no intention of telling them anything, except his name, so he was beaten nearly every day with askaris (police constables) wielding kibokos (Hippo hide whips) and they also, in their frustration, beat him with rifle butts.

After on particularly savage beating his interrogator, a very sadistic sergeant Jones shouted at him: 'This will go on until you tell us where that rabble headed by Kahinga is headed.' Kinua just spat at his feet and looked away, which resulted in another frenzied beating, rendering Kinua semi-conscious. A bucket of cold water was thrown over him, reviving him somewhat. 'You will die here, very soon, unless you tell us something,' yelled a frustrated Jones. This time Kinua answered in Kikuyu and was rewarded with a fist in the face from Jones.

The interpreter translated: 'I was prepared to die in the forests; it makes no difference to me if instead of that I die here, and you can go and fuck your mother.' Instead of further beatings Jones just stormed out.

A few days later Jones came back with a nasty but triumphant look on his face: 'Without your help we tracked that animal Kahinga down and most of his gang were shot dead.' Kinua didn't even look at him. 'Well, don't you want to know whether your friend Kahinga is dead or alive?'

Kinua looked him straight in the eyes and said in Swahili: 'The lion does not listen to the lying hyaena.' This resulted in a flurry of blows and Kinua was left lying on the floor in a pool of blood.

Within days Kinua was told that it had been determined (by whom he did not know) that he was 'hard core' Mau-Mau and that he would be sent to Hola. Kinua had no idea what Hola was or what horrors it held for him. The camp was located in semi-desert country, on the banks of the Tana River in the remote Northern Frontier District (NFD), about eighty miles from its mouth and far from any population centre. Rising on Mount Kenya the Tana is one of the longest rivers in Kenya, flowing north east off the mountain into the semi-desert of the NFD before turning sharply south and emptying itself into the Indian Ocean between the small seaside resort of Malindi and the island paradise of Lamu further north. The local population are all nomads who held no sympathy for the Mau-Mau, all of whom were Kikuyu or cousin tribes Embu and Meru. Escape was therefore impossible: if an escaped prisoner was not attacked by wild animals he would get no help from the locals and indeed they would probably kill him.

The authorities at Hola were quite out of control and the inmates were subjected to almost daily beatings. All the warders were other than Kikuyu and took a great deal of satisfaction in humiliating the Kikuyu, who under the protection of 'Pax Britannica' had become the dominant tribal force in the Colony, mainly because of their energy and intelligence; also the Kikuyu areas surrounded the capital, Nairobi, to the north, so they benefitted from their proximity to the white settlers and their technology.

At the prison camp, there were many attempts at trying to make the prisoners work, all of which were unsuccessful. There was a general agreement among the inmates of Hola that they would not work: this gave the authorities all the excuses that they needed to beat prisoners which they did almost every day. This was despite the instruction from Nairobi that the only occasion in which force could be used was if guards were physically threatened. The food was sparse and not very nourishing and many of the inmates just became weaker and weaker.

On a fateful day in early 1959 the prisoners were divided into three groups: one to the kitchens, one group went for medical treatment and the largest group of over eighty were assigned to dig a ditch. This was nothing new and all the men so assigned absolutely refused to work. Kinua was in the latter group and Kahinga who had now also been sent to the camp had, luckily for him, been assigned to the kitchen detail.

That day the beatings took on a new intensity and they were savage in the extreme with guards, encouraged by their white superiors, using kibokos, rifle butts, rungus (wooden clubs) and anything else that came to hand. Kinua could see what was happening and tried to organise some resistance but they had no weapons of any sort and his group was isolated and were then subjected to even worse brutality. Kinua was being held down by three warders whist another aimed a blow with his rifle butt at Kinua's legs which missed as Kinua squirmed away. One of the white warders more with an eye to preserving his own job and skin, than in protecting people under his care, could see that the situation was getting out of control and yelled suddenly: 'Stop, Stop,' just as the second very savage blow from a warder's rifle smashed down on Kinua's leg. There was an ominous crack and Kinua howled in pain. All four warders then just ran, leaving Kinua on the ground with what was obviously a badly broken leg. All the injured, including Kinua, were dragged off to the very inadequate hospital facility within the next three hours. The mayhem initiated by the authorities was stopped just too late: as it turned out, eleven of the prisoners died. Kinua's leg was never properly treated and he would walk with a limp for the rest of his days.

The British Government tried to claim that all the prisoners who died had all drunk from a water cart that had been contaminated. This was pure invention and was quickly shown to be the falsehood it was. Hola was closed down a few months afterwards and the prisoners were released and told to go home. No transport was arranged, the gates if the camp were opened and that was that. Kinua was still unable to walk properly and he was dumped outside the gates with his friend Kahinga, who was able to help him. Kahinga had taken as much food from the kitchens as he could manage and he made Kinua a makeshift crutch. They struggled along the dusty road trying to get help. After many failed attempts they managed to persuade a lone canoeist to take pity on them and he laboriously paddled them upstream to the small local centre of Bura. 'We have no money but we will pay you when we can get word to our families to come and rescue us,' said Kahinga.

'I will wait until they come,' was the answer in Swahili. They waited a day, then two three and four days. 'Where, where are these people of yours,' the canoeist yelled at them. 'If they do not come I will kill you.'

After a week a rather battered pick-up driven by N'guku and with Kinua's wife Sarah and Kahinga's wife Wanjiru as very anxious passengers found the pair under a tree in Bura, the only place that they had been able to find shelter. They had run out of food and the canoeist having refused any further help was sitting disconsolately nearby. The canoeist started to demand money: Sarah offered him fifty shillings and was prepared to go to one hundred shillings. The man then completely lost his temper, grabbed his spear and was about to stab Sarah when Kahinga who had been watching the process cracked the man on the head with a rungu knocking him unconscious. Kahinga flung the spear into the river, bundled the man into his canoe, stuffed the fifty shillings into the man's pocket and pushed the canoe out into the current travelling downstream. The canoe would be several miles away before the owner woke up and by then the Kikuyu would be well on their way home.

They all realised that leaving Bura was a priority after this incident, which they all hoped had not been seen by anybody else, but they needed food so Sarah went to a local shop to purchase some of the necessities. 'Why did you buy so little?' asked Wanjiru.

'Prices, as soon as they saw me they doubled the prices. We can get more in Garissa, these people are just thieves and they don't want us here.'

They were just about to go when a local policeman sauntered up and started examining the vehicle, which they could all see was not in the best condition. Kahinga whispered to Sarah: 'I need another fifty shillings.' She was about to ask: 'What for,' when he glanced at the policeman and she handed it over. He greeted the policeman politely in Swahili and surreptitiously handed him the fifty shillings. The policeman without even looking at Kahinga merely sauntered away.

'Come let's get out of here,' Kahinga said to N'guku and they drove off. They stopped for fuel and food in the local administrative centre of Garissa, about sixty miles upriver from Bura. Garissa was a larger place than Bura and the local population were used to all sorts of people visiting the town from the Somali to the east, the more local Boran and the Rendille and Samburu from the north-west.

Kinua was able to lie down in the back of the vehicle and Sarah helped to make him as comfortable as possible. Wanjiru and Kahinga were dropped off at Kahinga's village near Thika and then they drove all the way to Gil-Gil to the white owned farm where Zacharia, Sarah's father, was established. Sarah and her children had spent most of the years of the emergency with Zacharia, interspersed with a stint looking after Kamau, Peter and Rafiki Lawrence's son, whilst Kinua was fighting in the forests.

Zacharia had never had any time for Kinua or the Mau-Mau and he made life very difficult for the family after Kinua arrived. He had also heard rumours that all white owned farming land was to be purchased by the Government, including the farm that he had squatted on for forty years, and that black families would be resettled on that land. He was extremely anxious about this development since it threatened his own way of life and he wondered whether he would be able to stay where he was and if not where he and his now extensive family, would move to. So from the start his mood was anxious and hostile. As far as he, Zacharia, was concerned the advent of the white settlers had substantially benefitted him and his family and he could see that he might be losing all of that with the advent of Uhuru (independence).

'It is a pity that your miserable husband did not die in the mutoni (forest) or at Hola; he is useless and can't work,' was typical of the remarks he made to Sarah.

After two months and when Kinua had sufficiently recovered his health they contacted Kahinga who agreed that it would be better for Kinua, Sarah and their two children to move to Kahinga's village near Thika.

Zacharia's passing comment shouted at them as they left: 'Tell your no good father that he still owes me three cows as part of the bride price for Sarah.'

The whole ghastly episode surrounding Hola only emerged after the 1959 British election. If the terrible truth regarding Hola had been known before the election, the probability is that the Conservatives, who held on to power in that election, would have been thrown out as a result. If there had been any doubt, in Britain, about the wisdom of trying to maintain Kenya as a dependency those doubts were wholly dispelled by the events at Hola. From then on with Ian Macleod as the newly appointed Colonial Secretary Kenya was moved swiftly on towards independence, which was achieved on December 12th 1963.

CHAPTER 2

Peter Lawrence and his Kikuyu wife Rafiki knew that they would have to leave 'Naseby', Peter's farm in the Ol'Kalou district of the so called 'white highlands' of Kenya. A critical part of the Kenyan independence settlement was the purchase of most of the white owned farms in the Colony for resettlement by the burgeoning black population. Ol' Kalou was to be settled by Kikuyu, although prior to the advent of white settlement the area was used by the Masai as an emergency grazing ground. All the names in the district are Masai (Ol'Kalou, Ol' Joro Orok, Ol' Bolossat, Oleolondo and so on).

Ol'Kalou, in the Great Rift Valley at nearly eight thousand feet above sea level, is located on a plain a few miles from the extensive and pristine forests of the Aberdare Mountains (Nyandarua in Kikuyu) which forms the eastern boundary of the Rift in this part of Kenya. It is about thirty miles from Nakuru to the west through the Bahati forest and about one hundred miles northwest of Nairobi through Naivasha and Gil-Gil. The Great Rift Valley is a depression, formed millions of years ago, that extends from the Dead Sea in Israel to Lake Malawi in Central Africa.

Peter, having played a significant role in the independence settlement, was to be Minister of Agriculture in the new Kenyatta led Government, so he, Rafiki, Kamau, and John had to make a plan to move to Nairobi. Peter was a big man, six feet three inches tall; he was well built and weighed just less than 200 pounds. Although older and greyer than in his youth he still had an impressive physical presence.

Kamau was the now pre-teen son of Peter and Rafiki. He had spent much of the last few years in his grandfather's village near Thika in what had been the Kikuyu reserve. That was before Rafiki had been wounded by the security forces, convicted to be executed and then reprieved at the last minute. Prior to this episode, Peter had been banished from Rafiki's father's village and so had seen nothing of either Rafiki or Kamau during a large part of the emergency. John and his brother Robert were Peter's sons from his marriage to Jenny who had been killed in a horse riding accident, on Naseby, many years earlier. John was in his final years at the Duke of York School (for European boys, during the colonial era) near Nairobi and Robert was at Oxford University in England.

Peter was excited about his new role. He was comfortable that justice had been done with the settlement resulting in the independence of Kenya. This was despite the fact that he had had to leave the place where he had spent a large part of his life transforming an unproductive piece of African bush into a highly productive farm. He had never lived in a city before and was wondering how he would deal with that. He had savings from his now world renowned photography business and he knew that there would be some funds left over from the sale of the farm once he and paid off the associated loans and all this would be sufficient to purchase a house in Nairobi without recourse to a loan.

Rafiki had loved living on Naseby but she was quite happy to be moving on with her life. She had escaped being executed by the British by a mere minute and was determined to make the most of her situation. Always slim bright and very pretty, she had been brought up in a typical Kikuyu village in a grass hut, so the rather primitive stone cottage on Naseby was, in a way, a step-up for her, not that she ever considered it in that fashion. The houses that they considered purchasing in and around Nairobi looked like palaces to her so she relied on Peter's judgement. Her concerns were that she should not be too far away from the schools that the boys would attend. With the independence settlement and the desegregation of the schools Kamau would also now be able to attend The Duke of York, shortly to be renamed Lenana after the lesser of the two peaks on Mount Kenya.

John and Kamau were just excited by the move and they ran around the gardens of the various places they saw.

Peter eventually settled on a property in the outer western Nairobi suburb of Karen, which was only two or so miles from the school and ten miles from central Nairobi, but satisfied his need for space. He was wondering what to name the place, when Rafiki said to him: 'Sattimma, why not call it Sattimma. That will always remind you of the view you had of the main peak of the Aberdares from Naseby, one of the things that attracted you to the area in the first place. For me it will always remind me of what we fought for and those tough days in the forests for all those years.'

Sattimma was a large well laid out property; there was a long dusty driveway from the road and a row of sheds on the right for Peter's and Rafiki's cars. The house was a double story: the ground floor consisted of a big lounge and separate dining room together with an old fashioned but well appointed kitchen and scullery as well as two rooms that Peter and Rafiki would use as their offices. There were four bedrooms and two bathrooms on the upper floor. The lounge flowed out on to a well shaded verandah which in turn spilt out on to a large garden with trees and colourful flowers round the periphery and an undulating lawn that was kept green by constant watering. At the rear of the house was the line of Blue gums behind which there were a number of well appointed huts that would accommodate the servants for Sattimma, and there were several 'spare' huts as well. From the driveway one was able to enter the house from the back steps and a small verandah which opened out into the kitchen.

During the final drive from Naseby to their new home and life in Nairobi the whole family were silently aware in this the last time they would regularly make this journey and they each reflected on the real beauty of the place that they had called home.

On the way to Nakuru, as was often the case there was a family of the elegant Colobus monkeys, high up in the trees of the Bahati forest excitedly chattering at their vehicle as it drove past. The pink fringe of the flamingos surrounding Lake Nakuru was as spectacular as ever as they emerged from the Bahati and started the step decent towards Nakuru. The familiar drive from Nakuru, now on the tarred road that Italian prisoners of war had built, went past Lake Elementeita to the scruffy little town of Gil-Gil, still a major British military base. They had lunch at the Bell Inn in Naivasha and beyond that unattractive little place, were on the lookout for herds of Thomson's gazelle, Zebra and Giraffe grazing peacefully with the backdrop of the extinct volcano of Mount Longonot on their right. They all laughed at what they had known as the 'Bay of Biscay' describing the undulating state of the road in that part. As they started the steep and spectacular ascent from the floor of the Rift Valley, Peter asked if anyone would like to stop at the little church built by the Italians during their time constructing the road. There was a chorus of assent. The drive through Kikuyu to Dagoretti was less inspiring and Peter pointed out the massive overgrazing which had resulted in parts of the Kikuyu Reserve becoming little more than a dust bowl: 'It's just the growth in the population that is responsible for all this; there is not enough room for everybody anymore. As much as anything this is what led to the Mau-Mau and the resettlement that Naseby is now part of. Look at the size of some of those cattle, only a little larger than goats.' Rafiki kept her peace: she knew that the advent of the Mau-Mau was more complicated than that but she didn't want to spoil the day with any kind of disagreement. They drove down the Ngong road and all excitedly leapt out of the vehicle when they arrived at Sattimma, to be greeted by a cook and a housemaid who Rafiki had engaged.

While they were settling the family into Sattimma, Rafiki had been thinking about what she might do for the country and indeed for herself. She valued her life and situation, occasionally when she had a 'down' moment or an inkling of self doubt she reflected that she might easily have been executed by the British, so as far as she was concerned the fact that she was alive was a bonus to be used as positively as possible both for herself her precious family and the wider community. She had been visiting Njoki who had been a member of her age group and had been part of the same initiation ceremonies Rafiki had participated in. Rafiki, herself, now safely ensconced in a large comfortable house in the leafy suburb of Karen on the outskirts of Nairobi was conscious of her good fortune and how it could very well have turned out very differently.

She had eventually tracked Njoki down to a small poorly built cottage in the heart of Pumwani, just east of the Nairobi city centre, which was one of the largest of the disgusting slums that had grown up around Nairobi over the years to accommodate the ever growing population. The cottage consisted of two small rooms built from concrete blocks by the city council some years earlier. The cottage had no running water and no toilet. There was a tap fifty yards away for water and the bucket that they used as a toilet was emptied into the unmade street daily. Alternatively people made use of the communal toilet at the end of the street, which although it was cleaned every day by the community was often filthy and smelly, because it was wholly inadequate for the number of people using it. Rubbish was dumped into the street by all the residents and periodically this with all the other debris was swept up and collected by the municipality.

Njoki's husband had tried to get elected to parliament, but he was one of many and had so far failed. He had a poorly paid job as a clerk with the railways and commuted by a very crowded and not very reliable bus.

Initially Rafiki was horrified at her friend's situation but after her second visit she realised that once a visitor had accepted the slum as it was that there was a real community in the slum which had its own unofficial organisation, providing some support for those in need and it also helped to keep order. So instead of her initial perceptions of complete hopelessness she realised that the situation was far from hopeless and with a little help people could, through their own efforts, create a life for themselves and gradually improve their lot. Njoki somehow had coped with the situation, she made certain that her three children attended school every day and she was part of a group of women who made representations to the municipality on numerous issues, such as rubbish collection, bus services, medical facilities and so on. Her family were always fed and clothed adequately. She could see and naturally resented the difference between her own situation and that of another of their age group who was now a deputy Minister in the Ministry of Works: 'That Johanna Kariuki, he lives in a big house and his wife goes to Ulaya almost every year,' she observed during one of the conversations with Rafiki. She laughed: 'He was the one who cried when the witchdoctor cut his foreskin, and now look where he is.'

After a few visits Rafiki was starting to get an idea of how she could possibly help her people, a large number of the people in Pumwani were Kikuyu, mainly because the Kikuyu tribal areas adjoined Nairobi to the north, although there were also increasing numbers from the other tribal communities in Kenya attracted to the large city. So she kept asking: 'What does this community really need?' All sorts of ideas were put forward by Njoki and the many people who popped in to her house from time to time.

The people were especially curious about Rafiki; how she had escaped from death row, her now celebrated marriage to Peter, an M'zungu (white man), and her Nusu-Nusu (lit: half-half or half caste) son Kamau. When they realised that she was genuinely interested all sorts of ideas were put forward: bus services, sanitary arrangements, water, medical facilities and many others.

'What about clinics?' offered Rafiki on one occasion.

The three women that had crowded into Njoki's house looked at her curiously. 'What do you mean, clinics? Now, if we are sick we just go to the hospital.'

'Is that easy?' asked Rafiki. She thought that she knew the answer but she wanted to hear from them.

'Well you have to take a taxi if you are very sick, which is very expensive or you go on the bus, which takes too long and then you have to wait in a very big line, sometimes all day, to get seen by a doctor. Usually the doctor just gives you a few pills and then sends you away. Ugh, there are just too many people,' said Njoki and then she giggled. 'Maybe I am talking too much.'

'No, no,' said the others in chorus 'you are right, that is what always happens.' For ten minutes they all shared stories of their last visit to the hospital.

'So, if we set up a clinic here in Pumwani, would that be helpful?' asked Rafiki.

'Yes, yes,' was the chorus.

'What would we want the clinic to have?' she asked. They quickly came up with a list of basic things.

Then Njoki said: 'But who is going to pay for this clinic; the Government people, all they are worried about are their big cars and big houses and trips to Ulaya (England or overseas). They are not worried about clinics in Pumwani.' There was a chorus of assent.

'Are there any buildings here in Pumwani that are not being used that we might be able to make into a clinic?' asked Rafiki. There were some doubtful glances around the room.

Rafiki sensed fear. 'What's the problem,' she asked.

Njoki eventually responded quietly: 'Well there is this man Mwangi Mkubwa (big Mwangi), but he is a very kali (fierce) man and he does not listen to anyone but himself. He owns many places in Pumwani, shops and beer halls and other sheds and houses, many houses. Maybe he is involved in selling drugs, I am sure that he has places that could be used for a clinic but he will want a very high rent I think for such a place. He has these men around here, bad people, who beat us up if we don't do what Mwangi Mkubwa wants.'

'Have any of you been beaten up?' asked Rafiki.

'They were going to beat my husband up when the rent was late, but he paid quickly and so they did nothing. They are very kali,' said one of the women quietly.

'Where is this man, where can I find him?' Rafiki held up her hand as they were about to answer, 'and, can you first show me one or two of these places that he owns that might be cleaned up for a clinic?'

'He lives very close to here, there is a big place there with big walls and barbed wire around it; they say there is a big house in there as well as his office and some sheds. It is very difficult to go there, they have guards at the gate with guns and all that,' said Njoki.

'I don't think that such a place would be suitable for a clinic,' said Rafiki.

'No, but there are other places around that he owns, we can easily show them to you,' responded Njoki. They all went out and Njoki carefully locked the house. The main thoroughfare was an unmade road with potholes and little gullies running across the width of it; the gullies acted as drainage in heavy rain. A few minutes walk down the road they turned off and walked down another laneway where they came to a small shed. There was a man standing outside.

Rafiki asked: 'What does Mwangi Mkubwa keep in here?'

The man looked at her strangely with a faint trace of recognition and answered without thinking: 'Cow skins.'

'Can we see?' asked Rafiki. The man smiled, he now recognised Rafiki and he opened the shed. There were a few cow skins lying in one corner but the place was almost empty. They all looked around, there was plenty of space. 'This would do but it would need quite a lot of building work to make it into a workable clinic,' observed Rafiki.

They walked to another place close by; again there was a man standing around and appearing to be guarding the premises and Rafiki asked him the same question. 'Just cow skins,' was the answer.

'Can I see inside?' asked Rafiki. The man hesitated, looked at Rafiki and then opened the premises. The place needed cleaning up but it had a large space in the front and a number of small rooms at the back. There were a few cow skins in one of the rooms, otherwise the place was empty.

'I think that this place could be made into a very good clinic,' said Rafiki. They walked around the area a bit more; there were a couple of small but well stocked shops on the main thoroughfare nearby.

'Mwangi Mkubwa's shops,' observed Njoki.

'Are they expensive?' asked Rafiki.

'No, not really, Mwangi knows that we can go into town to buy food and things, so he keeps the prices down most of the time; he only puts the prices up when the other shops are closed.'

They went back to Njoki's house and discussed what they might do. 'I will just go and see this Mwangi, on my own I think. He will know that I don't live here and so he won't be able to bully me in any way. I will go now.'

So they all escorted Rafiki and showed her the main entrance to Mwangi Mkubwa's premises. There were two untidy looking guards clothed in what could pass a military style uniform lounging around inside a big solid metal gate all wound around with rolls of barbed wire, that could be opened to take deliveries. Next to that was a smaller gate, also solid and covered in barbed wire, for pedestrians. The men wore jackets that Rafiki assumed concealed firearms.

She walked up to the gate: 'I have come to see Mwangi Mkubwa,' she said to one of the guards in Kikuyu.

'He is not here,' was the surly answer.

Rafiki looked into the yard: 'So how many other Mwangi Mkubwa's are there then, all riding around in big black Mercedes cars, like that one over there?' She pointed to a car clearly visible in the yard. The man looked round uncertainly. 'Tell him that Rafiki Wainaina is here to see him, I will wait here.' The mention of her name generated considerable interest and both guards came to the fence and had a good look; one of them shuffled off to a building about fifty yards away. Within a few minutes he came running back, he unlocked the gate and escorted Rafiki to the building and ushered her inside. The guard vaguely indicated a door at the end of a short passage, before he returned to his guard duties. The passage was dusty but otherwise there was nothing in it so Rafiki walked the few feet to the door, knocked loudly and went in. She found a large room, surprisingly tidy with cupboards and steel filing cabinets lining three of the four walls. There was a large picture window on the fourth wall overlooking a yard in which a number of trucks were parked, one of which was unloading. In the middle of the room was a gigantic wooden desk and sitting behind the desk with his feet on it was a large very fat man who she assumed was Mwangi Mkubwa.

Mwangi was wearing dark glasses and had on a pair of cowboy boots, otherwise he was dressed conventionally in a black ill-fitting suit with a white shirt and red tie. He said nothing for a brief minute and then said in a deep voice in Kikuyu:

'Ah, so it is indeed the famous Rafiki, I wondered if someone was trying to imitate you but I see not.' He took his feet off the desk and indicated a chair. Rafiki sat down. He looked at her briefly and said generously: 'It seems that your husband Munyu did us all a favour by saving you from the British hangman; certainly if it wasn't for you and others I would not be sitting here now, maybe it would be me sitting in jail.' He laughed. 'I am surprised that you are here, firstly how did you find me and then how do you think I can help you. I can't think of anything that I would want you to help me with, and there are no people in the forests that need feeding anymore.' He laughed at his own humour.

Rafiki was a little taken aback by his rather forthright comments, but thought: 'Maybe I can deal with this man, he seems very open, I was expecting a very gruff uncompromising person.'

'I have some friends here who were in my age group during initiation, so I came to see them and they showed me where to come, you are well known in this neighbourhood.'

Mwangi grunted: 'Most people who manage somehow to get out of this place,' he waved his arm around disparagingly, 'never choose to come back, I like it here though, so I have stayed, so why else are you here.' He looked at her shrewdly.

'There is a desperate need for some simple medical facilities here in Pumwani and maybe some of the other poorer areas around Nairobi and to establish such a clinic I need premises.'

'You are going to run a clinic here in Pumwani?' Mwangi looked surprised.

'Yes.'

'Who is going to pay for this, the people here have very little money, and they will not be able to pay much.'

'They will pay nothing, it will all be free.'

'Are you getting money from Government for this?'

'No, they are too busy making themselves rich to worry about clinics in Pumwani.'

He laughed: 'So where is all the money coming from?'

'I will raise it, just watch me.'

'I don't have any suitable premises for a clinic, so what do you want from me?'

'Nonsense, I have just seen two places you own. One would be better than the other, but we could make them both work.'

Mwangi looked surprised. 'What premises?'

Rafiki explained.

'Yes but they are full of hides, cattle skins, you know,' was Mwangi's response.

'No they aren't, I have just been in to both of them and certainly a few skins are stored there, but if you moved all the hides into one place, it would still be only about twenty percent full with plenty of room for any more that you might want to put there. Then one of the places would be empty.'

'They let you in to those places?' he looked surprised.

'Yes, I think that they may have recognised me so when I asked they showed me round.'

'You can't rely on anyone these days, they will have to be dealt with,' he said threateningly.

'No harm was done, I am sure that they are very reliable people, it must be very boring just standing there all the time with nothing much happening,' said Rafiki, 'and my personal interest in hides is very limited.' The last thing she wanted was for the guards on those premises to get into any sort of trouble. 'Anyway, if you let me have one of them,' she described the second place that they had visited, 'we will clean it up and have it painted, we will look after the security.'

'What about rent? You will have to pay rent.'

'We won't be able to pay any rent, I was thinking that maybe if I cleaned up the premises and painted them and made sure it was secure then the premises would be given to us free of rent.'

Mwangi was genuinely taken aback. 'Free, there is nothing free in this world.'

'At the moment all these people,' she waved her arms around indicating the whole suburb, 'go to the big hospital when they are sick; they even go there when there is very little wrong with them. Then they buy everything they want while they are in the city and not in your shops here, because they think it is cheaper to do that and they have already made the effort to go there anyway...'

'What do you know about my shops?'

'Nothing, except that you own several shops in Pumwani,' Rafiki mentioned the location of one shop which was very close to the premises she wanted for a clinic.

'So what has that got to do with getting a place rent free for your clinic? Where all the people with nothing to do will hang about all day?' he said in a tone of disgust.

'Exactly that, the people will come to the clinic and then it will be very convenient for them to buy whatever they need at your shops, so you will sell more and maybe then you will be able to expand your shops and even put the prices up a little bit.'

'You think that your lousy clinic will attract people to my shop?'

'Of course it will; it will be free, it will be efficient, they will not have to wait as long as they do at the hospital. They will have more money to spend at your shops because they will not have to pay bus fares and they will have more time.'

Mwangi grunted, despite himself he was enjoying sparring with Rafiki.

'What are you personally going to make out of these clinics? You said that you were going to establish clinics, so there will be more than one?' he said enquiringly.

Rafiki tried to look surprised. She supposed that in his world nobody did anything without expecting some sort of a payback.

'I will make absolutely nothing, these clinics will be a charity not a business; and I will not be paid, although I expect to pay all the employees, nurses and cleaners and so on. If the first one is successful I expect that in time there will be others. I suppose that since my husband represents this area many people will give him some credit for the establishment of the clinics.'

Mwangi looked contemptuous: 'Mnn, and then when you get tired of doing all this, what happens? It seems to me that there is really no incentive for you to carry on year after year. There needs to be some incentive.'

'The incentive is to provide accessible medical facilities for people who don't have them at present. As you know despite the poverty, there is a thriving community here. Once the clinics are seen to be providing a vital service the community they will not let them disappear, whether I am here or not.'

Mwangi looked at her and then changed the subject:

'All these M'zungu, they have small pricks.'

Rafiki did not want to get into this type of discussion with Mwangi or anyone else. She sighed: 'Another Mwangi, many years ago now, in the forests tried to have this sort of conversation with me, unfortunately he died.'

'Oh, what did he die from?'

'A bullet wound to the chest.'

'Security forces?'

'No, me, I shot him. He wanted more than just a conversation and tried to force the situation.'

There was a brief silence. Mwangi Mkubwa was genuinely shocked.

'If we can have the premises for the clinic without paying any rent, I will certainly tell people that the premises have been given to the community by you. Your reputation is not very good here in Pumwani, this sort of action will be seen very positively here even though as I have pointed out you will actually be better off.' Rafiki swiftly changed the subject.

'What do you know of my reputation?'

'They all think that you are a bully and a thug.'

'All I do is to protect my interests,' he said glowering.

'Yes, and by allowing me to use those premises, rent free, will do a great deal to protect your interests. People will want you to stay here in Pumwani instead of wishing that someone would shoot you, and I expect that you will have no trouble from the police either.'

'I don't have any trouble from the police now.'

'Then that sort of relationship will cost you less in future.'

Mwangi was irritated and at the same time intrigued by this woman, who when she came in to his office looked so innocent and naive, dressed in a pretty floral dress with high heeled shoes and fancy hair style; he now realised that she was very tough, but she had also talked a lot of sense. He could see that having the clinic in his premises really was in his best interests.

'OK,' he said grumpily, 'you can have the premises for your clinic rent free. You will clean it up and paint it and keep it secure. I will move the hides and then you can have the key. You can collect the key tomorrow.'

'Thank you very much,' she leaned over and much to his surprise shook his hand. 'You can leave the key with your people at the gate; I will pick it up there. We will have a formal opening ceremony in a few weeks, I would be glad if you would come to that.'

There was no response from Mwangi and Rafiki let herself out and walked up to the gate. She smiled at the gatemen as they opened the gate out into the street.

Before she went back to Njoki's house she went into one of Mwangi's shops and bought a few staples, really just to check prices. Whilst they were slightly higher than the prices in Karen, to her surprise they were not outrageously so. She went back to Njoki's house and told her the good news. 'No rent? Did he want something else from you?' Njoki smiled knowingly.

'He tried, rather half heartedly, but when I told him that I had shot and killed another Mwangi who tried the same thing on me many years ago in the forests he suddenly lost all interest.' She laughed. 'He is not as tough as he thinks, but we will have to watch ourselves, he will certainly be up to something.'

Rafiki returned the following day, picked up the key and gave it to Njoki, who had arranged for a group of her colleagues to clean the place up. After a good look round the women decided that they could paint the place themselves, whitewash outside and a good gloss inside. Rafiki engaged a carpenter to erect some shelving and a large cupboard for storing medical supplies, as well as a locksmith-she made certain that two of the rooms in the back could be locked and she decided to change the lock on the front door as well. Finally an electrician was asked to make certain that all the electrics were safe and that the meter was only connected to the clinic premises.

Afterwards the electrician smiled at her and asked: 'How did you know that the shop next door was also metered to these premises?'

'Mwangi was always going to be up to something, he must have had it done almost as soon as I left him two days ago; if we leave things as they are he will be surprised when he gets the electricity bill for the shop, I expect that he thinks it will be nothing. So can you fix it so that the electricity for the shop is connected to another of his premises and not this one? I want him to continue thinking that he has put something over on me even though he hasn't.'

The electrician was genuinely intrigued by the conspiracy. 'Of course, he will never find out if I do it properly,' he replied.

While the premises were being cleaned up Rafiki made a list of some of the major white owned businesses in the city and told Peter that she intended to approach them for money to run the clinics, but it needed to be an on-going commitment not just a one-off contribution.

Sitting together near the log fire in their now well furnished sitting room that they had lit for the first time in months, Peter made several suggestions as to who she should talk to first and what her approach might be. They found Nairobi at five thousand five hundred feet above sea level, although temperate, much warmer than Naseby, where the top of the farm was at almost nine thousand feet. There was never an evening on Naseby when they did not have a fire and frosts were commonplace, despite the fact that Naseby was virtually on the equator After the conversation she went up to him and put her arms around him and said: 'Thankyou for that and thank you for not offering to 'phone them or go and see them first; I want this to be my project and I was wondering if you would be tempted to sort of take-over, if you see what I mean.'

'You have already done far more than I could possibly have done, such as dealing with that nasty piece of work Mwangi Mkubwa, who I know something of.'

'Yes, but the businesses I have listed in the City are really the 'white world' in a way, your world if you like, and I thought that you might think that you could do a better job if you ran that side.'

'No,' he replied smiling, 'I don't actually think that I could do a better job, you are clearly on the right track. Anyway, I am not necessarily the most popular man around town; many of the business people in Nairobi have not forgiven me for my activities in the emergency for example. Also they might think that I was trying to take advantage of my position as a Minister in the Government. I would then be tarred with the same brush as some of my ministerial colleagues, who seem to be doing just that.'

So Rafiki tried making appointments on the 'phone. She was unable to speak to any of the people she had targeted at all; they were too well protected by receptionists and secretaries. So she decided on a direct approach and just call in at their respective offices without making an appointment. The first one was a large milling company, located in a big new building in the centre of the city, whose main market audience had to be African. The receptionist just looked up at her enquiringly without speaking as if to say: 'What the hell are you doing here?' Rafiki smiled and said: 'I would like to speak to the Managing Director please, my name is Rafiki Wainaina.'

'He is not in yet…'

'He is a tall good-looking man with grey hair, wearing a smart suit and carrying a briefcase?' the receptionist nodded uncertainly; she had just realised who Rafiki was.

'Then you must have missed him,' Rafiki said evenly, 'I just saw him walk in, tell him I only need ten minutes.' The receptionist dialled a number and there was a brief conversation of which Rafiki only heard one side of course: 'She is standing here in reception, right in front of me.' There was a brief silence: 'She hasn't told me what she wants, but says she only needs ten minutes.' Another brief silence: 'No, her husband is not with her, she is alone.'

The receptionist nodded: 'He says that he will be a few minutes and then you can go up to the third floor, he will see you then.'

'Thankyou, I will wait here then?' asked Rafiki. The receptionist indicated a comfortable chair in the reception area.

After thirty minutes Rafiki returned to the reception and said: 'This feels like an African few minutes, I thought that when the Wazungu said a few minutes that is what they meant. Should I just go up to the third floor?'

'I will call him again,' said the receptionist tiredly. She listened and said impatiently: 'Certainly she is still here; she is standing right in front of me again.' Another silence: 'You said that you would see her, she is waiting, and no, I can't get rid of her.'

Rafiki looked around and then walked over to the lift which luckily was open and pressed the button for the third floor. She stepped out on what was the management floor and asked the Kikuyu woman pushing the tea trolley: 'The Managing Directors office please.' The woman looked startled and then indicated a corner office, so Rafiki marched confidently to the door and knocked politely. There was a brusque: 'Come in.'

As she entered the room he found the tall grey haired man just folding up his newspaper, he looked surprised. 'I am Rafiki Wainaina; your receptionist said you would give me ten minutes of your valuable time.'

The man was clearly flustered but his manners wouldn't allow him to throw her out so he said: 'Yes, yes of course, why don't you sit down.' Rafiki was dressed in a new business suit, her hair was smartly done and she was wearing high heels; she knew that she looked absolutely stunning, even to a middle aged white man, who was almost certainly, by his standards, expecting a frumpy black woman, probably something like one of his house servants. She also knew that her English was impeccable, which would also have been a surprise to him. He didn't introduce himself so Rafiki launched in to her prepared speech, hoping that it would all come out as she had planned.

'I am planning on opening clinics in Pumwani, the people there are all poor and if they get sick, which is often because of the unsanitary conditions in that place, they usually have to go to the hospital and that sometimes takes them all day, which costs them a day's wages plus the expense of a bus fare or taxi.'

'What has that got to do with me? Surely the Government should be providing money for such things as clinics?

'The Government thinks that it can be all things to all people, but that can never be the case. People need to do things to help themselves rather than waiting for Government. Providing clinics is one of the things that we can do to help ourselves in Pumwani.' Rafiki had a shrewd idea that this fitted in with the man's own personal philosophy, such as he had thought it through; his response was wholly predictable:

'Admirable I'm sure but I still don't see what that has to do with me or this company. I pay my taxes and the company pays its taxes.'

'Almost all your products are sold to the African population, and obviously over time because of the sheer overwhelming numbers of Africans in this country, the other population groups will become less and less relevant.'

He knew that, but it was a surprising statement from a person who he thought was an ignorant uneducated African peasant until a few short moments ago. He inclined his head signifying agreement.

'I see advertisements for your products on bill boards, in newspapers and magazines, mostly directed at a sort of generic African consumer who doesn't really exist.'

There was a very surprised look on his face, and he wondered what was coming next.

'There are fifty or so languages spoken in this country, across four different African ethnic groups; obviously Kikuyu, Luo, Kamba, Kipsigis are some of the main African languages and then of course there is English and some of the Indian languages, Gujarati maybe, so communicating individually with all those people must be very difficult.'

A secretary brought him a cup of tea. Rafiki was not offered anything.

'We advertise mostly in Swahili, you have forgotten Swahili in your list there,' he said with a dismissive wave.

'Mmm, the language of last resort; for many people the language of master servant relationships. I think that seeing an advertisement in Swahili often will result in the product being ignored or sometimes creating a hostile attitude towards the product advertised.'

He almost choked on his tea. Rafiki could see he was off balance, but she didn't want to put him completely off side, so she continued before he could say anything:

'Anyway I'm sure that you didn't expect a discourse from me on how to direct your advertising, just to say that if the clinics in Pumwani were associated somehow with your excellent products, that would appeal to all your African consumers regardless of their ethnic roots, and would create a very good impression right across the whole African population.'

He now started to listen.

His secretary bustled in to the office: 'Your next appointment is here; should I bring him up.'

He looked up briefly: 'No, see if you can put him off, I expect to be a little while yet.'

The secretary started to say something, and looked at Rafiki in exasperation as if to say: 'What on earth could she be saying to him that could be so interesting?' but before she could open her mouth he waved her away. Rafiki then knew that she had his full attention.

'A businessman in Pumwani is allowing me to use one of the premises he owns there, free of charge. We are at present cleaning the place up and painting it. I intend to recruit several nurses, who of course will need to be paid, and I am hoping that some doctors will give me possibly a half day a week on a pro-bono basis. My services are altogether voluntary, Mr Watson.' (She had seen his name on the door).

Don Watson didn't know of any businessmen in Pumwani.

'What do you really want from me?' he asked.

'Well what I really need is an on-going source of revenue so that I can run this and perhaps a few other clinics properly. We do not want Government interference, which means no Government funding. We need to do this for ourselves and if it is done properly it will make a very significant difference to the people of Pumwani. I was hoping that many of the businesses in this city would be willing to come together and help fund this project. Maybe it would help if I took you to visit this place to show you that we are serious about this.'

In his thirty years in Kenya Don Watson had never been near Pumwani or any of the poorer areas.

Don hesitated for a moment, and then he said: 'Frankly I'm intrigued; I would like to see the proposed clinic in Pumwani and maybe have a look at the estimates of what you think it will cost to run.'

'Well I have an estimate of the costs as I see things, right here.' From her handbag she pulled out a piece of paper with rows of figures neatly written out. Peter had told her this was the first thing that any businessman would ask, if they were at all interested. Kinua's wife, Sarah had helped her putting together the estimates and Peter had cast his eye over it and told her that as far as he was concerned it looked fine.

Don really did not expect that Rafiki would have thought of preparing estimates, he assumed that she just wanted to run clinics, so was really impressed when she produced her figures. He spent ten minutes going over them with her: 'Here, what's this, this number for contingencies? It seems quite big compared to the rest of the figures.'

'Well, see that estimate for medications,' replied Rafiki, 'which is just an estimate for all the medicines that we will be using. I have not yet seen the drug companies and I am hoping that I will be able to persuade them to either give me the drugs for nothing or at the very least give them to me at their own cost. That figure assumes that they will not cooperate and I will have to pay full price and there may be other things that I have forgotten.'

'I would like to go to Pumwani,' said Don after having had a good look at the figures, 'tell me when you can manage it and I will see what fits in.'

'I can manage almost any time,' said Rafiki. 'I could take you now or maybe tomorrow or another day to suit you.'

'Now would be good,' he said. 'How long will it take?'

'Two or three hours, I can have you back here at lunch time, no trouble.'

'Can I have those cost estimates, please, I will have my secretary type them up and I would like my accountant to cast his eye over the figures.' Rafiki handed over the figures again.

'I think that it would be better to go in my car,' said Rafiki smiling. 'It attracts no attention in Pumwani for obvious reasons as you will see. I imagine that your car might attract the wrong sort of attention, it is better to leave it here.' She laughed.

Don hesitated. He wondered what sort of a wild ride he was in for. Then he thought: 'Peter Lawrence's wife! Maybe he taught her to drive properly; after all he must have had an influence on her impeccable English'

As they got in the car, Rafiki said: 'I take the kids around in this thing so I make sure it is well maintained.'

'Where are the kids at school,' asked Don.

'We have the eldest at Oxford, and John and Kamau are both at Lenana, which is just down the road from where we live. They will both be boarding though, their choice.'

Don had never considered that the black Africans had similar goals to the one's he and his family aspired to and Rafiki was a black African, despite the fact that she was married to a white person. His own children were at school in England, he thought that it most unlikely that they would ever be admitted to Oxford though. All his dealings with the local African population in Kenya had been as servants or lower level employees such as his own personal driver. He helped some of the house servants with school fees, but he imagined this was for some village school in one of the reserve areas, not a place where they could aspire to major universities overseas. He wondered how many more Rafikis there were in the world outside his own experience.

Rafiki competently eased in to the mid-morning traffic, turned left at the main railway station, crossed the mainly Indian area of River Road and turned right into what was the slum area of Pumwani.

After a fifteen minute drive the road became rougher and as they entered Pumwani proper Don found that they were travelling along a rough unpaved road with rubbish littering the guttering all the way along. He did not disclose to Rafiki that he had never been in to the slum before. He was quite shocked with the mean little houses, some of which were built out of concrete blocks but others were erected from pieces of discarded corrugated iron and wooden and cardboard boxes. 'There is no running water or electricity in most of these places,' explained Rafiki, noticing his discomfort, 'and you can see that at the end of each street there is a communal toilet block and a tap where people have to collect their own water.'

'What about all this rubbish?' said Don waving his arms in the general direction of the rubbish strewn everywhere.

'The municipality sweep it up when it gets too overwhelming, often with a bulldozer or a grader. There is no proper rubbish collection; and then they try to burn it so there is the smell of burning rubbish almost all the time.'

The approach to the clinic's proposed premises was equally depressing but Rafiki was pleased to see that there was a largish area around the clinic that had been cleared and that they were getting on with whitewashing the outside. The inside had been transformed and was now beautifully clean; the main front room had been painted and was now gleaming white and the other rooms were in the process of being cleaned up and painted. A carpenter was making some large cupboards and had erected shelving.

Rafiki explained: 'The people will have to line up outside, we will have a nurse receptionist who will take down basic symptoms and then direct the patient to one of three nurses who will prescribe appropriate medication. I am hoping to have a doctor on duty most of the time. Any really serious cases will still have to go to the hospital of course, but most cases will be treated here.'

'When do you expect to open?' asked Don Watson.

'As soon as we can, but I would rather delay things a little and have everything as well organised as possible, before that. When we have been running for a few weeks and we have ironed out all the problems, we will have an opening ceremony. Anyway I still have much to do: I need to make sure that we have enough money to run the thing properly, I need to recruit people...'

'Who is paying all these people at the moment?'

'I am paying the carpenter and electrician; all the others are voluntary, but I would expect to pay them when we are properly funded. The volunteers are people that have been involved with me from the beginning and feel committed to the project; they see it as a community initiative as much as anything.'

'Community?' Don looked around at the surroundings as if to say: 'how can there be any sense of community in such a poor place?'

'Oh yes, there is a real sense of community here, I would not be able to do this if that was missing.'

'Who is this businessman that has let you have the premises for nothing?'

'Mwangi Mkubwa, he is known as, he owns the shops that you see on the main thoroughfare amongst other things.'

They walked over to the nearest shop. The shop assistants knew Rafiki but were intrigued to see a white person in the shop, something that had never happened before in their experience. Don looked around: 'This is a well stocked place, despite its small size; there are many of our products on the shelves here,' he said picking up a packet of mealie meal. 'Reasonably priced as well. I am sure that we don't have any directly supplied customers in this area; I suppose he gets his stock from a wholesaler. Can I meet this Mwangi?'

Rafiki tried to put him off, so she said guardedly: 'You will have to be a little cautious in dealing with this man; he is not a very straightforward businessman.'

Don got the message and did not pursue the matter. 'Something for the future,' he thought.

Rafiki returned to the city giving Don a whirlwind tour of the mean streets of Pumwani and the neighbouring slum of Shauri Moyo: 'You can see the need just by looking around,' she said, as she drove carefully up River Road and parked outside the modern office block that housed the company that Don ran. During the journey Don asked who else Rafiki had seen or wanted to see in the business community. She gave him a few names: 'You were the first, just because of the products you sell.'

'Can you leave this with me for a few days, what I have in mind is that possibly I can gather a group of Nairobi business people together and at least help with the finances,' said Don thoughtfully.

Rafiki glanced at him: 'Yes of course, that would be wonderful, I still have a lot of other things that need to be done, I would be very happy to leave some of the financial arrangements to you.'

Rafiki went back upstairs with Don when they arrived back at his office. She was given a neatly typed version of the figures that she brought with her in the morning, together with what now looked like a rather scruffy piece of paper containing her own estimates. She left her phone number with Don and with his secretary, who now seemed a little more accepting of Rafiki than she had been in the morning.

✕　✕　✕

Chapter 3

Kinua had spent the previous ten years firstly in the forests of the Aberdares (Nyandarua) as part of a group of Mau-Mau under the leadership of his long time friend and colleague Kahinga and then in detention, mostly in Hola, when the Mau-Mau had been militarily defeated by the British.

The first years in the forests were not too bad. Although it was often very wet and they had to be careful of the wild animals, they did have enough to eat and the raids into the white farming areas had been exciting. The latter years in the forests had been very hard. The British and the settlers had virtually destroyed the Mau-Mau "passive wing" and with it an assured supply of food, and the security patrols had gradually increased in intensity until towards the end the bases that he and Kahinga had so carefully set up had been overrun and they had been relentlessly hunted down like wild animals.

After he had been released from Hola, Kinua had then spent two frustrating and unproductive years in Kahinga's village near Thika, firstly recovering from his ordeal and then thanks to the ministrations of his wife, Sarah, he had recovered his health.

Kinua was now a driver in the Ministry of Agriculture. His old boss Peter Lawrence (Munyu to the Kikuyu), now Minister of Agriculture in the new independent Government of Kenya, had found him this job when he and Kahinga had gone to see him just after Uhuru (independence). Both he and Kahinga had worked for Peter as tractor drivers on Naseby, this was before they had left and made their way into the forest as part of the Mau-Mau insurgency.

Kinua, his wife Sarah and their two teenage children were now living at Sattimma. The hut Kinua lived in was much the same as the one he had lived in on Naseby. Certainly he had food in his mouth and some money but really began to wonder what the previous ten years had been all about.

One Friday night he and Kahinga, who also lived with his wife and family on Sattimma, were enjoying a gourd of beer expertly brewed by Sarah. This beer was very special honey beer or Njahe. Sarah said it was in celebration of Kinua's birthday. Kinua had no idea of his birth date or even the precise year he was born; nevertheless, it was a good excuse for a drink and a chat with his old friend. At least now they didn't need to obtain beer permits from their employers as they had had to in colonial times. After some discussion on what Munyu had been up to (Kahinga was Peter's personal driver, Kinua was just in the "pool") Kinua brought the conversation round to what was on his mind.

"More than ten years ago we left Munyu's farm and went into the forest to fight for Uhuru."

"Eh-heh," answered Kahinga. He belched quietly in appreciation of the beer and wondered what was coming next.

"We spent many years in the forests and then many years in the camps."

Kahinga nodded.

"This place," he gestured around him, "is the same as I had on Munyu's farm."

"Eh-heh," Kahinga thought he understood where Kinua was coming from.

"I have no cattle, no land of my own. If I don't work for Munyu in the Government I will have nothing, nothing," he started to get angry.

"Munyu is a good man," responded Kahinga. "He has suffered like us, and he has helped us."

"Yes, yes, but don't you see: all those fat arsed baboons who stayed in their huts and helped the Sirkali (Swahili for British official), they are now in Government, and they have all the land in the reserves. We did all the suffering, all the work; they have had all the rewards."

Kahinga started to say something.

"And my children, what do you think they will do, they just went to the farm school in the last ten years, and they have nothing. Can they go to Lenana, no; this is reserved for sons of ministers and civil servants. Poor people like me cannot afford such a place."

Kahinga nodded. He actually felt much the same although he was enjoying working for Peter.

"Even though Nusu-Nusu can now go to a proper school," Kinua was referring to Kamau and his attendance at Lenana.

Kahinga drank his beer.

"I thought all the Wazungu (whites) would go, there seem to be plenty of them in the streets of Nairobi, even now," Kinua continued.

Kahinga then said, "Maybe you could get some land in the 'Million Acre Scheme'. Many of the whites have left now they have got their money from the British Government. Munyu is looking after this scheme; maybe he can help you out."

Kinua spat contemptuously. "I went there to apply; they told me I would need some money for a deposit, maybe three thousand shillings. This is another scheme for the fat arsed baboons to make themselves rich. Where do I get three thousand shillings?"

Sarah brought more beer. The conversation continued onto more cheerful subjects. Kahinga returned to his hut. He had to be up early the next day to drive Peter out to part of the 'Million Acre' resettlement scheme on the Kinangop.

The next day Kinua was sitting disconsolately outside his hut enjoying the sun but still wondering what life was all about and whether in another ten years he would still be sitting in the same place with the same thoughts.

Rafiki came through the screen of gum trees that separated the big house from the huts occupied by the servants and now Kahinga and Kinua and families.

They greeted each other warmly in Kikuyu. Kinua had always had a lot of respect for Rafiki. In the early years of the Mau-Mau she had organised food for the people fighting in the forest. After she had been wounded and captured, and then nearly executed, the food had dried up and the real hardships had started.

They briefly passed the time of day.

"Kinua, please can you help me, the car won't start and I must take Kamau to the school for Rugby practice."

Kinua got up and with his usual limp walked with Rafiki through the trees. He fetched the heavy toolbox from Peter's garage, and dumped it next to Rafiki's car parked in the driveway.

Within a few minutes he had it going.

"Look, that thing needs a service, from the looks of things it also need some real attention. When you come back I'll take a look at it for you and get the spares from the wholesaler in town." Kinua told Rafiki, who was only half listening.

Just as Rafiki and Kamau were about to drive off the woman from next door came through the little gate that separated Sattimma from its neighbouring property, and approached them nervously. She was white and had only recently moved in. When she saw two black people and a coloured child she almost wished she had stayed where she was. She had met Peter once, briefly, but had no idea what the domestic setup on Sattimma was.

"I'm Joan Sims," she stammered, "I'm having terrible trouble with my car and I need to go into town urgently. I wondered if Mr. Lawrence was about and if he would mind helping me start the thing."

"I'm Rafiki Lawrence and this is our son Kamau and a friend Kinua," Rafiki tried to put the woman at ease. "Peter is not here, but I can take you into town and Kinua could take a look at your car."

The woman looked doubtful.

"Kinua has just got this old banger going," Rafiki thumped the car. "Maybe he can do the same for you, but if you are in a hurry just come with me."

The woman had never heard a black person speak such good English.

"I'll just get my handbag, maybe Kinua can come with me and I'll show him the car," said Joan.

Kinua picked up the toolbox and followed Joan through next door. She trustingly gave him the keys.

Kinua happily spent the rest of the day lovingly doing what he could for the Sims' battered Peugeot. As with most Kenya cars, the suspension had been ruined by bad roads and the exhaust was loose. Kinua nevertheless got the car going and cleaned the engine up as best he could. He was just driving the car round the yard when Joan's husband Geoff drove in and saw this unknown black man driving round in his wife's car. He immediately assumed the worst.

"Hey," he shouted, "Who the fuck are you?"

Kinua tried to smile, but there was no mistaking the man's hostility.

He tried to explain what he was doing in Swahili.

Geoff spoke no Swahili; he'd only been in the country six months.

Luckily for everyone Joan and Rafiki came through from next door just at that moment.

"Car thief," yelled Geoff. "I found this bloody man just about to drive off in your car."

"No, no," said Joan. "He was just helping us fix it; anyway you know damn well the thing wouldn't start this morning."

Geoff calmed down.

Kinua then produced a rather greasy, crumpled piece of paper on which he had got Sarah to write the spares he would need to properly fix the vehicle (Kinua was illiterate).

"What's this?" asked Geoff.

Rafiki explained.

They managed to decipher it all.

"I just had the bloody thing serviced in town," fumed Geoff. "They claimed to have replaced half the stuff in here."

Rafiki translated.

Kinua shrugged.

"It's all old," he said.

Kinua and Geoff went to the wholesalers in town with a list for the Sim's car and Rafiki's car. Between them they managed to make themselves understood and they found they could get most things on the list.

Kinua spent a happy weekend, fixing first Rafiki's car and then the Sims'.

Geoff came over on Sunday evening and found Kinua.

"How much?" he asked.

Kinua didn't understand. He hadn't even thought of it. Eventually Sarah said to Kinua in Kikuyu, "I think he wants to pay you for the work on the car."

They all went to see Rafiki who then told Geoff what to pay.

"This is ridiculous," said Geoff. "That bloody garage charged me ten times that figure and did nothing. I know where I'll be bringing my car for service in future."

Kinua was thrilled with the 100 shillings in his pocket. He thought nothing more of it.

One evening Sarah said to him, "Why don't you fix all the Wazungu's cars?"

"If they bring them I will fix them," answered Kinua.

"But they don't know you are here."

Kinua shrugged.

"Look, that Indian who owns the store, he has an empty shed there, maybe he would let you use that," Sarah continued.

"I don't like Indians."

Sarah started to get impatient. "He probably doesn't like Kikuyu. That doesn't matter, it's just an arrangement. You clean up the shed and use it, it will bring more customers to his store, and maybe he'll let you have it for nothing."

"And the Wazungu will bring their cars there for me to fix." Kinua's eyes lit up.

"Yes."

It took them two weeks to set up. Somehow Sarah persuaded H.Dass, the Indian storeowner, to let them have the shed for nothing for a year. He had no use for the shed and Sarah was right, the place would be cleaned up and he was certain to attract more customers to his store.

Peter helped by lending Kinua money for the tools and heavy equipment he would need. He also persuaded the major wholesaler in town to extend a week's credit to Kinua.

Rafiki painted a big sign: "Kinua's Garage", which was hung up on the corrugated iron shed that constituted his garage.

Kinua also brought a scooter, which he would need to run backwards and forwards into town to buy spares.

The first customers were the Lawrences and the Sims.

Sarah ran the business end of things. She understood the need to charge customers properly and added 50% to all the costs of spares; she also charged Kinua's time out at twenty five shillings an hour. Kinua thought this was exorbitant. Nobody objected. Old spares that had been replaced were always left in the car. Within a very short time they had a booming business; everything was paid in cash. Peter showed Sarah how to open a bank account. Kinua worked like a slave from morning until night as well as all day Saturday. He and Sarah and the two boys Karanja, now sixteen and Isaac, thirteen, spent most Sundays in the place cleaning up and making sure everything was in working order for the onslaught of customers the next Monday morning.

The conversations with Kahinga over a beer on Friday nights now never mentioned the injustices done to them. Kahinga was pleased for his friend. Dass the storeowner was delighted; business had increased; maybe Kinua would even be able to pay him a small rent next year.

※　※　※

CHAPTER 4

One Friday night Kinua had stayed behind for an hour to complete work on a vehicle which was promised for the next day. As he locked up he was thinking how his life had been transformed over the past few months. He wondered whether he could afford to replace the scooter with a motorbike or even a small pick-up truck.

Suddenly two men in balaclavas came out of the shadows, grabbed him and smashed him against a wall of the shed. All the breath was knocked out of him and a knife was put to his throat.

"Listen you son of a stinking Kikuyu jackal," the knife was pressed into his neck, it drew some blood. The words were in Swahili, Kinua thought his attackers were probably Wakamba. "You value this business, do you?" said the voice.

Kinua struggled.

"Of course."

"Then it needs protection," said the voice.

Kinua was silent. He knew what was coming.

"I want one hundred shillings by Monday night," said the voice.

"I need more time. I'll give you two hundred shillings but I need two weeks."

The grip relaxed slightly.

"Two weeks when?" asked the voice.

"Two weeks today, here at ten o'clock at night."

The grip tightened.

"You, your pretty wife, the children, this stinking place," there was the sound of a kick against the wall of the shed, "will all go up in smoke if you don't deliver."

Kinua thought of going to the Police. He looked down—boots! This was the Police. They let him go and melted into the night.

Kinua shakily started his scooter and drove slowly home.

He ate his meal in silence; Kahinga would come round later to drink beer with him, he would know what to do.

"Police, you say?" questioned Kahinga when Kinua told him the story. Kinua nodded.

"Kamba Police; I expect Dass and all the rest of the shopkeepers are paying them off as well."

"We will stop this right here and right now," said Kahinga determinedly. "You say we have two weeks?"

"Two weeks tonight; I said ten o'clock at night."

"Good. You remember we buried some rifles and ammunition in the back of Tembo base, years ago?"

Kinua nodded. Towards the end of their sojourn in the Aberdare Mountains he and Kahinga had buried some rifles and other weapons and ammunition in the very back of the cave that made up their main base camp Tembo. Only the two of them knew of the arms cache and he was pretty sure that nobody would have found them. Tembo had been overrun by the security forces weeks after they had created their cache. The arms would be in good condition; they had covered them in grease, wrapped them in animal skins and the cave was dry.

"I will fetch them and bring ten of our men; we'll sort these stinking, thieving Kamba out."

"It's going to be difficult for me to come with you," said Kinua, indicating his leg: he still walked with a distinct limp from his injuries sustained whilst he was incarcerated in Hola.

"Karanja will come with me. I don't want anyone else to know about our secret." Kahinga's eyes glinted. Kinua could see the adrenalin flowing.

"Karanja is a good boy, he's also very strong. I'll tell him," said Kinua.

Kahinga needed a few days off; he also needed transport. He went to see Peter the next day, Saturday. The conversation was all in Kikuyu.

"I need a few days off," he told Peter.

"Ok, what for?"

"Some business in Nyeri."

Peter didn't think Kahinga had ever been to Nyeri before, he certainly couldn't remember him ever having mentioned it.

"I also need another favour."

Peter inclined his head.

"Can I borrow Rafiki's car? It will take too long if I have to go by bus."

Peter hadn't seen Kahinga so animated in a long time. He smelt a rat.

"I'll ask Rafiki," he said, "but I expect it will be OK especially if you arrange for one of the pool drivers to take your place."

Kahinga spent the next two days making contact with five of his most trusted followers from the Mau-Mau days. They were told to steal a pick-up truck, hide it and be at Kahinga's hut a week the following Wednesday.

"Don't get caught and don't let Munyu see you," ordered Kahinga.

Kahinga and Karanja set off early on the Monday morning in Rafiki's car.

He drove through Thika and then the back way to the Kinangop; he wanted to make sure that nobody saw them. He already had a feeling that Peter suspected something. Without much trouble he found the spot where, years before, he, Kinua, and Rafiki and that double crossing Nderobo, Witu, had first entered the forest to set up his bases. He thought he remembered Kinua telling him that Witu had had his throat cut. He deserved no less in Kahinga's view. (Witu had at first helped Kahinga set up bases in the forest and then he had gone to work for the British security forces.)

He parked the car, and he and Karanja cut branches from nearby bushes and painstakingly camouflaged the vehicle. He was certain that it couldn't be seen even from a few feet away.

At five feet six inches tall, Kahinga was average height for a member of his tribe; he had a sturdy build. His round open face and broad toothy smile were completed with a typically flat African nose and a pair of bright, brown, sparkling eyes. He had natural authority and was a born leader.

Both he and Karanja were well equipped with flexible "jungle boots" from an army surplus store in Nairobi plus good thick khaki trousers and shirt; each had a sweater, a greatcoat and a balaclava. Kahinga had also purchased two large Bergen rucksacks from the same army surplus store. They carried food now but would be filled with arms and ammunition on the way back.

They made their way into the forest. Kahinga was again entranced by the wildness and majesty of the place that had been his home and his protection for some years, but it also brought back dark memories of hunger and privation especially in the latter days of the conflict with the British. The cloud had lifted but it was, as always, slippery underfoot as they scrambled along the once familiar game trails. There was absolutely no evidence of any human activity at all: not a footmark, nothing.

Karanja was really quite frightened; he had never been near the forest before. During the years that his father Kinua had spent in the forest and in detention, he had lived with his mother in his grandfather Zacharia's village, on a white owned farm. He nearly leapt out of his skin when a bushbuck crashed across the path in a desperate attempt to get away from the now unfamiliar human presence. At one stage Kahinga held him by the arm and they crept forward. Kahinga pointed; Karanja could see nothing at first, then he heard a rumbling sound and suddenly saw the large grey shapes of the small herd of elephant in the path in front of them. The herd were moving slowly and eating as they went; the rumbling was from their stomachs. The two men watched for a few minutes. Then Kahinga signalled and they quietly withdrew and continued on another path.

To Karanja the forests were quite alien—eerily silent one moment and full of noise the next. The sound of the tall bamboo noisily creaking and clattering against one another was something he had no experience of. The trees were tall and forbidding and in many places the sunlight barely penetrated to the floor of the forest. He found the game trails very hard to follow and wondered if he was on his own how he would cope; he was certain that he would become lost very quickly. Had his father and Kahinga really spent years in this forest fighting the Wazungu? He shuddered and wondered how he would survive days here, let alone months and years.

For Kahinga the place was like an old friend. He no longer had security patrols to worry about. He enjoyed all the familiar sights and sounds; the wild animals, the occasional snake, many familiar landmarks and the clean damp smell of the place.

They spent the first night under an overhanging rock. Kahinga explained to Karanja how the women led by Rafiki had brought food in here for the fighting men in the forest. They lit a small fire and cooked and ate some of the food they had brought. Kahinga then rolled himself up in his greatcoat and went straight to sleep. Karanja barely slept a wink; when a hyrax started its eerie racket close by he leapt up, panga in hand, ready to fight to the death. Kahinga didn't even stir. Karanja looked about him; he couldn't believe how alive the forest was at night. He saw the eyes of animals attracted by the firelight. He eventually sat shivering in the cold damp air huddled in his greatcoat, panga in hand and waited for morning.

Just as the dawn came up Kahinga stirred, got up and Karanja could hear him noisily urinating a few yards away.

"Best sleep I've had in years," ventured Kahinga.

Karanja just looked at him.

"Did anything happen in the night, it looks as if you spent most of it awake," laughed Kahinga.

"Many noises," volunteered Karanja.

"None of the animals will come near if they smell woodsmoke," Kahinga told him.

They ate some more of the food they had brought and then Kahinga showed Karanja how to bury the fire and eliminate all the signs that anyone had been there.

"Why do you do that?" asked Karanja.

"We did it to confuse the security patrols; now maybe it's better if there is no sign of humans."

Karanja looked at him thoughtfully. He hadn't the faintest idea of what Kahinga was talking about.

They moved on, continuing to climb upwards along the steep, often slippery, paths and within a day and a half they came to the entrance of the cave which Kahinga and his followers had occupied as Tembo base, at eleven thousand feet above sea level. Kahinga's natural caution made him watch the entrance to the base for thirty minutes before they went in. They followed the little game trail at the entrance and silently crept into Tembo, keeping an eye out for any danger. The place was much as Kahinga had first seen it ten years earlier, completely quiet and with no sign of any sort of habitation.

Kahinga showed Karanja around in a very proprietorial way. He took Karanja right into the back of the cave and showed him the secret way out. Then they went to the front of the cave and climbed the large rock from which one could look back into the area in front of the cave and, if one looked the other way, out into the more open areas of the Rift Valley. These areas, once occupied exclusively by white farmers, were now being settled by his people, the Kikuyu. This was what he had fought for, all those years in the forests and in detention. His anger surged again; how unfair it was that the rewards of independence had all gone to the so-called black loyalists, the people who had actually fought for the whites against him. Yet it was he, Kahinga, and his fellow fighters, who had made the British give back their country. He, Kahinga, his friend Kinua and thousands of others like him, had fought and made sacrifices but had gone unrecognised and certainly unrewarded.

They climbed down the rock and Kahinga then went straight to the area where he and Kinua had concealed their arms cache. They had hidden two spades in and old ant-bear hole nearby; Kahinga found these; then he and Karanja moved a large stone from over the site of the cache and dug for ten minutes. They found everything as it had been left all those years before. The arms were in perfect order, covered in layers of grease. Kahinga sorted them out: there was a Bren gun; he'd forgotten about that, he would have to leave that behind. There was the hunting rifle that he'd taken from Bob Halway's farm; the first M'zungu they had attacked and killed. He'd leave that behind too, as he wanted no evidence around linking him to a specific murder. There were several dozen Smith & Wesson .38 revolvers that he had stolen from the Naivasha police station in the early part of the emergency. He selected six of them. There were four Patchett sub-machine guns that they had taken off a security patrol, ideal for what they wanted to do. He left the Sten-guns: "They always jam," he said to Karanja.

Kahinga lovingly cleaned all the weapons he had chosen, and then selected an old tree stump about fifty yards away and started testing the weapons. He instinctively hesitated to do this, as, particularly in the later stages of the emergency, they had always tried to keep quiet for fear of attracting attention from the security forces. He then reminded himself of their present circumstances; they were alone and the forest was deserted.

They were not alone.

Njiri, a little Nderobo, a cousin tribe of the Kikuyu, at about four and a half feet, was typical of his people, who traditionally lived as forest dwellers. He had re-established his family in the forest with his two wives and several children, when all the shooting and bombing in the forests had stopped. Beside the two ramshackle huts, they had a small patch of maize and vegetables, protected as well as possible by bushes that Njiri had gathered over months and which surrounded his establishment, which his wives cultivated, and, despite the depredations of the local wildlife, provided an adequate food supply, supplemented from the now abundant resources in the forest: honey, porcupine, and the occasional antelope which he shot with his poisoned arrows and then followed until the victim collapsed. He was content with his lot and entirely comfortable with his environment. The shooting and bombing in the forests during the emergency had driven him away and he had spent two years working with the security forces as a tracker. At that time all the human activity in the forests had frightened the animals and made them more difficult to anticipate. Now things were back to normal, he and other isolated members of his tribe, had almost the whole Aberdare range to themselves. He knew its every mood and all the little game trails and he could identify every living thing there: the elephant, rhino, the occasional leopard, the very nervous okapi, bushbuck, and all the snakes. If he and his family were short of food he knew of plants and berries they could eat. He did not want any encroachment. As far as he, Njiri, was concerned they could keep their cars and roads and European style clothes, he wanted none of it.

Njiri collected his spear, bow, and quiver of arrows, told his wives that he would be back in a few days and went off into the forests—his forests. He was dressed in a cloak of animal skins that his wives had made for him and he was barefoot.

Njiri found the tracks about two hours into his journey. He'd been following a bushbuck; then he saw the bootmarks. The horror of the years of the emergency returned.

"Boots," he thought to himself, "must be Wazungu." He quickly identified that it was two people he was following, he could see where they were going and he found the area under the overhanging rock where Kahinga and Karanja had spent their first night. Njiri scouted round. He was surprised to find so little evidence of occupation; he eventually dug up the fire, now cold, and found a few scraps of mealie meal. "Not Wazungu," he thought, "they normally eat from cans and leave them lying around, harming the animals." He thought for a minute: "Must be Wakikuyu, ex Mau-Mau familiar with the forests. I wonder what they are up to." It was years since anyone had been back in this area.

Njiri followed the tracks on the run and found his way to Tembo base. The Nderobo normally steered clear of the place, there were many legends depicting the cave as a source of evil; certainly the experiences during the Mau-Mau emergency had confirmed all his prejudices against the place. He crept down the game trail and glimpsed two black men digging something up at the back of the cave. He crept through the bushes using all his very considerable skill in keeping himself concealed and eventually found a vantage point behind a rock with a small bush growing through it.

The men had dug a hole and there were guns strewn around. Obviously they had dug the guns up. Njiri watched.

He saw the older man select a number of the weapons from the pile, take each selected weapon, and after carefully cleaning and loading, fired each one at an old tree stump about fifty yards from him. He was a very good shot. Njiri was familiar with the weapons from his time in the security forces; he had never handled one though.

Kahinga loaded the pistols he had selected and fired them one by one at the tree stump. He fired a thirty shot magazine from each of the Patchetts. He remembered his lessons from his time in the forests and only filled the magazines with twenty-two rounds, as the weapon tended to jam if filled to capacity. Everything was in fine working order. He took one hundred rounds of ammunition for each weapon; if what he, Kahinga, had in mind worked, the weapons would not be fired very often in any case. Kahinga was tempted to try to teach Karanja how to shoot but he remembered his own first lessons from Munyu where he didn't get to fire a shot for two weeks after the lessons started and he decided against it.

Kahinga decided it would be best to spend the night at Tembo base and then leave at dawn to return to Karen with the weapons. He and Karanja carefully wrapped the remaining weapons up again and re-buried them. They replaced the large rock on top of the cache and hid the spades again. They then swept the area to try to make it look as undisturbed as possible.

Karanja had collected a small amount of wood and they lit a fire and cooked some of the food they had brought.

Njiri saw that the men in the cave had decided to spend the night there. There was no chance he himself would spend more time than was necessary in that evil place. He would catch up with his quarry in the morning. It was obvious to him the two men were up to no good, but what should he do about it? There was only one person in the outside world that he thought he could trust and that was Munyu. He didn't really know him, as he had seen him only once and that was in Nairobi outside the courthouse when Rafiki was being tried for her life. He knew his reputation well, however, and his instincts told him that Munyu could be trusted.

Unlike the previous night Kahinga stayed awake and spent some time telling Karanja what he and Kinua had done during the Mau-Mau emergency and in particularly what Tembo base meant to them. It had once been a refuge but it was also a place of death.

Karanja had always regarded his father and Kahinga as sort of irrelevant and old. He didn't think much of their jobs as drivers in the Ministry of Agriculture. He had been intrigued by the success his father had made of the garage. Karanja was frightened of the forest and did not see Kahinga's skill in dealing with that environment as having the slightest possible relevance to his own young life. Kahinga's skill in handling the firearms, though, truly impressed Karanja. He could see the power that proper use of the weapons could give one. He made Kahinga show him how the revolvers and sub-machine guns worked. He was sure he could manage them by himself and was piqued when Kahinga said to him, "You will need proper training before you can be let loose on these weapons, I'll teach you to use them another time."

As before, Kahinga went straight to sleep once he lay down. Karanja stayed awake and managed to filch a dozen rounds of revolver ammunition. He would find a way of taking a revolver at some stage later. Karanja got more sleep the second night in the forest, and found Kahinga was up and about and preparing breakfast when he woke.

"We leave as soon as it starts to get light," Kahinga told him. "We must try to get to the place we parked the car before it gets dark, tomorrow night."

They packed the rucksacks full of the weapons and ammunition, cleaned up the campsite, took the food that was left and as the sky started to lighten, and left Tembo base. The rucksacks were heavy and it was, as usual, slippery underfoot. They made slow but steady progress, now thankfully mostly downhill.

Njiri came into the campsite vacated by Kahinga and Kinua some two hours after their departure. He looked around; nobody but an expert would know that there had been any visitors. Njiri guessed that the older man had been a member of the Mau-Mau and he had obviously spent time in the forests; the other one was too young. He wasn't worried about the start his quarry had. With the weight they had to carry he would soon catch up with them. He had a good idea where they were heading, so he decided to cut through the forest and wait for them further down the track.

Kahinga and Karanja wound their weary way through the sometimes poorly defined game trails. Kahinga was unused to this amount of physical effort and needed constant rests. During one of the stops when Kahinga seemed to be sleeping Karanja managed to slip one of the revolvers into his pocket. After a day and a half they made their way to the car arriving there just before dusk.

Njiri had waited for them a few hundred yards from the car, which he had found earlier that day; he heard his quarry clumping about some minutes before they appeared.

Kahinga still had all his wits about him. He had had a sixth sense that they were not alone in the forest and twice he had doubled back on his own trail to see if anyone was following. To no avail of course. He watched the area round the car for ten minutes before emerging and finding everything as he expected it. They removed the bushes covering the car and drove back to Nairobi.

Njiri had watched from a safe vantage point just fifty yards away. He would have to make a plan to see Munyu. He needed to make sure his family were looked after and then he would have to find Munyu. He wasn't certain how.

Kahinga and Karanja had arrived back late at Karen and Kahinga had taken both rucksacks and put them in the storage hole he already had in the floor of his hut. Wanjiru gave him a troubled look. He didn't have time to check the contents.

Apart from his normal duties, Kahinga had much to do over the next week. He checked with his colleagues that the small pick-up had been stolen and had a load of sand, cement, some wire netting and a forty four gallon drum of water loaded in the back; everything they needed to make concrete. The truck had been hidden in the Ngong forest and could be retrieved whenever they wanted it. Kahinga told them he had collected some weapons. He did not tell them where from.

CHAPTER 5

Peter was used to rising early to attend the morning milking on Naseby and he saw no reason to change his habits now he was an 'office wallah' as he sometimes thought of his situation. Besides he saw no value in becoming stuck in the morning rush. Actually Nairobi had four 'rush hours' a day because people often went home for lunch so there was a morning and evening rush and two rush periods at lunch time.

So Peter was in the office by six thirty on most mornings often after having completed an early morning run in the cool and pleasant atmosphere of Karen.

Kahinga usually drove him the ten miles to the office down the Ngong road past Lenana School round Dagoretti corner, further along the Ngong road then Valley road, past All Saints Cathedral leading into what was still Delamere Avenue, shortly to be renamed Kenyatta Avenue after the country's President and Peter's boss. The statue of Lord Delamere at the top of the avenue named after him was eventually removed to Soysambu, the huge Delamere estate near Lake Naivasha. Peter's office in the Parliament buildings was a right turn off Delamere Avenue just out of the city centre down Uhuru Highway.

During his occasional lunchtime strolls round the centre of the city Peter sometimes reflected on the leading role that Lord Delamere had played in establishing Kenya as a Colony. Delamere had, to his credit, invested most of his fortune in Kenya and had persuaded a sometimes reluctant British Government to change Kenya's status from a Protectorate into a fully fledged Colony in 1919 thus encouraging settlement, with people mainly from the United Kingdom, but other places as well, such as South Africa. He often thought: 'Did we, the white invaders, have any business being in Kenya at all?' Most of the settlers had left or were about to leave at the time of Independence in 1963, bought out by the British Government, so the strategy of encouraging settlement had in the long run amounted to nothing. Few if any of the skills that the settlers brought were directly transferred to the local population. Certainly the whites had brought peace to the area as well as railways, roads, schools and indeed a democratic Government. He reflected that the legacy that the whites had brought was a very mixed blessing, with the destruction of many of the local African traditions being unthinkingly trampled and replaced by poorly understood traditions from Europe.

During their regular trips into his office in town Peter politely asked how Kahinga's visit to Nyeri had gone. He got very non-committal answers, although he could see that Kahinga was excited by something in the background. There was definitely something going on and he was determined to find out what it was. He knew that Kahinga had the capacity to be far more than just his driver and Peter helped him with literacy lessons which Kahinga lapped up like a young child. Peter just hoped that Kahinga could find something legitimate to engage with, knowing that his real skill was leading men in what had been a very dangerous escapade.

Mweleli and Munyao, the two Wakamba policemen, had as usual on a Friday evening done the rounds of the businesses they "protected". Ten businesses at one hundred shillings each. One thousand shillings. They saw very little of this and were normally allowed to keep just ten shillings each. Their immediate superior Inspector Kiprogot expected them to deliver the loot by midnight every Friday night. The inspector knew of the ten businesses and he in turn had to account for the takings upwards to his superiors, and, it was rumoured to the very highest levels. Kiprogot did not know about Kinua's garage nor did Mweleli or Munyao have any intention of telling him. If they could share the "takings" from the garage every week, within a year or so they could retire to their tribal land in the Kamba reserve area near Machakos, south-east of the capital, and forever forget about the Police and their boss, whom they hated mainly because he was from another tribe.

Kinua waited inside the garage with the promised two hundred shillings on the appointed Friday night. He really had no idea what Kahinga was going to do although his friend had indicated that he would do something. At just before ten in the evening he went outside and stood under the bare bulb of the single outside light.

"Here," murmured a voice in the shadows. Kinua could just make out two figures. He went over to them holding the money. They were dressed as before in Police overcoats and balaclavas.

Kinua was just about to hand the money over when four figures came round the corner out of the darkness, and ruthlessly overpowered the policemen by knocking them unconscious with rungus.

There was a shrill whistle and within a minute a small truck appeared from around the corner.

Kahinga leapt from the cab, leaving the driver in the cab with the engine running.

Rummaging through the pockets of the two policemen, Kahinga found what he was looking for; one thousand shillings in cash and more importantly a list. His literacy lessons meant that he could make out the names on the list and the amounts. He grunted in satisfaction.

Completely business-like he said to his companions: "Put them in the truck, and drive towards Naivasha. On the way there, kill them. One bullet in the back of the head will be enough. Burn the clothes separately. Wrap the bodies up in the wire netting, then make concrete and fill the wire netting with the concrete. Throw the bodies in Lake Naivasha and the heads separately into Lake Elementeita. Come back here Sunday night and we can share the money."

"Clean the truck out and dump it down River Road," he added as an afterthought.

"Now go," he instructed them.

The unconscious forms of the policemen were loaded into the back of the pick-up and four Kikuyu clambered in after them. Wanyoike banged on the roof of the cab.

"Naivasha," he yelled.

The vehicle drove off.

The men were all armed with the firearms Kahinga had provided. Wanyoike and the driver had revolvers; the other three had Patchett sub-machine guns. All had been in the forests with Kahinga.

Kinua went back inside the garage. He was just about the put the money back in the drawer. Kahinga had followed him in.

"You must pay too," said Kahinga.

Kinua was completely non-plussed.

"Pay?" he asked.

"Yes, pay, all the businesses round here pay one hundred shillings a week."

"You are going to collect money, the same as those stinking Kamba policemen did?" Kinua couldn't believe his ears.

"Yes, if anyone wants protection they will have to pay. You asked for protection, you will have to pay. I did get rid of the Wakamba for you."

Kinua stared at his friend. Then he started to understand.

"How much?" he asked.

"Same as all the others, one hundred shillings a week."

"What happens when the Police come back?" asked Kinua.

"The same thing that happened tonight."

Kinua handed over one hundred shillings. At least he had saved a hundred shillings.

Kahinga went outside.

Kinua locked the rest of the money in the drawer, switched all the lights out and went outside and locked up.

He drove Kahinga back to Sattimma on the back of his little scooter.

Nothing was said. Kinua wondered if the relationship would ever be the same again. He had thought he was getting rid of the Wakamba, not just replacing them, albeit with his friend.

Kinua had found a niche in the society, and all he really wanted to do was to go on developing that without interference. It seemed that was an impossible dream.

Inspector Kiprogot was now becoming more and more anxious; it was after three in the morning; his other protection groups had reported as usual, but the normally reliable Wakamba in the Karen area had not. This had never happened before. As far as he, Kiprogot, knew, they had always accounted for every cent they had been paid and were always on time. He wondered what had happened. He would certainly have some explaining to do to the Superintendent the next morning, now only a few hours away.

Wanyoike and the Kikuyu were in the meanwhile on their way down the escarpment into the Great Rift Valley. They had stripped the two policemen and with his revolver muffled in one of the greatcoats, he had executed both of them as Kahinga had suggested. There was only very light traffic and any passing car might have thought that the noise of the pistol shot was the truck backfiring as they went down the steep hill. When he fired the first shot the driver swerved in fright.

The Kikuyu then wrapped the bodies up in the wire netting and made concrete in the back of the vehicle as best they could. They stuffed the concrete into the wire netting with their hands. Just after midnight they had arrived in the very deserted town of Naivasha. The driver turned down towards the lake; he had worked there in the days before the emergency and he knew of a farmer there who had kept a boat on the lake. An hour later they found the farm, still in the hands of the original European owner, and had crept down the track to a small jetty on the edge of the lake. Sure enough, there was a rowing boat. The place was completely deserted; there were no lights, but the quarter moon reflected on the surface of the water; there was an occasional quack from the innumerable ducks resting among the reeds.

Wanyoike decided to stay there for a while to let the concrete set; they all also needed a sleep. They finished concreting the bodies. Wanyoike and the driver slept in the cab, two of the others slept under the pick-up and one was left on guard. At about four in the morning Wanyoike woke everyone up and they attempted to move the now solidly concreted bodies from the back of the truck. All the concrete had set so the bodies were stuck in the back of the vehicle. An hour later they had managed to prise one body loose and carry it to the boat. It needed all five of them to do that; they dumped it in the boat.

"It will need two trips," said Wanyoike.

"Take the boat out quite far," he added. "We'll fetch the other body."

He then remembered Kahinga's instructions about the heads. "Too late," he thought, "anyway nobody will find them here."

The two people paddled the boat out into the lake most inexpertly. Neither of them could row and the boat kept going in odd directions and getting tied up in patches of reeds. About one hundred yards out they decided to dump the body. They got it onto the gunwale of the boat with much effort; then the boat turned over, dumping them and the body into the water with a great splash. Luckily for them the water at that point was only about four feet deep so they righted the boat and clumsily pushed it back to shore.

"What happened?" asked Wanyoike.

They explained.

He wasn't too worried; even if the body was only in a few feet of water, he doubted whether many people came down here and the chances of them finding the body, safely wrapped up in wire netting and weighed down with concrete, were remote. He was determined that the second one would be further out.

They loaded the second body into the boat and this time Wanyoike took the boat out himself.

Robin Hillsborough had owned his farm on Lake Naivasha for many years, as had his father before him. The land was not suitable for African settlement and it seemed that he would be able to stay on the farm. He and his family had accommodated themselves to the new political dispensation in Kenya; it seemed they could stay put forever and still enjoy the country that they had grown up in and loved. One of his great pleasures was to go down to the lake in the early morning with his shotgun and dog, and take the little boat out into the lake and shoot a few duck for the pot as the birds rose from their resting place in the reeds and made for the feeding grounds in the middle of the lake. He often walked the three miles or so.

On this particular morning the dog started growling when they were still a good two hundred yards from the jetty. They crept up and saw the pick-up truck parked with three black men hanging about. He couldn't see what they were doing.

Then there was a great splash from some way out in the lake. The dog couldn't contain itself any longer, and it went rushing towards the truck, barking furiously, followed by Hillsborough.

The Kikuyu round the truck were already nervous; two of them were soaking wet and cold. Hillsborough came within about ten metres of the trio and said in Swahili, "What are you people doing here, this…"

The burst from the Patchett took him in the chest and the second burst took the dog out.

"What's up? What's going on?" yelled Wanyoike from the water. The boat was now coming closer.

"The M'zungu came, he was shot," was the answer.

"Is he dead?"

"Yes, I think so, hurry up we must leave now."

The driver started the pick-up and turned it round.

Ten minutes later Wanyoike returned to shore. He had dropped the second body further out, but still in only ten feet of water.

They now had a real mess on their hands; there was a dead M'zungu, which was certain to attract police to the area. He wondered how long it would be before they thought to search the lake. He looked around.

"Don't touch anything, we must go back to Nairobi and dump the pick-up. Maybe they will blame the Indian who owns it. We'll be back in Nairobi before they find the M'zungu's body."

They drove back to Naivasha and were on the main road back to Nairobi before there was much activity on the road. Opening the tailgate of the pickup the remains of the sand and cement were scraped on to the road as they went along. They then washed the back of the vehicle with the rest of the water from the forty-four gallon drum. The empty drum was thrown off the back. They still had the policemen's clothes. Being short of clothes, it seemed a pity to burn clothes which were in good condition. They shared them out and threw away some of their own clothes.

They drove to Pumwani and unobtrusively made their way to their shacks.

Wanyoike went with the driver and made sure that the pick-up was dropped off in the River Road area. Maybe the Indian would just be pleased to have his vehicle back. They rarely reported thefts of this nature to the police, as the last thing they needed was to attract attention.

Wanyoike wiped the cab down to try to eliminate fingerprints.

Inspector Kiprogot as usual went to see the Superintendent at his house on Saturday morning. He handed over the cash. It was carefully counted.

"Where's the rest of it?" demanded Nyamita.

"Those stinking Wakamba didn't show up last night. I can't find them," was the answer.

Nyamita was an enormous Jaluo from the Kisumu area of Lake Victoria. He had always used his size to intimidate people and to get his way. He stood up, came over to the well built but much smaller Kipsigis inspector and slapped him hard across the face. The inspector went flying across the room.

"Don't come in here with crap like that, we want more money, not less. You had better find a way of replacing that money by this time next week."

"How? I don't know where they are. They have probably run back to Machakos," the inspector mumbled.

"Then find them in the Machakos, don't come crying to me."

Nyamita was angry. As soon as he had replaced the M'zungu Superintendent he had set the scheme up. It required very little administration; he collected the bulk of the money but passed some of it up the line to keep his superiors happy. He already had a large sum of money in a Swiss bank account, arranged for him by one of the larger Indian traders. Another five years of this and he could live like a king in Europe for the rest of his life. He had always doubted the wisdom of releasing the Mau-Mau detainees; he now wondered if they were getting fed up with their lot in the new post-Uhuru society. He would have let them rot. He had his spies and informers out in Pumwani. At the first sign of any Kikuyu having more than the normal amount of cash he would pounce.

The phone rang. Nyamita listened.

"Shit, a bloody M'zungu, shot to bits near Lake Naivasha you say? Shot with what? A sub-machine-gun? Anything else, nothing except pick-up truck tyre marks you say?"

He thought for a minute. He knew this would hit headlines around the world. If ten blacks were killed none of the Western Press would give a goddamn; one worthless M'zungu and they would be asked if the country was falling out of control.

"I'll be down there with the forensic people before lunch. Just block the site off; nothing is to be touched. What did you say? The wife has already taken the body back to the house? Told you, you were a useless bloody kaffir! Well, we'll see about her, she's obviously upset, doesn't make our job any easier."

He made three calls.

The first was to his mistress to tell her he wouldn't be there to see her in the afternoon.

The second was to the President to tell him what had happened. He managed to tell him before the press did. Foreign investment he knew was important; if this issue was mishandled the loans could dry up for a while.

He then phoned forensics, which was still run by a European. They arranged to meet at Dagoretti and drive down together.

After an hour at the murder site Joe Crawford, the head of forensics, came to Nyamita and said, "Looks like a group of four or five came down here in a pick-up truck to dump something in the lake. There are some scraps of wet concrete and some blood spots in the boat. It also looks as if we have some fingerprints in the boat. Hillsborough probably just disturbed them. We'll have to drag the lake; my guess is they were perhaps dumping something in the lake."

"OK, organise it. I'll go and see Mrs. Hillsborough."

He drove up to the farmhouse and knocked.

A tear-ridden, haggard looking white woman opened the door. She would have been pretty once, thought Nyamita.

"My name is Superintendent Nyamita." He drew himself up to his full height of six foot two.

"Oh, how do you do, Superintendent, please come in."

"You are Mrs. Hillsborough?" questioned Nyamita.

"Yes," she said nervously.

"I'm truly sorry about what happened today, ma'am."

She looked at him blankly.

"We think your husband must have stumbled on some people who were up to no good and they shot him just because he was there."

"I see."

"We do need the body, ma'am; to find out who the killers are we need an autopsy."

"I see; I only took the body away because that nincompoop of a local inspector didn't seem to have any idea what he was doing."

The body was taken away.

"But that bloody woman called me a useless kaffir," wailed the inspector.

Nyamita couldn't stand whiners.

"Shut the fuck up will you, has it ever occurred to you that she might be right.'

Within two days they had recovered both bodies. Inspector Kiprogot identified them as his two Wakamba policemen.

Wanyoike and his partners in crime duly appeared at Kahinga's hut on the Sunday evening. He collected all the weapons and examined them.

"This Patchett has been fired," he looked at them.

"So it was you who killed that M'zungu down by the lake," he observed. "That means the whole place will be crawling with police. I hear the Superintendent went down there himself yesterday. Still, if you hid the heads separately it will take them time to identify the bodies."

There was a tense silence.

"You mean you drove the truck to Naivasha, murdered an M'zungu and dumped the bodies of the policemen in the lake. Why didn't you also run around Pumwani telling everyone what heroes you are?"

There was silence.

He gave them fifty shillings each.

"Get out of town; don't come back for a year. Go to Tanzania. If nothing has happened in a year come back and I'll give you the other fifty. Maybe the police will find the truck and blame the Indian."

A month went by.

Little Njiri the Nderobo had firstly looked after his family and made sure they had enough to eat. He then told them he would be away for a month. He didn't say where he was going.

He still had some ill-fitting Western clothes from his days with the Security forces in the emergency. The family all laughed at him when he put them on. He knew he looked ridiculous but he would look even more ridiculous in his normal forest clothes of monkey skins in the streets of Nairobi. He made his way to the local Indian owned duka or store on the Kinangop and after sitting around for two days managed to negotiate a ride into Nairobi on the back of a vegetable lorry. The lorry dropped him off in Pumwani, and he asked where Munyu could be found. He spent the night happily foraging for berries in the Ngong forest having been told to go to Karen. Eventually Njiri found himself at Sattimma having been directed there from Dass's shop. He sat on his haunches under the shade of a large tree and watched unobtrusively. Nobody noticed him, not even the dogs.

Rafiki went in and out, she had picked Kamau up from the school in mid-afternoon; there was a cook and a housemaid in the house, the two gardeners were busy at the front of the house. He saw nothing of Peter. Karanja came wandering jauntily down the driveway. Njiri stiffened and moved further into the shade; this was an unexpected development. Eventually he went to the back steps of the house and waited.

The cook came out, noticed him and asked him what he wanted.

"Munyu," he answered, "I've come to see Munyu."

The cook was by now used to all and sundry appearing at the back door. In the past he would have sent most of them on their way but after much patient counselling from Peter he had been persuaded that Peter actually wanted to see them all.

"Why does a big bwana like you want to speak to all these 'shenzi's' (shenzi is the Swahili word for those of lower breeding)," he asked. "I would beat them and send them away."

Peter always laughed at this.

"But this is democracy; all these people must be listened to."

The cook was troubled by this.

"All these 'shenzi's' have a vote too?" he asked many times.

"Yes," said Peter.

He shook his head. The value of the vote was severely diminished in his eyes from that point.

Njiri was allowed to squat on his haunches near the back steps under the watchful eye of the cook. He was even given a tin mug of very sweet milky tea and half a loaf of bread.

Eventually at dusk Kahinga drove Peter into the yard. Peter got out carrying a briefcase. Kahinga drove the car into the garage. Njiri watched; although it was dusk he was certain he recognised the profile of the elder man in the forest. This was really troubling. Could it be that Munyu was involved in this thing as well? If he was, Njiri might as well go back to the forest. He was sitting there thinking about it when the cook came out and roughly told him that Peter would see him now.

The cook took him through the house. He had never been in an M'zungu's house before and he nervously trod down the polished wooden floor in his bare feet and looked curiously at the unfamiliar sight of pictures on the walls.

Peter was sitting on the front steps with a cup of tea talking to Rafiki.

"Your visitor," announced the cook in a loud voice, hoping to make the little Ndorobo as uncomfortable as possible.

Peter immediately understood what was happening, realised that his visitor was probably a forest dweller and took Njiri into the garden.

Njiri squatted on his haunches and Peter sat on the bottom step. Rafiki was intrigued so she sat with Peter.

Peter greeted Njiri in Kikuyu and asked him about his family and the crops to try to put him at ease.

Eventually Njiri said, "The forest is now peaceful again, after all the shooting and bombing during the troubles."

Peter nodded.

"The shooting and bombing made all the animals nervous."

Peter nodded again.

"I don't want all that shooting in the forests anymore."

Peter said, "All that is over; all the people have left the forests; all is quiet again."

"Yes," said Njiri," but two moons ago I saw people in the forest; they collected guns."

Peter was genuinely surprised.

"How many people?"

"Two people, Kikuyu."

"Will you recognise them if you see them?"

"Yes," Njiri squeaked nervously. "I have seen them, they are here."

"Here?" Peter was dumbfounded. "Which people?" he asked.

"The one who drives your car, I saw him in the forest, and another younger one, I saw him earlier," answered Njiri.

"Kahinga, my driver!" choked Peter. "Tell me exactly when this was."

Njiri tried to and Peter worked out that it must have been when Kahinga had had those few days off.

"Shit," he thought, "Now what?"

"Describe the younger one," asked Peter.

"Sounds like Karanja," said Rafiki, after Njiri had given a brief description.

Peter nodded.

"I wonder what he is up to. There was that Hillsborough murder a few weeks back and then they found the bodies of those two policemen; maybe he is linked to that somehow."

"I think we should confront Kahinga and Karanja with this fellow and see what happens," Rafiki volunteered.

Peter agreed. "I'll go and find them," said Peter.

Peter wandered back through the house and across the dusty yard and went through the trees.

He knocked on the door of Kahinga's hut.

"Who is it?" asked Kahinga's muffled voice.

"Munyu."

The door opened.

Kahinga looked startled.

"I've got a visitor for you from the forest; bring Karanja with you."

"Karanja?"

"Yes, Karanja, I'll see you both back at the house, but be quick; my visitor is nervous."

Ten minutes later Kahinga and Karanja came anxiously round the side of the house.

"That's them, that's them," said Njiri excitedly.

"Njiri, tell them what you saw," asked Peter.

The Nderobo then described how he had followed the boot marks to Tembo base, saw Kahinga and Karanja dig up the guns and return to the car.

"I even saw them put the guns into the car you are driving," he turned to Rafiki.

"Explain yourself," Peter looked at Kahinga. "This all happened when you said you were going to Nyeri. You've never been to Nyeri in your life—where are the guns now?"

Kahinga was silent.

"Tell me now or I'll call the police," Peter said firmly.

"Damn this little Ndorobo," thought Kahinga.

The fuss over the murders had died down and he, Kahinga, and another of his previous henchmen had collected protection money from the Karen shops for the past five weeks now.

Rafiki unobtrusively left the scene.

"Come on, who will you talk to, me or the police?"

"The guns are in the hut," said Kahinga truculently.

"Why do you need them?"

Rafiki had gone through the house and found Wanjiru, sitting nervously outside their hut.

She greeted her politely.

"Why has Kahinga got these guns?" asked Rafiki.

Wanjiru then burst into tears.

"They collect all this money from the shops in Karen, ask Kinua; he also pays."

"Come,"

They walked the few yards to Kinua's hut and knocked. Kinua emerged.

"Why do you pay money to Kahinga?" asked Rafiki.

"Protection," answered Kinua eventually.

"What protection?" asked Rafiki, "what are the police for?"

"Police also ask for protection."

"Police?"

Over the next hour the story gradually emerged. Rafiki, Kinua and Sarah then went back to Peter. Njiri had disappeared.

Kahinga, Karanja and Peter were sitting on the front steps in animated discussion.

They abruptly stopped when Rafiki and the others appeared.

"I've got the story," said Rafiki.

Peter nodded and she told them what she knew, speaking of course in Kikuyu.

"So you killed the policemen and Hillsborough," said Peter eventually.

"No, no," said Kahinga, "I did not go to Naivasha, the two police were alive in the truck when I left."

Eventually they had the whole story. Kahinga denied having anything to do with killing the Wakamba policemen or Hillsborough. The rest he admitted.

"Wanyoike and the others are all in Tanzania," he added.

Peter eventually dismissed them all. He and Rafiki went into the house to a very agitated cook who told them that they had completely ruined all the hard work that he had put into the meal.

Peter could hardly eat anything.

"See," said the cook in Kikuyu. "Ruined. If you can't eat on time I might as well go home early."

Peter made conciliatory noises.

Normally the place was a haven of tranquillity. Tonight Peter was in turmoil.

"The stupid, stupid fuckers," he swore.

"I have an idea," said Rafiki.

"What?"

"That fat Jaluo pig Nyamita is obviously up to his neck in all this."

Peter nodded.

"Wainaina's (Rafiki's father) younger brother is high up in the police, we can find out exactly what's going on from him."

"If he says anything."

"He will, don't worry."

She phoned him and within an hour a very nervous Chief Inspector Wacheera, Rafiki's uncle was round at the house. By three a.m. they had a written deposition from him. It turned out he was slated to benefit from the scam but was uncomfortable about it. All the money he had received was untouched in a separate bank account. He was, however, absolutely terrified of Nyamita.

"Please don't tell him," he said.

Peter and Rafiki eventually went to bed.

The next evening Peter said to Rafiki over dinner, "Now what?"

"I have an idea."

"O.K."

"We have all the evidence to put that fat Nyamita and a few others in jail for a very long time," said Rafiki.

"Who will then be replaced by another bunch of fat, stinking, corrupt cops who will do the same all over again," said Peter.

"Exactly."

"So what do we do?"

"I need money for my clinics, and maybe in time, schools and hospitals in Pumwani."

"Yes," said Peter doubtfully.

"You bring Nyamita in here, present him with all the evidence and tell him you are going to the papers with the story; he'll crap himself."

"And then?" asked Peter.

"Tell him you want half the proceeds."

"That puts us on the wrong side of the law," said Peter.

"Not if the police pay the money directly into an account that is a registered charity," responded Rafiki.

Peter looked doubtful.

"Look, this fat bastard is ripping the country off and is probably sending large sums of money to some Swiss bank account. If he gets found out it won't take long before the whole process starts again and some other fat bastard does the same and so on."

"It still puts us on the wrong side of the law," said Peter stubbornly.

"Stop being so bloody M'zungu," said Rafiki impatiently. "We need African solutions for African problems. This seems quite reasonable, he gets some of what he wants and we get money for the impoverished people in Pumwani—your constituency for heaven's sake. Look, if we can make this thing work nobody will dare touch it or you or me; the whole of Nairobi would go up in flames."

"Maybe we could muscle in on a few more of these schemes," said Peter thoughtfully. "For the same reasons, I already have Stanley, you remember Stanley who was with me on Naseby, in the finance ministry finding me stuff that I'm not supposed to see. Maybe I should try to find people in all the ministries doing the same," said Peter.

"Yes, but let's deal with this first," said Rafiki.

Chapter 6

Nyamita as usual on a Saturday had spent a very enjoyable afternoon in the bed of Ziporah, his young Jaluo mistress. She was young, she was pretty and he gave her everything she wanted. He could not understand why some of his colleagues chose to sleep with white women, they all seemed very insipid to him. Earlier than usual he started to make moves to leave.

"Why so early?" she pouted.

"I have an important appointment with Munyu tonight, I can't be late."

"That M'zungu who saved Rafiki, a few years back."

"The very same."

"What do you want with him, he's not enough of a crook to be of interest to you," she giggled.

Nyamita glowered at her and heaved his huge frame out of the bed. That was precisely what was worrying him; the invitation was quite specific; he was invited alone for a "get to know you" evening. He got the feeling though that if he turned the invitation down he would greatly regret it; he was unused to this situation, it was normally he, Nyamita, who issued such invitations.

Nyamita arrived at Sattimma at eight o'clock precisely. He told his Luo driver to wait for him; the driver would be fed but would not socialise with any of Lawrences' staff, who, he was certain, would all be Kikuyu.

Peter came out to the car to greet him and took him round the side of the house and up the steps to the veranda and the front of the house where Rafiki was waiting.

Rafiki had made a really special effort that evening. Without really knowing Nyamita she had guessed that the pleasures of the flesh were high on his list of indulgences. Nyamita was knocked out by Rafiki's appearance. He quickly saw the white blouse and maroon skirt showed off her black skin to its best. In his mind he quickly imagined what she would look like naked.

"Pity it's wasted on a bloody M'zungu," Nyamita thought to himself.

The evening was indeed very pleasant; the cook had excelled himself after much persuading from Rafiki. When he had first been told who the guest was he had been contemptuous:

"Those Jaluo, they have no teeth, you can just give him soup and mealie meal," was his first reaction, (many Luo have all their top front teeth removed so they can be fed if they contract tetanus or 'lockjaw' which is a not uncommon occurrence).

After the meal and coffee and a snifter of cognac Nyamita relaxed; maybe his suspicions were unfounded and it genuinely was a "get to know you" evening.

Peter had done his very best to make Nyamita feel at home and they swapped stories about the colonial days in Kenya. Rafiki could see that Nyamita found her attractive and really made sure he felt he was the centre of attention.

Once the meal was over, Rafiki ushered the servants out and locked the back door. There was certainly no need to complicate the proceedings with eavesdropping.

Over the past few weeks Peter and Rafiki had done their homework well. During a brief break in the conversation Peter said, "Superintendent, we have some information that we would like to share with you."

He handed Nyamita ten pages of charts with some typewritten paragraphs and figures on them.

Peter then went on to explain in minute detail how the protection rackets that Nyamita was involved in worked, including specific information of what every shop paid every week and how the proceeds were shared out. Nyamita was astounded. Every detail was correct; it even included the payments made by the shops in Karen although he hadn't seen any of that for weeks now. He was also absolutely furious, but he kept his cool; he looked up and said nothing.

They sat in silence for a few minutes; eventually Nyamita decided to call the Lawrences' bluff.

"You can't prove any of this, it won't stand up in court," he said.

"It may never get to court," said Peter.

"So all you've brought me here for is a share of the action," Nyamita thought he understood.

"Not exactly," answered Peter.

"Then what the fuck do you want?" said Nyamita explosively; he was now getting impatient.

"Firstly, you should understand, everything in those papers is the subject of a deposition or a statement written down on people's behalf for those involved who are unable to read or write. One copy is in the hands of a solicitor here in Nairobi and one copy in the hands of a solicitor in London. None of the lawyers have the faintest idea of the contents since they are in sealed envelopes. A single instruction from either Rafiki or me and they will be released to the press, or if anything happens to Rafiki or me the same will happen."

"Yes, and what do you now want from me?" Nyamita demanded.

"Seventy five percent of the proceeds will be paid into…"

"Seventy five percent?" bellowed Nyamita. "You can't be serious."

"Seventy five percent of the proceeds will be paid into this account," Rafiki dropped the bank book of the Pumwani Clinics on the table.

"And every paying in slip will have a police stamp on it," she added.

"No, no, bloody no!" yelled Nyamita.

"You either agree now, or I'm making two telephone calls, one local and one to London. It makes our job very easy. I have people standing by now; if I make those calls everything will be in the paper tomorrow, including the number of one of your Swiss bank accounts"

Nyamita started to sweat.

Peter went to the phone and picked it up. He gave the telephonist at the Karen exchange a Nairobi number.

"Hello," a voice answered.

"Mr. Singh?" asked Peter.

"Yes, speaking."

"Lawrence here, you (he was about to say: release the papers)…"

The phone was snatched out of his grasp and slammed down. Nyamita was standing there glaring at him.

"I agree to your bloody conditions," he said quietly.

Nyamita started to leave.

"Not so fast, not so fast," said Peter. He gave him the bank paying in book.

"Just remember," said Peter, "One, there will be a police stamp on every paying in slip. Two, we know exactly what you are up to so any shortages will result in those letters going to the papers. Three, just so as you are in no doubt, the money is going to develop clinics, and possibly later, schools and hospitals in the poorer districts, starting with Pumwani and Shauri

Moyo, something the Government could afford to do if it weren't for corrupt officials like you. Four: We know all your men; they will all be shadowed, so don't think that you can get away with anything—you won't."

Nyamita glowered.

He grabbed the bank book and stormed out, seething and trying to think of some way of turning the tables.

Rafiki looked up at Peter and smiled.

"You were fantastic. We're going to have to watch ourselves though; Nyamita will be looking for every which way to get back at us."

"I know; we need to have a plan to send him on his way; maybe a friendlier person will succeed him."

They were too excited to go to bed.

"I really need that money for the clinics," said Rafiki. "In the past few weeks we have had a few men in with what they call 'the thin disease'."

"The thin disease?" questioned Peter.

"They just waste away, and get sicker and sicker; the witchdoctor says it comes from the monkeys," said Rafiki.

"I've told you about Stanley," said Peter.

"Well, you mentioned him, what is he doing now?"

"He works in the Finance Ministry and he's passing me all sorts of interesting things. I'm afraid that our friend Nyamita is not alone in his quest for personal wealth," added Peter.

"Oh," said Rafiki.

"It seems likely that the arrangements we made tonight may have to be done again and again."

"I know the problem is that Government and Parliamentary salaries are quite low, us being a developing country. However you M'zungu have a certain standard of living and all Ministers and Government employees think that is what they are entitled to. They have to steal to maintain anything like that standard of living and also the expectations from their extended families are enormous. We are lucky; you have the proceeds from the sale of Naseby and the income from your photography, not to mention your ministerial salary."

"What's the answer then?" asked Peter.

Rafiki shrugged.

"At least some of the money is now going to help the people of Pumwani," she said.

In the morning they found Kahinga and told him what was happening.

"How will I pay my people?" he asked.

"The clinics will employ them as security guards," said Rafiki.

Peter then explained to him.

"No more killing, do you understand?"

"Yes, maybe," Kahinga was hesitant.

"You will shadow the police, but they will do all the cash collection; do not get involved, and that includes the shops in Karen."

"O.K." said Kahinga looking uncomfortable.

"You will not become rich but you will see the poor people and your Mau-Mau colleagues benefit."

"O.K."

"Wanyoike and the others may not come back. Tell them to stay where they are."

"What, never?" asked Kahinga.

"Never."

The guns in Kahinga's possession were never talked about. Peter had decided that he really did not want to draw any unnecessary attention to himself or his family.

✳   ✳   ✳

Chapter 7

Don Watson did a great deal more than he had promised. He organised a number of businessman in Nairobi to contribute a set amount each month to fund the Pumwani clinic. Rafiki was sitting in his office, where she had now become a welcome visitor:

'What has been promised will pay for at least one clinic and then some, if the estimates are correct. I suggest that all the money be paid in to us here and that will save you the trouble of having to chase people for contributions. Also I suggest that my accountant keeps the books here. What you need to do is to authorise each invoice for expenses by signing it and then sending the invoices here for payment. We can arrange to pay wages from here also. He, the accountant, will be responsible for preparing a set of accounts for you on a monthly basis.

People are very happy to contribute money to such a cause,' Don continued, 'and they obviously want it to go to the front line so to speak, which is clearly what you are doing. So what you have done is to create trust, and that needs to be maintained, so what I suggest is that I will arrange for a set of audited accounts to be prepared every six months and that can be circulated to the contributors. It would make them more comfortable if you were prepared to write a short report to accompany the accounts.'

Rafiki was quite overwhelmed; to some people what Don Watson had suggested might, in a way, be seen as ensuring that no money 'leaked' from the system. Rafiki had absolutely no intention and no need to do that so she was not in the least bit sensitive on the subject. So as far as Rafiki was concerned Don Watson had really solved the biggest problem for administering the clinics and that was an on-going supply of money to run them, as well as ensuring a full accountability so that there was no hint of anything other than what Rafiki had promised. In the weeks leading up to this she had arranged for a number of the potential contributors to visit the site of the clinic, which had rapidly been transformed into a gleaming, new looking facility. She had 'phoned each contributor after the visit to make certain that all their questions had been answered satisfactorily.

'I can't tell you how much these arrangements mean to me and the clinics. It means that we can concentrate on running the clinics and not have to worry too much about the financial aspects. I can certainly write a short report whenever it is needed,' responded Rafiki.

Don was relieved; as far as he was concerned he had promised all his colleagues that the operation of the clinics was totally above board as far at the financial aspects were concerned. The arrangements he had now agreed with Rafiki would allay any fears that they might have had: 'I am certain that everyone gains from this arrangement, you can concentrate on running the clinics, something which we have no knowledge of, and as I am sure you know the level of corruption in the country, is increasing all the time and my colleagues will be very supportive with this arrangement in place.'

Recruiting staff had been easy, people were thrilled to be working in the clinic, right in the community there and for some of them it was closer to home. She had managed to persuade only three doctors to give up some of their time, but that was a start as far as she was concerned. Most of the drug companies and other suppliers had also come to the party.

Four short weeks after she had first visited Don Watson the clinic was open and ready to serve the people of Pumwani. Rafiki knew that there was great deal of interest in what she was doing so she just put the word out that it was to open on a certain day. They had decided that the facility would be open from six am to eight pm so that people could come before and after work, so right from the start she needed two shifts and another shift covering weekends. They were not sure what to expect at the beginning but from five-thirty am on the opening day there were already people lining up for attention and after that there was a steady stream of people waiting to be served.

Rafiki was there from dawn to dusk for the first month making certain that all was running smoothly. After that she was able to let the senior nurse run the facility, although Rafiki was always available on the 'phone when needed.

The Minister of Health was invited to formally open the facility. Rafiki asked Peter if he wanted to make a speech: 'No, this is your show; you should be making the speech.' The Minister made a gracious speech, followed by Rafiki who thanked all the contributors. Among the five hundred people who had gathered for the ceremony Rafiki noticed Mwangi Mkubwa talking to Don Watson. 'Mmm,' she thought, 'I have warned him and he is obviously capable of looking after himself.' Meaning Don Watson; she was certain the Mwangi was more than capable of looking after his own interests.

The Minister, despite his speech was clearly uncomfortable that the Government had not been consulted about the project and seemed determined to involve himself at least in obtaining some credit for the initiative. 'I am worried that the finance ministry may wish to tax the income that you are raising for this project,' he said. This was said as more of a threat than as a concerned participant in the project. 'Also all this free advertising of all these products on the walls of a clinic, I am not certain that this complies with the health regulations.' He was referring to the signs that Don's company and other contributors had, at Rafiki's behest covered the clinic walls inside and out.

'Don't worry about the tax stuff,' said Don afterwards when he was told of the conversation. 'Our finance people are on to that and we will ensure that all the proper registrations are in place, so that the project will be treated as a charity. We will make certain that the project will in any event not show any profit. I am concerned about his attitude though, we really need the Government on-side; otherwise they may make life unnecessarily difficult.'

'We obviously have the political connections,' said Rafiki, 'we will try to find out what he really wants; it may be something quite simple, not necessarily connected to the clinics at all.'

The money from the share of the protection rackets started to flow into the clinics bank account shortly after the opening ceremony, which meant that Rafiki started to plan a second and a third clinic almost immediately. Peter had suggested that rather than just running the clinics in an informal way like they had been maybe there was room for a board of some sort, which would meet quarterly and would include Don and one or two of his colleagues and he wondered whether they should ask the Minister of Health to be the Chairman: 'I will ask him if you think it is good idea, after one of our regular cabinet meetings; perhaps you could check with Don to see what he thinks and then I can take it from there.'

Don thought that having a board was the right thing to do, so that major decisions could be formalised. He made it clear that Rafiki would still be running the show. He then raised the question of the contributions from 'the police' as he saw the situation: 'If you had known about this potential source of income, would you have come to me?' he asked.

Rafiki shrugged: 'Yes I had always intended to approach the business community in Nairobi, this additional income from police sources just means that we will be able to open more clinics, sooner than we expected to.' Don looked at her shrewdly during this exchange and decided that the less he knew about that particular source of income the better; whilst the paying in slips had police stamps on them he decided that there was no need to worry too much.

The Minister accepted the position as the Chairman of 'The Pumwani Clinics'. Peter made it clear that there was no payment involved and that all the participants on the board gave their time voluntarily as did Rafiki. 'I got the impression that he was slightly disappointed by that but he accepted the situation quite gracefully; I had told him in a previous conversation that you gave all your time to this project for nothing so he was aware of the situation,' he said to Rafiki one evening at the dinner table.

'Do you want to be on the board?' asked Rafiki.

Peter looked surprised: 'No, not particularly, I actually think that I can be more use to you outside the formal operation. Anyway I don't want to be seen interfering publicly in areas that should not concern me.'

Rafiki mentioned her conversation with Don regarding the new payments from the police protection rackets: 'I think that he suspects that those payments are not entirely above board, but he seemed to be satisfied that everything was alright if the paying in slips had police stamps on them.'

Chapter 8

Nyamita had stormed out of the Lawrence house, Sattimma, and sat down heavily in his car. He slammed the door violently.

"Home," he shouted at the driver.

All his plans laid to waste by that stupid M'zungu bastard Lawrence, he thought. Somehow he would get his own back on him, plus that Kikuyu upstart Rafiki.

It hadn't always been like this. He'd started off as a young recruit in his hometown of Kisumu on Lake Victoria. He'd been lucky enough to go to a local mission school and his academic ability had created a few options, one of which was the police. He'd started off as an eighteen year old and, after a year at the police training school, he'd been attached to a large police station under a rather dour but very competent Scot, Chief Inspector McLoughlin, who had from the beginning taken Nyamita under his wing.

Nyamita was taught from the start the values of good policing and total honesty in his dealings with the public. For ten years under McLoughlin he was entirely happy; he became a good policeman and he managed to get regular promotions. It was when he was promoted to Sergeant that the pressures on him began to build, mainly from his family. He always knew he would be expected to share his good fortune with his extended family; this was the Luo tradition and indeed the African way. As soon as he was promoted to Sergeant his father demanded a new bicycle. He'd gone home one weekend just after the promotion had been announced and there was a rusty wreck of an old bicycle parked in a prominent position outside his father's hut. Nyamita had looked at it suspiciously; he'd never seen it before but he could guess what was coming.

After the normal greetings his father took him outside and said, "The father of Sergeant Nyamita can't ride such a machine; it would be a disgrace to the family for such a successful son to allow his old father to ride such a bad looking bicycle…" and so it went on.

Nyamita bought his father a new bicycle; then his mother wanted a sewing machine. He had to pay school fees for this brother, medical expenses for an auntie. The pressure never relented.

He had married and had a couple of children. Luckily the police provided housing; otherwise he would not have been able to manage financially. With that assistance he was able to maintain a reasonable balance between his obligations to his own immediate family and his wider obligations, all on his police pay.

It was on his promotion to Inspector that the situation he was in, hit him. He was one of the very few African Inspectors; most of the others were White or Indian. He knew he was at least as competent as they were but he was still living in the police compound in Kisumu. His white and Indian colleagues all lived in comfortable bungalows, many of them on the lakeshore. His white colleagues had their children educated at schools in England. He began to realise that something was seriously amiss. The issue was raised with Chief Inspector McLoughlin, who was entirely sympathetic and promised to bring the issue up with police headquarters in Nairobi when he next had the chance.

A conversation he overheard between Mcloughlin and a bureaucrat from Nairobi really made his blood boil:

"Look, the munts (derogatory English slang for African or black man) need less than we do, they're quite happy in their primitive huts with no sanitation or water laid on. They've never known anything else. Anyway, there's nothing I can do, this is all decided down at H.Q."

"Bollocks," said Mcloughlin.

"Bollocks, what?" said the bureaucrat, surprised.

"Bollocks to all that, I have Inspector Nyamita who does at least as good a job as any of my other inspectors and he's paid less than a quarter of what they get. We're storing up a packet of trouble I can tell you," responded evenly.

"Nonsense, my dear chap, you talk nonsense, they're still all a bunch of savages at heart, give them a decent bungalow and they'd still continue crapping in the garden and lighting fires in the middle of the sitting-room. We don't want to spoil them you know."

"Bollocks, bollocks and more bollocks," said McLoughlin evenly. "Nyamita has been to my house many times and frankly he has better manners than many of his white colleagues. He's never got drunk or been sick in the garden for example."

The bureaucrat was offended, "You are being painful now, the policy is laid down; anyway he's probably got herds of cattle and large acreages and several wives in the reserve."

"Bollocks, again! He has one wife, no land in the reserve and he lives here in the police compound. He can't afford to go anywhere else. I also know he has enormous demands from his extended family. Open your fucking eyes man! Not spoiling these people, as you so naively describe the situation, will just lead to them taking advantage of the situation and that as far as I am concerned is the beginning of the end. Your attitude will only cause trouble," Mcloughlin became quite heated.

"You've become quite a little wog-lover in your old age," quipped the bureaucrat. "Quite a little wog-lover," he continued threateningly. "I'll tell Nairobi what you think."

"Don't worry, I've already submitted my recommendations; here is a copy for you," he said.

The discussion went on to other matters.

Nyamita moved away; he was fuming. His salary was adjusted upward a little. He wondered what he should do. He certainly aspired to a so-called white lifestyle with a decent house and well educated children, even a motor-car. He could see that his present style of operations would get him none of these, even with the salary increase, certainly while the whites were in charge. He seriously considered leaving the force.

Shortly afterwards, he was on a trip to Kakamega, north of Kisumu, on the trail of some bank robbers, which involved staying with a colleague in that town. Kakamega was the only source of gold in Kenya and for that reason attracted some of the more lawless elements in the society. Nyamita noticed that his colleague, although only a sergeant, had a considerably better lifestyle than he himself had. After a few nights and a few beers a mutual trust and a mutual respect was established. One evening the question of money and lifestyle was raised.

"That's the reason I came here," said his colleague. "Out of sight of the bosses in Kisumu. I have a sort of understanding with the local M'zungu inspector."

"Oh, what's that?" asked Nyamita.

"Well, we share."

"Share what?" asked Nyamita

His colleague looked exasperated. "We provide protection to the wealthy Indian businessmen in the town and we split the proceeds."

"They pay you?" Nyamita was astounded.

His colleague nodded.

"And if they won't pay?"

"Well sometimes in a case like that their shops burn down, by accident, in the middle of the night."

Nyamita was horrified. He wondered what McLoughlin would say if he knew. He kept his own counsel. What this man was doing was against everything he had ever been taught. His first instinct was to arrest him and have him charged but then another voice said, "Well, why not, these Wazungu all live in fancy houses and I still live in the police compound, maybe this is the only way out."

And so it started, at first in a small way in some out of the way locations in the Kisumu area. Later, as Nyamita was promoted, the scale of his operations became more extensive. Now, since independence from Britain, there were no inspector McLoughlins around to tell Nyamita what to do, so he did what he liked and he had become used to the fruits of his corruption. Besides, there was considerable evidence that his colleagues in senior position throughout the administration were also benefiting in a similar way. He felt no remorse or guilt anymore. Peter Lawrence and Rafiki had challenged him, and he would bring his considerable ability and resources to bear on exacting his revenge.

Chapter 9

Rafiki was busy from morning to night doing her best to administer the Pumwani clinic and finalising plans to start other clinics. Peter was even more of a hero in the area than he had been before. Many of the other members of Government jealously watched the progress in Pumwani and wondered where the money was coming from and how they might get their hands on some of it. Clinics for them were not a priority; keeping up with the demands of their family and home village were of paramount importance and then putting some money away in a Swiss bank account in case things went wrong.

The loss of three quarters of his cash flow from the protection rackets had severely embarrassed Nyamita. He had promised his village chief near Kisumu a new house which he could no longer pay for, his mistress was pouting since he had had to move her to less expensive accommodation, and the funds flowing to his Swiss bank account had altogether dried up. What was more, some large debts he had incurred with an Indian moneylender were almost due, and he knew he could not possibly repay them unless something drastic was done. He had tried withholding some of the money, but the first time that happened, he had an immediate call from a very threatening sounding voice saying that if the money was not paid into the Pumwani clinic bank account within two hours, the promised articles would be released to the press in Nairobi and London. He could not risk calling their bluff, so the money was paid in.

One Saturday he had as usual spent the afternoon with his mistress. She was in an ugly mood and had forced him to tell her the story of how he was now running his protection racket largely for the benefit of "the low life Kikuyu in Pumwani" as he put it.

Bhang," she said. (Bhang is the local and very potent form of marijuana).

"Bhang, what do you mean bhang, speak sense woman," he said impatiently.

"Grow bhang in the mutoni (forest) and then sell it in Nairobi; it should be easy," she said.

Nyamita was intrigued.

"Who would grow it?" he asked.

"I know some people, they just need protection," was the answer.

"Who would sell it?"

"You have people visiting shops every week to collect protection money; sell it through them or some of them anyway." She had obviously thought quite deeply on the subject.

"Where do I find the people who can grow this bhang?" he asked eventually.

"Come tomorrow; they will be here," was the answer.

Nyamita gave brief consideration to his position as police chief. He shuddered when he thought of his mentor Chief Inspector McLoughlin and what he might say if he ever knew what his protégé was now up to. He easily cast these considerations aside. He, Nyamita, had problems; he had debts to pay off and his home village to look after. His primary responsibility was and always had been to his family his village and tribe, in that order; what did he care about the thieving Kikuyu and the rest of them.

True to her word, Ziporah produced a very unsavoury looking character the next day. When Nyamita arrived he was very disconcerted to see an old man with thinning grey hair, a wispy beard, tattered clothing, and car tyre sandals. He was sitting on his haunches outside Ziporah's back door. He gave Nyamita a very crooked grin that exposed a few yellow teeth, as usual being a Luo his top front teeth were missing; his smoky, brown eyes were expressionless. Nyamita let himself in quickly.

"That, that animal out there, is that your bhang grower?" he said anxiously to Ziporah.

"Sh, sh, he's just had a run of bad luck that's all, just give him a chance," she answered soothingly.

"Looks like a jailbird to me," observed Nyamita.

"He was let out three weeks ago," she answered.

"Who is he then?"

"He is my father's brother, he was involved with some Kisii stone cutters in the forest and someone got killed. He had to spend ten years in jail. He says he was not responsible for the killing. They were growing bhang and there was a fight," said Ziporah stoutly. The man shuffled uneasily into the kitchen.

Nyamita greeted him gruffly in Luo; at least he was the same tribe.

The contrast between the two men could not have been starker. Nyamita was large, somewhat overweight and six foot two. He was the epitome of power and authority. He was as usual dressed in a European style suit with tie and gleaming black shoes.

Ziporah introduced her uncle Amon, who apart from being unkempt was short at five foot six and thin. Amon coughed uneasily.

"So, you want to grow bhang in the forest," said Amon.

"Maybe," answered Nyamita.

"I know the very place, the plants will grow easily and it is well hidden," said Amon helpfully.

Nyamita grunted.

"We could share the profits half, half," suggested Amon.

"Half, half," bellowed Nyamita. "You'll get ten percent if you are lucky."

They eventually settled on twenty percent with Nyamita providing the transport and the marketing (by courtesy of the police).

"We will need some labour," suggested Amon.

Nyamita said he would arrange for some convict labour to be made available.

The next weekend Nyamita commandeered a police truck and went with Amon, five convicts, a police guard and his driver. Amon directed them to drive the back way to Kijabe, through what had been the middle of the Kikuyu reserve, past the Sasamua dam to Kipipiri and then by a small farm road into the foothills of the Aberdare mountains. Nyamita had never really been into the Kikuyu areas before and was quite unfamiliar with the forest areas of the Aberdares. The land from Kipipiri onward had been owned by Europeans in the past but was now in the process of being resettled, mainly by Kikuyu. A police truck aroused no suspicion whatsoever, as there were always numerous official-looking vehicles all going about their business.

Amon showed them where to park the vehicle, at the extremity of what was once a white owned farm where he had worked. They had driven down a very overgrown track and had found the now abandoned stone quarry, which was the source of much of Amon's grief in the past. Amon scouted around and found the path into the forest.

Nyamita had come dressed for the occasion with proper police issue jungle boots and green fatigues plus his service revolver. Amon and the convicts went barefoot, the convicts still in their prison garb. The driver and the guard had on normal police issue leather boots, which they removed and went barefoot after a few minutes on the slippery path. Amon led the way from the quarry with Nyamita bringing up the rear. The path wound its way steeply up into the mountain. Despite the damp, Nyamita started to sweat profusely and he found the going very difficult.

After two hours they came to a glade, which, much to Nyamita's surprise and joy was already full of bhang plants. Many of the plants had gone to seed and the place was very overgrown but he could see the potential.

Amon explained that ten years previously he and the Kisii stonecutters had planted the grove of bhang with the idea of supplementing their income. The whole thing had gone sour when one of the Kisii had been killed. He thought that they could weed the glade and get the whole thing operational within a few weeks. There were some huts at the stone quarry, which could be cleaned out and made habitable, and Amon thought that they could dry the bhang leaves and bag them there at the quarry.

Nyamita was thrilled; he could see some sort of income coming from this operation within weeks. They returned to the quarry, opened up the huts and unloaded the food they had brought with them. Nyamita and Amon supervised the convicts, who made one of the huts habitable. One of the convicts made a fire and just as it got dark they all tucked into a meal of ogalie (maize meal cake), vegetables and some rather tough meat they had with them. Nyamita thought they would need the convicts for a couple of weeks now and then again for short periods when the crop was ready for harvesting. He wondered if the convicts would try to escape. He doubted it; the forest seemed very inhospitable and they were all from Lake Victoria so would not be shown much sympathy by the new Kikuyu settlers in the neighbourhood. Besides, he promised them all a reward when the crop was harvested. Amon seemed quite at home and Nyamita arranged to bring his wife the following weekend. As far as he, Nyamita, was concerned it looked like a viable proposition; he could almost see his fortune being restored within a year or two. Nyamita spent the night there and then he and the driver returned to Nairobi leaving Amon, five convicts and the police guard behind. He promised to be back the following weekend.

The following weekend Nyamita and the police driver arrived early on the Saturday morning with Amon's wife as well as Ziporah, who was curious to see the place, plus a truckload of beds, pots and pans, blankets and some maize seed. The party were pleasantly surprised to see a small patch of ground had been cleared near the newly thatched huts to grow the maize. When they made the two-hour climb to the plot of bhang they found that almost half the area had been weeded; it certainly seemed that Amon had done a great job, and Nyamita was pleased. After a brief inspection Nyamita, the driver and Ziporah left with the promise of returning the next weekend to collect the convicts. They would also bring some small bags into which they would pack the dried bhang.

Njiri's life in the Aberdares had remained almost undisturbed since he had spotted Kahinga and Karanja digging up the guns at the old Tembo base. Every now and then he went to Tembo to check that there had been no more visitors. Njiri had, for some time, known of the glade that Nyamita now wanted to exploit. He passed by it once every six weeks or so in order to renew his own small source of the drug. A few weeks after Amon had moved into the stone quarry, Njiri was horrified to find that the plot of bhang was now being intensively cultivated again and that there was evidence of the presence of at least ten men. He followed the path down to the quarry and watched over a two-day period. He saw Nyamita come and go and then all that seemed to be left one weekend was the old man and his wife and one of the people with the prison clothes. He wondered what he should do. He thought that if one lot of people could come and cultivate the area, what was to stop more people coming, and then his world, his tranquillity, the animals he lived among would be disturbed forever. "Well," he thought, 'Munyu seemed to sort the last problem out; maybe I should go back to him."

A few weeks later Njiri again found himself at the rear of Sattimma. He spent most of the day waiting for Peter and as before the cook fed him some bread and tea. Both Peter and Rafiki listened to the story.

"Sounds like a job for Kahinga and some of his henchmen," said Rafiki.

"They can go tomorrow, and take Njiri back with them," said Peter.

It was late in the afternoon so the next day Kahinga and six of the his associates together with Njiri were on their way to the Aberdares in Kinua's pickup truck, who agreed to lend it to Kahinga after having been told that Peter knew what was going on and had asked Kahinga to go into the forest to confirm Njiri's story. They made their way into the forest from the Kinangop where Kahinga and Karanja had entered the forest on their way to collect the guns.

All the men had been in the forest during the Mau-Mau uprising with Kahinga, so like him they considered it almost a home from home. They had strict instructions from Peter: "Find out who is behind all this, that is the most important thing, and don't let them see you. Also, if there is nobody about then destroy the crop—destroy it completely." The party led by Njiri made rapid progress through the forest; all slept at Tembo base for old time's sake, except Njiri, who would not sleep there and made his own arrangements. Then, making sure that the traces of their habitation were eliminated made their way by early afternoon to the glade where the bhang was being grown. They all stayed in the forest and watched for a while; there was no movement. Njiri had already told them that there was a man and a woman living at the stone quarry. Kahinga thought for a minute:

"Njiri and I will go down to the quarry. The rest of you should pull up every plant and make a few small piles of bhang and burn it. We will be back by nightfall." Kahinga and Njiri made their way quickly down the path, stopping every now and then to listen. They did not want to be seen by people coming up the path, although they thought it unlikely that anyone would be going up to the glade this late in the day. They found their way to the quarry and crept closer, making sure they remained unseen. After having viewed the site from several vantage points all they could see was one oldish man and a woman. There was a quantity of bhang leaves drying on a slab of rock and the man had packed some of the dried leaves into small paper bags. Just as they were about to leave to go back to the glade a very battered pick-up truck arrived at the quarry, the packed bags were loaded into the front of the vehicle by the lone driver and the old man and then in what seemed like an inordinate hurry the truck retraced it's steps. From the appearance of the people and the snatches of conversation that he had heard Kahinga determined t the people were Luo. This in itself was unusual, the Luo were not forest people; they were from the Lake near Kisumu. After a few more minutes Njiri and Kahinga left and just as the short equatorial dusk was falling they arrived back in the glade. All the plants had been pulled out and there were a few small fires burning.

Kahinga wondered what he should do. His people always shadowed the police on Friday nights when they picked up the protection money from the various retailers. Maybe on this Friday night he could leave the situation to take care of itself, after all there had been no problems for months now. Kahinga's party spent the night in the forest near the glade and made sure that all the fires were fully burnt out. The next day they made a final inspection of the site and made certain that all the plants had been destroyed and all the fires completely extinguished. Kahinga had decided that whoever was behind this exercise would probably appear at the weekend, however, as a precaution he left one of his more reliable men at the site to keep watch. The rest of them went back to Tembo base and Njiri went home and promised to be back at dawn in two days, which would be Saturday.

Nyamita was excited, he had renegotiated the use of five convict labourers and he was going to go to the forest today to harvest the first crop of bhang. He also expected that Amon would have some samples for him at the quarry. The party arrived in the police truck early on the Saturday morning in good cheer. As soon as Nyamita stepped out of the vehicle his instincts told him that something was amiss. Amon was very nervous although there were a good number of small bags filled with bhang for Nyamita to take away. His police training instinctively made him cast his wary eyes around the site. He then saw the tyre trucks of the vehicle that had been there a few days earlier. "I'll kill that little bastard Amon if he's cheating me," he thought. Amon had hoped that the normal rain showers would wipe away all traces of the vehicle and had only made a clumsy attempt to sweep away the tyre tracks. Ziporah's brother had been cut into the deal; the arrangement was that Amon would take a portion of the crop and sell it through Ziporah and her brother; his share of the profit would then be one third instead of the measly twenty percent allowed him by Nyamita.

Nyamita decided to keep his own counsel and within a short time Nyamita, the convicts, Amon, the police driver and the guard were on their way up the path to the glade.

Kahinga was well prepared; he his men and Njiri were in place not long after the sun had burnt away the mist that usually enveloped the mountains at night. Njiri was detailed to go down the path and warn Kahinga if and when anyone was going to appear. The weapons had all been cleaned and inspected and test fired at Tembo base and Kahinga's men were all at vantage points overlooking the glade. Njiri darted back into the glade, found Kahinga and told him that a party of about ten men would appear in a few minutes. The men round the glade were on full alert.

Nyamita, puffing and panting, led his group of men into the glade. He simply could not believe his eyes. He was prepared to find that Amon was cheating him a little on the side but he was totally unprepared for the sight that now confronted him. There was nothing left in the glade, not one bhang plant. Amon staggered into the glade; he too was truly shocked. A few days ago he had been up here, harvested a few plants for himself and returned to the quarry. Nyamita stepped up to Amon and with all his considerable strength slapped Amon in the face. Amon crumpled. When he recovered he said, "No, no, it was all O.K., even a few days ago, I picked some plants and dried them down at the quarry as you said; this was done by other people."

Nyamita eventually calmed down. They started looking around and found many footmarks. The party suddenly felt very vulnerable; the only weapons they had were Nyamita's revolver and the guard's .303 rifle. After a few more minutes they collected in the centre of the glade and tried to discuss the next steps.

The appearance of Nyamita at the glade amazed and surprised Kahinga. He wondered what to do. He could take the lot of them out now, bury them in the forest and they would probably never be discovered. When he thought about it further he was certain that Munyu would do nothing, but then Munyu was an M'zungu, and this was just a bunch of Jaluo. Eventually the decision was taken out of his hands; the clouds had been building up all morning, and suddenly there was a loud clap of thunder and within seconds there was a torrential downpour which restricted visibility to a few yards. Kahinga saw Nyamita's group slip away down the path. He took his own men back to Tembo. Njiri went home.

His men looked at Kahinga curiously when they were back at base.

"Who was that big fucking Jaluo?" one asked.

"Nyamita, Police chief," answered Kahinga.

"Eh heh, now we understand why we didn't shoot all of them."

They all went back to Sattimma and life returned to normal.

Kahinga reported in full to Peter the events of the week and what he had seen.

"Can I have a share of the profits from the dope as well?" asked Rafiki, jokingly.

"Mmm," said Peter, "The clinics are doing very well from the protection money. I think that what we should do is to formally report the existence of this activity to the police and make sure that Nyamita himself is made aware that we know of the existence of the bhang plantation. We will then see what action he takes."

"You are beginning to think like a true African," said Rafiki admiringly.

Peter decided to write a formal letter addressed to Rafiki's uncle Chief Inspector Wacheera, notifying him of the existence of the glade and its precise location and telling him that he had been advised of the existence of the bhang plantation by an Ndorobo who lived in the forest somewhere in the vicinity of the glade. Within a few days he received a call from Wacheera: 'There are of course many illegal bhang plantations all over the country,' he said, 'we try to destroy them when we find them, but is there something special about this one?'

'This is a big plantation and therefore obviously warrants some attention, maybe you could discuss it with the chief?' replied Peter disingenuously.

The small number of samples that Nyamita had taken away with him sold very easily through the protection racket network at a premium price. This made Nyamita even more determined than ever. He arranged to replant the glade and as the plants came close to maturity he sent two of his more trusted police constables to stay with Amon, firstly to keep an eye on the latter and secondly to make sure there was a daily inspection of the now maturing crop in the glade.

Nyamita was quite taken aback when, weeks later, Wacheera came to see him and told him that he thought they should send a police detachment to destroy the plantation. 'Yes of course we should but we are rather busy at the moment, I don't see the urgency, it can probably wait a little while. Anyway leave it to me.' Wacheera left Nyamita's office and unthinkingly gave him Peter's note which gave the location of the glade where the bhang was growing. Nyamita was furious when he saw that it was Peter who had written the note alerting the police to the existence of the plantation. He realised that in sending the letter to Wacheera Peter had assumed that it would be brought to his, Nyamita's, attention and it was his way of indicating to Nyamita that he knew what the Police Superintendant was up to. 'I will get that interfering bloody M'zungu,' he said to himself. He was determined not to let anything interrupt his plans for harvesting and selling the drug: 'I will just have to make sure that I harvest it a bit sooner than Amon thought was the ideal time,' he thought. 'Damn that bloody Munyu, I will get him one day.'

The fact that Peter had made it clear that he knew that Nyamita was involved with bhang plantation made him even more determined to continue with what he was doing there: 'No bloody M'zungu is going to stop me now,' he thought, 'this is our country now, not theirs anymore.'

Njiri had come to see Peter again and told him of the renewed activity at the glade; this time Peter tried to put him off. They wanted to see what, if anything Nyamita would do. Although the drug was now illegal in Kenya it had been used from time immemorial, as Rafiki put it, "Some of our people have smoked this stuff for centuries now. Why should we worry about a silly law the Wazungu have put into place."

Njiri was disconsolate and went to see Kahinga, who had in any event been thinking about the potential of the crop, for himself, he now knew was being grown in the mountains. Kahinga told Njiri that he would "sort it out" like he had before.

The crop of bhang grew well and quickly; both Kahinga and Nyamita were constantly aware of its progress. Kahinga knew that he would have to get in ahead of Nyamita and that he probably had one day to strip the crop, pack it into bags and get out. Nyamita's plan was to strip the crop, dry it in the quarry and gradually ship it to Nairobi, but in view of his conversation with Wacheera he realised that that would not work and that he would have to make another plan. Nyamita of course had no knowledge of Kahinga or his plans.

Ten of Kahinga's men were sent through the mountains via Tembo base. Their instructions were to overpower Amon, his wife and the two guards and then wait for Kahinga and the rest of his crew. Kahinga just hoped that he had judged it correctly and that Nyamita was only planning to harvest the crop a week or two later. He of course knew nothing of what Peter had told the police and Nyamita's reaction to that.

Kinua refused Kahinga the loan of his pickup; he had heard enough from Sarah and thought that Kahinga was probably up to no good. So they stole a truck down River Road, drove to Kipipiri and continued down the track towards the quarry in the early hours of the morning. The last part of the journey was done very slowly without lights so as not to attract any attention. The vehicle crept into the clearing to the stone quarry, and one of Kahinga's men came out of the shadows and gave the thumbs up. Kahinga now had sixteen men; they were all well armed either with rifles or Patchett sub-machine guns and they were all wearing balaclavas and dark clothing. Kahinga needed to check the bonds of the four prisoners and then they would be on their way. One man was to be left behind to make sure Amon and the others did not escape.

Suddenly they heard the distinct noise of a truck making its way down the little track.

"Damn," thought Kahinga, "that can only mean one thing, Nyamita."

There was no time to back-off. Kahinga quickly placed his men in positions around the quarry but before he had time to get into position himself Nyamita's police truck came hurtling into the clearing. Kahinga shattered the windscreen with a burst from his Patchett, killing the driver and severely wounding Nyamita. In the dim light of the very early morning the rest of Kahinga's men then opened up. The police and convicts in the back jumped off and scattered in all directions. The convicts rushed into Amon's hut to hide, where they found Amon and the prisoners tied up. The guards and Amon were released and raced off into the surrounding bush. Eventually one of the police removed the dead driver from the police truck, managed to turn it around, regroup and get two of the remaining police into the vehicle; Nyamita was bleeding profusely and one of the men tore strips off his shirt in an attempt to stem the bleeding. They hurriedly drove off. A couple of the others who had come with Nyamita managed to clamber on to the back of the pick-up; the rest were left to fend for themselves.

In the half light of the early dawn Kahinga and his men gradually assembled when they thought the mayhem was over. Amon and the guards and convicts had escaped so apart from the one dead driver there was nobody else about. Kahinga was surprised that there were no other casualties, but put the thought out of his mind; he and his men needed to get away quickly They carried the body of the dead policeman a hundred yards into the bush and buried him in a deep grave: Kahinga made certain that the grave was covered with leaves and other forest debris so that it would be undisturbed by wild animals and virtually impossible to find. Kahinga, relieved that the casualty rate among the police contingent was so low, supposed that was due to the poor light. Kahinga's men had all been well hidden and had suffered no casualties. After the burial they cleaned up the area, making sure all the spent cartridges had had been retrieved, and made it look as if there had been almost no activity at all. They all squeezed into the pick-up and by mid-afternoon they had abandoned the stolen vehicle and had all disappeared into the slums of Pumwani. A day later a low level contingent of police from Gil-gil, alerted by the injuries sustained to Nyamita made their way to the quarry and looked around. Much to their surprise they found very little sign of any activity but they did eventually follow the now well trodden footpath to find the glade with a thriving crop of bhang, which they destroyed.

The headlines appeared in the Nairobi papers:
"HEROIC POLICE CHIEF SEVERELY WOUNDED IN ATTACK ON DRUG SMUGGLING GANG"

Nyamita was to spend many months in hospital and was then expected to spend a long time in rehabilitation; it was uncertain whether he would ever walk again.

'I suppose that that stinking Kikuyu, Wacheera, will have to act in my place, until I am well again.' He mused once he was on course for recovery.

After a great deal of fuss Rafiki's uncle, Chief Inspector Wacheera was made acting Superintendent.

"Good," said Peter," now we have a chance to clean this whole thing up." He had been uncomfortable with the arrangements for Rafiki's clinics to share in the spoils of the police protection racket right from the beginning. He had always considered that they were operating on the wrong side of the law.

Rafiki was flabbergasted.

"What about my clinics?" she yelled. "Don't you understand that my uncle Wacheera will now have much bigger obligations back at our village; how do you think he is going to pay for that on his miserly salary? No the protection business will continue, it is in everyone's interests that it is so."

"But if everyone in power is ripping off the system what happens to this country? You'll end up having another revolution, also Wacheera is not altogether comfortable about this racket, and he now passes all the money that is supposed to come to him, to your clinics." Peter argued.

Rafiki shrugged. "I don't know. This Wazungu system is maybe part of the problem. What I do know is that Wacheera will be expected to help his village to show favour otherwise he can never go back. They might even want to kill him," said Rafiki.

"But this is ridiculous!" Peter became quite heated. "There must be another way, all that's happening is that instead of the Wazungu dominating the scene a few privileged Africans are doing the same thing. The rest of them can starve for all anyone cares."

Rafiki just looked uncomfortable.

So the protection racket continued. Rafiki felt quite safe; her uncle was after all now nominally in charge of the Police. They didn't want Kahinga to think that anything had changed, so the surveillance operation continued as if as if nothing had happened.

Wacheera paid one visit to Nyamita, really as a courtesy. Nyamita although still in a bad way managed to convey to Wacheera that he thought that they should take their time on investigating the incident: 'There are many other crimes that need attention,' said Nyamita, 'I think this one can take a back seat, until I return to my duties.'

'But what about the injuries to you and there is one policeman missing, surely that is a priority.'

Nyamita changed the subject: 'Has the plantation been destroyed?'

'Yes of course, I arranged for it to be destroyed the next day.' Nyamita nodded. He waved Wacheera away.

Wacheera pondered over Nyamita's behaviour: he could get no information out of any of the people who had accompanied Nyamita on the raid to the bhang plantation. They all had the exactly same story which in itself made Wacheera suspicious. Also his conversation a few weeks earlier with the chief, who had said that dealing with this particular plantation was not urgent and then suddenly going off on his own with a contingent of police, notably all Luo, ostensibly to destroy the plantation, just made no sense. He came to the only possible conclusion: he was now almost certain that Nyamita himself was responsible for growing the bhang. Wacheera was aware the protection racket, now funding Rafiki's clinics had significantly reduced Nyamita's income, so he assumed that growing bhang was a way of recovering some of what had been lost. He knew that he needed to tread carefully but this realisation made him determined to stamp out corruption where he found it.

Peter felt more and more uncomfortable with what was going on, both with the protection racket and what he knew was going on in other government departments. Much of his information came from Stanley. Stanley, who had grown up on Naseby, attended the farm school there and had accompanied Peter on some of his hunting trips. Later he had managed to complete his education at Nairobi University. During the Mau-Mau emergency Stanley, then still a youth, had been helpful to Peter on several occasions. Now Stanley had a mid-level job in the Finance ministry.

From time to time Stanley used to come to Sattimma with copies of documents and snippets of information from the Finance ministry; because of his position he had access to files relating to most of the departments of government. Over a two year period Peter and Rafiki had become aware of "leakage" of government funds from almost every ministry, probably for personal use. The burgeoning civil service was witness to the fact that the relatives and associates of those in authority were generally being looked after.

Peter really understood the issues. He and Rafiki had after all found a very effective way of ensuring that the people in his constituency felt they were being looked after by their chosen representative, namely Peter. None of his constituents gave any consideration to the fact that the Lawrences gained no personal benefit from the arrangements. Most of Peter's fellow ministers and Members of Parliament represented constituencies where there was a core of loyal supporters, however for their loyal support they expected material benefits to flow their way in the form of jobs or other compensation. If the jobs or benefits stopped flowing, the particular M.P would almost certainly lose the next election. In extreme cases Peter was aware of M.P's who had died in mysterious circumstances to be replaced by others who presumably were more able to accommodate their supporters' needs.

"It's a sort of vicious circle," he explained to Rafiki. "The country needs economic growth to provide jobs especially with the increasing birth rate, but we won't get economic growth if there is no investment from both outside and inside the country and whilst there is a perception that corruption is rife the investment will be limited."

"The Wazungu countries should give us foreign aid," offered Rafiki helpfully.

"What, so that people like Nyamita can steal the aid and put it away in Swiss bank accounts?" said Peter.

Rafiki pouted. She didn't really understand all the mumbo-jumbo about growth. She could however see that certainly in Pumwani the number of people without a steady income was growing and that the crime rate was increasing in leaps and bounds. She, more than anyone, understood the pressures.

"Maybe we should chuck all this up and go live in Ulaya (England)," Peter said one day in a cloud of despondency.

"Me, live in Ulaya! I would be a second class citizen because I am black, and anyway, what would all the people in Pumwani do when I am gone? Do you want them all to die?" Rafiki answered heatedly.

"Isn't there anyone else who can do your job?" asked Peter. "Are you the only one?" And then he added more as an afterthought," No, of course I don't want them to die, I think you do a wonderful job."

※　※　※

Chapter 10

Stanley had now presented Peter with a large dossier of information that involved a number of Ministers in what were clearly corrupt practices. Peter spent many sleepless nights wondering what to do about the information, after all these were his colleagues and they were supposed to have a shared trust, a shared responsibility to run the Country in the interests of the Country, not a lot of sectional or individual interests. Eventually he shared it all with Rafiki.

'Maybe we could just do what we did with that fat Jaluo pig, Nyamita, and return it all to the people through my clinics.' She suggested.

'How many clinics do you run?' He knew the answer perfectly well, but just wanted to emphasise the point.

'Well two at the moment, but I would like to increase that to five.'

'With what I have here there is enough money for at least a thousand clinics.'

Rafiki was silent for a moment. 'What?' she said in disbelief.

'You heard, and I am sure that what Stanley has here is just the tip of the iceberg. This is really too big for us, it is not just a petty protection racket, they are stealing the country blind.'

'And this is not all of it; there are an ever increasing number of Government employees: Ministers, top civil servants, people at all senior levels employ relatives and members of their community, whether they are competent or whether they are needed. None of that is included in these figures.'

'Even the Minister of Agriculture does some of these things' joked Rafiki.

'Meaning Kahinga and Kinua, I suppose you are right, although they were needed and competent. Anyway Kinua has made his own way and is now not part of this situation.'

Peter threw up his hands: 'what do you think I should do?' he asked.

'We could hand it all over to the Police,' said Rafiki helpfully, 'that is what you would do in one of your Wazungu countries isn't it?'

'If we took all this to Acting Superintendent Wacheera, what do you think he would do?' asked Peter.

Rafiki laughed: 'Uncle Wacheera? Perhaps try to prosecute some of the small fry involved. I actually doubt if the Police have many of the skills needed to really understand and prosecute these cases. If he started on any of the major figures he would probably be assassinated.'

'So, do we just let it go?'

'I really don't understand all this and what it means; how serious is all this? Does it matter that some money is being sidetracked for personal use? Please don't tell me that this sort of thing never happens in Wazungu-land.'

'It is very serious indeed. The way things are going they will substantially affect the long term prospects for this country, with money being sent illegally to Swiss bank accounts, money which should be used for development. There are a couple of other issues: the international community either are already aware of what is going on or soon will be, so aid money will dry-up and it appears that there is a sort of competition building up among senior people as to who can filch the largest amount of money, which has to be very unhealthy.'

'If we just go on as we are, me running the clinics, you doing your best as Minister of Agriculture, what then happens?'

'In the short term-nothing. Sooner or later though someone will get greedy and this thing will escalate and whatever we do, attempts will be made to compromise us.'

Rafiki's shoulders slumped: 'I thought that after Uhuru all our dreams would come true and with the Mzee's (Jomo Kenyatta) development thrust of 'Harrambee' (all pull together), we would really start to go places as a country. Now I wonder. Maybe we should just go through the papers that Stanley has given you, while I think what we might do to change the situation.'

So they spent the rest of the day going through everything that Stanley had given them. Rafiki then selected two cases and they went through them in more detail so that Rafiki had a really good understanding of what was going on.

'What are you going to do?' asked Peter.

'Maybe I will go and see these people.'

'Should we go together?'

Rafiki shook her head.

'This person, Johanna Kariuki, I know,' she said waving a collection of papers at Peter, 'he was in my age group when I was growing up. I think that I can deal with him. He was the one who cried when the witchdoctor cut his foreskin off. He is weak.'

'Be careful,' said Peter. 'You know how dangerous a cornered hyaena can be.'

Rafiki nodded.

'I will ask Kahinga to drive me.'

'Could you ask Kinua, firstly he is no longer connected with me and to be honest with you I am a bit worried about Kahinga at the moment. I think that he is up to something.'

'Kinua will not be able to help me much if I get into trouble with Johanna. Kahinga will be able to, with his people.'

'It will take more than one meeting for Johanna to realise how much trouble he is in. Just play it cool this time.'

Peter's suspicions were justified: Kahinga was now certain that Nyamita was out of the way at least for the time being and he contemplated taking over the bhang plantation for himself; he was hopeful that Peter knew nothing about his involvement with the death of the policeman and the wounding of Nyamita. He was still Peter's personal driver, so he had to be careful and to make sure that any of his absences were well explained. Rafiki made a call to the Ministry of Works the next day and asked to speak to deputy minister Johanna Kariuki. She was told he was in a meeting. This went on for a few more days and there was no call back. Rafiki then got fed up and arranged for Kinua to take her into the city to the ministry early one morning. They arrived just before 8.30 and Rafiki marched through the building as if she owned it. The security guard at the entrance recognised her—the Pumwani clinic had helped his wife—and after some very brief pleasantries he told her that the Deputy-Minister's office was on the fifth floor. Security was lax and she rode in the lift to the appointed floor and marched confidently to the Deputy-Ministers office. There was nobody about so she walked into the office, looked around and then sat down in the Deputy-Ministers chair, after having closed the door. It was a large corner office as befitted the status of the occupant, with wood panelling and photographs of a pretty woman and a couple of children. The desk was almost bare. At just after 10am the door opened and in marched a very confident sleek looking Johanna, dressed in a suit and tie, with polished black shoes, he was short and fat. He didn't see Rafiki until she stood up and greeted him in the traditional Kikuyu way.

Johanna almost jumped out of his skin. 'I have been busy' he stammered, 'I was going to phone you today.'

'Well I just thought that I would save you the trouble.' said Rafiki evenly. 'You look very well, after all your troubles.'

'Yes, some years ago now', said Rafiki evenly, 'you have done well for yourself' she continued; looking around the office.

Johanna had done little in the emergency, having spent most of the time at university in England. He had always been in awe of Rafiki and her heroic role in the emergency had exacerbated that feeling.

They spent five minutes reminiscing about the past and their upbringing in the village near Thika.

'I am sure that you have a busy day ahead of you,' said Rafiki, 'I just wanted to share, with you, some knowledge that has come my way.'

Johanna just smiled. He had no idea what was about to hit him. Rafiki pulled out a sheaf of papers from her handbag. As soon as he saw them, the smile dropped from his face and he went ashen.

'All these companies,' she waved the papers in his face, 'either belong to you or to members of your family. None of them have any employees. All of them have an address that does not exist. The box number on the invoices is your private box number.—Building works—this invoice says. What building works and so it goes on. You personally have authorised every invoice. What is all this about?'

Johanna tried to retain his composure.

'Where…?'

'What are you talking…?'

'You have no business…?'

'I did think of giving all these to Wacheera, but I thought that I might come and see you first,' continued Rafiki as if Johanna had said nothing.

'If I do anything with them it will be back to the bicycle for you, perhaps with a spell in the 'Hoteli ya Kingi Georgie' (Rafiki used the Swahili term used in colonial times for prison-lit: King Georges Hotel) just to cool your heels.'

Johanna just looked at Rafiki with his mouth open. He had no idea how she had come by the information and really no idea how to deal with the situation. He was absolutely terrified though—his nice suburban house, his children at a private school, annual overseas trips with his wife, none of which he could possibly afford on his ministerial salary. As far as he was concerned he had come a long way from a grass hut in what was the Kikuyu

Reserve; most of his age group were either still there in the Reserve area near Thika or more likely living in some ramshackle shack in Pumwani with a labouring job that had no prospects and paid little, if they were lucky. He had no intention of returning to that situation under any circumstances. He had always been intimidated by Rafiki and had envied her. She had also done well, by marrying Peter Lawrence. He knew Peter from attendance at cabinet meetings and had been impressed by his sincerity but he had avoided any social contact—Peter just seemed to come from another world with what he had gone through in the emergency and with his almost mystical reputation. The fact that he, a white man, represented one of the poorest areas in the country and was clearly popular there was intimidating in itself-he knew that he, even with his background was almost unknown in Pumwani and that there was no possibility that he could do what Peter was doing created another barrier in his mind. In the brief silence that ensued after Rafiki's barrage he started to gather his thoughts. He knew in his heart of hearts that it would be useless trying to deny the accusation but instinct made him start there anyway:

'Those worthless bits of paper you have, prove nothing, if they are authorised by me then they are legitimate invoices for legitimate services provided by those legitimate companies. All this stuff about me owning the companies is just invention on your part. What have you got against me anyway?'

Rafiki said nothing and looked at him.

'I think that you should go now and while you are about it you can give me those papers and we can forget about this whole unfortunate episode. I won't tell your husband.'

Rafiki just smiled. 'I am sure that you have copies of these papers here or at your home. I will probably just give them to uncle Wacheera; it will save me making another copy.'

Johanna just glowered at her as she stood up to go.

'Wait, what do you really want?' he asked as she moved towards the door.

'When you have had a chance to think about things, give me a call. We can talk further later.'

She left.

When Peter returned that evening, Rafiki related the whole incident to him.

'He will fight to keep his ill-gotten gains; his lifestyle would collapse if he lost access to this source of income. Same as Nyamita. Johanna might even try to threaten or intimidate you. Anyway we should increase the security round here and you need to watch yourself and Kamau around town. Dear God, I thought that all this security nonsense was long gone; it seems not.'

'What about this other case?' asked Rafiki

'That one and many others; let us just see where this one leads and then we may be able to come up with a plan. Otherwise we might find that we are taking on the whole world.'

Peter then spoke to Kahinga.

'I need more security around here.'

'OK, what would you like me to do?'

'Two people outside from about 10 O'clock at night until dawn, and one inside the house, for the next three months.'

Kahinga raised an eyebrow. 'Has someone threatened you or Rafiki?'

Peter was vague; 'Well, sort of, there may be trouble, soon I think.'

'What sort of trouble?'

'Well, I'm not really sure, we just have to be careful, that all.'

'What about the dogs?'

'They will both be outside, as usual. We need to make sure that they recognise the guards of course.'

For the next few weeks all was quiet. There was no contact from Johanna at all.

'Maybe he thinks that this will all go away,' Rafiki said to Peter one evening.

'Not sure about that; at a recent cabinet meeting he sat as far away as possible and glowered at me.'

'Maybe I should 'phone him?'

'Why not, the die is cast anyway.'

Rafiki 'phoned and 'phoned and eventually got through on the tenth attempt.

'What do you want?' asked Johanna gruffly.

'I think that you should stop stealing from the Government, you should stop what you are doing and help this country develop instead of lining your own pockets'

There was a contemptuous grunt from the other end of the line.

'You and that M'zungu husband of yours should watch your step, if you tread on too many toes you may get more than you bargained for.'

'Both of us have been stepping on toes for years now, as I'm sure you know. You of course were sitting around in Ulaya drinking beer while some of us were risking our lives.'

There was a sharp intake of breath.

'You are living in the past, Rafiki, now is the time for more modern men…'

'To steal the country blind,' interrupted Rafiki. 'It seems that I will have to give all I know to uncle Wacheera.'

'You need to make your mind up what you want from me,' came a more conciliatory reply. 'Maybe we could meet somewhere.'

Rafiki was ready for that.

'You can come here, after 10 in the morning. Tomorrow.'

'I can't make tomorrow.'

'Then I go to Wacheera.'

'What's the hurry?'

'This has gone on long enough. Either you come here tomorrow or I go to Wacheera in the afternoon.'

She put the 'phone down.

Later that day when Rafiki was on the way to the clinics in Pumwani she kept noticing a particular car, which seemed to be following her. She decided to test the situation and turned down a side street and waited a few minutes. Sure enough there was the car just creeping along, obviously looking for something or someone, probably her. She let it go past and then went back the way she had come. Within a short time, there was the car again, immediately behind her. 'I'll show them,' she thought and using the skills she had learned during her time in the emergency, she overtook three cars in a very tight situation, amid a lot of hooting and gesticulation from the other drivers, ducked down a side street and made her way to Pumwani on the back roads.

She knew that this was only the beginning and that she had to get a message to Kahinga and if possible, Peter. Acting quickly, she commandeered the little motorbike that they used for emergency deliveries. She saw the car that had been following her, driving slowly, obviously looking for her: hopefully they wouldn't notice her on the bike despite that fact that she wasn't wearing a helmet. She raced back to Karen.

In the driveway at Sattimma, to her surprise, she saw two unfamiliar cars; there was nobody about. Parking the bike she ran round to the huts occupied by Kahinga and Kinua and their families. The scene that greeted her reminded her of the very worst of her memories of the emergency. Wanjiru and Sarah were naked and tied up; the children were all running around yelling. She untied them as quickly as she could. There was no sign of Kahinga. 'They took him, into the house. I think that they will kill him. They were looking for papers, I heard them say,' said Wanjiru as she scrambled into her clothes.

'How many?' asked Rafiki.

'Five or six.'

'Where is Karanja?' She knew that Kinua would be away at the garage. They shrugged.

Rafiki went racing round to the other huts and found Karanja tied up in another hut. He had been badly beaten up.

He fumbled in a rucksack at the back of the hut, when Rafiki untied him, and emerged with the pistol that he had taken when he was with Kahinga in the mountains.

'Here give me that,' Rafiki snatched it away from him, before he could object.

'I know how to use this, you don't. Find a panga and come with me.' She checked that it was loaded and found some more ammunition in the rucksack.

She raced round to the area where the cars were parked, with Karanja limping behind her. She shot out two of the tyres in each of the strange cars, and waited.

She did not have to wait long. Within a few seconds of the sound of gunshots five men came rushing out of the rear of the house, dragging Kahinga, who had blood all over his face. Rafiki was about to confront them, when there was a sudden burst from what she determined was a sub-machine gun. Turning around she saw Karanja clutching one of the Patchetts, which he and Kahinga had retrieved from the Aberdares. He had no idea how to handle the weapon, the few shots that he had managed to fire off had harmlessly gone into the roof of the house and then the gun had jammed. The sight of Karanja and the weapon had galvanised the five intruders: they dropped Kahinga; three of them just took to their heels and ran off into the bush. The other two made the mistake of trying to start one of the cars; Rafiki just stuck the revolver into the front of the car and yelled: 'One more move and I will shoot. Just get out of the car with your hands up, very slowly.'

The men knew Rafiki and her reputation and had no doubt she would do as she said. Sarah and Wanjiru had now appeared, fully clothed, shaken but unharmed.

'Help me tie these two 'shenzi's' up will you. Kahinga may need some help and then we should 'phone Munyu.'

Peter arrived in a flurry of dust about forty minutes later; he had had the foresight to alert Kinua on his way home; Kinua arrived shortly after him.

They tried to patch Kahinga up but it was clear that he needed some expert attention.

'Take him to the clinic in Pumwani,' suggested Rafiki. 'They will fix him up.'

Kinua and Wanjiru helped him into the front of Kinua's new pick-up and rushed off to Pumwani.

'So what is all this about?' asked Peter when they had looked through the shambles that had been made of Peter's office, obviously in search of something.

Sarah and Karanja then described how the five men had suddenly descended on them all, how they had beaten Wanjiru, Sarah and Kahinga up and demanded to know where the papers were.

'What papers?' Kahinga had asked.

'Munyu's papers lying about Minister Kariuki.'

Kahinga had shrugged. He knew of no papers.

They beat him and then Sarah and Wanjiru. When Karanja unexpectedly appeared on the scene he was given the same treatment.

'They were obviously looking for the invoices that I showed my friend Johanna in his office the other day, we should talk to those two baboons out there,' said Rafiki.

The two prisoners were sitting back to back on the floor of the kitchen under the disapproving and watchful eye of the cook. Their hands and feet were still tightly bound.

Peter went into the kitchen and sat himself in a chair facing the elder one.

'You know who I am?' he asked

There was no answer, but there was a flicker of recognition on the man's face.

There was a whimper from the other man, who was scarcely more than a boy.

Peter repeated his question with the same result.

'Maybe we should just call the Police,' he said to Rafiki in Kikuyu.

There was an agitated look on the faces of both the prisoners.

'No, no Police,' the elder one eventually stammered.

'Then tell us what all this is about,' said Peter evenly.

There was no answer.

The matter was taken out of their hands. A police car with a sergeant and a constable arrived quietly and there was a knock on the back door. Peter went out.

There were the usual polite greetings in Swahili; the policemen obviously knew who they were talking to.

'There were reports of gunshots, and we see that two cars outside have had their tyres shot out' observed the sergeant politely.

'There was an attempted robbery; we have two of the men inside, three people escaped.'

The men were bundled into the police car and Peter, Rafiki, Sarah, Wanjiru Karanja and the cook were all asked to go to the local police station to make statements. Somehow Kahinga was overlooked.

As soon as the Police arrived Rafiki had made sure that the firearms were well hidden. The gangs cars were eventually laboriously loaded onto police trucks and taken away for 'further examination'.

As they were trying to tidy up Peter's office Peter said:

'We really must take this whole thing to Uncle Wacheera, clearly this was an attempt to find all the papers you waved in front of Johanna Kariuki and he is trying to retrieve them.'

'I will 'phone him now, but I have no confidence in the process especially if he follows Nyamita's example.' answered Rafiki

'This is too big for us now; we will just end up on the wrong side of the law unless we are very careful. You must remember that Wacheera is not taking any advantage of the protection racket that funds your clinics.'

'Maybe that is just to confuse you, if he is to support his village he will have to have other sources of income,' said Rafiki.

'What did you do with the guns by the way?'

'Karanja was asked to return them to Kahinga's hut, he needs to clean and hide them again.'

'Mmm, maybe that is for the best, hopefully the Police won't ask too many questions.'

'I said in my statement that I used the licensed pistol that we have here in the house, to shoot the car's tyres out,' added Rafiki.

Two days later they went to see Acting Superintendent Wacheera in the Central Police station located the opposite side of the city centre to Peter's office in the Parliament buildings. Ironically Wacheera occupied the same office that Peter had visited many years earlier to try to persuade the British authorities of the seriousness of the Mau-Mau insurrection.

Wacheera at about five foot six was typical of his tribe. He was very black, which was unusual for a Kikuyu. His very smart starched uniform suited his slim body. Wary but intelligent eyes peeked out from under a pair of bushy eyebrows.

'Is this about the problem that you had at your house in Karen two days ago? He asked.

'It is related, we think, but the issue is much wider than just that incident.'

The whole conversation was held in Kikuyu and Peter and Rafiki then laid out everything that they had found regarding Minister Kariuki and gave the Superintendent copies of all the documents that they had.

Rafiki then described her visit to Minister Kariuki and how he had reacted.

'It seems to us that the raid on our place is somehow connected, the people were obviously looking for something in the office, and it was not just a burglary. They kept asking about papers, which the people at Sattimma had no knowledge of, of course,' said Peter.

'Yes, I have read everyone's statements,' responded Wacheera. 'Where did you get these documents?'

'Certain people, including me, are extremely concerned about the level of corruption within Government and they produced the documents and came to me for advice; I'm afraid that I am unable to tell you any more without compromising the sources of information. I wonder if these documents would, in any event, be allowed as evidence in a court of law, I suppose that in order to prosecute there would have to be an independent investigation.'

'Quite so, I'm not sure that we have the resources to investigate such stuff. It seems that we may have to find resources from elsewhere.'

Peter looked enquiringly at Wacheera.

'Surely there is enough evidence to arrest Minister Kariuki here, together with the raid on our property.'

'Maybe; we haven't yet picked up any of the others involved in the raid, if any of those people tell us that Kariuki is involved we will then be able to take action. At the moment there is only sufficient evidence to charge the two we have in custody with attempted burglary, if this goes to court without further evidence they may not even get a prison sentence'

'Would you contemplate asking the British to help with the investigation on a confidential basis?' Asked Peter

Both Wacheera and Rafiki pulled a face.

'Maybe, I would have to brief M'zee (Kenyatta's colloquial name) though and this may compromise the investigation, depending on how many people he chooses to take into his confidence.'

'With your permission, Superintendent, I may be in a position to provide some very confidential assistance. If you give me a few days I will come back to you with a proposal.'

Wacheera nodded.

After a few pleasantries Rafiki and Peter left.

※　※　※

Chapter 11

'I thought that we were going home,' said Rafiki. 'We seem to be going in the opposite direction.'

'I just wanted to show you something—there.' They had pulled up outside a very modest bungalow in the suburb of Westlands, north of the city centre and just beyond the National Museums.

Peter pointed. 'That is the Wacheera residence; it really does not look like he is enjoying the fruits of corruption.'

'I have never been to his house, he kept his distance when I was in jail and my father has held that against him ever since. Maybe we are wrong and he is not in any way corrupt, despite our assumptions; maybe he is in a position to help root out some of what is going on.'

'We should pay a visit to your father and raise the question of Wacheera and what he is doing for the village, we may be very surprised.'

The following Sunday they picked Kamau up from Lenana School and went to Rafiki's home village near Thika north east of Nairobi. John had decided to stay at the school and study to help him gain admission to a British university. Kamau had a soccer ball and a rugby ball with him. Kamau had inherited some of his father's genes so was big for his age. He was now involved in his new passion, rugby, which his brother Robert, now living in England also excelled at. Kamau rarely missed an opportunity to visit his grandfather's village a place where he had spent most of the years of the emergency, while Rafiki was organising food drops for the Mau-Mau.

'Maybe I can teach the village boys rugby now,' he said by way of explanation.

The year before when Kamau was almost fourteen, he was about to go to Lenana.

In the meantime he had had to go through the Kikuyu initiation ceremonies at his grandfather Wainaina's village. Kamau had become the leader of his age group and had led his peers into all sorts of adventures particularly in regard to the practice of 'ngweko' where male and female initiates are encouraged to lie with each other and play sexual games without full intercourse taking place. With Kamau's encouragement the group went way beyond what was envisaged by the village elders. (Authors note: for a full description of the initiation ceremonies please refer to the third book in this trilogy: 'No Peace for the Wicked.')

So whilst Kamau still went to the village regularly, rugby and other sporting interests took up much of his time, but when the opportunity arose he still enjoyed his visits to the village, where he was always regarded as a bit of a hero partly because of his exploits during initiation.

Rafiki's father Wainaina greeted them warmly. In the early days of Peter's relationship with Rafiki Peter was ostracised from the village and indeed it was only after Peter had played a leading role in rescuing Rafiki from the gallows, that Wainaina had relented and realised that Peter was genuinely fond of his daughter and that he, Peter had suffered just as much in the emergency as many of the Kikuyu.

Kamau tore off to play with all his friends and from the noise level that ensued it seemed that at least that part of the visit was a success.

The first part of the visit, as always, involved long discussions about Wainaina's cattle, which Peter had helped to upgrade by giving him bull calves from Naseby before the farm was purchased for resettlement as part of the 'million acre scheme'. This involved walking amongst them while out grazing and admiring many of the individual beasts; Wainaina, of course, knew each of them by name and he was very proud of his attractive and substantial herd. Peter recognised many of the offspring of his own herd and was able to tell Wainaina some of their related history.

Peter reflected that he had been happy building up the farm from what had been a piece of untamed bush, but he was now involved in a much more significant role in helping to build up the country; he was determined that greed would not be allowed to wreck his efforts.

Rafiki's mother said to Peter: 'If we had known you were coming I would have brewed something special, but now you will just have to make do with the ordinary home brew.'

'The ordinary home brew, as you describe it, mama, is very special to me, so I am very happy, thank you.' As always she beamed, Peter was now regarded as a very celebrated member of the village, apart from his help with the cattle he had provided a school room and even paid for the teacher—just the sort of thing that a successful son-in-law was expected to do. He had also sponsored several of the village boys to Lenana.

After long discussions with Wainaina and the elders Peter managed to turn the conversation round to Wacheera. Rafiki had crept into the conversation; the men tolerated her because of her role in the emergency; none of the other women would have dreamt of taking such liberties.

There was a stony silence.

'He is now a Police chief,' said one, 'maybe we should be proud of him.'

'He did not help Rafiki when the Sirkali put her in jail,' said Wainaina.

'He is a big man now, but does nothing for this village, we never see him,' said another.

Peter kept quiet. He had an idea of what Wacheera earned and without 'supplementing' his earnings he thought that financially things would necessarily be fairly tight.

'We cannot do anything since he is part of the Police, if he was in the Parliament we could vote for someone else.'

'Minister Kariuki, who was born in this village, he does many things for us; even Munyu does many things, but Wacheera—nothing. Maybe we should kill him.'

Peter flinched.

The debate went on. There was no doubt that the feeling against Wacheera was very high and that because of what was seen as his good fortune in becoming a Police chief that he should be doing something to help his village.

'The Police do not have any money to help individual villages; their job is to make the country safe from criminals,' interjected Rafiki.

There were a few shrugs around the group.

'Minister Kariuki is able to help, why not Wacheera?'

As far as the village was concerned both of them were part of 'Government' and had similar authority; anyone who was in a 'high position' was able to help his home village.

The discussion was interrupted by Kamau and a few of the village boys who came running into the group. They were covered in dust and Kamau had a torn shirt.

Rafiki started fussing and dusting him off.

'Mum, we need to go, I have to be back at the school by six, I think.'

So they left in rather a rush.

'It seems that Uncle Wacheera is doing the right thing by the country but as a result of that he has put himself offside in a big way with his village,' offered Peter.

'Maybe we should talk to him, just to see how he feels,' said Rafiki.

So they did.

Rafiki 'phoned him at home.

'Would you and Auntie come to dinner at Sattimma sometime in the next week or so,' she asked.

Wacheera was hesitant. 'Is this official?' he asked suspiciously.

'No, not really. We seem to have lost touch in recent years and it would just be a chance to talk.'

'OK.' They made a date.

Wacheera arrived on his own, with a driver.

The cook had made a really special effort.

'It is good to have a Kikuyu as head of the Police now and not one of those other people; I will make sure that we have something special.'

The driver who was also a Kikuyu was invited into the kitchen, fed and made a fuss of.

'Auntie could not come tonight,' said Wacheera as he was welcomed by Rafiki, 'she had another engagement.'

Actually he had not told her where he was going; he found that she tended to complain about their own relatively modest establishment if she went to a place that was much better.

'This is what we can afford on my salary,' he would explain.

'Then they must pay you more.'

'I am paid much the same as anyone else.'

'Then why do they all have bigger houses and trips overseas?'

'Maybe they steal.'

'Maybe you should steal as well, just look at the house that fat Jaluo pig Nyamita has, it is twice the size of this one.'

' My job is to stop people stealing, not to join them.'

'Just a little would do no harm.'

'If everyone steals, just a little, as you say there will be nothing left.'

She just shrugged.

The evening went very smoothly and Rafiki reminisced about her childhood and the village generally.

'I don't go to the village very much anymore,' volunteered Wacheera.

They looked enquiringly at him.

'They want too much, just because I am high up in the Police they think that I have plenty of money, so I get requests to pay for school fees and for school buildings and many other things. On my salary I am unable to do much more than pay my own way. I have quite a small house anyway,' he said unhappily. 'Not like this place.' He looked around pointedly.

Peter ignored the comment; he thought that Wacheera probably understood the basis of Peter's finances perfectly well.

'Some of the other people in Government positions seem to have bigger houses,' offered Rafiki.

Wacheera nodded: 'They steal from many places, Government, protection rackets and so on.'

'Is there anything that you can do about it?' asked Peter.

'Yes many things, but I need help, such as the information that you brought me the other day.'

'Is your boss involved in any other rackets?'

'I'm not certain but obviously I know that most of the money from the protection racket that we all know about goes to Rafiki's clinics in Pumwani, and that Nyamita takes some of it. I don't know how much you take.'

Peter blanched:

'Nothing, we take nothing, all the money goes to the clinics and is paid in there by the Police. Nyamita takes the rest.'

Rafiki chimed in: 'All the financial arrangements for the clinics are run by a large traditional and very reputable company in town here. Many, mostly white owned, businesses contribute on a regular basis and I have almost nothing to do with the administrative arrangements. The money that is paid in includes all the funds from police sources. This is done so that not only is everything above board but so the contributors are reassured that it is above board as well. Because of this the number of people willing to contribute is growing all the time.'

Wacheera nodded approvingly and then said:

'If we are serious about stopping and preventing corruption, then the protection racket that we are all aware of should now stop as well.'

'What about my clinics and the people of Pumwani?' asked Rafiki furiously. 'I have opened another clinic recently as a result of the amount of money coming in now.'

'What about Minister Kariuki's children's education and what about many other things; if we are to stop all this then it must all stop, not just some of it.'

'The trouble is that if the protection racket that funds the clinics stops then within weeks another one will have started up, taking money from the same people and just filling up another bank account,' observed Peter.

'What happens in Ulaya?' asked Wacheera.

'The same problems exist, of course, but it seems to be on a smaller scale. Also some people have been jailed for such things.'

'We have much to think about,' said Wacheera. 'I am sure that you know I am involved in none of these things. Any money that is supposed to come to me I now send to the clinics. I don't even interfere in the Police recruitment process, something which Wainaina has asked me to do, he wanted village boys to be taken into the police whether they are suitable or not.'

'If you do start investigating some of the corruption, how much support will you get from Government, do you think?'

Wacheera shrugged. 'It depends on how high the investigation goes, if it gets into very sensitive areas I may be in trouble.'

'What sort of trouble.'

'They will try to stop the investigation, at least. They may even kill some people.'

The conversation then drifted on to some more cheerful topics and quite early Wacheera took his leave.

They had certainly broken the ice with Wacheera and a degree of trust was emerging.

Before Rafiki could say anything Peter said: 'We need to find another way to fund the clinics. Wacheera is right; you can't allow some corrupt practices and not others. I will ask Giles what he thinks.'

A few days later Peter made a call to England, something he did very rarely, due to the cost and apparent extravagance of such an activity. Giles Dingley-Ferris was married to Louise, Jenny's sister.

After the usual greetings, Peter then tried to explain the complexities of the protection racket and how they were now funding Rafiki's clinics in the slums of Nairobi.

'Why don't the Government just fund the clinics,' asked Giles.

Peter laughed. 'They do some of that but by and large they are too busy stuffing their own Swiss bank accounts with as much as they can get away with.'

'The arrangement seems most unusual; I can't say that I have ever had such a dilemma before,' said Giles in his understated English way.

'I suppose that you are surprised that we are involved at all in such a scheme?' Asked Peter.

Giles ignored the question. Over the years he had ceased to be surprised by his Kenyan brother-in –law, most people in Peter's position would have abandoned the ex-colony years before. He knew that Peter would always put the interests of the country before his own.

'But you say that Rafiki's clinics would suffer if you no longer had access to these funds.'

'These or other funds.'

'I suppose that you could just continue as you are,' said Giles reluctantly.

'Yes, but it could put us on the wrong side of the law, Rafiki's uncle who is now acting Police chief certainly knows of the scheme, firstly since we have discussed it and at our insistence all the paying-in slips have a police stamp on them. Also the actual Police chief, who is recovering from a very severe injury from an apparent drug bust, still benefits substantially from the scheme; it was after all he who set the scheme up in the first place, we just muscled in on it. Wacheera, Rafiki's uncle personally is not involved in any corruption and is paying the price for such reticence.' He briefly explained Wacheera's comparatively modest lifestyle and the attitude of his home village. 'He is keen to try to stop as much of the corruption as he can since he sees that it is holding the country back, but he needs help and if apparent allies such as Rafiki and me are obviously involved in what looks like a corrupt scheme, where does he start.'

'Well what about the United Nations, maybe they could help your clinics?'

'I know nothing about how they operate; I would be surprised if there wasn't a massive amount of bureaucracy involved though. At present, the whole thing is very simple, neither Rafiki nor I take a cent from the scheme or any of the other funds that we raise so all of the money goes straight into the front line, where it is needed.

'What about individual church groups.'

'That could work, but it would need to be several groups acting together to raise enough money.'

In the end Robert came to their rescue.

He and several colleagues at Oxford had decided to raise money for charity; which charity they had not yet identified.

On a weekend visit to Giles' Belgravia mansion he mentioned the project to Giles and Louise during dinner.

'Have you mentioned this scheme to your father?' Asked Giles.

Robert looked surprised.

'I thought that he had some fancy scheme with the Police or something.'

'Yes, I think that that is right, but it may be coming to an end.'

Robert raised his eyebrows.

Giles tried to explain the scheme that funded the Pumwani clinics and why it needed to stop.

'Obviously that will have an enormous effect on the operation of the clinics; they might even have to close some of them. That could affect my father politically I suppose,' mused Robert.

'Yes, I'm sure that that is right.'

To start with the amounts of money that were sent were quite small and not enough to replace the funds from the protection racket.

'If we stop the protection money now I will have to close clinics,' said Rafiki one night over dinner.

'How much would you be short, if we stopped the protection business?'

She told him.

'I will be able to fund that for one year from some savings that I have but you should try to see if there are any places where you can maintain services but make some savings.'

Rafiki nodded.

'Wacheera is going to try to shut the scheme down within the next few weeks I think.'

'I wonder how soon it will be replaced by another scheme,' observed Rafiki cynically.

'We should just watch what Nyamita does.'

❊   ❊   ❊

CHAPTER 12

Nyamita recovered slowly from his wounds. As soon as he could sit up in his hospital bed he asked Ziporah to find Amon. He urgently needed to rescue his financial position.

'What has happened to the bhang plantation?' He asked Amon without any preliminaries.

Amon shrugged. He had not been near the place since the shootout.

'You must go there and see what is happening; do we know who those people were that tried to kill us?'

'Maybe some Kikuyu.' Amon was just guessing, he really had no idea. 'If you want me to go, I will go but how do I get there?' he added.

A few days later a small Police truck drove slowly to the stone quarry with Amon sitting uncomfortably in the front next to the driver.

The driver turned the vehicle round and said to Amon:

'I will stay here, you go and look around but if there is any trouble I will leave even if you are not here.'

From his vantage point in the truck it seemed to Amon that nothing much had changed since the shootout; nevertheless he cautiously emerged from the vehicle and scouted around the area. There were no footprints and when he opened the unlocked door of the hut he had occupied, it seemed that all his meagre possessions were untouched. 'So far so good.' he thought.

'I will now go up to the plantation, maybe you can come with me,' he said to the driver.

'I stay here.' Was the firm response.

'I will be a long time; it is a two hour climb up to the plantation.'

The driver just shrugged.

Amon slowly climbed up the now partly overgrown path to the plantation.

To his unpractised eye there was little or no sign of any human activity, so much to his surprise when he arrived at his destination two hours later there was the bhang plantation growing again. It looked as if it was almost ready to be harvested. He started to walk around the area. Suddenly he was knocked to the ground and he felt the barrel of a gun in his neck.

He was silently brought to his feet and his hands tied behind his back, he was then pushed down to the ground again.

'We should just shoot him now and bury him in the mutoni (forest) nobody would ever find him'. The words were in Kikuyu as far as Amon could make out.

'Kahinga said not to kill or hurt anyone but if they came up to the glade then we should take them prisoner and bring them to Tembo and keep him there until he comes next week.'

Amon could make out very little of what was said; he did register the word 'Kahinga' though.

'I will go to Tembo with this stinking piece of Jaluo shit. You will go down to the quarry and see what is there. Don't kill anyone. Just go, look and come back and tell us what you saw. Nothing else,' said Macharia, who was nominally in charge, speaking to N'guku.

Amon was roughly dragged to his feet and pushed along a path going up the mountain.

N'guku made his way uncertainly down the path to the quarry arriving just before dusk; he quietly scouted the area. He could see the police truck but there was no sign of anyone around. He crept up to the truck, wondering what he should do. Then he heard a light snoring sound coming from the cab. A quick glance showed him a man in a police uniform sound asleep lying on the front seat of the truck. 'I should just shoot him and leave' was his first thought. Then he remembered what he had been told by his colleague. 'I can't just do nothing,' he thought.

He collected four short twigs. Going to the back wheel away from the open driver's window he undid the tyres' air-cap and inserted one of the twigs; there was a loud rush of escaping air. He quickly withdrew the twig, since he did not wish to wake the driver, and inserted it more gently. This time there was a much quieter release of air. He judged it would take about fifteen minutes for the tyre to deflate. N'guku then did the same to all the other tyres and found the spare and completed the exercise. He waited for all the tyres to deflate, quietly withdrew all the twigs and replaced the air-caps. He wondered if there was a puncture mending outfit in the vehicle and a pump but decided that those items would have been lost or stolen months or years earlier. He supposed that he should just return to Tembo, but he thought that he would have some fun first so he gently shook the truck. There was a sudden flurry of activity from the cab. N'guku quietly withdrew to the safety of the nearby bush and watched in the gathering dusk. The police driver got out of the vehicle looked around, looked around the quarry and the mean little hut, shrugged his shoulders re-entered the cab and started the engine and tried to drive off. Within a few yards he stopped looked at the rear tyre on the driver's side, scrubbled around underneath the driver's seat and pulled out a jack and wheel spanner. Half an hour later he had successfully changed the wheel and was ready to drive off again. He stopped again within a few yards and this time having seen that the tyre that he had changed was also flat he carefully walked around the vehicle. He then stood and scratched his head. He put a stone under the rear wheel to stop the vehicle rolling away and started to walk down the track, obviously to find help. N'guku waited for about thirty minutes, and then he opened the bonnet of the truck and pulled out all the plug leads and distributor cap, which he threw into the bushes. N'guku then made the now arduous journey back to Tembo in the dark, which held no fears for him since it had been his home during the years of the emergency.

Amon was taken to Tembo and kept tied up apart from meal times and when he needed to relieve himself. Even if he was untied the last thing on his mind was escape; he found the whole atmosphere terrifying, all the night noises with many squeals and crashes continuing throughout the night. Also he had no idea which way to go.

Nyamita was beginning to get impatient. There was no sign of Amon or the Police vehicle. Then about a week later Ziporah came with the news that the Police driver had eventually returned to Nairobi and there was a garbled story about the vehicle having all its tyres let down and its electrics wrecked.

'Tell the driver that I want to see him,' demanded Nyamita.

'He has been sent back to Kisumu, Wacheera's personal instructions.'

'What about Amon?'

'Missing, he has just disappeared.'

'What do you mean disappeared, what did the driver say.'

'I didn't speak to the driver, nobody was allowed near him before he was transferred back to Kisumu.'

'Transferred, you say, not sacked.'

Ziporah nodded.

'Then you must find him; speak to Inspector Boniface who will help you.'

Normally on a Saturday morning an envelope with a wad of cash arrived for Nyamita, this had even continued while he was in hospital. He wondered for how much longer.

Nyamita was beside himself with worry and irritation. He was not due to be released from hospital for weeks yet and there was little that he could do until that happened.

Kahinga managed to get a few days off from his job with Peter at the Ministry of Agriculture. One of his colleagues stole a vehicle in River Road and they made their now familiar journey into the mountains and Tembo base.

He was surprised to find that they had a prisoner there.

'What is all this about,' he asked N'guku, who explained the situation. Wisely N'guku had told nobody about his exploits at the quarry, somehow he knew that it would not be popular.

Kahinga went up to Amon, sat on a rock and asked, in Swahili:

'So who sent you to the quarry?'

Amon just looked at him.

Kahinga got up and pointedly put a panga in the fire.

'Was it that fat Jaluo pig Nyamita?' he asked again.

This time Amon nodded. He had no intention of taking any more heat for Nyamita. He really wondered if he would get out of this Kikuyu hideout alive, he was now focussed on his own survival.

'Was it you that planted the bhang originally.'

Amon nodded.

'What is your name?'

'Amon.'

'Where is Nyamita?'

'In hospital, he was shot.'

'How long before he is discharged from the hospital.'

'Many weeks, I think.'

Kahinga went and sat on a stone a few yards away and thought.

'We should just shoot him and bury him here,' offered N'guku, in Kikuyu, waving his arms at the surrounding forest. 'He now knows what we all look like and he will report us to Nyamita, who when he gets out of hospital will come and arrest us.'

'Maybe, but maybe he can help us.'

'But he is Jaluo, how can a Jaluo help us,' was the response.

'Let me think, we will do nothing at the moment. Except that we need to get organised to harvest the bhang before anyone else gets there.'

Kahinga and his followers spent the next two days stripping the bhang plants and bagging the results. He made Amon help with the whole process.

'We will hide the bags near the quarry and then bring them out as soon as we can.'

'What about this jackal?' asked N'guku, pointing at Amon.

'He will take some of it to Kisumu, it gives us another market.'

'You trust him?' N'guku was incredulous.

'Some Kikuyu that I know have opened shops in Kisumu. They will keep an eye on him.'

N'guku just walked away shaking his head.

Three days later Kahinga arrived at the quarry with two stolen pick-up trucks.

'These ten bags go to Nairobi. These three go with you, N'guku and Amon to Kisumu. N'guku, you will drive to Kisumu.'

The arrangements were simple. Amon was to get twenty-five percent of everything he sold and submit the funds through a Kikuyu shopkeeper that had been a colleague of Kahinga's. N'guku was to spend a few weeks in Kisumu just to keep an eye on things.

'If I see you back in Nairobi or if you go anywhere near the quarry, I will kill you. Do you understand? Also have no dealings with Nyamita. If I find out that is what you are doing the same thing will happen to you; your body will be dumped in the mutoni here for the hyaenas to eat,' Kahinga spoke quietly to Amon just before N'guku started the pick-up.

Amon almost wet his pants. He nodded. As far as he was concerned this was a much better arrangement than the one offered by Nyamita: he would be at home in Kisumu, bhang would be delivered to him on a regular basis and all he had to do was sell it, something that he had been doing in the past, and he would be away from this hateful forest. Best of all he would make some money, maybe in time he would be able to afford another wife.

Kahinga drove the stolen pick-up to Sattimma, arriving after midnight, quickly unloaded the ten bags of bhang and then sent one of his henchmen with the vehicle to dump it back in River Road. With luck it would not have been reported missing and the Indian owner would just be glad to have the vehicle back.

A very tired Kahinga reported for work the next morning.

Kahinga was most anxious to dispose of the ten bags of bhang before

Peter found out that he had them, so after work he found his way to River road and the Indian shopkeeper that he thought he had made arrangements with to unload the bhang.

'Samples,' asked the shopkeeper.

Kahinga produced a grubby little paper bag containing s few leaves of bhang.

'Undried, I have no facilities to dry this stuff.'

Kahinga shrugged.

He was offered a very low price.

'I can't give it to you for this price, I have to pay people.'

The shopkeeper shrugged.

'But we had an arrangement,' said Kahinga plaintively.

The shopkeeper shrugged.

Kahinga picked up the sample and walked away.

※　※　※

CHAPTER 13

Peter decided to visit Wacheera in his office. He was greeted warily, but there was a sense of expectation in his demeanour. After the usual greetings and discussion about the weather, Wacheera looked at Peter expectantly:

'We are now ready to stop the protection racket, I am receiving funds from Ulaya and I have agreed to make up any balance from my own funds. Rafiki and I agree that all this corruption must stop and we cannot make any exceptions, whatever the final destination of the funds.'

'Nyamita will go ballistic, I have made certain up to now that he gets his little envelope every week,' Wacheera smiled.

'The question is, as soon as we stop this business someone else will try to muscle in and start the same thing again, which just destroys the whole purpose of what we are trying to do.' Peter looked at Wacheera.

'I have rearranged the Police patrols, with people that I can trust, they will visit each week as if they are collecting money, but they will collect no money.'

'All Kikuyu, are they?' Peter asked.

'Absolutely not, they are all from different tribes and I have made certain that in each patrol no pair will be from the same tribe.'

Peter nodded. 'At least this has a chance of working,' he thought.

'You must stop Kahinga monitoring these people.'

'OK.'

There was a brief pause; it seemed that Wacheera expected Peter to take his leave.

'What about Minister Kariuki?' asked Peter.

'One thing at a time, I need more time on that one please. That person who you brought from England and is working with us has been very helpful but we must have a watertight case.'

Johanna Kariuki had worried himself to death over what was to happen to the information that Rafiki had and what he should do about it. His attempt at rescuing some of the evidence that Rafiki had confronted him with had failed and two of the thugs that had been sent to raid Sattimma were still in police custody; luckily the arrangements were made through an associate so the people being held by the police did not directly relate the raid with him. He had heard rumours that Rafiki's Pumwani clinics were largely funded by some sort of protection racket taking money from small shopkeepers; somehow the police were involved. He wondered if he should go to see Wacheera, but quickly discarded the idea since he had been told of Wacheera's rather modest lifestyle. He then wondered if he should go to see Nyamita, but again rejected the idea mainly because he was a Jaluo. Johanna's wife was putting pressure on him for more money: 'I see the wives of even junior ministers are making trips to Ulaya and are buying many things at the big store in London.'

'You mean Harrods,' he said helpfully.

'Yes, that is the place.'

'We must be careful; especially now that Rafiki has come to me with information that could put me in jail.'

'Rafiki,' was the contemptuous response, 'she is up to her neck in all this, how can they afford that house in Karen and they have children at Lenana and one in Ulaya.'

'The new acting Police Superintendent, Wacheera, is Rafiki's uncle, we must be careful or they will give all that information to him and who knows what could happen then.'

She went quiet for a minute. 'That thieving Jaluo pig Nyamita is still the Police chief, how much longer will he be in hospital?'

'Maybe some weeks, still but I think it will be months before he can resume his responsibilities if he ever does.'

'I am sure he is not just lying in bed doing nothing, maybe he is worried about what Wacheera might do to some of his little schemes.'

'What do you know about his schemes?' asked Johanna.

'He and Rafiki have some sort of protection racket going where they take money from shopkeepers ever week.'

'How do you know this?'

'Rumours, but I think that they are true. Also maybe Nyamita is not such a hero, you read all the stories about how he stopped drug traffickers and that is how he was shot.'

Johanna nodded.

'We the truth is that he was one of the traffickers and he was shot in a sort of a gang war with some Kikuyu.'

'More rumours?'

'Yes, but I think that you should go to see him, he has an expensive lifestyle, maybe he can help you.'

'Why is a Jaluo going to help me, maybe he would like another Jaluo in my place anyway.'

'Maybe he would but with the M'zee at the top, he is lucky that a Jaluo such as him was chosen for that position. Maybe he needs friends like you.'

Johanna mulled over this discussion for a number of days.

He then found out where Nyamita was in hospital, what the visiting hours were, and since he had no other method of contacting him he just went to see him.

Nyamita was, as Johanna expected, in a private ward. He knocked politely and entered. He saw a very large man propped up in bed with a young attractive woman sitting quietly beside the bed. Nyamita looked surprised but said nothing. The woman made no sign of even having seen Johanna.

'I am...' began Johanna.

'I know who you are mister Deputy Minister,' was the aggressive response.

Johanna hesitated. Maybe this was the wrong move; there was no mistaking the hostility emanating from the man in the bed; he was about to turn away and open the door.

'What do you want, why are you here?' asked Nyamita.

'I thought that maybe there were some things that we could usefully discuss.'

The whole conversation was in a mixture of English and Swahili since neither of them spoke the other's home language.

'What personal things could I possibly want to discuss with a stinking Kikuyu jackal like you?'

Johanna again considered walking out, but then he thought what his wife might say if he did that and he grew a bit of backbone.

'Well you know that we have to maintain a certain style of living?'

There was a faint spark of interest on Nyamita's face. He nodded without saying anything.

'I have been told that that bitch Rafiki and her disgusting M'zungu husband have compromised one of your schemes that helps maintain the standard of living that we need.' It was a statement rather than a question.

Nyamita wondered what sort of a trap was being set for him to fall into.

'The scheme funds some of the clinics that the bitch runs in Pumwani; she is also trying to compromise a scheme that I run to keep my children in school.'

'What scheme?'

Johanna ignored the question.

'She has threatened to take all the information on my scheme to her uncle Wacheera who is now acting Police chief in your place.'

'So?'

'If they prosecute maybe I will be forced to resign.'

'And possibly end up in 'Hoteli-ya Kingi Georgie' that would certainly reduce your lifestyle back to a grass hut and a bicycle,' Nyamita said unkindly.

'That Rafiki has got too big for her boots, she needs to be sorted out, and I thought that maybe since our interests are similar, we might have a better chance of succeeding if we helped each other,' responded Johanna evenly.

'Like what?'

Johanna shrugged. 'I was wondering if you had any ideas.'

'Let me think about it; it will cost you though, you need to understand that.'

Johanna nodded and left after having agreed that he would return in a few days.

Nyamita turned to Ziporah with a questioning glance. She hadn't understood all of the conversation, since her English skills were at best rudimentary.

'He wants to kill Rafiki?' she asked.

'Maybe not kill, but at least make sure she stops all her nonsense.'

'What about Munyu?'

'Difficult, if we hurt him then when the Kikuyu find out that person will be in very big trouble.'

Ziporah made as if she was about to leave.

'Not so fast, not so fast. Have you contacted Inspector Boniface yet?'

'I tried but he was not there.'

'Try harder. I must know what is going on in Kisumu.'

Ziporah was terrified by the turn of events; she had contacted Boniface who had told her what had happened at the quarry and that Amon was now selling bhang in Kisumu. She didn't know what to do. She had introduced Amon and the whole concept of growing the bhang and it had now all gone sour. From previous incidents she knew that Nyamita was totally ruthless and if he decided that she was to blame she would certainly be punished and maybe killed. She was almost completely dependent on Nyamita for everything, without him she would just have to return to her disapproving parents in Kisumu. Her prospects of marriage had more or less disappeared since she had taken up with Nyamita. When Nyamita found out what Amon was doing, all Amon could expect was to end up as crocodile fodder in Lake Victoria. Somehow she had to warn him, he was after all her uncle and in the end her loyalties lay with her family. In any event she was considering how much longer her relationship with Nyamita would last-from her perspective the last few months had been most unsatisfactory, being moved from her luxurious apartment into a much more modest place and now the landlord was complaining that the rent had not been paid. Nyamita had been convalescing for weeks and weeks now and she wondered whether he would ever recover.

A few days later Ziporah happened to be passing by the first of Rafiki's clinics in Pumwani. She was worried sick and had not been to see Nyamita in hospital since their last conversation. She was just about to walk past when she saw Rafiki entering the clinic, so ignoring the lengthy queue she dashed into the clinic and touched Rafiki on the sleeve. 'I need to talk to you, it is very important,' she whispered in Swahili.

'Just join the queue; you will be attended to in turn.'

'No, I don't need any medical attention, this is more personal.'

Rafiki turned around and saw a comparatively well dressed young Jaluo woman looking terrified and almost pleading with her. The usual clients at the clinics were often dressed in rags. There were so many special cases that normally Rafiki would have made her go to the end of the queue but there was something different and desperate about this woman so she said quickly: 'OK come with me,' and they went to a small office in the rear of the building, furnished with just a desk and two chairs.

'Now relax, just sit down quietly and I will get you a mug of tea.'

A short while later Rafiki emerged with two tin mugs of sweet milky tea and sat down opposite Ziporah. 'Take your time,' she said, 'take your time.' They both sipped their tea in silence for a few moments. Rafiki waited.

'This is very difficult for me,' said Ziporah.

'OK, just tell me slowly and I will listen.' Rafiki was quite used to dealing with traumatised people; poverty brought out the worst in human behaviour she thought.

'You know Nyamita, the Police chief,'

Rafiki was suddenly on full alert. She nodded.

'These clinics are paid for by that scheme that the Police run for you.'

'Not any more they don't, that all stopped last week, instructions from the acting Police Superintendent.'

That was bad news for Ziporah.

'I am a friend of Superintendent Nyamita,'

Rafiki nodded. Who was she to judge, bearing in mind her relationship with Peter for years before they were married.

'I was with him a few days ago in the hospital and there was an unusual visit from Johanna Kariuki, who I think you know.'

Rafiki was very surprised.

'Yes I know Kariuki; we grew up in the same village.'

'He and Nyamita are planning to harm you and Munyu, because of the trouble you have caused them.'

'What trouble?'

'The trouble with the money that funds these clinics and some other problem that you have with Kariuki.'

'Why are you telling me all this?'

'Nyamita is a very dangerous man; he is not going to play any more games.'

'Yes but why are you telling me this, surely if you keep your mouth shut nothing will happen to you.'

Ziporah started to shake. 'I am in trouble with him as well.' She then explained the bhang plantation and the involvement of her uncle Amon and the fact that she had introduced Amon and the idea of growing bhang to Nyamita. She also explained what she knew of the shootout at the quarry. 'Nyamita is not a Police hero, like the papers said; he was trying to harvest that crop of bhang, grown by Amon. Someone else just got in before he did.'

'Where is this Amon now?'

'In Kisumu.'

'Doing what?'

'Selling Bhang.'

'Provided by Nyamita?

Ziporah shook her head. 'No, Amon tried to start up the plantation again, on behalf of Nyamita, but he just disappeared. We thought that he had been killed, but then I found him in Kisumu.'

'You found him, how?'

'Through the Police in Kisumu, Inspector Boniface.'

It all started to fall into place.

'Nyamita doesn't know any of this yet,' added Ziporah.

'Who provides the bhang?' asked Rafiki.

'Boniface says maybe it is some Kikuyu, the same ones that shot Nyamita up in the first place.'

'What happens to Amon when Nyamita finds out?'

'He will be killed and thrown into Lake Victoria.'

'And you?'

'Maybe the same.' Ziporah started shaking uncontrollably.

'OK, what do you want from me?'

'I need to go to Kisumu to warn Amon to go far away, and then I need a place to stay and maybe a job.'

'You say that you need a job, what can you do?' asked Rafiki.

Ziporah looked slightly discomfited.

'I can cook, I can read a little.' She responded lamely.

'I will try to find you something, maybe as a cleaner and then we can teach you other things. Come back here in about a week and I will be able to help you.'

'I have no money; I need to pay for the train to take me to Kisumu.'

Rafiki looked at her. 'You really are in a mess,' she thought and then she thought of her relationship with Peter and if he had chosen a different path how she could have ended up in a similar or even worse situation, in fact she would probably have been hanged by the British.

Without saying a word Rafiki handed over enough money for the train fare to Kisumu and then added enough for meals and other expenses.

Ziporah left, looking relieved. Rafiki wondered whether she would ever see her again.

When she told Peter of her discussions with Ziporah, Peter immediately went to see Wacheera at his house after dinner. It was a perfectly adequate but modest bungalow in a very ordinary street in Westlands. Wacheera himself came to the door and was surprised but quite pleased to see his visitor. The house was neat and well kept: 'Much nicer that the house we had on Naseby,' he thought. He was offered a cup of tea by Wacheera's wife, who had greeted him like a long lost friend although he had never met her. He often forgot that many Kikuyu regarded him with awe because of his reputation in saving Rafiki from the gallows and generally for the even handed way in which he had handled himself during the emergency. Peter noticed that she was a large and apparently very traditional woman; she had dispensed with her earring bangles although she still had long ear lobes hanging down. When the tea had been served she made herself scarce.

Wacheera looked at Peter curiously, and he now regarded Peter as a kind of ally. He just waited patiently.

'There has been a serious development and I think that Rafiki and I and possibly our children are in danger, you as well probably.' He then explained Ziporah's visit to Rafiki and what had been learned about the visit of Johanna Kariuki to Wacheera's old boss Nyamita.

Wacheera responded very quickly: 'I am not quite ready to arrest Minister Kariuki, but I will put both him and our friend Nyamita under surveillance. I do not have the manpower to provide you or your family with security though, or the clinics. Maybe you can look after that. I can look after myself, of course.' He smiled, 'now the fun starts.'

'What about Inspector Boniface and Ziporah and even Amon.'

'I hope that Boniface can be persuaded to understand that his real interests lie with the Police service, who after all is his employer. Amon will get what is coming to him, it would be better for him to go to Uganda, so he is out of the way. Ziporah needs to keep out of Nyamita's way, but you seem to think that Rafiki will look after her in the clinics somehow.'

The next morning Peter called Kahinga quite early and was surprised to see the look of apprehension on his face, which disappeared when he told him his purpose. 'I wonder what he is up to now,' he thought.

'Kahinga,' he said, 'two things, one, the collection of money from the small shopkeepers has been stopped by Wacheera, so you don't need to monitor them anymore.'

'What about the clinics, who will now pay for them?'

'Money is coming from Ulaya for the clinics, from Robert.'

Kahinga looked surprised, but said nothing. He thought: 'These Wazungu are crazy, what can the people in Ulaya gain from such an arrangement.'

Peter continued: 'Two, there is going to be big trouble, here and at the clinics and maybe with my children at Lenana, so I need to increase the security even more.'

'Can you tell me the reason?'

'Well, stopping the collection of money from the small shopkeepers will not please everybody. Some people will be very upset.'

'Nyamita?'

Peter was surprised at the response, but he supposed that very little passed Kahinga by and he probably knew where all the money went.

'Any other reason?'

'Well there are many people in responsible positions in Government who are stealing from Government, this means that Government has no money and are unable to look after such things as the clinics that Rafiki runs and maybe some roads do not get built or looked after and so on . Rafiki's uncle Wacheera is now the Police chief and wants to stop it all, so some people may try to blame us for some of this.'

'Oh yes,' responded Kahinga. 'Rafiki's visit to Minister Kariuki, I hear bad things about this person.'

Peter ignored the comment, but he thought that Kahinga might be worth pumping for information at a later date.

'How many guns do you have?'

Kahinga hesitated: 'six revolvers and four Patchetts,' he said eventually.'

Peter didn't turn a hair. 'We need to increase the security at the clinics, instead of just the one guard at night, I need one person on guard all the time at each clinic, so one during the day and one at night, they must be armed so you can give them the revolvers. They must keep out of sight but they must be ready. The clinics could be attacked at any time. I need security here: one guard on in the day, you can arm him with a revolver, but at night I want one in the house, in the kitchen, and three outside. The one in the house can be armed with a revolver the one's outside should be given the Patchetts. Again they must keep out of sight. Now the school… '

'Don't worry about the school, many people in the school were with me in the forests, nobody will be able to get anywhere near the boys, Munyu's children.' He said pointedly.

'The clinics will pay for the guards on duty at the clinics and I will pay for the guards here at Sattimma. Are all the weapons clean and tested?'

Kahinga grinned: 'Of course, like you showed me all those years ago, but maybe we could go to the Police firing range just to make certain.'

Kahinga returned to his hut and retrieved the weapons that he had brought back from the forest. 'Only five revolvers,' he thought. He looked again, definitely only five. 'Ah,' he thought, 'bloody Karanja.' Karanja was already at work with his father Kinua. Kahinga went quickly to Karanja's hut and looked around the dark interior for a few minutes, then he looked in the Bergen rucksack that Karanja had taken up the mountain with him, tipped it upside down and out fell the revolver and some ammunition. He picked up the weapon and ammunition, put the rucksack exactly where it had been and went back to his own abode. The revolver had not been cleaned since the previous incident when Rafiki had shot the tyres out of the cars belonging to the people who had raided the house a few weeks earlier. The gun was loaded and the empty cartridges from shots that had been fired remained in the chamber. He just shook his head. He cleaned all the weapons, collected all the ammunition he had and put them all safely in a rucksack and took them to the boot of the car.

Peter and Kahinga went to the Police shooting range. Once they had announced themselves no notice was taken of them. The officer in charge of the range knew Munyu and he was totally trusted, so he and Kahinga just got on with what they were doing. They tested each weapon and made certain that they were all in working order, firing a few shots. 'How much ammo. do you have?' asked Peter.

'Enough for the moment, but we will need more quite soon I think.'

Kahinga was clearly enjoying himself.

'Just like the old days,' he ventured. 'When we were camping at the wheat farm you had for a few years, where I was bitten by the snake, and then when we went on Safari with that mad bwana Athill.'

Peter laughed. They both had good memories of those days.

They returned to Sattimma and on the way back he said to Kahinga: 'Maybe we should get those weapons properly registered.'

'Yes, in my name though, they are my guns, I worked very hard to get them,' said Kahinga fiercely.

Peter didn't enquire any further, but he managed to get Wacheera to register the guns in Kahinga's name. Wacheera buried his discomfort at the request; he had much bigger fish to fry.

Chapter 14

Part of Peter's responsibility as Minister of Agriculture was the administration of the 'Million Acre Scheme' where all or most of the white farmers were bought out by the British Government and the land was resettled by African farmers on small plots ranging from seven to fifty acres each. He had never had the courage to return to Naseby, wondering what had happened to the farm that he had lovingly tended and developed from a rough piece of African bush to a highly productive farm. Always hoping for the best but fearing the worst. He had no problem with the political developments in Kenya and the fact that the land had been returned to the local Africans, but human nature dictated that he wanted to see his efforts to bear fruit for somebody.

He and Kahinga made sure over a few weeks that the security environment was operating correctly at the clinics and at Sattimma and he asked Kahinga what the arrangements were at the school.

'There are twenty people working at the school who were with me in the forests, they are working in the kitchens, gardens, even one teacher. They are always watching your boys, nothing will happen to them. Also nobody else knows anything about the arrangements that are in place, so please don't worry. Your boys are very popular at the school, especially Kamau; all the other boys will look after them as well.'

They set off for Naseby, early one morning stopping for breakfast at the Bell Inn at Naivasha. The place was dirty and the breakfast barely edible. Peter said nothing, but it was not a good omen for the rest of the day.

'Did you bring one of the revolvers with you?' asked Peter when they turned off the main road and turned up a still well kept dirt road in the small ugly township of Gil-gil, which mostly consisted of a row of shops on the Nairobi to Nakuru road.

'Yes, I left the guard at Sattimma with one of the Patchetts and told him to keep out of sight and to keep the gun hidden under his coat.'

They passed under the low railway bridge and the freshly painted sign for 'Pembroke House' which was a long established primary school catering mainly for pupils who wished to qualify for the entrance exams. to English public schools.

The dusty east road twisted and wound much as Peter remembered it, over the narrow wooden bridge and then up the hill past Oleolondo station. The bush was mainly leleshwa, a greyish green bush that grew to a height of about ten feet and had little nutritional value. There was not much evidence of farming although the land was occupied with huts built haphazardly in every spare corner, a few women tilling small patches of mealies and many children running about. After about three quarters of an hour they came to the church on the outskirts of Ol' Kalou; the church that Peter had helped to build. He wondered whether to visit the churchyard, but was unable to help himself and asked Kahinga to stop the car. They both got out: Jenny's little grave was well tended and there were fresh flowers on it much to his surprise. 'I wonder who does that' he asked almost to himself.

'The memsahib was always admired and liked,' said Kahinga quietly.

'But none of the people that were with us on Naseby are here anymore, it's interesting and I'm pleased.'

They both stood there for a minute and then left. Peter wiped a tear away: 'I wonder what she would have made of all that has happened?' he thought.

They passed the Police station looking unkempt and rather forlorn and once they were in the village the stopped outside Shah's store, which brought memories for both of them.

Inside the store there was a young Indian man who greeted them both warmly.

'Business good?' asked Peter casually.

'No,' was the straight answer. 'There is very little activity around here anymore. Soon we will sell up and go home.'

'Last time I was here, just about the time the first farms were taken over you were about to move to Bristol in the west of England.'

'I am the last, soon we will all be there, we are just waiting for the vouchers, as you know there is a limit of fifteen hundred per year for Kenyan Indians to settle in England.'

They left and made their way up the steep dusty road to what both of them had known as Naseby. To Peter's dismay all that was visible from the road were some huts, a few unkempt patches of mealies and not much else.

They called in to where the dairy had been; most of the farm buildings had been destroyed and the stone used to build small stone cottages. A woman came out of one of the huts and instead of the usual Kikuyu greeting they were assailed with requests for food. Peter gave her twenty shillings.

'Why can't she grow some mealies or vegetables,' asked Kahinga.

Peter shrugged.

They passed the big water tank on the side of the road and stopped.

Peter turned to admire the view, the same view that he had enjoyed all those years before, just before he had purchased the farm. Mount Kenya was just visible through its small table cloth of cloud drifting around the peak and the Aberdares looked much the same with its blanket of forest. The Wanjohe valley (the famous 'happy valley' of the nineteen thirties-where the expression 'are you married or do you live in Kenya' was coined) floor was now a sea of huts as far as the eye could see. He knew that the political developments that had occurred were just; he worried that what had once been productive farmland had now been reduced to subsidence and what he, Peter, could do about it.

Kahinga crossed the road and jumped up on to the rim of the tank. 'Just mud,' he said, climbing down.

There were a few curious onlookers; opposite the tank was an unofficial bus stop where a somewhat irregular bus service took people into Nakuru, some twenty five miles away.

Peter found a disgruntled man who said that he lived and worked in the vicinity. 'What is that thing there for?' he asked

'That is something that the Wazungu put there, I don't know what it is for.'

Kahinga became impatient.

'That tank is for water that was pumped up from the borehole, over there,' he pointed to a broken down shed across the next valley. 'Does the borehole still work?'

'No borehole has pumped water since I have been here which is seven years now. There is no engine, there is no pump and we filled up the hole with rocks so that children could not fall down the hole.'

'Do you own land here?'

'No, I work for a man that lives in Nakuru, when I get paid I think that I will leave.'

'How much money are you owed?'

'Six months,'

Kahinga didn't tell him that he would always be owed a few months wages and that was the strategy to keep him where he was.

They went on and stopped by the borehole. It was as the man said: no engine, no pump and the top of the hole was blocked with a large rock.

'Wouldn't take much to sort that out,' said Peter, 'eight inch hole and plenty of water down there.'

The roof on the nearby cattle dip had fallen in and all that was visible was a puddle of muddy water. All the wooden races to corral cattle prior to dipping had been removed; Peter presumed for firewood.

They drove on over the very rough track, made their way on to the stone track that Peter had carefully laid across an area of swampland now more than twenty five years earlier. The track was severely potholed but still serviceable. They drove down to the little cottage where Peter had spent seventeen years of his life.

During the drive both Peter and Kahinga looked about them, there were many huts all built in an apparently haphazard way. There was nothing left of any of the fences that Peter had so carefully constructed and there were a few unkempt patches of mealies and vegetables surrounding the huts. There were some bedraggled looking cows. Neither of them said anything.

There was a well dressed man on the front veranda of the cottage who greeted them stiffly. He soon warmed up when Peter and Kahinga introduced themselves in Kikuyu.

'You are fortunate to have found me here,' said the man. 'I actually live in Nakuru and come up here about every two weeks to collect the cream, which I take to the KCC in Nakuru.' He waved a small one gallon can which was clearly not full.

'How much cream?' Asked Kahinga.

'Nearly one gallon,' the man said proudly.

'Anything else here?'

'No, I only have twenty five acres, with a man and his family looking after the place. They grow some mealies and vegetables and I provide them with posho (mealie meal) and sometimes meat.'

Peter briefly reflected on the three hundred gallons of milk he used to send to the KCC in Naivasha every day, from Naseby, and the ten or so bacon pigs he sent to Uplands bacon factory every week and the annual wool clip from six hundred sheep. Even if one multiplied the one gallon of cream each fortnight by fifty, what was being produced on this acreage now was literally drop in the ocean compared to that.

'Why are you here?' asked the man.

'This is Munyu,' explained Kahinga, 'he used to live here,' he gestured at the cottage. 'So did I, I used to work here for Munyu driving tractors.'

'Munyu, Munyu,' the man's eyes almost popped out of his head and he rushed over and said: 'if it wasn't for you I would never own such a place.' He grabbed Peter by both hands and shook them warmly. 'Come in, come in.' Peter and Kahinga accepted a cup of tea. The chairs were as Peter had left them, just a bit the worse for wear.

Kahinga was looking around him.

'What are all these holes in the wall?' he asked.

'Bullet holes, 'said Peter, 'we were attacked by the Mau-Mau under general Waichagga after you had left. They had about sixty people out there'

'Sixty people and they didn't get inside.'

'No, John got away on a horse and raised the alarm, they were just in time; I was wounded, quite badly.'

Kahinga shook his head. He knew Peter had had a rough time in the emergency, but he had never been told the full story of the attack on Peter and his family.

After they had finished their tea they took their leave and went on their way. As they were driving onto the main road they came across a small herd of reasonable looking cattle herded by a Kikuyu man who still wore the 'old' uniform: KAR hat, army greatcoat, car tyre sandals. He was smiling broadly. He had a long conversation with Peter and Kahinga: yes he owned fifty acres, yes he was very happy and his cattle were doing well, yes he lived on the place, yes he earned more than enough selling milk to neighbours and selling cream to the KCC in Nakuru, he also grew mealies and vegetables for his own use and he or one of his three wives sometimes sold any surplus on the main road. 'Any problems?' asked Peter.

'Water, sometimes there is not enough water for the cattle to drink,'

'What about the borehole at the top of the hill.' The man didn't know what he was talking about.

As they drove off Peter said: 'I thought I might pay a visit to officials here responsible for the settlement and development of the Ol'Kalou salient, but I will do that another time, I think that I have seen enough for one day. We should go to Nakuru and then back to Sattimma.'

They drove through what little was left of the once magnificent Bahati forest. It was now being destroyed and Peter could see that within a few years it would be almost completely denuded of trees and was being settled with a myriad of huts and patches of mealies. He shook his head: 'Population growth, if there is no room for people the wild animals and trees and everything else just disappears, we often saw Colobus monkeys on this drive here, now I suppose they have all been eaten.'

'Yes,' said Kahinga unsympathetically, 'they make very good eating, especially if you have nothing else; we ate them in the forests of the Aberdares when we could find and shoot them.'

Nakuru was teeming with people and they made their way to the 'Stags Head' hotel. It was worse that the 'Bell Inn' in Naivasha; they were too late for lunch and nobody could be found to provide them with sandwiches and the toilets were messy and the drains blocked.

'I must get out much more often,' said Peter on the way home. 'There is much to be done.'

The drive home took them just over three hours for the one hundred miles. The once pristine road, built by Italian prisoners during the Second World War was now potholed in many places. 'Another sign of corruption,' sighed Peter.

CHAPTER 15

Peter was still certain that Kahinga was 'up to something' so he kept his eyes open for unusual behaviour. Eventually Kahinga's wife Wanjiru came to see Rafiki, while she was sorting school clothes out for Kamau; they chatted for a while and Wanjiru eventually came to the point:

'You and I were both brought up in a grass hut like all the other Kikuyu.'

'Eh-he,' Rafiki could see what was coming.

'Now you live in this big house with this M'zungu, Munyu.'

Rafiki nodded.

'I still live in a grass hut like I did before.'

'Eh-he,'

'Since Uhuru many Kikuyu are now living in big houses like this one. Even Kinua is building a big house (Kinua had been given permission to build a brick house near 'Kinua's Garage') and now Kahinga wants to live in a big house.'

'What do you want, Wanjiru?'

'Maybe I want to live in a big house with a maid and a cook?'

'So how are you going to do that?'

'All these big Government baboons, like Kariuki, he did nothing in the fight with the M'zungu, and he now lives in a big house. Kahinga spent years fighting in the forests and he just has the small job with Munyu.'

'Does he want to do something else?'

Wanjiru looked uncomfortable.

'I think soon he will go to jail.'

'Why what has he done to go to jail.' Rafiki was intrigued.

'He has these guns, which he brought from the forest, which you know about, and now he has bhang, which he wants to sell in River Road and he is trying to dry it outside our hut and he is afraid that Munyu won't like it.'

'The guns are now licensed, so there is no problem with those, and he has organised security for Sattimma and the clinics. I don't think that the bhang is a good idea though. Where does he grow it?'

'Somewhere in the mutoni,' she hesitated and then went on: 'that fat Jaluo pig Nyamita is also wanting the same bhang from the same place. They had a fight and that was when Nyamita was shot.' A tear crept out of her eye, which she impatiently wiped away.

'Who else knows about the fight with Nyamita?'

'Nobody, just the people who were there.'

'Tell no one else, not Munyu not anybody, this is very dangerous knowledge. I will not even tell Munyu myself. If this becomes known Kahinga will certainly go to jail. How can we now stop him thinking about growing and selling bhang?'

There was a faint smile on Wanjiru's face and the she looked sheepishly at Rafiki:

'Well you know that Kinua set up his garage when he had fixed your car and the car of the M'zungu next door.'

'Yes, he has put all that fighting behind him and has a very good little business. He can now send his children to Lenana and he has a pick-up truck of his own,' said Rafiki encouragingly.

'Now that Kahinga is providing guards for your clinics in Pumwani and here at Sattimma, I thought that maybe he could do the same for other people, like the shops in Karen. There are many of the people that were in the forest with him just sitting around in Pumwani and stealing and getting into trouble, so they could work for Kahinga. Also he has more guns in the mutoni, maybe Munyu could help him get these guns a licence and then he will be too busy to worry about bhang and we can leave it all to Nyamita.'

'Whew,' responded Rafiki. 'That is a really brilliant idea.'

Wanjiru looked pleased and relieved.

'Now the children are bigger and at school maybe I can get a smart dress and go and tell all the people who need guards that Kahinga will arrange guards for them if they want. Maybe I need a scooter or motorbike so I don't have to take the bus and then I can see more people.'

Rafiki looked at her with admiration.

'What will you charge? She asked.

'Well, we need to pay Kahinga something for doing all the work and we need to pay for the scooter and maybe I need to be paid as well and maybe there will be other things. I was speaking to Sarah and she says that there are many small things that she has to pay which she did not think about in the early days at the garage, so I think that we will charge for two people when we provide one person and the extra charge will be for all the things that I have discussed.'

'I think that you will need a telephone, as well.'

'A telephone?' Wanjiru looked at Rafiki incredulously. She had never considered that she would ever have a telephone.

'The costs for the clinics and Sattimma will have to go up if we are to be fair to all the other people, at the moment we just charge what we pay the people and we get nothing for finding the people and organising everything,' Said Wanjiru shyly.

'Yes, of course.' Said Rafiki, 'Munyu will need another driver I suppose, if Kahinga wants to do all this. Have you spoken to Kahinga about your idea?'

'Not yet, I wanted to understand what you thought about it first.'

'OK, you speak to Kahinga and then I can help you set the business up properly.'

When Peter came home that night Rafiki mentioned the discussion she had had with Wanjiru.

'Bhang you say, I knew he was up to something, he will have to get rid of it and quickly but this idea of a firm providing security is a very good one and should keep him out of trouble. On our trip I also had another idea. When we went to Naseby the other week I told you that apart from the disappointing use of most of the land that neither of the boreholes was working.'

'So, that is hardly a surprise, there is nobody there to maintain them and I don't suppose that anyone has the interest or the resources to provide water for the whole community.'

'Exactly. Just as we left there was a oldish fellow who appeared to be thriving and when I asked him if there was one thing that I could do to help he said that often there was a shortage of water, which we of course know about, that was why we needed the boreholes in the first place.'

'OK,' said Rafiki uncertainly.

'Well getting the boreholes going should not be a problem; all they need is a suitable engine and a pump. There must be hundreds of such boreholes all over the farms that were taken over.'

'What is your idea then?'

'Well there are two issues, firstly money to purchase pumps and engines and secondly someone to install and maintain everything afterwards.'

'The Ministry of Agriculture ought to be able to provide the money,' said Rafiki firmly. The last thing she wanted was more of their own resources being directed to something the Government should be financing.

'Yes and perhaps I could persuade some of the other ministries to share some of that cost.'

'And you thought that Kahinga could organise the resources to install and maintain the boreholes in the farms that were taken over.' Rafiki sighed with relief.

'That's pretty well it. If he is interested I will start him off with the two on Naseby to try to understand the practicalities involved. He knows what to do, as you know he used to help me maintain those boreholes when he was with me on Naseby.'

Peter raised the question of his idea regarding the boreholes with Kahinga on their way to the office the following week.

Kahinga looked bemused: 'Also Wanjiru has suggested that we should start a security business since we already have two customers, you and Rafiki's clinics. I think that I will be too busy to fix many boreholes.'

'Maybe you could fix the boreholes on Naseby just for me to understand how difficult such a scheme would be to start and keep going?'

'Maybe?' was the non-committal reply.

'And one other thing,' said Peter quietly. 'You won't have the time to worry about that patch of bhang in the Nyandarua forests any more. You know that uncle Wacheera is going to be much tougher on that type of thing than Nyamita has been, and you don't want to end up in jail do you, that could put a stop to any of your schemes of running a security company or helping to fix boreholes.'

Kahinga looked at Peter anxiously.

Rafiki told Peter that evening that the cook had told her that a pickup truck with a covered back had come in to the yard during the day and within a few minutes had loaded a few bags of something and driven off in a hurry.

'I asked Wanjiru what all that was about and she looked pleased and said 'bhang-all gone', something you said to Kahinga apparently.'

✕   ✕   ✕

Chapter 16

Ziporah made the twelve hour journey by train from Nairobi to Kisumu sitting uncomfortably on the wooden slatted seats in one of the very crowded third class carriages towards the rear of the train. She was resentful of the turn that her life had taken: 'Only a few months ago I was the mistress of the head of the Police force living in a fancy house in a good suburb in Nairobi and now I am scared that he will kill me. He was nearly killed in that bhang scheme that went wrong and now all I will be able to do is to live in a slum like Pumwani and I will be the cleaner in a clinic run by the Kikuyu.' A tear slipped out of her eye.

She barely noticed the teeming crowds on the stations they passed through, Kikuyu, Limuru, Kijabe and the other very crowded Kikuyu areas, previously reserved by the British administration for the Kikuyu when the population was less than one tenth of current levels. Down into the Great Rift Valley, in the distance they passed the extinct volcano of mount Longonot, then Naivasha, Gil-gil, the train ground on the with two big Garret engines belting out smoke as they puffed their way along the what was the floor of the Rift to Nakuru. She managed to find something to eat on the station at Nakuru where the train stopped for almost an hour. The train then began its laborious climb up the western slope of the Rift, to almost nine thousand feet at Mau Summit. Ziporah huddled under a thin blanket against the cold, lent to her by a kindly fellow passenger. The long descent followed, to the steamy shores of Lake Victoria and the Kavirondo Gulf at Kisumu, which is at a comparatively low altitude of three and a half thousand feet above sea level.

Ziporah scrambled out of the train along with all the other passengers clutching a small bag with her few possessions. She waited a long time for a bus which took her to a little house on the outskirts of the town where her parents lived.

She was greeted warmly by her mother and given a large meal. There were no questions. She knew they would come when her father returned.

'Amon,' she said 'I must find Amon, he is in big trouble.'

'Hmm,' ventured her mother. 'He seems to have too much money for someone that has spent most of the last ten years in jail.'

Her large cheerful father, Okongo, arrived from his job with a local fishing company. As with most Jaluo of his age all his top front teeth were missing.

'So you are not staying with that heroic policeman friend of yours.' He said sarcastically. 'I hear he is still in hospital.'

Ziporah just looked uncomfortable. 'I must find Amon, he is in big trouble.'

'Amon is always in big trouble, what is it this time?'

'I think that he is selling bhang for the Kikuyu, when Nyamita finds out I am sure he will kill him.'

'What has that got to do with Nyamita? I thought that your friend Nyamita was the big drug busting hero, from what you say am I to understand that he is now a big dealer as well. Anyway, someone has called Amon, he will be here soon.'

'No, no don't bring him here; you will then be in trouble as well. Take me to him. We need to get him out of Kisumu, maybe he should go to Uganda where they won't find him.'

Okongo looked serious for a minute and then went out and returned thirty minutes later.

'Amon will not now come here, we will leave and go to another house in ten minutes and you can tell him what you know. I have only seen him once recently and he told me that there was a Kikuyu man following him and keeping an eye on him. There are too many Kikuyu in Kisumu now, most of the Indians left I think to go to Ulaya and the Kikuyu have come here and set up shops now. We thought that the shops would belong to the Luo but that is not so, I think that all these Kikuyu should go back to Nairobi and set up their shops there.'

The equatorial dusk had within a few minutes turned to dark. Okongo peered out into the poorly lit streets and then beckoned to his daughter to follow him. They stayed in the shadows and then found a vantage point a few hundred yards from their little house. They waited ten minutes and while there were a few passersby there did not seem to be any sign of anyone following them. They went in to the back gate of another mean little house and waited. A dog barked, then Okongo knocked on the back door and when it was opened he pushed Ziporah inside saying:

'Amon will be in there, tell him your business and then come back here, I don't want to hear any of it, then we can go back to your mother and you can tell me what you are now going to do with your life.'

Amon was sitting by himself in the small but neat kitchen, where Ziporah found herself. He was looking quite prosperous, wearing new clothes and he seemed quite pleased with himself.

'Ah Ziporah,' he greeted her. 'So what is all the secrecy about? First I was told that I was to meet you and my brother Okongo at his house and now he won't even talk to me and we have to meet like this in secret.'

'Look Amon, you are in danger, big big danger. I don't know what happened to you in the forest but Nyamita is trying to find out where you went. So what are you doing?'

'I am doing what I have always done; I just supply a few of my friends and now some of these new Kikuyu shopkeepers with a little bhang. I keep some of the money and I am now living properly and soon I will have a house of my own.'

'Nyamita is not supplying the bhang?'

'Not this time but you can ask him if he wants to send me some bhang I will sell that for him as well. I do not need to go back to the mutoni anymore and grow bhang; that is all over. I have the protection of the Police here as well; there is this Inspector Boniface...' He stopped talking when he saw the expression of absolute horror cross Ziporah's face.

'Boniface is Nyamita's man you stupid 'kichwa ya marenge', (lit. Pumpkin head). I was told to contact Boniface to find out what you were doing but when I didn't come back Nyamita must have made another arrangement to contact him. You are in deep trouble, where does Boniface think you are getting the bhang from?'

'I told him it was coming from Nyamita's plantation in Nyandarua.'

'And you think he believed you. You have just told me that it is not Nyamita who is supplying the bhang, so where do you get it from?'

'Just some Kikuyu,' said Amon resentfully. He considered that he had just re-established himself in his home town and here was this jumped-up niece of his telling him he was a 'kichwa ya marenge'.

'Amon, please believe me, if you do not leave here now, even tonight you will end up being fed to the crocodiles in the Kavirondo Gulf. You must go to Uganda on the next bus or train. I am not joking, Nyamita is very angry with me and with you. Inspector Boniface knows that you are selling the bhang from the plantation that Nyamita regards as his own. He thinks it is a gang of Kikuyu that is selling it to you, possibly even the people who shot him up.'

'Boniface is my friend, I am paying him off, I have made my life here and I will not run away to Uganda or anywhere else.'

'Amon, I came all the way from Nairobi just to warn you.'

The back door suddenly burst open and Okongo just grabbed Amon and hustled him out of the mean little house. 'We must be quick; there is a policeman and a number of thugs out at the front of the house. I heard them planning to kill Amon.' They ran out of the back with Amon protesting all the way, back to Okongo's house.

Okongo was furious: 'You stupid little shit Amon; as usual you are in, way above your head. Right now I will take you to the bus station and you will go to Kampala and if you come back, they will kill you and maybe all of us as well.'

'No,' shouted Amon. 'I will go to Inspector Boniface, he will help me.'

'That was the famous Inspector Boniface outside that house; you stupid fool, planning to kill you. Come you must go right now. And Ziporah, just stay here, we must talk.'

He grabbed Amon by the collar and went out returning three hours later.

'Well, I got him on to one of the buses to Kampala; he will have to walk around the border post since he has no papers. I said that I would send him all his papers when he sends me an address. If he comes back here he will be killed,' announced Okongo.

Okongo then turned to his daughter: 'I suppose that it was you that got Amon involved in the bhang business in the first place. I told you a few years ago that Nyamita had gone bad and had completely betrayed his people, the Jaluo, and he has made many others here in Kisumu bad as well, probably also that Boniface.'

'I am finished with Nyamita now, I think that he will kill me if he finds me,' Ziporah was crying.

'What will you do now, are you going to stay here in Kisumu and marry a nice Jaluo boy,' asked her mother kindly.

Ziporah couldn't think of anything worse than being married and living a life of genteel yet respectable poverty like her parents. She shook her head: 'I am going back to Nairobi; I have a job in one of the clinics in Pumwani run by Rafiki Wainaina. Nyamita will not be able to find me there.'

'That Rafiki who is married to that M'zungu, Munyu they call him.'

Ziporah nodded unhappily.

'What do you know about clinics? What will you do there? You are more likely to kill people than help them with anything medical,' said Okongo unkindly.

'I don't know yet, maybe just a cleaner to start with, but they can teach me things.'

Her parents looked at her uncomprehendingly.

Amon had no intention of being sent on the bus to Kampala. As soon as he was certain that Okongo was out of sight he persuaded the bus driver to stop and he scrambled off the bus and walked back to his shack where he arrived at nearly three o'clock in the morning. As he opened the rickety door he knew that there was something wrong and he tried to escape but strong hands grabbed and dragged him inside. It really was a shack; with bits of cardboard and corrugated iron somehow shoved together to give him some shelter from the torrential rain that was commonplace in that part of the world. There were three men in the shack which was dimly lit by his own rather smoky Dietz paraffin lamp. Inspector Boniface was sitting in the only chair. 'Ah Amon,' he said. 'We wondered when you would turn up. Come with us.' They dragged him to a quiet jetty a few hundred yards away and they all piled into a small motor boat. 'This is a bit crowded at the moment but it will be easier on the way back,' said Boniface. Amon crapped himself. 'No No what do you want, I will give you all my bhang, no no please please.' He was like a gibbering idiot.

'OK,' said Boniface. 'We just want to know one thing and then we may be able to let you go.'

Amon nodded.

'Who is supplying you with the bhang?'

'It is from the plantation that I grew for Police Chief Nyamita.'

He got a very hard crack from a rungu (wooden club) on the back of his head as a response. 'Crap, Nyamita has no source of supply,' there were another couple of blows and Amon nearly fell out of the boat into the dark murky water. 'Careful, careful, we still need some information from this idiot,' said Boniface trying to balance the boat.

He asked the question again and then it all came out: 'They took me to some big base in the mutoni and forced me to sell the bhang for them here in Kisumu; they are watching me all the time.'

'Who forced you?'

'There is this Kikuyu called N'guku.'

Another crack on the head from the man with the rungu.

'We know about that little jackal, he is nothing, who is supplying you with bhang.' He was beaten again.

'This Kahinga, he was the man who forced me.' Amon stammered. 'They were going to kill me and bury me there in the mutoni, in that awful place.'

'Who is Kahinga?'

'I don't know, I have never seen him before.'

'Where is the place they took you?'

'I don't know, I think it may have been a base for the Mau-Mau.'

The boat went on a little way.

Boniface nodded to his companions. Amon was unceremoniously shoved off the boat where he yelled and splashed about for a few short moments and then there was a powerful splash a swoosh, a muffled yell and then silence. Boniface indicated that they were to return to the jetty.

'Burn the shack,' was his final instruction. 'Make sure that there is no bhang left, otherwise there is nothing of value there. Don't hurt his wife though, if she is still around, maybe she has had enough sense to make herself scarce'

Ziporah and her parents were blissfully ignorant of what had happened to Amon. Ziporah spent a few more days in Kisumu and then she returned to Nairobi, went straight to the clinic and found Rafiki.

'I was wondering what had happened to you' said Rafiki. 'All went well?' Rafiki thought that the less she knew about Ziporah's grubby little business the better. 'Yes,' said Ziporah. 'Uncle Amon should be safely in Kampala by now, out of harm's way.'

The clinic was a modest whitewashed brick building with a corrugated iron roof, down a rubbish filled laneway off one of the main unpaved thoroughfares in Pumwani. There was no sign on the outside apart from the advertising posters of the firms that helped fund the clinic, but during the daytime there was always a queue of people waiting patiently for attention. Inside there was a small reception area where basic records were kept; for any new patient some essential information was recorded on a card and then any treatments that were prescribed were listed. For existing patients the patient together with her or his card went to one of three nurses each of whom occupied a small room behind the reception. Most of the time the nurses were able to deal with the ailments presented: cuts, stomach complaints, birth control, colds, flu and so on. For more serious ailments they made an appointment for the patient to see a doctor. Rafiki had now persuaded several of the doctors at the large hospitals and even a few in private practice, to give their time free for half a day a week. So most of the time there was a doctor on duty and Rafiki had made it her business to try to schedule the doctors attendances so there were no major gaps or clashes. There were quantities of medical supplies stored in a back room; Rafiki tried to keep an eye on the usage of the medicines, but with two clinics already in operation and three more in the planning stage she was unable to monitor usage very satisfactorily and she thought that it was more important to treat patients than to set up some cumbersome bureaucratic operation that would control usage better. There were no charges for any treatments given.

Ziporah was given a uniform and an array of cleaning equipment and Rafiki spent the first day with her showing her the ropes. There was also a shower with hot water. At the very back there were two rooms with beds in them. Ziporah had also noticed a smart looking Kikuyu in what she took to be some sort of uniform. 'Security,' was all that Rafiki would say. 'If you have nowhere to stay for the moment you can use one of these rooms,' Rafiki added. 'Security is here all day and all night.' Ziporah was relieved that she didn't have to ask about accommodation.

CHAPTER 17

Kariuki visited Nyamita in hospital on several more occasions, each time whilst they felt wary of each other there was a growing comfort in that they seemed to have some common interests.

'This scheme of mine where small shopkeepers pay for protection has now been stopped,' offered Nyamita.

'Maybe we could start it up again?' enquired Kariuki.

'I think your colleague Wacheera has his eye on that situation for the moment, he will not allow it to happen. We could think of it again some-time later when all the excitement has died down. I think that the bhang plantation has more promise.'

'But you say that there are others interested in that place?'

'Maybe?' was the noncommittal answer.

'We need to teach that Wacheera to mind his own business and stay away from our interests' added Kariuki.

'And Munyu and Rafiki,' said Nyamita.

'Maybe we should deal with Munyu and Rafiki first, so that they will no longer interfere with us.'

'What do you have in mind?' asked Nyamita.

'Well, there are those clinics and that fancy house in Karen and then there are those two children at Lenana.'

'Two, I only know of the 'Nusu-Nusu' one. What other children do they have?'

'There is another one called John, he is all M'zungu, from before Munyu took up with Rafiki.'

'Are they both at the boarding establishment at Lenana?'

'Yes,' answered Kariuki.

'Maybe we should take one of them into the forest and tell Munyu that all the activities against us must stop or the boy will be killed.'

'Which one?'

'Nusu-Nusu. He belongs to both of them; they will panic if he disappears,' said Nyamita after some thought. 'I have some people who can help with this. When this is done do not forget how I have helped you.' He looked threateningly at Kariuki.

Nyamita had had a string of visitors during his convalescence one of whom was an old friend who had grown up in the same village on the shores of Lake Victoria. Otieno was now a cook at Lenana. Most of Otieno's visits were innocuous and he brought Nyamita the occasional gift of food from the kitchens at Lenana. 'I get bored with the food here, it seems to be what the Wazungu eat, bring me some proper Jaluo food,' was the entreaty. This time it was slightly different:

'I need some help, with something very special and private' he told Otieno. Otieno had for many years been in awe of Nyamita and the fact that he had become a chief of Police meant that in Otieno's eyes Nyamita could now do no wrong.

'That Munyu and his Kikuyu wife Rafiki are interfering with some of my private business and they need to be taught a lesson.'

Otieno continued to listen.

'We are going to take their son, that Nusu-Nusu, and hide him for a few days until they agree to stop interfering, then we will let the boy go. We will not do the boy any harm; we just need to make sure that they understand that we are very serious.'

'I know the boy; he eats the food that I cook. He is quite a nice boy and is very popular with most of the other boys and also the staff.'

This was not necessarily what Nyamita wanted to hear, but he continued to brief Otieno: 'An Inspector Boniface will come to the school within a few days and find you; you will then show him where the boy sleeps. You will then go with Boniface and two other Jaluo that I have picked and make your plans to take the boy in the middle of the night. This will only last a few days and then we will hear nothing more of those Lawrences and you can go back to work at Lenana.'

They talked of other things and Otieno left.

Boniface paid a very private visit to Nyamita, still in his hospital bed, although he was a taking a short walk each day and expected to be discharged within a few weeks. Boniface decided that in the mid-afternoon when things were generally quieter would be the best time and he managed to creep into Nyamita's room unseen. Firstly they talked about Amon:

'He was selling bhang from the forest, the place that you want to supply bhang from; some Kikuyu were selling it to him.'

'Which Kikuyu?'

'Some old Mau-Mau, they have a base somewhere further up the mountain.'

'Any names?' asked Nyamita.

'He said there was a man called Kahinga; I think that was his name.'

'Kahinga was one of the Mau-Mau leaders in the forest, if I had had anything to do with it he would still be in jail. He now works for Munyu, as a driver I think. The new Government has ignored him and he is trying to make money in other ways. We will deal with him later. What about Amon?

'Crocodile food, he will not trouble us again.'

'And Ziporah?'

'She has disappeared, I think that she was in Kisumu, maybe to try to warn Amon, but we did not find her. It seems that she was too late to warn Amon.'

'We will deal with her later too, but I have something much more urgent for you today.'

Boniface looked doubtful, he wondered how much more trouble he would now be getting into on behalf of his once respected superior officer: 'I think that I should return to my duties at the police station, they will be wondering where I am.'

Nyamita said threateningly: 'You have just admitted to me that you committed murder, be very careful, my friend,'

Boniface blanched; he wondered what Nyamita would or could do to him. He knew that this man in the bed opposite him could be absolutely ruthless, so he backed off and said: 'What do you need me to do?'

'This M'zungu, Munyu and his wretched wife Rafiki have now destroyed one of my schemes and I think that they are going to interfere with other schemes, also that minister Kariuki has told me the same thing.'

Boniface was surprised: 'But that Kariuki is a Kikuyu!'

Nyamita waved his concerns away: 'Yes, but we now have a common interest in teaching those two a lesson that they will not forget and then we can go on running this country as we wish without interference from a settler.' He emphasised the word settler. 'Maybe after this they will go to Ulaya and stay out of our way.'

Nyamita continued: 'We will take the boy Nusu-Nusu from his school at Lenana and hide him away. Kariuki will then make a 'phone call to Munyu or Rafiki and tell them to stay away from all our schemes or the boy will be killed. When they agree we will release the boy.'

Boniface looked very doubtful, he thought: 'Ridding the country of a no good drug dealer like Amon was one thing, but kidnapping an innocent boy and possibly hurting him was something else altogether.'

Nyamita said soothingly: 'You will only have to hold him for a few days, this boy is very precious to them both, I am sure that they will agree very quickly and then the boy will be released. He will not be killed.'

'But what happens if they do not agree?'

Nyamita started to get agitated: 'I have just told you, they have a very comfortable life and this boy is very important to them. I know them, they are weak and I am sure that they will see that interfering with things that do not concern them will only get them into trouble. They will see that risking everything that they have created here in Kenya will just destroy them, and that nobody gains.'

Nyamita knew that he was overstating the case and he also shuddered when he thought of the Lawrences reaction to what he was proposing; he knew that to describe them as weak was lulling him and Boniface into a false sense of security.

Boniface still looked doubtful.

Nyamita persisted: 'This will only last a few days and when Munyu and his disgusting wife have come to their senses, they will back off and we will release the child. Maybe Munyu will leave the Government and concentrate on his silly pictures,' (He was referring to Peter's wildlife photography business which had been put on hold so that he could concentrate on his Ministerial duties).

'OK, what should I do?' was the reluctant response.

'We must be quick,' he said to Boniface. 'You brought the driver who has helped in the past?'

'Yes, but…'

'You will go to Lenana and find this Jaluo, Otieno, who is a cook there; he can show you where this 'Nusu-Nusu' sleeps. You will then take the boy and make sure that he cannot make any noise and take him to the place in the mutoni and keep him there. Do not hurt the boy in any way. When I have what I need I will tell you and you can let him go in a place that I will determine at that time. Otieno will go with you and one other, who will be at Otieno's house by now waiting for you.'

'But…'

'No buts just get on with it; when you have the boy you will 'phone me here, I now have a telephone.'

'What about payment?' blurted out Boniface.

Nyamita waved him away. 'We'll talk about that later. If you get this right, payment will not be a problem.'

Nyamita had by now lost all perspective; the fact that he was still nominally the head of the Police force and the main upholder of law and order in the country had been superseded by his personal considerations. He briefly thought of his mentor, Chief Inspector McLoughlin and shuddered; he put the thought out of his mind entirely as quickly as he could.

Boniface and the driver made one exploratory visit to the school in the middle of the day when most of the pupils were in the classroom. He knew that there would be people moving around the school and his presence wouldn't arouse any suspicions. The driver stayed with the vehicle that they had stolen in Kisumu, and Boniface, after a few polite enquiries found a very nervous Otieno and another man in Otieno's small house on the school property. The African servants were housed in the original labour lines as they had been in colonial days. The three of them walked the half mile through the well kept grounds, with many trees and beautifully manicured grass verges to the kitchen in which Otieno worked and they passed unobtrusively past the single story dormitory that Kamau occupied along with twenty five other boys.

'His bed is third from the end on the other side' Otieno pointed, 'lights are out by half past nine and normally all is very quiet by about half past ten.' They were largely unnoticed, but they got a very curious glance from a boy walking past.

'Are the outside doors locked at night?' asked Boniface.

'No, there is no danger and they are kept unlocked in case of fire so the boys can get out easily.'

Boniface looked around: 'Seems easy enough,' he thought. He saw that they could bring a vehicle right up to the door of the dormitory block and they would have Kamau out of there within less than a minute; he hoped that Kamau would not be missed until morning. The three of them strolled around the grounds: Boniface wanted to make certain that he understood the lie of the land and that if things went wrong there was an escape route. They all went back to Otieno's house and he cooked them a meal while Boniface fetched the driver. They hung around, making sure that they kept out of sight until well after dark and then quietly left the house and drove the pick-up back towards Nairobi.

By ten o'clock they had parked the pickup and left one of the men looking after it, near a row of small shops. A few streets away Boniface found a large unlocked saloon car in a driveway and within less than half a minute the driver had hotwired the vehicle and Boniface leapt into the front seat with Otieno jumping into the back. They drove off quietly past Dagoretti corner and along the Ngong Road where they turned into the long driveway to Lenana, between the two murram (gravel) hockey pitches and then up the short hill up to the main school buildings. Boniface indicated a left turn and the driver drove down a very short incline and parked outside the dormitory. The driver kept the engine running and Boniface and Otieno quietly and confidently opened the door of the block and entered the dormitory. All was very quiet; there was one light on in the corridor so they could see. Otieno and Boniface briefly stood at each end of the bed that had been indicated and lifted the complete bed and without bumping into anything carried it out to the car. Boniface held a dirty piece of cloth soaked in chloroform over Kamau's face and after a few snuffles Kamau collapsed. They wrapped Kamau in a blanket and bundled the sleeping form into the back of the car.

Boniface thought that they were about to make a clean getaway, when there was a yell from the dormitory and all the lights went on: 'Hey, Kamau's bed has gone and he's not there,' came the shout. A boy came out and took one look at the car and yelled: 'He's in there, in the car, someone has just taken him away,' Boniface told the driver to move as fast as he could, they drove round the school and away down the driveway.

There was pandemonium at the dormitory. Someone called the house-master who called the headmaster who immediately alerted the police. John, who slept in a next door dormitory with more senior boys, had kept his head; he dressed when he heard the news and started to ask the other boys if they had seen or heard anything. 'They drove away in a large Rover and I have some of the registration number but not all,' said the boy who had raised the alarm. John wrote it down. Some of the Kikuyu workforce had started to gather, since they felt responsible as they had been alerted by Kahinga some weeks earlier that something might happen to the Lawrence boys. The Police arrived and John gave the senior man the information that he already had; the Police of course wanted to interview the boy for themselves. John had in the meanwhile asked all the other boys if they had seen or heard anything. Eventually a boy came forward and said that he had heard a strange conversation that afternoon: 'Something about the third bed from the other end,' he stammered.

'That's Kamau's bed,' yelled John: 'Did you know any of the men?'

'Yes, one was one of the cooks in the kitchen here.'

'Do you know his name?' The boy shook his head.

John thought for a minute and then asked: 'What language were they speaking?'

'Oh, Jaluo I think, I understand some of their language although I am Kikuyu,' he said irrelevantly.

John thought again, he knew most of the staff: 'There is only one Jaluo cook in this kitchen, Otieno,' he said. Kahinga's people were listening intently to this conversation. 'Get Otieno, bring him here, now,' went the cry.

John then went to the headmaster who was nearby. Beside himself with anxiety, he was due to return to England within a year and hand over to the handpicked African who he was busy training; he had had a few very good years in Kenya after independence and did not want anything to spoil his record. 'If anything happens to this boy it will be a total disaster,' he thought. 'These Lawrence boys, more trouble than they are worth,' he thought uncharitably.' So he was rather short with John when he approached.

'Yes, Lawrence, can't you see I'm busy.'

John looked at him coolly. 'I need to 'phone my father, now,' he said forcefully, 'he and Rafiki need to know what is going on.'

The headmaster was somewhat taken aback by John's aggressive stance but saw the sense in his approach and quickly pushed aside his own personal feelings and said: 'Yes, yes of course. Come with me to the office.'

'Peter picked up the 'phone at the first ring.

'It's the headmaster here,'

Peter went cold. He knew then that it was one of the boys in trouble, the deepest possible trouble there was.

'Yes,' he said shortly.

'They have taken Kamau, your son,' stammered the headmaster.

'What do you mean, taken,' Peter asked calmly, much more calmly than he felt. By this time Rafiki was beside him wiping the sleep from her eyes.

'He has been kidnapped; three men came in and just took him away in a car.'

'Just took him away?' he said unbelievingly. 'When?'

'About forty minutes ago.'

'Have the Police been called?'

'Yes, they are here.'

'Is John OK?'

'Yes, I'll put him on.'

'John, are you OK?'

'Yes, I'm fine, look Dad, I think it was some Jaluo who have done this,' he went on to describe the conversation that he had had with the boy who had overheard Otieno and Boniface easier in the day.

'Where is this Otieno?'

'They have gone to find him.'

'We will be over as soon as we can.'

The 'phone was put down.

As quickly as he could he filled Rafiki in with all the details. Rafiki's eyes went bigger and bigger, then a white hot fury took over:

'If they touch a hair of his head, I will cut their…!

'Look, to give him a chance we must really keep ourselves together. Maybe you could 'phone Wacheera and I will go and get Kahinga. One of us at least needs to go to the school.' He dressed while Rafiki spoke to Wacheera on the 'phone. 'He says that he will meet us at the school,' she said as Peter rushed down the stairs.

A very sleepy Kahinga emerged from his hut, but he was all action once he heard the news. Peter, Rafiki and Kahinga had a brief council of war before they decided what to do.

'It has to be something to do with Nyamita,' said Rafiki. 'What do you think they will do with him?'

'Someone wants something,' said Rafiki. 'I wonder if we will get a 'phone call sometime in the next twenty four hours.'

'I am sure we will, we should get the post office to monitor our 'phone.'

Peter phoned the Minister of Posts and Telegraphs with whom he had always had constructive dealings.

A very sleepy voice answered.

'Peter Lawrence here,'

'Who? Ah yes Munyu, it must be very important to have phoned me this late.'

'It is.' Peter explained the situation.

'How terrible, I suppose you are hoping that someone will 'phone and tell you what they want. We will monitor your 'phone. I will set it up immediately. I hope that you find the boy quickly, he has put up with a lot in his short life.' The 'phone was put down.

'What about the newspapers; maybe we should 'phone the newspapers,' suggested Rafiki.

'OK, you do that I will just try to gather up a few people with Kahinga and then we will see what we can do.'

The four security guards were called in and were briefed: 'If it is Nyamita,' suggested N'guku, who had now returned from his sojourn in Kisumu, 'he does not know the mutoni very well, the only place he knows is the quarry and the place where the bhang is grown, that is if he takes the boy to the mutoni. Maybe they will stay in Nairobi or even take him to Kisumu.'

Peter's shoulders slumped briefly.

Rafiki joined them in the lounge: 'I have 'phoned the press. It will of course be headlines in the papers in the morning, being that he is my son, poor boy, but we must find him and quickly. If you are going into the forest I am coming with you, since I know it better than most of you anyway.' She had already started to think what they might need in the Aberdares. 'Peter, why don't you go to the school, they will still be scratching about like a lot of old hens anyway. When you have found out what you can, come back here, by then we can make a plan and we will have gathered some more of Kahinga's people, which will certainly give us a few options. It is obviously important to keep the police on side though.'

Boniface and his cohorts drove quietly down the long driveway and turned left into the Ngong Road, as they got to Dagoretti Corner; half a dozen Police cars raced the other way towards the school. They drove to where they had parked the pick-up. They were busy transferring some of the things from the car to the pick-up assuming that Kamau was still groggy, but they did not know the boy very well. He was by now alert and aware that he was in trouble; he crept out if the car and started running, somewhat unsteadily, down a nearby road. Boniface saw him and although Kamau had a fifty yard start his four pursuers quickly caught up with him. Kamau kept his head, turned around and tripped up the leading pursuer who was the driver, who came crashing down on to the pavement and the other three clumsily fell over him. Kamau ran on and dashed into a house where the lights were still on. The door was unlocked and he rushed inside right into a middle aged white woman in her night things, who screamed blue murder. Her husband made a grab at Kamau and subdued the somewhat groggy and out of breath boy. 'Who are you and what are you doing here?'

'Kidnap,' panted Kamau. 'They are trying to take me away, from the school...'

At that moment Boniface appeared in the doorway and he presented his Police warrant card and politely said to the couple: 'The boy has escaped from a remand centre, he is very big trouble, thank you for apprehending him but you can give him back to me now and I will deal with him.'

The couple saw a coloured boy, dressed in only his pyjamas, and a black policeman, apparently on official duty and saw no reason to disbelieve the story, so he was handed over to his pursuers. 'Speak to Pet...' –he tried to say Peter Lawrence—Kamau tried to yell but a large hand was clamped over his mouth. Kamau tried to struggle but Boniface had a firm grip on him and he was dragged unceremoniously out of the door and down the road to the pick-up where he was flung into the back with two of his abductors.

The couple looked bemused: 'Bloody people, just can't control themselves,' said the man unsympathetically. They were due to return to England within months and couldn't wait to get out of the country; this incident convinced them that they were on the right track.

Peter went to the school and found the gaggle of people outside Kamau's dormitory. John rushed up: 'The cook, Otieno that I mentioned in the 'phone call, disappeared this afternoon and did not show up at the evening meal.'

Wacheera arrived and was immediately approached by the Police inspector in charge who gave him a quick briefing. Peter and Wacheera and the inspector moved a few feet away from the rest of the group. The first newspaper reporter arrived. Peter said: 'We think it has something to do with Nyamita, you know the background regarding the protection racket and now, the fact that there were people discussing where Kamau slept, in Luo earlier in the day seems to point in that direction.'

'What are the press doing here?' asked Wacheera. Nobody said anything. Wacheera looked suspiciously at Peter who was talking to John.

'Some of Kahinga's people work at the school,' said John. Peter replied: 'Yes, he told me that was one of the reasons that we thought you would both be safe, we wondered if something like this might happen.'

'You should have told us,' said John evenly. 'We might have been more prepared then.'

'Yes, but there is nothing we can do about that now. We need to find him and quickly; we have an idea where he might be taken.' He turned to Wacheera: 'As I said this has all the hallmarks of a Nyamita activity, what do you think we should do?'

Wacheera responded: 'We will go to see Nyamita tomorrow morning.' He hesitated when he saw Peter's face. 'No maybe we should send somebody right now, a senior inspector.' He called one of his men over and started to brief him.

The inspector looked at his watch: 'Nyamita, at this time of night in hospital?' he said questioningly.

'Yes, time is the most important element now; if we can find the boy before they reach a settled hiding place then we have a better chance.' The inspector left with a sergeant.

'I have sent people to Nyamita's house, I hope that his wife will not be too upset, and we have the address of the place that his mistress occupies.'

Peter chose his words carefully: 'You remember the place where Nyamita was shot up, by that drug gang in the Aberdares?'

Wacheera looked at him warily: 'Yes.'

'Well I have credible evidence that Nyamita was actually responsible for cultivating the bhang that was being grown there, it was his people on the ground; that was one of the reasons that I formally wrote to you on the subject.'

'What's the point?' asked Wacheera warily, he did not mention that it was also his view that Nyamita was somehow involved in growing bhang.

'Nyamita does not know the mutoni that well so if he is going to take the boy to a safe hiding place outside Nairobi, he will probably go there.'

'Do you know how to get to this place?' asked Wacheera.

'No, but I can find out.'

Peter went over to where some of Kahinga's people were standing around rather disconsolately and had a brief conversation with them. He went back to Wacheera. 'There is one man over there, who says he thinks that he might be able to find the place. We should probably understand that he is somewhat reluctant to tell you or anyone in the Police that he knows the place in case you try to link him with the shootout with Nyamita; I am, however, certain that he knows the precise location of the place we are talking about. If the boy has been taken there we also need to approach it very carefully, we don't want the kidnappers to panic and harm him.'

Initially Wacheera was irritated by Peter almost taking over what should have been a Police function, but then he reflected for a moment: 'Peter is remarkably calm for a person whose son has just been kidnapped, everything he has suggested makes perfect sense, he is just trying to help as much as possible, also he has had a great deal of experience of difficult and dangerous situations. The Police have ignored his advice in the past, much to their regret.' Wacheera thought for a moment; he then decided to really make Peter a partner in this episode.

After a brief consultation with Kahinga Rafiki first drove Kahinga to Kinua's new house and dropped him there. He expected to be able to persuade Kinua to drive around with him in his pick-up truck to some of the poorer suburbs and collect as many of his 'followers' as he could and take them to Sattimma. Rafiki took her car and fetched the guards that were on duty at her various clinics.

Ziporah appeared at the clinic in Pumwani, rubbing sleep from her eyes. 'What's happening?' she asked.

Rafiki reflected for a moment and then took her into one of the consulting rooms and told her what had happened. 'We think that Nyamita may have something to do with this, can you tell me some of the possible places where he could take the boy.'

Ziporah looked terrified and then said: 'Maybe that place in the mutoni where the bhang was grown, where Nyamita was shot.'

Rafiki nodded: 'Anywhere in Nairobi?' After some thought Ziporah gave her three addresses in Nairobi. 'Kisumu?' she asked. There was some hesitation and then she was given Amon's address. 'Anywhere else, Mombasa, Malindi?' Ziporah shook her head; she had never been to the Kenya coast.

As Rafiki returned to Sattimma, she was joined by Kahinga and then Peter. By now it was three am and they had a quick council of war. Rafiki 'phoned through all the information that she had gleaned from Ziporah, to the command centre at Police headquarters Wacheera had set up. There were now some twenty five of Kahinga's followers hanging around Sattimma.

Kamau, cold and frightened, in the back of Boniface's pick-up wondered what sort of trouble he was in. His captors were strangely uncommunicative and he had been given a very brutal clout round his head after he had been recaptured by the man in charge whose name he had understood was Boniface. Kamau had determined that his captors were speaking Luo; the driver and the two in the back with him were wearing balaclavas, but Boniface had to remove his when he had approached the couple who had recaptured him, so he had had a very good look at him, a face that he was sure he would never forget. The pick-up kept stopping at what Kamau thought were telephone boxes, with Boniface leaping out of the vehicle and then rushing back again and slamming the door. After a few of these episodes Kamau thought that he was trying to make 'phone call and all the 'phone boxes he had found were broken. Eventually there was another stop and Boniface was away for almost half an hour.

Inspector Orinda went to the hospital where Nyamita was recuperating.

Approaching the main desk, he produced his warrant card, and asked if he could see Nyamita: 'It is very urgent; I know that it is after midnight but I must see the patient now.' The attendant was uncertain what to do, but she was a Luo and spoke the same language as Orinda, so told him where to go. Orinda said to the sergeant: 'Look up the register of visitors for the last two months or so, they would be bound to keep one especially for such an eminent patient.' He went off in the direction indicated by the desk attendant.

Orinda found the room that had been indicated and waited for a minute outside the door, where there was the sound of a voice, seemingly on the 'phone. He opened the door a crack to see if he could hear what was being said. He could hear Nyamita's big booming voice in Luo, 'No, no...' There was silence for a few seconds and then Nyamita shouted anxiously: 'Who is there? Who is there?' he hesitated and then said: 'Call back in twenty minutes, there is someone at the door.' The 'phone was slammed down. Orinda disappeared down the passage for ten minutes and then confidently marched up to Nyamita's door, knocked and entered. The huge bulk of Nyamita was lying in the bed looking anxious, but he made no pretence of being asleep and the light was still on.

He looked at Orinda as the latter produced his warrant card. 'What the fuck do you want, I know who you are you stupid fool, have you any idea what time it is,' he yelled before Orinda could say anything. Orinda calmly sat down; the 'phone call was certainly suspicious but not proof of anything. Orinda then went on to explain the kidnapping.

'Why are you telling me this at this time of night' Nyamita yelled. 'I'm stuck here in this bed and have been for months now, how do you think I could be involved in such a thing, my job is to uphold the law not kidnap worthless children of worthless parents. Now get out, I shall be making a formal complaint to Acting Superintendent Wacheera.' He emphasised the word 'acting'. He rang the night bell and a nurse appeared. 'Get this man out of here,' Nyamita ordered. Orinda meekly complied: but he had seen and heard enough, if Nyamita had been entirely innocent the reaction would have been more measured and Nyamita's eyes, although blazing with apparent anger were also full of fear.

Orinda returned to the reception where the sergeant was waiting. 'Here look at this,' said the sergeant waving the visitors book: 'Ziporah, I think that is his mistress, Amon, a convicted criminal, and now this Kariuki, maybe that is the minister Kariuki, no wife , no children, that is very strange. We will take this book, we need it for evidence.' He waved at the desk attendant who protested mildly, but by then they were gone.

The 'phone call came through a few minutes after Orinda had left: 'That was the idiot Inspector Orinda,' Nyamita said to Boniface. 'They already suspect that I had something to do with this. So don't go to the mutoni for a few days; that will be the first place they look. Go to this address.' He gave Boniface an address in Parklands, in Nairobi. 'The house is unoccupied but leave early, before six o'clock in the morning, and then 'phone me during the day when I will tell you what to do.'

Boniface asked: 'Where should we go during the day?'

'I don't know,' Nyamita bellowed, 'Use your sense man, maybe you could go to the Ngong forest.'

Peter and Rafiki had decided that whatever happened they needed to see if Kamau was taken to the quarry, so Kahinga and eight men were to go through the forest and approach the quarry from there. Rafiki and seven men would drive to the area and then approach the quarry on foot for the last mile or so. Peter was to stay at Sattimma with ten of the men in case there were any developments.

Peter and Rafiki arrived at the command centre at Police headquarters just after six am. Wacheera had already arrived so he was able to give them a full update. Wacheera had organised teams to visit all the addresses in Nairobi and Kisumu that Rafiki had given them the previous night. Peter quietly told Wacheera about the two groups that were being sent to the quarry; he made certain that only Wacheera knew about this activity: 'The fewer people that know about this the better, they require no police resources and if they find nothing then there is no need for anyone here at police headquarters to know about them,' he told Wacheera.

Wacheera hesitated and then nodded, he thought: 'Although they are not Police, they know what they are doing, it is their son and this helps with resources.'

'Are you going to arrest Kariuki?' asked Peter. 'Presumably you have enough evidence on the other matter to arrest and charge him and now he seems to be involved somehow with Nyamita, maybe he is even an accomplice in the kidnapping, you say he has visited Nyamita in hospital several times in the last two weeks or so.'

'We are not quite ready to arrest him, although the person you provided to help us put the case together has been very useful, we are still building the case. Also I am sure that Kariuki is not going anywhere. We could arrest him but I think that the best thing would be to keep a very close eye on him and see what he does, he may further incriminate himself if he is involved with the kidnapping,' responded Wacheera.

Peter and Rafiki looked at each other and then Rafiki said: 'That makes good sense, do you need anyone to follow him?'

'No,' said Wacheera. 'I have very good people, who will watch him twenty four hours a day. I will brief them after this.'

'Peter said: 'I will be at home, hoping for a telephone call from the kidnappers and I still have ten good people waiting there if they are needed.'

Wacheera nodded.

Nyamita had not been able to sleep and as the dawn broke he 'phoned Kariuki at home hoping that he would not get his wife; as far as Nyamita was concerned the fewer people that knew of the contact between the two the better. 'Hello,' was the uncertain response to the first ring.

'Is that minister Kariuki,' asked Nyamita.

'Speaking; is that Superintendent Nyamita,' the voice was almost a whisper.

'Yes,' and he added after a brief moment of hesitation: 'We have the boy.'

'Yes, I know, it is all over the papers, which have just been delivered here.'

'Do they say anything about who they suspect?' Asked Nyamita.

'No, there is just a lot of sensational stuff about the kidnapping and about the background and of course Rafiki and what she had to endure at the end of the emergency and so on.'

'You must now make that call to the Lawrence place and tell them what we want,' said Nyamita.

'Me, I thought that you were going to do that.'

'Look the police have already been here, in the middle of the night, so they suspect me. If you make the call in Kikuyu that will confuse them.'

'What should I say?' asked Kariuki, who was already regretting his involvement. Approving false invoices was one thing; Kariuki had no stomach for kidnapping innocent children.

'Tell them what we agreed, that they should stop interfering with our schemes or the child will be killed.'

'And when we let him go, what happens then.'

'Tell them that if they continue to harass us we will kill him and their other son, tell them they can see what we can do and we will not hesitate.'

'OK,' said Kariuki reluctantly. I will 'phone you when I have any news.' The 'phone was put down quietly.

The couple who had handed Kamau back to Boniface were horrified at the headlines. They looked at each other when they had seen the photograph of Kamau on the front page of all the newspapers. 'This was the boy that ran in here last night,' said a very nervous Mrs. Terry, 'we will have to go to the Police.'

'No,' said her husband. 'They will blame us and then I will lose my pension, I don't want to be involved, we'll be shot of this place in a few weeks and then they can't touch us. I just don't want to be involved.'

'That poor boy, surely we must help, they will probably kill him.' she repeated. They went on arguing for the next thirty minutes and then Mr. Terry had to go to work. Mrs. Terry sat down for ten minutes on her own to think and then she determinedly got into her car and drove to Police headquarters where she was quickly directed to the kidnap command centre. After a few minutes Wacheera was called and she explained the whole episode to him.

'Can you describe the boy?' She gave him a full description of Kamau, including the fact that he was barefoot and was wearing pyjamas.

'Can you describe the person who took the boy away?' asked Wacheera. She gave him a detailed description of Boniface.

'Would you recognise him in a line-up?'

'Yes, I expect so,' was the response.

'Did you see the vehicle they were driving?'

'No, but I think it was down the road, the boy had been running and was out of breath.'

'Without doubt the boy who was kidnapped is the person who ran into your house, and the man you have described is certainly one of our Police officers, who seems to have got himself into very bad trouble. I must apologise for him on behalf of the Police.'

'So we are not in trouble then?' asked a troubled Mrs. Terry.

'No, quite the opposite, thank you for coming forward, we may have to contact you later.'

Police were sent to the area in which the Terry's lived and found the very confused owner of the Rover used for the kidnap. After explanation the car was removed for examination and finger printing, with the owner's full cooperation.

Boniface and his cohorts took Kamau to the address mentioned. They had to force their way in through a back window. They found a stale loaf of bread which was consumed in a few seconds, even Kamau was given some. Kamau was firmly locked in a room by himself. The windows were barred so they were confident that there would be no escape. They all went to sleep.

Kamau looked around but was unable to see how he could possibly escape, so he went to sleep in the unmade bed. At six in the morning he was roughly dragged out of the bed and dumped in the back of the pick-up again and they drove off. After more than forty minutes, he saw that they were in the Ngong forest where Boniface found a very secluded hiding place. He left Kamau with Otieno and one other kidnapper with strict instructions not to let Kamau out of sight. 'I will bring some food and I need to 'phone Nyamita for instructions,' he told them, out of Kamau's hearing.

Kamau had started to examine his captors, there was certainly something familiar about one of them, although they were both still wearing balaclavas, so Kamau bided his time and when Otieno bent down to pick something up Kamau made a grab at his balaclava and pulled it off. He recognised Otieno immediately: 'You,' he shouted, 'why you, what have I done to you?' Otieno flattened Kamau with a vicious clout with the flat of his bony hand and he retrieved the balaclava and put it back on without a word. Nothing more was said.

Boniface with the driver went to the little village of Ngong and was one of the first customers at the Indian owned grocery store where he bought provisions for immediate use and for a few days at the quarry. The shopkeeper was delighted with the large order and helped Boniface carry it all to the pick-up. Something in Boniface's demeanour made him memorise the licence plate number of the vehicle, which he immediately wrote down when he went back inside.

When asked if there was a telephone nearby he directed Boniface to the public 'phone box around the corner. Boniface 'phoned Nyamita and asked for instructions: 'Did you find the address that I gave you last night?'

'Yes, it was fine; we are now in the Ngong forest as you suggested, where do you think we should go.'

'I don't know yet,' was the answer. 'Phone back later.'

'Maybe we should just go to the quarry.' suggested Boniface.

'No, not yet, as I said 'phone back.' The 'phone was put down.

Later in the morning a very nervous Kariuki made a call to Sattimma from a public 'phone. He tried to disguise his voice by holding his nose and he spoke the language of an uneducated Kikuyu. Peter answered the 'phone since Rafiki and Kahinga had already left. 'Hello, Peter Lawrence speaking can I help you?' he knew that if one of the kidnappers 'phoned he needed to keep them talking for as long as possible so that the post office could trace the call.

'Munyu is that Munyu' said a muffled voice in Kikuyu.

Peter responded in fluent Kikuyu: 'Yes, Munyu speaking, this is Munyu here, what can I do to help you, if you wish to come and see, me we can make an appointment if that is convenient.'

'Munyu, if you want to see that Nusu-Nusu alive you will stop doing what you are doing.'

'Explain what you mean, I don't know what you mean, what things are you referring to?' This was the kidnapper, or one of them, he must keep him talking, he thought. There was hesitation on the line so Peter continued: 'What things, I don't know what you talking about?'

'The protection business that funded the clinics; that must now continue.'

'The Police have stopped that, I have nothing to do with it; I can stop nothing or start nothing.' There was heavy breathing on the line. 'Look,' said Peter, 'you, whoever you are, you are in very big trouble, just by making this call, please give yourself up and tell us where to find the child; maybe you have children, how do you think they would be able to deal with being kidnapped.' There was a whimper on the line and then the 'phone went dead.

The post office had traced the call almost immediately and the information had been excitedly transmitted to the command post. Within ten minutes of the call, although the caller had long gone, a policeman had sealed the 'phone box and was waiting for the finger print experts.

Boniface and the driver took the food back to his hideout. Otieno cooked the posho and meat purchased by Boniface, over a small fire. Kamau eat as heartily as the others, much to their surprise. One of the kidnappers, still with his face partially covered said to him: 'So you eat our food as well, not just the Wazungu food.'

Kamau responded in Swahili: 'This is my food, I was brought up in a Kikuyu village near Thika, and this is what we ate.'

Boniface and the driver went out again in mid-afternoon. He thought that he would make for the 'phone box at Ngong where he had bought the provisions, but just as they was about to turn in he noticed a police van parked there, so he drove on to the shops in Karen and 'phoned Nyamita: 'You must go to the mutoni now, I have a person on the inside, who has told me that the police have been to all my houses in Nairobi, they also have a description of you and they know the licence plate number of the pick-up you are driving; all this from an Indian shopkeeper in Ngong, and some M'zungu where the boy almost escaped to. There has been no mention of the place in the mutoni, maybe they don't know about that or have forgotten.

You should go there now, that is the safest place.'

Boniface proceeded to give Nyamita an explanation of what had happened at the Terry's house the previous night, but was roughly interrupted. 'There is no time to talk; but you should go as soon as it gets dark. But you must not harm the boy, under any circumstances.' Boniface was now terrified, the whole idea which seemed so simple was starting to unravel, he wondered whether he should just give himself up and go straight to the police, but then he thought of Nyamita and what he might do, so he instructed the driver to return to the hideout in the Ngong forest. As the equatorial dusk turned quickly to dark, they bundled Kamau and themselves into the pick-up and drove off.

Kahinga had gone to the forest in the Aberdares and had walked his men all night by the light of an almost full moon. He was lucky that most unusually the night was clear and there was no cloud, so they were able to walk along the game trails almost as if it were daylight. They deliberately made some noise in order to scare any wild animals who might innocently be walking along the same trails. Within twenty four hours they were stationed above the quarry. On his own, Kahinga carefully manoeuvred his way down and looked around; the place was deserted and there was no sign of any recent habitation. He looked into the huts; one of them had the few possessions that had been there since his last visit. He jumped as there was a rustle in the bushes and swung Peter's precious .416 Rigby hunting rifle in the direction of the sound.

Rafiki emerged from the bushes holding her hands up. She said: 'I stopped by two of the huts in the nearest settlement, as it happens the woman I spoke to was one of my food carriers during the fight with the British. She is really thriving and says that she has a lot to thank me and you and indeed Munyu for all her good fortune. I asked her if there had been any vehicles or any other activity down here at the quarry recently and she said not for some weeks now. I told her what was going on and that these nasty people had kidnapped Kamau. She was truly shocked and was really concerned about Kamau. She has put a watch on the road twenty four hours a day and will warn me if there is any vehicle movement. As a result of that I was able to bring my truck quite close to here, it is well hidden, and all the people that came with me are hiding within two hundred yards of here.' Kahinga told her that all his people were lying in concealed positions not far away, but on the hillside just above the quarry, all had clear views of the quarry.

Kahinga said: 'I have told them, no noise, no fires; they are all pretty tired anyway having walked for twenty four hours, so I have one on guard and hopefully the rest are sleeping. It's again almost like the war against the British.' He shuddered: 'I hope that we never have to do any of that again.' Then he became more businesslike: 'We must make sure that there is no evidence of us being here, so if you go back to your people, I will just make certain that the place looks really deserted,' he smiled: 'again I am an expert at that.'

They agreed that they would meet in two hours just on the periphery of the quarry. 'Of course this may all be for nothing,' said Rafiki unhappily. 'They may not be coming here at all.'

'We'll see.' was all Kahinga would say.

They both went back to their people and spread them out so that the quarry was surrounded by well concealed people. They were all very disciplined having been in the forest during the emergency, so there was no noise, no fuss, they ate what was available and most of them just slept where they were, unless it was their turn for guard duty.

Rafiki and Kahinga met just before dusk at the place they had agreed and waited. Periodically they went back to their people and checked that all was in order. They were becoming despondent and wondering whether all this was a wild goose chase when Rafiki's friend quietly approached her through the bush and said: 'There is a pick-up truck parked a little way from my hut, he came with no lights on and is facing back the way he came, the engine is still running. There is a man walking along the track, I think that he is just making sure that there is nobody at the quarry.'

Rafiki said: 'Can you somehow block their way out of here, with tree branches or something so that if they do decide to run away or go somewhere else, they will not be able to use the vehicle. You must do it quietly though, and some way down the track, we don't want them to get suspicious.' She then took a deep breath: 'Could you see how many in the vehicle and if Kamau was with them?'

The woman shook her head: 'Too dark to see anything and I did not want to get too close.' Rafiki nodded and the woman slipped back into the bushes. Rafiki knew that she could rely on her as she had done in the past.

Boniface had cautiously approached the settlements leading up to the quarry. He knew that all the new settlers in the area were Kikuyu, so they would either be hostile to him or at best unhelpful. He had waited until midnight when as far as he could see there were no lights still visible and all the flickering fires had been extinguished. The moon was shining brightly and he had made the driver turn the vehicle round so as to make a quick escape should the need arise; he told the driver to keep the engine idling. Walking the almost half mile to the quarry, he stopped periodically to listen. He shone his torch down on the track: there were no signs of any recent vehicle tracks. If he had been more of a bushman or had better knowledge of the wild he may have noticed the uncanny silence; there was not a peep from the numerous wild life that abounded in the area, they had all instinctively moved a little way into the bush to avoid the now strong presence of humans. He walked cautiously on until he came to the quarry. He entered the unlocked hut, it seemed undisturbed and as far as he could see there were no bootmarks in the area surrounding the huts. He walked back to the vehicle, clambered in and told the driver to drive as quietly as possible to the quarry.

Rafiki and Kahinga made certain that all their people were alert and awake. 'Do not do anything until you are told and if Kamau is with them the most important thing is that he comes out of this unhurt. If possible all of the kidnappers should be taken alive, if indeed they are kidnappers. Whatever they are they are certainly up to no good,' said Rafiki. Kahinga told his people much the same thing.

They waited and waited for what seemed like an interminable time. The pick-up appeared with just its parking lights showing. It was driven close to the huts and parked facing back down the track again. The full moon provided sufficient light so they could all see most of what was going on. They saw four adults get out. 'What, no Kamau,' thought Rafiki almost in panic mode. Then one of the men lent into the back of the pick-up and pulled a small figure out. Boniface stepped up and hit Kamau hard with the flat of his hand on the side of his head. Kamau staggered a little and then there was a lot of gesturing but Rafiki was unable to hear what was said. She thought: 'Oh, my poor baby, but don't worry we'll have you back very shortly.' Kamau was then pulled roughly a few yards away and he pulled his pyjama trousers down and squatted.

'I am going to take the bastard out,' said Kahinga to Rafiki as this was happening, aiming the Rigby.

'We need him alive,' whispered Rafiki, 'Can you see well enough, you mustn't hurt Kamau in any way.'

Kahinga nodded: 'I can see quite well, the moonlight, it's almost like daylight.'

'Leg; get him in the leg, then,' said Rafiki quietly. She knew that Kahinga was a good shot and she thought that she would just have to rely on that, even in the poor light. Kahinga took careful aim while the large figure of what appeared to be the man in charge was standing away from Kamau, two of the men had gone into the hut, and the fourth man stood to one side in the doorway. Kahinga carefully squeezed the trigger; the report seemed devastatingly loud in the quiet of the quarry and Boniface crashed down almost on top of Kamau clutching his right leg screaming in pain. Kamau jumped up and ran into the bush as all seventeen of the rescuers rushed the huts in the quarry. The man outside was dispatched without mercy with a burst from one of the Patchetts in the chest and the two that had gone into one of the huts rushed out with their hands up.

Rafiki just had eyes for Kamau and ran after him calling: 'Here we are, it's all alright now.' She caught up with him and hugged him; there was a short struggle until he realised who it was and then he clung to her. The two men who had surrendered were firmly tied up.

Kahinga went over to Boniface who was screaming in pain: 'Shut up or I will finish you off right now,' he waved the Rigby threateningly at him. The screaming was reduced to a whimper.

Kamau, still in his pyjamas, was absolutely filthy. To Rafiki he seemed quite calm and said very little but just clung to his mother. 'I must get Kamau cleaned up and we must get this lot to the police,' said Rafiki. She went over to Boniface, whose leg was bleeding profusely. 'We had better try and tie this up; otherwise he may die before we get him to hospital, not that he deserves any better.' With Boniface cringing and whimpering she roughly ripped a piece off his shirt and tied his leg up carefully, to stop the bleeding. Boniface and his two live companions and the one dead one were then flung unceremoniously into the back of their own vehicle. Just before that happened Rafiki stuck her revolver into Boniface's face and growled at him threateningly: 'This was Nyamita's doing, wasn't it?' Boniface nodded unhappily.

The back of the kidnapper's vehicle was locked. Kahinga smashed the cabs rear window and smoothed out all the bits of protruding glass with the tyre lever that he found under the seat. Two of his men were instructed to get in to the cab with one of them kneeling facing backwards into the rear of the vehicle with a Patchett cocked and ready to fire. 'Any attempt to escape or do anything except sit still and you will all get a gut full of lead,' said Kahinga in Swahili.

'I need a crap,' said one of the men.

'Then do it in your pants,' was the curt reply. 'I am going to police headquarters in Nairobi,' he said to Rafiki. 'You can take a few in your pick-up and I will arrange transport for the rest, anyway you should all be welcome in the nearby settlement.'

Rafiki, Kamau in his bare feet and all the remaining men walked back to the village where they were greeted with some apprehension until Rafiki told them what had happened. They had heard the gunfire and seen Kahinga drive off. Despite the late hour they were then given a huge meal and some traditional beer. Kamau was able to have a thorough wash in very cold water and he put on clean clothes that Rafiki had thoughtfully brought with her. Kamau somewhat hesitatingly then told Rafiki what had happened to him in the past very traumatic three days. Kamau seemed quite calm. At four am Rafiki decided to set off for Nairobi in her borrowed pick-up with Kamau and one other in the front and four in the back; the rest would have to wait for the transport that Kahinga had promised, but they weren't unhappy with that; all they wanted was sleep. Rafiki stopped at South Kinangop and banged on the door of an Indian trader until he reluctantly opened the door of the shop. He recognised Rafiki immediately and looked surprised and apprehensive: 'You heard about my son's kidnapping,'

'Yes, it's been all over the newspapers,' was the response.

'Well, we have got Kamau back and captured those responsible, I have him in the pick-up, but I just need to 'phone my husband and tell him, so please can I use your 'phone.'

'Got him back, that's wonderful, we have all been worried about the poor boy, yes please use the 'phone, it's a pleasure to have you here.'

Peter picked up the 'phone at the first ring, he had only been sleeping fitfully, for obvious reasons. 'I've got him back,' said Rafiki joyfully, 'unharmed, at least on the outside, he seems fine.' She explained what had happened and also told him something of Kamau's ordeal. 'We will come straight home, Kahinga is taking what appears to be a policeman and his cronies to police headquarters, they should be almost there by now, there is one dead and one, the policeman is badly wounded and will need hospitalisation.'

Peter was overjoyed and he said to Rafiki 'They arrested Kariuki yesterday, but Nyamita has disappeared. I will 'phone Wacheera and pop down to police headquarters, but come back here and I will see you in two hours or so. Can I speak to the boy?'

Rafiki put the 'phone down and rushed outside and waved at Kamau who came to the 'phone.' 'Hello Dad, yes I'm fine,' there were few more teenage grunts and the he said: 'See you at home.' He put the 'phone down. They drove back to Sattimma.

As they left the shopkeeper excitedly phoned the major paper in Nairobi and was soon put through to the editor. Within an hour a somewhat garbled but reasonably accurate story of the kidnapping and rescue was out on the streets of Nairobi.

Peter arrived at police headquarters at the same time as Wacheera and they waited for Kahinga's arrival, half an hour later. There was an ambulance and a police escort waiting to take Boniface to hospital and a mortuary van for the deceased; the other two kidnappers were immediately taken into custody. Kahinga and his men were told to go home and return later to make statements. 'I suppose that we had better make a statement to the press,' said Wacheera thoughtfully, just before a copy of the daily paper was thrust into his hand.

He took one look at it and showed it to Peter: 'Must have been that shop-keeper on the Kinangop,' said Peter. 'Rafiki 'phoned me and the shopkeeper would have overheard the conversation. I had better get back to Sattimma; it is going to be a complete circus.'

'They will all have to come and make statements,' said Wacheera to Peter's departing back. Peter turned around: 'Could you come to Sattimma and do that, all Kahinga's people will be there and it is going to be difficult getting in and out over the next few days. We may need your help to deal with the press as well.' Wacheera nodded.

Chapter 18

Rafiki was expecting a quiet and joyful reunion with Peter, assuming that he would have collected John from the school and she thought that they might have a few hours together before anyone knew about the rescue. Although it was still quite early, just after dawn, there was a surprisingly large amount of traffic and as she turned into the driveway at Sattimma chaos greeted her; there were cars parked in every available space with people running around waving cameras and shouting. Peter was not to be seen, although she caught a glimpse of Kahinga. Then the throng saw that she had arrived and flocked to the pick-up: she had cameras and microphones thrust at her and Kamau all asking questions.

There was a burst of gunfire from the direction of the house and the crowd scattered. Peter and Kahinga emerged: they had fired shots into the air just to get some attention. Peter held up his hand: 'We understand that there is a great deal of interest in what has happened, I can tell you though that Kamau has been rescued and is physically unharmed. If you will give us an hour just to sort ourselves out, we will then be able to answer any questions that you might have. In the meantime you may be more comfortable on the front lawn of the house. If you go round there hopefully we will be able to serve you a cup of tea, but please be patient and please let Rafiki through.' He indicated the direction everyone should take.

Rafiki was able to drive the vehicle close to the house and she and Kamau managed to get out and dash up the back steps. At the top of the steps they instinctively turned around and arm in arm waved to the throng, waiting there briefly before disappearing into the house. This image would appear in all the local papers and some of the overseas papers who had been following the story. Peter was waiting for them and crushed them both to his large frame and then John who had been unnoticed up until then joined in together with the cook and housemaid.

'OK,' said Peter. 'We had better get organised.' He had anticipated something like this happening during the excruciating wait over the past few days, so he and the cook had several tables which they had set up on the front lawn with three large urns for tea plus packets and packets of biscuits. The cook took charge while Peter went inside to look after the family. Kamau and Rafiki were bathing. John went to find Kahinga and his men: 'They were part of this as much as anyone,' he said.

Kamau and Rafiki emerged looking fresher and they all sat down in the sitting room for a few minutes to gather their thoughts.

Wacheera arrived soon after and quietly took charge: 'We must deal only with facts, no speculation; by all means tell them what happened to you, young man,' he glanced at Kamau, 'but just facts nothing else. Please no mention of Boniface or any of the names of the other kidnappers.' Kahinga appeared. 'That applies to you as well, and from me and the police, thank you for a job well done. The best thing is just to answer questions, don't try to give them anything else. OK, it's going to be difficult, but I will stop any nonsense.'

Wacheera directed the group to walk outside and sit on the wide steps of Sattimma, with Wacheera in the middle and Rafiki sitting next to Kamau on Wacheera's left, and Peter, John and Kahinga sitting on his right.

Wacheera said in English: 'Thankyou for coming, we will answer as many questions as we can, but please be aware that this young man has just had a most awful experience.' He indicated Kamau. 'We will take one question at a time.' Peter translated into Swahili. The crowd was orderly and Wacheera pointed to a man at the front: 'Kamau, can you just tell us what happened to you?'

Kamau looked uncertain and then said, after a nod from Wacheera: 'Some men came to the school and took my bed outside and then they must have had chloroform or something so I don't remember what happened for a while. I remember being in this big car and while they were trying to move me into another pick-up I managed to get away and ran to a house that was close by. But B'...-he was going to say Boniface but remembered what Wacheera had told them—'the big man in charge told them that I was a runaway from a remand centre and took me away again. Then we drove around Nairobi while the big man tried to find a telephone that worked and when he did we went to a house somewhere, I don't know where, and stayed the night there. We left very early in the morning and went into the forest at Ngong where we stayed all day. The big man then went away for a long time and came back with food. Later when it was nearly dark we drove for a very long time and came to the place where I was rescued.'

'Who were the people that kidnapped you?'

Kamau shrugged.

'What langue did they speak?

Kamau looked at Wacheera.

'We have some Luo people in custody,' answered Wacheera.

'What did they say to you, did they say why they were kidnapping you?'

'They spoke very little; I don't know why they took me.'

'Who were the people that you escaped to?'

'An old Wazungu couple.' There was an intake of breath.

'They have come forward and have been very helpful,' added Wacheera quickly. 'I can't name them.'

'Did they treat you badly? The kidnappers I mean.'

'I was hit a few times.'

'We saw the big man hit Kamau hard just before he was rescued,' said Rafiki sharply.

'Did you have enough to eat?'

'No.' There was general laughter.

'OK. Enough questions for Kamau,' said Wacheera firmly. He was relieved there was no mention of Boniface.

'How did you know where to go?' the question was directed at Rafiki.

'We had some information.'

'Where from?'

'Police sources, we can't answer that question, 'said Wacheera.

'Munyu, why didn't you go on the rescue? Why did your wife go?'

'She insisted, and she has wide experience of this type of activity.' More laughter.

'Isn't this more of a job for a man.'

'I was the right person, I knew some of the people in the nearby settlement and I thought that Kamau would need his mother when he was rescued, he might have been hurt,' interrupted Rafiki, 'anyway we had plenty of men.' She pointed at Kahinga.

'Why didn't the police go to this place where the boy was rescued?'

'We agreed that the police would concentrate on the leads we had in Nairobi and Kisumu; Kahinga runs an official security company and he knew the place that we thought that these people were likely to hide out. It made sense to use his resources and skills, and it produced the result that we all wanted,' answered Wacheera 'Yesterday you arrested a minister of the Government.'

'That has nothing to do with this case,' said Wacheera dismissively. 'There will be separate announcement regarding that issue in a few days.'

Amid a cacophony of further questions the Lawrences quietly withdrew into the house and Wacheera and his police then asked the assembled throng to leave and that there would be more announcements within the next few days. When all the people had gone he came into the house and spent some hours there collecting everyone's statements, including those of Kahinga and his men. He asked everyone not to speak to the press any further.

Kamau just slept for the next few days spending time with Peter and Rafiki and John, They 'phoned Robert and Giles in London.

Much to Peter and Rafiki's surprise Kamau did not have a very bad reaction to the incident; they were expecting some tears, perhaps bad dreams, long moody silences, but none of that happened. He just behaved as a normal teenager would; he played with the dogs in the garden, spent time with Kahinga and thanked him for coming to his rescue and spoke to some of the rescue party. John went back to the school as a boarder. After a week the headmaster paid them a visit. 'We need you back at school,' he said to Kamau, 'the rugby teams are missing your talent and leadership. Perhaps you could live here at home for the time being and be a day scholar.'

Kamau just shook his head: 'No, I liked being a boarder and I think that I am ready to return next week.'

Peter had to take Kamau to the hospital and the jail, respectively where Boniface and his cronies were being held. He was able to identify Boniface and Otieno: 'The other two always kept balaclavas on,' said Kamau in explanation, 'I never saw their faces properly.'

✕   ✕   ✕

Chapter 19

Once all the drama of Kamau's kidnapping had died down Wanjiru decided, after some consultation with Kahinga that she was now in a position to see if she could find some more custom for their security firm.

Rafiki had shown her how to open a bank account and how to manage it. 'Maybe you could pay me one month in advance,' she suggested to Rafiki, 'so that I can pay all the guards every week.' So this became the normal method of doing business. She had bought a second hand scooter which Kinua serviced and made roadworthy and she was then taught how to ride it by Rafiki, firstly just around the driveway at Sattimma and then out on the local roads. Rafiki then helped her get a learners licence.

Wanjiru's first call was to H.Dass, the owner of the grocery store at Karen. He was standing outside the store and was very surprised to see a smartly dressed woman ride up to the store on a motor scooter and park; she took her scarf off. He had a vague recollection that he had seen her somewhere before. He was even more surprised when she said to him in Swahili:

'Mr. Dass, can I see you for a moment, I think that I have something that might interest you.'

Dass was about to dismiss her out of hand, but then he remembered that Sarah, Kinua's wife had helped Kinua start the nearby garage, which was now a thriving business which had certainly brought more custom to his store and was now paying him some rent. So Wanjiru was invited into his small office, a glassed in cubicle which looked out across the store. He did not invite her to sit down.

'Mr Dass, I was thinking that you need guards here at night, and I and my husband run a small business providing guards,' said Wanjiru confidently.

Das completely misunderstood her proposition and he had had just about as much as he could take with people offering to 'protect' his premises, so his first reaction was to yell at her: 'No, No, No I have just sorted out the last of all these protection rackets, you just wait here I am going to call that Superintendent Wacheera, who promised me that all that nonsense was a thing of the past.' He started looking around for the piece of paper that Wacheera had given him with his 'phone number.

Wanjiru was slightly taken aback by the man's reaction, but kept her head and said: 'This is not protection, Mr Dass, like you, and Kinua and all the other people here were paying. That has all been stopped, I know all about that and my husband and Rafiki and Munyu helped the police to stop it.'

'What, what are you talking about, what does this have to do with the Lawrences?'

'They and my husband went to Superintendent Wacheera and helped him stop it. Maybe it is one of the reasons that the boy Kamau was kidnapped; the people that were benefitting from the so called protection did not like what the Lawrences did.'

Dass then sat down heavily on his chair and then said: 'What are you talking about; you mean that the Lawrences knew about this racket and had it stopped.'

Wanjiru just nodded. She had got Dass to listen to her and she didn't want to say any more than she had. Kahinga had told her the story and she hoped that she had the facts right.

'So what are you offering then?'

'Nairobi is full of robbers and other criminals, and I thought that this whole set of shops here might want armed guards at night to keep the robbers away. I have looked around and I think that two would be enough. We already have guards in all Rafiki's clinics.'

'These people would be armed?'

'Yes, all the people have licensed firearms.'

'Licensed?'

'Yes, Munyu helped us get all the right licences.'

'What has Munyu got to do with this? I thought that he was Minister of Agriculture.'

'Nothing except that he didn't want us to break the law, so he and Rafiki helped us.'

'So are all these guards going to be Kikuyu?'

'Yes.'

'Who has trained them; do they know how to fire a gun?'

'My husband trained them all; they were all in the forests with him.'

Dass looked doubtful: 'all Mau-Mau?'

'Yes, but that is all finished now that we have Uhuru.'

'Who trained your husband?'

'Munyu, we were on the farm with him, before the men went into the forests,'

'Munyu again. OK, so tell me what the arrangement is, how much will you charge, what hours they work, and what they do if there is a problem.'

Wanjiru had a sample invoice with her with what would be charged for two guards seven days a week. 'I am asking that I am paid one month in advance,' she said, 'and if there is a break-in, there is a 'phone box here so they can call the police. They have also been told to fire their guns in the air, then the robbers will probably run away.'

'And if they don't run away?'

'They may have to shoot them, but I don't think that will happen very often.'

'I will talk to the other shopkeepers, the charges are OK but I don't think that you will be paid in advance, not for a service that we know nothing about.'

'If everything is OK after three months, will you then pay in advance?' asked Wanjiru.

'Maybe, we will see.'

Wanjiru, still standing said: 'I know that Kinua will sign up, he had a break-in a few weeks ago and they stole some spanners, anyway you should speak to Sarah about that, Kinua only knows about engines and getting himself all greasy.' She smiled: 'I will come back in one week, if that is enough time to talk to the other shopkeepers.'

Dass nodded: 'One week then.'

He went back to his work and Wanjiru let herself out. She was elated and said to herself: 'This is going to work, this is going to work.'

A few days later Sarah came to her and told her that Dass had spoken to all the shopkeepers and that she should go and see Dass, they all wanted to start the patrols as soon as possible.

Once the arrangements had been functioning at Karen for a few weeks, Wanjiru started to approach other areas. To start with she asked Dass if he knew any of the shopkeepers at a certain location and if he would be prepared to 'phone them to tell them his experience with the service at Karen, which he did on several occasions.

Kahinga, for his part, visited all his guards every night at varying times, partly to keep them on their toes and partly to see if they were all alright. He went back into the mountains on several more occasions to retrieve more weapons as they were needed. He ensured that they were all licensed before they were allocated to any of his guards.

Kahinga also found time to see what was needed to repair the boreholes on what had been Naseby. He had spent a few hours with Peter and together they decided what equipment was needed for both boreholes. This was then provided by the Ministry of Agriculture. Kahinga borrowed a three ton truck from the Ministry and together with N'guku drove to Naseby. It took them two days to remove all the debris from one of the boreholes and install the pump and the diesel engine to run it. All the foundations were still in place although there was no sign of any of the equipment that had been left behind when the farm had been taken over. They had gathered a number of curious onlookers from the new settlers. At the end of two days Kahinga started the engine and within minutes, amid cheers from the crowd, water gushed out of the pipe leading from the pump. He let it run for a while and then switched off the engine.

They had spent the nights with one or other of the Kikuyu who had been settled in the area after the farm had been taken over; as always they were provided with meals and somewhere to sleep and there was no thought of them having to pay anything. Naseby had been split up into fifty acre lots and almost all the owners lived in Nakuru or one of the nearby towns; most of the people who actually lived there were caretakers and did very little farming, really just enough to keep themselves alive.

'There was a pipe here leading up to the tank there,' Kahinga pointed up to the stone water tank on the next ridge. 'Does anyone know what has happened to that pipe?' People looked slightly embarrassed and some of them started to drift away.

Then the man that he and Peter had seen now months earlier happily tending his herd of cattle came up and said: 'The pipe that you are talking about was taken by many people from here. At that time there was no water from this borehole, the engine and pump had been taken by the man who now owns this piece of land and I think he sold them in Nakuru, which is where he lives; he told me that it was better for him to sell those things before they were stolen and sold by someone else. The tank over there, we did not know what it was for, but it is on another person's land and in between here and the tank, the land belongs to yet another person, who also lives in Nakuru. The pipe was just left and over many months pieces of it just disappeared, so now there is no pipe. We need more water, sometimes this place is very dry and all the rivers and streams stop running, but if you leave that engine and pump here the man who owns this place will do what he did before and take the equipment and sell it in Nakuru.'

Kahinga just looked bemused and then he said: 'I told Munyu that I would see if the boreholes could be fixed, as you can see it is possible to fix this one at least, but I will not leave this engine and pump here just to be taken away. It seems to me that the people need to be fixed as much as the boreholes and I can't do that.'

So much to the consternation of the people now watching he laboriously disassembled the equipment that he brought and he and N'guku loaded it all back on the truck. Thoughtfully he had brought with him a steel cap which he installed over the hole and he said to anyone who was listening: 'This is so you don't have to put rocks down there any more to block the hole, you will need someone with the proper equipment to remove it now, maybe that can happen when Munyu has fixed the people.'

They went to the other borehole, almost a mile away. This time, although none of the original equipment was there all the piping was still miraculously intact and the man who now owned the land watched on in fascination as water was pumped from the borehole to several points, still on his land, once the installation was complete.

'What happened to the original equipment that was here,' asked Kahinga.

'It stopped working, so I sold it,' said the man.

'Why didn't you get someone to fix it for you?'

The man laughed. 'There is no one here to fix such a thing, anyway there is no diesel.'

Kahinga frowned: 'But you can buy diesel from any store in Ol' Kalou.'

There was a shrug: 'I have no car or truck like you to fetch the diesel, also I have no money to buy diesel, and there is too much water from this borehole. I need some water but not so much. I only have fifty acres and two cows and some mealies; that is all.'

'What about water for the house, I see that you have a nice stone house over there.'

'Yes the house was built from stones that the Wazungu who lived here had used, I think, to keep some pigs. We don't have any pigs so we knocked all that down and built a house. We carry water from the river for the house.'

'But that river sometimes dries up and it is far away, and the water is not always clean,' observed Kahinga.

The man shrugged. As far as he was concerned the water was collected by the household women as they had done from time immemorial.

'If you have too much water from this borehole can't you share the cost of diesel with the neighbours and let them have some of the water.'

'Maybe, but some of them are like me and have no money and no truck to fetch diesel. Also many of them live in Nakuru and Naivasha and other places and only visit once a month or less often, so it is very hard to find them to talk to. So if I give them water it will be very difficult for me to get them to pay for water or diesel or whatever.'

Kahinga and N'guku then disassembled all the equipment he had brought and started loading on to the truck. The man looked disconsolate. 'You come here to fix this borehole and now you are taking it all away again.'

'Well,' said Kahinga, 'you just told me that if it breaks down there is nobody to fix it, you can't buy diesel for all the reasons you have given me. If I leave all this here, will it still be here when I come back in three months time, maybe not.'

'You are coming back in three months time?

'I don't know; Munyu asked me to see if the boreholes could be fixed, which I have done but the problems are with the people and that is something that I cannot fix. I will tell Munyu what I have found here.'

With that they finished loading the truck and they drove back to Sattimma, after having placed a cap on the borehole as with the first one.

Kahinga unloaded the equipment and stored it all neatly in one of the garages on Sattimma. He returned the truck to the ministry and went on to attend to his burgeoning security business, so it was almost a week before he was able to report back to Peter on the matter.

'The boreholes are working, you say?' asked Peter.

'The boreholes are easy to fix,' said Kahinga, 'the problem is the people.' He went on to describe the conversations that he had had with some of the people in the district. 'What they really want is for the government to fix the boreholes and provide water to all the small farms in the district for nothing.'

'We don't really have the resources for that,' said Peter. 'The people were sold the land for very low prices and resettled, but we need to see that they are going to do more than just live on the land and grow a few mealies; there won't be any more handouts from the Government.'

Kahinga said: 'You Munyu have helped with this security business and

I am now very busy, thanks to you but if you want me to fix boreholes for you I can do that, but you first need to fix the people. If you put engines and pumps in those places they will just be stolen unless there is security and an agreement with all the people who will be given water from those boreholes. You also need someone to repair the boreholes when they break down.'

And then he continued: 'When I was a child in the reserve we had plenty of food and we, as children could all run around and play with the other children in the village. We could also go into the forest and hunt for porcupines or honey, and there was plenty of firewood and room for the cattle to graze. Then the place became too small; we had to go a very long way to collect firewood, the water became dirty, and there was nothing for us to hunt in the forests any more. Also there was no grass for the cattle and the mealies did not grow every year. Many people then went to work on the farms owned by the Wazungu like you; otherwise we would not have had enough to eat.'

'Yes, well the population increased year by year and the so-called reserve areas were then far too small for the number of people,' responded Peter.

'Well the same thing is happening on Naseby and as you saw in the Bahati. There are just too many people. Everyone has to go very far for water and firewood. The water is dirty, and there are too many cattle so they are now quite small, some just the size of goats. Also there are too many children, maybe some of them go to school but I don't know where. Naseby is looking like the Kikuyu reserve did all those years ago, almost like a desert. When the Wazungu left their farms many people left the reserve and went to live in places like Naseby, so there was suddenly more room in the reserve again. But now there are just too many people and there is nowhere for people to go; all the Wazungu farms have been settled again by the Kikuyu and there are no more Wazungu farms left. I don't know what will happen. Also I was speaking to a Masai at the duka (shop) in Ol'Kalou and he said that all the land the Kikuyu now have in this district should be given back to the Masai. All the names are Masai, and he said that the original Wazungu chased the Masai away before the war when the Bula Matari (Germans) were in Tanganyika (First World War).

'Yes, that is why we need to find a way of making those farms more productive again. Also the country needs to find ways of creating jobs; not everyone can live on a farm and with all this corruption around it will put investors off. They will just go somewhere else to invest their money,' said Peter.

Peter changed the subject and continued: 'Yes, thank you for doing what you did with the boreholes. It has been most helpful and I have much to think about.' Then he looked Kahinga in the eye: 'You now have a real business, like Kinua has and you can see that it will work for you and Wanjiru. Please, one word of advice, leave all the illegal stuff behind, no more bhang or protection rackets. Wacheera has his suspicions about some of your activities in the past, but with your efforts during the Kamau rescue he will turn a blind eye to all those other activities, but they may come up again if you step over the line. OK.'

Kahinga just nodded. He reflected briefly on his relationship with Peter or Munyu as he preferred to think of him: Peter's quick action after the snake had bitten him had undoubtedly saved his life. Peter had taught him many things—how to handle a gun—most of his ability with things mechanical resulted from working with Peter-and he had taken him in after the emergency, when his own people had discarded him. He would heed that advice; almost always any advice given from Peter was sound as far as he Kahinga was concerned.

Peter, in a conversation with Rafiki one evening said: 'the 'million acre scheme' really just provided a simple political solution to the burgeoning population. The trouble is that the population just keeps growing and even now the same problem of overpopulation exists and it will just get worse.'

✳ ✳ ✳

CHAPTER 20

Nyamita had always kept his ear very close to the ground. During the height of the drama of the kidnapping, his mole, Sergeant Odhiambo, at police headquarters had kept him updated with current developments. Odhiambo of course had no knowledge of Nyamita's direct involvement in the plot but had faithfully informed him of the suspicions that he, Nyamita had masterminded the plot; Nyamita was of course aware of that because of the visit of Inspector Orinda. At that stage, having spoken to Boniface and given him clear directions to go to the quarry, which he was sure the police knew nothing about, he felt secure. There was no knowledge at police headquarters regarding Kahinga and Rafiki's proposed visit to the quarry, since they were not using any police resources. But then he had a call from Sergeant Odhiambo that really frightened him for the first time in many many years.

Odhiambo had been asked to 'phone Nyamita at regular intervals during the day with developments, especially regarding the kidnapping, and he had given a full report. At that stage there was really no progress and Kamau was still in the hands of Boniface, but almost as a throwaway line to complete the call Odhiambo said: 'Oh by the way they have arrested deputy Minister Kariuki on fraud charges.'

Nyamita was silent for a moment and then said: 'Fraud charges, what sort of fraud charges?'

'I'm not really sure, something about invoicing the Government for work that was not done, I think.'

'Any connection with the kidnapping case?'

'No, not as far as I know.'

Nyamita thought for a moment and then asked: 'When are you off duty?'

'Later tonight.'

'See if you can get off early and then come to the hospital, I will need you to do something for me. Come in the back way, there is no need to report at the front desk, and come in civilian clothes, leave your police uniform at the station,' he added before the phone was put down. Nyamita knew that he was done for unless he got away quickly; he was certain that Kariuki would crumble under pressure and give the game away.

Odhiambo arrived just after ten in the evening, in civilian clothes as he had been instructed. Nyamita had dressed himself and was sitting uncomfortably in one of the chairs in his room. He handed Odhiambo a set of keys and an address: 'Please go to this address, these are the keys to my car, which as you will see is a large black Mercedes. Do not let anyone at the house see you and please bring the car here. I will tell you what we are going to do after you come back. There is no particular hurry.'

'There are some people outside this hospital, who I have seen before; I think that they work for us, the police. I made sure that they did not see me, but I think that it will be very difficult for you to leave here in your car without being seen and identified. ' said Odhiambo.

Nyamita thought for a moment. 'Just leave it to me, 'phone before you return.'

Well after midnight Nyamita struggled downstairs and went to the front desk, who he knew would be attended by a young Jaluo woman.

She was very nervous but Nyamita turned on the charm for a few minutes. He then said to her: 'Do you want to earn a bit more money; I need a rather urgent favour.' The girl looked worried, but nodded. 'Is there a back way out of here?' She looked warily at him. He handed her one thousand shillings.

She nodded her understanding. 'The back gates will be open between midnight and four in the morning, nobody will see anything,' she said.

Odhiambo was used to obeying orders and he had driven Nyamita on many occasions that involved clandestine destinations so he did not question what was happening, after all as far as he was concerned, he was obeying orders from the head of the police.

Odhiambo rode his bicycle to the address indicated, and kept it under surveillance for thirty minutes before he made his move. There was nobody about. The car, recently washed and polished, was in a car port and Odhiambo quickly unlocked the vehicle, managed to stow his bicycle in the ample boot. He adjusted the seat and the mirror to suit him and without switching on the lights quietly drove the car out on to the road. Driving home to a modest cottage in one of Nairobi's less affluent suburbs, the bicycle was unloaded. He packed a few personal things into a cardboard box. His wife had produced a meal and by two in the morning he was on his way back to Nyamita. He told his wife nothing; she was used to him going off on what was described as 'police business' so asked no questions. Odhiambo struggled to find a 'phone box that worked, so just drove into the main entrance to the hospital.

Odhiambo was stopped by Wacheera's surveillance crew on his way into the hospital, but he said that all he was doing was to deliver a message at the front desk, so he was let through without further question. He went up to Nyamita's room and told him what the situation was.

'I could not find a 'phone that worked and it was getting late so I came straight here,' explained Odhiambo.

'OK, don't worry but listen. Take the car out the front way and let them search it, then drive around the back, you will have to go the long way round, so you won't be seen; the gates will be open, drive in without lights and park and then come up here and fetch me,' instructed Nyamita.

Odhiambo did as he was told. Wacheera's surveillance crew were very suspicious and searched the car thoroughly but found nothing except Odhiambo's meagre possessions, so they noted the make and licence plate number of the car and let him through, although they never identified Odhiambo as a member of the police force. He eventually found his way into the rear of the hospital, after having taken several wrong turns. He parked the vehicle in a shadow and ran up to Nyamita's room.

Nyamita looked at Odhiambo enquiringly but said nothing. Odhiambo then helped Nyamita pack all his clothes and personal effects into several large suitcases which he laboriously dragged down to the car and stowed in the boot. Shortly before four am he helped a still rather sore and unsteady Nyamita down the back stairs into the rear seat of the car. As unobtrusively as possible they drove out of the hospital; as far as they could see there was nobody about and it seemed that they had managed to get away without anyone knowing. 'Namanga, but don't get there before six,' was the sole instruction. In twenty minutes Odhiambo navigated his way to the main Nairobi Mombasa road. The relatively lush terrain of Nairobi quickly turned to thorn scrub on the way to Athi River where they took the well signposted right turn off to Namanga and the Tanzanian border. The one hundred or so miles to the border was an easy drive on the well maintained dirt road and they were well in sight of the border just before six.

'Maybe we could get some breakfast at the hotel,' suggested Odhiambo.

'No, just wait here, we can go to the border at six, when it will be open,' said Nyamita.

'What about papers?' asked Odhiambo.

'We will tell them we are on police business, our warrant cards will get us through,' responded Nyamita.

At six they approached the border where there were several buses bulging with passengers with bundles of luggage and crates of live chickens on their roof racks. 'Quick, see if you can get ahead of all these people. Take our warrant cards, tell them I am unwell and if they want to see me they will have to come out here.'

Odhiambo returned a few minutes later saying: 'They recognise you, so we can proceed, also they have 'phoned the people on the Tanzanian side and they will let us through quite quickly I think.' The single boom gate was raised as they approached the border and much to their surprise the same thing happened on the Tanzanian side without them having to produce any form of identity.

Neither Nyamita nor Odhiambo were in the mood to admire the view which was dominated on their left hand side by Mount Meru at an impressive fifteen thousand feet, but completely overshadowed behind, by the towering snow-capped peak of Mount Kilimanjaro, at nineteen thousand feet the highest peak in Africa, and the tallest single mountain in the world, with the sun just peeking through, creating a beautiful pink tinge in the early dawn.

Nyamita told an uncomprehending Odhiambo that at one stage in the late nineteenth century Kilimanjaro had been part of the British protectorate of Kenya, but that the English Queen Victoria had given the mountain to her favourite uncle Kaiser Wilhelm, the German Emperor to be part of the German territory of Tanganyika, on the basis that Kenya had two mountains(mounts Kenya and Kilimanjaro) and Tanganyika none and so the gift evened things up with each territory having one mountain: 'So that is why the Bula Matari (Germans) owned this mountain, which really should belong to Kenya,' he explained.

Odhiambo was more interested in his hunger pangs and managed to persuade Nyamita to stop in Arusha for breakfast and some twelve hours later they arrived in Dar-es-Salaam via Bagamoyo, the original colonial capital. They spent one night in a seedy little hotel on the outskirts of the city. Nyamita made one call the next day and they were then directed to a magnificent house overlooking a beach. Nyamita was greeted like a long lost friend by a person who looked just like him, and who turned out to be his brother.

Nyamita then said to Odhiambo: 'You will go back to Nairobi, by train, do not tell anyone I am here.' He gave him one thousand shillings. 'They will take you to the train station.' referring to two 'assistants,' standing nearby. And with that he was dismissed. When he arrived back at police headquarters in Nairobi, three days later, after lengthy questioning they accepted that his absence had been caused by illness. Nobody connected him to Nyamita's disappearance.

Wacheera's surveillance crew were questioned at length when it was discovered that Nyamita had left the hospital. They produced the record of the black Mercedes having entered the hospital grounds and leaving shortly afterwards. By this time the police were aware that it was Nyamita's personal vehicle.

'The car was searched thoroughly, there was nothing at all in it, the man said that he was just delivering a message,' they reported when questioned.

'What about the rear entrance?'

'Always locked at night. We saw it being locked at ten o'clock; the key is kept at reception, so nobody could have taken it without being seen.'

Some months later Kahinga received a letter from Wanyoike, who had exiled himself in Dar-es-Salaam on Kahinga's instructions, telling him that he had seen Nyamita on several occasions in the street and had followed him back to where he was living. He gave Kahinga the address, which was passed on to Wacheera.

Chapter 21

Boniface felt completely abandoned; there had been no word from Nyamita at all and there was no news about anything. Boniface and the surviving members of the gang had been charged with the serious offence of kidnapping and had been remanded in custody awaiting trial. Wacheera decided to leave him and Otieno to stew in their own juice for a while and then he personally conducted their interrogations. He started with Otieno, who he mistakenly thought was the weaker of the two.

The interrogation was conducted in Swahili since Wacheera spoke no Luo and Otieno no Kikuyu.

'Otieno, do you ever want to see your wife and children again?' There was absolutely no response.

'Did you understand the question? Do you want to see your wife and children again?' Again there was no response.

Wacheera thought that he would try another tack:

'We have many witnesses who have told us that you and Inspector Boniface and two others abducted Kamau Lawrence and took him to a place in the forest. Why did you do that?'

'Superintendent Nyamita told me to go with Inspector Boniface and take the boy. He told me that Munyu and Rafiki were interfering in his affairs and that they should be taught a lesson. They said that we should hold the boy for a few days and then let him go. Those Kikuyu came and found us before we could let him go. Superintendent Nyamita said that I could go back to work at Lenana afterwards. I would like to do that now.'

'Did you not think that taking the boy from his bed in the middle of the night with no clothes except his night things and beating him was wrong? What if the same thing had happened to one of your own three children?'

'I just did what I was told to do by Superintendent Nyamita.'

'Tell me how it all happened, from the beginning please.'

Otieno looked at Wacheera balefully:

'I have known Superintendent Nyamita since I was a small boy. When I heard that he had been shot by those drug dealers I went to see him in hospital and sometimes took him some food. A few weeks ago he told me that this Inspector Boniface would come to me at Lenana and that I should show him where Kamau sleeps so that we could take him away and hide him for a few days until Munyu and Rafiki stopped interfering with his affairs.'

'What affairs, did he tell you anything about which affairs he was talking about?'

'No.'

'You still think it was the right thing to do, to capture the boy and take him away?'

'I did what I was told to do by Superintendent Nyamita.'

'What if it had been one of your own children?

'I am not interfering with any of Superintendent Nyamita's personal affairs, so there would be no need to take any of my children.'

'And if you had been, you think that Nyamita had the right to take one of your children.'

Otieno remained silent.

'I can tell you that you will never go back to your job at Lenana. Kidnapping is a very serious offence and you will spend many years in jail. Have you heard from Nyamita, has he been back to you to explain why it all went wrong and why you have ended up in jail and not him?'

Otieno shook his head.

'When Nyamita was giving you instructions to take the boy did he mention anyone else?'

'Yes he told me that Inspector Boniface would come and find me at Lenana, which he did.'

'Anyone else?'

'No, just those two who came with us. One was shot by those Kikuyu.' He said resentfully.

'Are you sure there was nobody else involved?

'Nobody else was involved.'

He then made Otieno go through everything from his last visit to Nyamita to when they were captured by Rafiki and Kahinga. He wrote it all down.

The surviving member of the kidnap gang corroborated what he could of the story that Otieno had told him.

A day or two later he interviewed Boniface, this time he had inspector Orinda with him, a person he trusted. Again and for the same reasons as with Otieno the interview was conducted in Swahili. Boniface was still hobbling with his leg in plaster, using crutches to walk. It seemed doubtful if his knee would ever be quite normal again; the slug from the .416 had smashed it to pieces and whilst the medical attention had been adequate there was not much that could have been done with the dozens of bone fragments that had been the result of Kahinga's accurate shot.

'Inspector Boniface, I just want to understand your role in the kidnapping of Kamau Lawrence...'

He was immediately interrupted by a blustering Boniface:

'We were just going to take him back to Lenana, those thieving Kikuyu just set us up, we found him and had seen some of the newspaper reports and were just taking him back to the school.'

Wacheera looked at him as if he was completely out of his mind.

'We have evidence from Otieno and your other colleague that you went to the school and took Kamau from his bed, drove around Nairobi half the night and then spent the next day in the Ngong forest. We have found the place there where you hid in the forest. You then went to the place in the mutoni where you were captured. You had just hit Kamau Lawrence when he was pulled out of the pick-up truck that you stole in Kisumu, by the way. There isn't a shred of evidence to suggest anything else. What about that Wazungu couple who you persuaded to hand the boy back to you, by telling a whole lot of lies. You had better come to your senses very quickly or I will have you sent to Mathari (the local lunatic asylum) for the rest of your life.'

Boniface just glared resentfully.

'Come on; let us just go through everything that happened from the time you went to Kisumu. Why did you go there, your post is here in Nairobi?'

'Superintendent Nyamita sent me to Kisumu...'

'On some private business,' interrupted Wacheera. 'You perfectly well understood his position; he was not active in any way in police matters, and there are some issues that we need to talk to you about relating to your unauthorised visit to Kisumu, but that can come later. Tell us what happened after you stole that pick-up.'

'The pick-up was lent to us, we did not steal it.'

'Be that as it may, that is not what the owner told us, but go on, what happened after that.'

'I went to see Nyamita in his hospital.'

'We can find no record of that visit; you had signed the visitor's book all the other times that you went there, why not this time.' said Wacheera quietly.

Boniface looked non-plussed for a moment and before he could say anything Wacheera continued: 'This was when he told you to go and kidnap that boy Kamau, wasn't it? Otieno had been there a few days before and you were told to go and see him at Lenana.'

Boniface just looked glum and said nothing.

'This is what happened isn't it, since you seem to have lost the use of your tongue as well as your leg: Nyamita told you of the scheme, he told you to go and find Otieno at Lenana, which you did and then you went with Otieno to the boy's dormitory with another man, the one who was shot. You then waited until late and you the driver and Otieno went back to the school and took Kamau Lawrence from his bed and the rest of it we know. We have all the evidence to put you away for a very long time indeed, but if you help us with one other matter related to this kidnapping we may ask the Judge at your trial to exercise some leniency.'

Boniface looked up hopefully.

'We have looked up the records of people visiting Nyamita in past weeks and suddenly a rather surprising name appears in the record, many times in the past few weeks in fact. Can you guess who that was?'

Boniface tried to look thoughtful, he knew perfectly well who that might be but he wondered whether disclosing the name would do him any good at all. He decided that since Wacheera was a Kikuyu it might help to disclose the name:

'Minister Kariuki came to see him I think.'

'You think,' yelled Wacheera suddenly, 'You lying fool, you know perfectly well I'm talking about Kariuki. What do you think they were discussing, remember that your answer might affect your jail sentence; so be very careful. Also we have Kariuki here in jail as well, so it will be very easy to confirm your story.'

Boniface was now terrified, he saw himself spending the rest of his life in the hellhole of a Kenyan jail.

'Nyamita told me that Minister Kariuki would make a 'phone call to Munyu or Rafiki, after we captured the boy, and tell them that they should stop all their nonsense or we would kill him.'

'What nonsense was that?'

'I don't know, he did not tell me, he just mentioned schemes.'

Wacheera now had Boniface here he wanted him, whatever he might have hinted at there was no question of any leniency and he now thought that he had some leverage against Kariuki.

'Inspector Boniface, you really are a disgrace to the service, you a serving police officer involved in a scheme to kidnap a young boy for some personal reason and you did not even try to find out any details of what the issue was. I am ashamed of you, from today you will be stripped of all your police rank and authority and your pension. I hope that you spend the rest of your life in jail, but that is for the Judge to decide.'

Wacheera stormed out and signalled Orinda to follow, Boniface just sat there with his mouth open:

'You continue the interrogation; get the full story on the kidnapping and the involvement of each party of course. Also there is now this story about a bhang dealer in Kisumu, who had some dealings with Nyamita, who just disappeared when Boniface was there; maybe he had something to do with that as well.'

CHAPTER 22

Johanna Kariuki's trial was a sensation, with extensive coverage in all the media in the country and there was also considerable interest from overseas media as well. The trial only dealt with his involvement in the kidnapping of Kamau, the fraud charges were slated for another occasion.

The evidence centred on his visits to Nyamita in hospital, the phone call to Peter and Boniface's testimony.

Under questioning by the prosecution he was asked:

'You went to visit Superintendent Nyamita on many occasions while he was in hospital, why was that?'

'I was concerned for his welfare; he had been shot in a drug raid?'

There was general laughter from the public gallery; the people in the gallery obviously thought that this was a ridiculous proposition.

'Please be quiet in the gallery or I will have everyone removed,' said the Judge quietly.

'Had you ever met the Superintendent before?'

'Maybe once.'

'Where?'

'I don't remember.'

'You only started to make these visits some months after the Superintendent was shot. If you were so worried about his welfare why did it take you so long to find your way to the hospital?'

'I was busy.'

'Really, you made six visits in a very short period, just prior to the kidnapping of Kamau Lawrence, were you not busy then?'

Kariuki remained silent.

'I submit that you and Nyamita were upset by some of the activities of Mr.

and Mrs. Lawrence and you decided to teach them a lesson by kidnapping their son and threatening to kill him.'

'We discussed nothing of the sort,' retorted Kariuki.

'What did you discuss then?'

'His treatment…'

'His treatment!' the prosecutor was incredulous, 'can you tell me what you studied at University?'

'Commerce,'

There was muted laughter from the public gallery, which the Judge chose to ignore.

'So based on your commerce degree, which presumably gave you no insight into anything medical whatsoever, you spent six meetings with Superintendent Nyamita discussing his treatment in detail.' The prosecutor threw his papers on the floor in real anger. 'And you expect us to believe that; this is nonsense.'

Kariuki started to say something.

The prosecutor held up his hand. 'Spare us any more of this.' He then hesitated: 'I have a deposition here in front of me from Rafiki Wainaina, the mother of Kamau Lawrence, the little boy that you helped arrange to be kidnapped…'

'Objection,' from the defence.

'Please rephrase,' asked the Judge.

'…the little boy who was kidnapped. That she went to see you regarding what she considered to be payments made to companies that you or your family control that appeared to be fraudulent.'

Kariuki tried to say something. He was waved away by the prosecutor. 'Did Rafiki Wainaina come to see you and raise those issues? And I want a yes or no answer, nothing else.'

'Yes, but…'

'The answer is yes, she did come to see you.'

'Yes,' was the whispered reply.

'Louder, so the court can hear,' the prosecutor held his hand up to his ear looking at Kariuki.

'Yes.'

'How long after this discussion with Rafiki Wainaina, did you go and see Superintendent Nyamita?'

'Objection, this is not relevant,' said the defence.

'Upheld, why is this relevant?' Asked the Judge.

The prosecutor hesitated: 'I have another deposition here this time from Superintendent Wacheera stating that he had stopped a protection racket run by Superintendent Nyamita, again a scheme that Rafiki Wainaina and her husband had drawn to his attention…'

'Objection, this is not relevant.'

'Objection upheld.'

'I put it to you Mr Kariuki that the only reason that you established a relationship with Superintendent Nyamita was that you both had reason to believe that the parents of Kamau Lawrence, the boy who was kidnapped, had done you some damage and that kidnapping the boy and threatening to kill him was your way of demanding that they stop what they were doing.'

Kariuki could see at this stage that the prosecution case was weak and that all they were doing was to try to get him to confess:

'We discussed nothing about anything like that, all we discussed was his treatment and when he was likely to be able to return to his position as police chief, nothing else.'

'During the height of the kidnapping, a 'phone call was made to the boy's father, Mr Lawrence, demanding that he and his wife 'stop your nonsense' to quote Mr. Lawrences written deposition.'

Kariuki said nothing.

'This call was made from a 'phone box close to your office.'

Kariuki remained silent.

'When the police examined the 'phone box, your finger prints were found, fresh finger prints. Did you make a call from that 'phone box?'

'Maybe, I sometimes make calls from that box for personal reasons.'

'Did you make a call to Mr Lawrence's house during the kidnapping?'

'No.'

'You are lying; I ask you again did you make a call to Mr. Lawrence's house?'

'Objection, the defendant has already answered the question.'

'Sustained.'

'No more questions.'

All the defence wanted was to get him off the stand as quickly as they were able.

'Please call Inspector Boniface.' asked the prosecution.

Boniface limped in, walking with the assistance of a stick.

'I have a confession here signed by you that based on conversations you had with Superintendent Nyamita, that you and others arranged the kidnapping of Kamau Lawrence. Do you recognise this?'

Boniface barely looked at it. He nodded. He looked utterly defeated. He had already been sentenced to life imprisonment for his part in kidnapping Kamau.

'During your discussions with Superintendent Nyamita regarding the plot to kidnap the boy, was Minister Kariuki's name mentioned at any time.'

'Yes it was,' answered Boniface.

'How, in what context?'

'Nyamita said that Minister Kariuki would make a 'phone call, once we had captured the boy.'

The court was dead quiet.

'To whom would he make the call?'

'To Munyu or Rafiki.'

'Do you know what he was supposed to say during this call?'

'That we had the boy and that he would be killed if they didn't stop interfering with the schemes of Nyamita and Kariuki.'

'No more questions.'

The defence had no questions.

'I call Munyu to the stand,' said the prosecution.

When Peter appeared the people in the gallery started clapping.

The Judge just glared at them.

'Mr Lawrence, there is a deposition from you that sometime in the morning after the kidnapping you received a telephone call threatening to kill your son unless you stopped doing certain things; can you tell me what the caller was referring to and can you tell me what language they were speaking.'

'The language of the call in question was Kikuyu, which I speak fluently. The caller referred to a protection racket that Superintendent Nyamita had set up mainly to benefit himself. We became aware of it and referred it to Superintendent Wacheera, who closed it down.'

'Did you recognise the caller's voice?'

'No, it was muffled and it sounded that the caller was holding his nose in order to disguise his voice.'

'No more questions.'

The defence asked: 'Mr Lawrence, you say that the scheme was set up mainly to benefit Superintendent Nyamita, who else benefitted from the scheme.'

'Objection, we are not here to try or discuss Superintendent Nyamita's affairs.'

The Judge asked: 'Can the defence show that this question is relevant to the trial of Mr Kariuki?'

The defence asked: 'permission to approach the bench?'

There was a whispered conversation.

'Mr Lawrence, please answer the question.' said the Judge.

'We, that is Rafiki and I, became aware of the scheme when one of my ex-employees who now runs a successful garage business in Karen was asked to pay protection money to the police. The people involved threatened to burn his premises down if he didn't cooperate. We collected evidence from all concerned and confronted Superintendent Nyamita, who was the main beneficiary of the scheme, with the evidence, having already discussed the matter with then Chief Inspector Wacheera. You will appreciate that there is no purpose in stopping a scheme of this nature for it to be replaced by a similar scheme within a few weeks. So the scheme continued, with the full cooperation of the police; seventy five percent of the funds from this protection racket were paid into the funds of the Pumwani Clinics, which Rafiki set up. Every single paying–in slip has a police stamp on it. The advent of the additional funds has resulted in at least two more clinics being opened.'

There was a deathly hush in the courtroom.

'May I continue?' asked Peter.

The Judge nodded.

'Once Superintendent Wacheera was in a position to shut the scheme down permanently, he told us that was what he was going to do and we were able to replace the funding for the clinics from the scheme with funds collected by my son in England.'

'As far you are aware was Mr Kariuki in any way involved in this particular scheme?' Asked the defence.

'No.'

'No, what? Please answer the question fully.'

'None of the evidence that I saw involved or implicated Mr Kariuki in any way as far as this particular scheme goes.'

'No more questions.'

'I have some further questions,' said the prosecutor standing up.

'Please proceed,' said the Judge.

'Are you aware of any other corrupt schemes, involving Mr Kariuki.'

'Objection,'

'Not upheld, please answer the question Mr Lawrence.'

'I have become aware of a scheme where Mr Kariuki was involved in invoicing Government for work that was not carried out. All the details are in the hands of the police; I believe that was the original reason he was arrested.'

'No further questions,'

The defence stood up:

'I have some supplementary questions.'

The Judge nodded.

'Why were you involved?'

'Information came into my hands, and Rafiki confronted Mr. Kariuki with the evidence.'

'Why Rafiki?'

'She was a member of his age group during initiation and so knows him well.'

'What happened after that?'

'We passed the information on to Superintendent Wacheera.'

'What was Mr Kariuki's response to all this evidence?'

'I had no discussions with Mr Kariuki on the subject.'

'Did Rafiki have any further discussions with Mr Kariuki regarding these allegations?'

'Perhaps you should ask her that question.'

'How did you acquire this information?'

'A personal source, a great deal of information comes my way, as a member of Government and in my private capacity. You should be aware that the information that Rafiki and I provided Superintendent Wacheera has now been superseded by his own enquiries and my understanding is that that this new information will be the basis of the prosecution in this case.'

During these proceedings it was clear to Rafiki that the prosecution case against Kariuki was circumstantial and weak and it seemed as if he might be found 'not guilty' of the kidnapping charges, although she was convinced he was guilty. She was instructing Ziporah, who had turned out to be a quick learner, on an administrative procedure when the subject of the trial came up during a break over a cup of tea. 'I was there once when this Kariuki came to see Nyamita in hospital,' offered Ziporah.

Rafiki was all ears: 'Really, this could be very important, what was the discussion.'

'I didn't really understand it all, but they were both upset with you and Munyu and said that you were both interfering with schemes that they had running. I really only understood the Swahili part of the conversation, some of it was in English, which I don't understand all that well. I asked Nyamita after Mr Kariuki had left if he wanted to kill Rafiki; he said no, but that she 'Needs to stop her nonsense.'

Rafiki immediately 'phoned Wacheera and told him of the conversation.

When the trial recommenced the prosecution immediately requested the introduction of another witness and Ziporah was called to the stand:

'Ziporah Okongo, you were with Superintendent Nyamita when Mr Kariuki came to visit him in hospital one day.'

'Yes.'

'Was this the first time that Mr Kariuki had visited Superintendent Nyamita.'

'Yes, he had not been to the hospital before and Nyamita had not mentioned his name before.'

'What was the subject of discussion?'

'Once they and made their introductions...'

'What do you mean by that, did they not know each other?'

'No Mr Kariuki came in and said: 'I am... and then Nyamita interrupted and said: 'I know who you are Mr Deputy Minister. It seemed to me that they had never actually met before.'

'What was the subject of discussion?'

'Both Nyamita and Mr Kariuki were angry with some of the things that Munyu and Rafiki were doing that had upset some of their schemes.'

'What schemes?'

'Mr Kariuki did not say which scheme but he did say that a scheme that he had to maintain his standard of living had been upset by Rafiki. Munyu and Rafiki made Nyamita pay most of the money to Rafiki's clinics from a scheme he had which collected money from many shops for police protection. Sometimes I had to pay the money into the bank account owned by the clinics and I was told that it was most important that the paying –in slip had a police stamp on it.'

'What else did they discuss?'

'Nothing really, they just said that Rafiki and Munyu needed to be taught a lesson so that they would stop interfering in other people's business.'

'Did they discuss Nyamita's hospital treatment?'

Ziporah looked surprised: 'No.'

'Did they say what they were going to do?'

'No.'

The defence had questions:

'Did they at any time discuss any of the Lawrence children in any context whatsoever?'

'No,'

'What is your relationship with Nyamita?'

Ziporah hesitated; she had been told by the prosecution that she would be asked this question and that she should answer it truthfully.

'I was his mistress, not any more though.'

'What does that mean?'

'Nyamita provided accommodation for me and he used to visit me several times a week, he sometimes stayed the night.'

'You say that this arrangement has ceased.'

'Yes, I now work in the Pumwani clinic.'

'Why did the arrangement cease?'

'Objection.'

'Upheld.'

'No more questions.'

In his summary the prosecutor emphasised the fact that Peter and Rafiki had upset Kariuki by exposing the allegedly false invoices that had been paid by his department. He referred to the meeting between Nyamita and Kariuki and that both of them wanted the Lawrences to be taught a lesson and he said that it was clear that Nyamita and Kariuki had not met before Nyamita was shot. He also mentioned that it was obvious that Kariuki was lying when he said that they discussed Nyamita's treatment; the only possible reason for Kariuki's visits were the fraudulent schemes that had been disrupted by the activities of the Lawrences. There was reference to Boniface's evidence and the 'phone call that Kariuki was supposed to make after the abduction of the boy:

'This man is undoubtedly guilty and should be sentenced accordingly.'

The defence said that the prosecution case was weak and solely based on anecdotal and circumstantial evidence:

'There isn't a shred of evidence to link this man directly to abduction of Kamau Lawrence and he should be found 'Not Guilty'.'

The Judge and his two assessors spent two days considering the evidence and returned to a quiet courtroom. The Judge summarised as follows:

'The abduction of Kamau Lawrence was a dastardly act and the perpetrators deserve to be punished with the full force of the law. Whilst there is some evidence of unusual discussions between the defendant and

Superintendent Nyamita, who has unfortunately left the country so this court has been unable to question him, there is no direct evidence linking Mr Kariuki with the abduction of Kamau Lawrence so this court finds that the prosecution case has not been proven beyond reasonable doubt. Mr Kariuki is therefore found NOT GUILTY of involvement in the abduction of Kamau Lawrence.'

There was a deathly hush in the court which lasted a full minute. Then the public gallery burst into a continuous shout of 'BOO'. Almost everyone in the gallery thought that Kariuki was guilty and wanted him convicted. The Judge was furious: 'Clear the court, clear the court.'

Peter and Rafiki were not in court to hear the verdict but Rafiki received a call within the half hour from Wacheera: 'Rafiki, I am sorry but the court has found Kariuki not guilty of involvement in the abduction.'

'Hmnn, I wondered about that, although he is undoubtedly guilty. What happens now?'

'Well there are two things that we need to do: one, we must try to get Nyamita back from Dar-es-Salaam and two we must make certain that Kariuki is convicted on the fraud charges,' answered Wacheera.

'I will tell Peter, if there is anything further we can do please let me know.'

She 'phoned Peter: 'Yes someone has just put his head round the door and told me; he's as guilty as hell. So what do we do now?'

'Wacheera will concentrate on nailing him on the fraud issue, and I think that he will now try to get Nyamita back from Tanzania, although when he starts that process I wonder if our friend will just move somewhere else,' responded Rafiki, 'we can talk later. I will go to the school now and tell Kamau; he does seem to have put it out of his mind now though, he seems more interested in rugby.'

Rafiki had tried to remain calm but the more she thought about it the angrier she became: 'The bastard is guilty and if the courts won't do anything about it then maybe we should,' she said to Peter that evening.

'There is no doubt that he is guilty, but our strength lies in getting him convicted by the courts, not taking the law into our own hands. The key is to get that animal Nyamita back here to face justice. If we can get him and Kariuki in the same room it will like two cats fighting, they will destroy each other.' He put his arms around her: 'now I have some other plans for the rest of the evening...' she snuggled up to him. 'Don't you ever think of anything else?' 'No, not while you are around.'

The next morning the housemaid found a trail of clothes leading from the lounge all the way up the stairs and in to Peter and Rafiki's bedroom. Peter was hurriedly getting dressed: 'I'm late,' he muttered. 'It's only half past seven,' said Rafiki sleepily from the bed.

CHAPTER 23

Kariuki was still being held in custody pending his trial on corruption charges. Wacheera had recovered from the disappointment that Kariuki had escaped conviction from the kidnapping case; he thought that there was really no question that he had been involved. He therefore made doubly sure that the evidence in the corruption case was completely watertight.

A few days after Kariuki was found 'not guilty' on kidnapping charges Wacheera was woken up in the middle of the night with a 'phone call. This was unusual in that he had left strict instructions that except in dire emergencies he was not be contacted outside normal hours:

The voice was muffled and it seemed that every attempt was being made to disguise the identity of the caller: 'Wacheera,' the voice called disrespectfully, 'the new charges against Minister Kariuki should be dropped. This comes from the highest levels of the leadership. The charges against him for the kidnapping of that 'Nusu-Nusu' Kamau Lawrence were trumped up and should never have got to court. So drop it now or you and your family will suffer.' The 'phone was abruptly put down before Wacheera could respond in any way.

Wacheera registered the call when he arrived at police headquarters the next morning and he increased security at home by having two police constables on duty twenty four hours a day. His wife and children were now always to be accompanied by a constable.

A few days later Wacheera had a visit, at his home, from three elders of his home village, a place he had learnt not to show his face any more. They were much more polite than the caller, but the message was the same:

'Minister Kariuki has brought much honour to the village, he also helps the village in many different ways,' said the spokesman.

'So I understand,' responded Wacheera.

'He was tried for the kidnapping of Kamau, and found 'not guilty'.

'Yes.'

'So now he is in jail on another charge where he will be found 'not guilty'.

'That is for the court to decide.'

'You have a very senior position in the Government.'

'No, I am not part of Government; the police are separate from normal Government, which is elected. The police are not elected.'

There was a look of distrust and a complete lack of understanding among his visitors.

'You do not do anything for the village; the village that educated you and helped to make you into the police chief.'

'That is certainly correct, I cannot afford to help much on my earnings, I have explained that many times.'

'But Minister Kariuki helps the village in many different ways and Munyu, even Munyu he helps the village, but you do nothing.'

'Munyu has money from his photography so that helps. As for Kariuki, you will see at his trial how he can afford to spend the money he does. His wife travels to Ulaya every year and his children go to special schools; he has a very big house. I know approximately what he earns, it is much the same as I earn. I do not have a big house and my wife has never been to Ulaya and our children go to ordinary schools. My job is to stop people stealing, not to encourage them and I will stop people who steal from anyone including the Government. I am not at liberty to discuss the case any further with you.'

'But you are from our village; your job is to help people like Kariuki, not to put them in jail.'

'If Kariuki has been stealing from Government then the court will decide what happens to him, not me. You must remember that it is my job to stop people stealing, even if they come from the same village.'

'But you can stop the case.'

'No, it is in the hands of the prosecution, I merely provided the evidence.'

There was a look of utter frustration on the faces in front of him and they obviously did not believe him. They all stood up.

Wacheera said to them just as they were leaving: 'What you have suggested is illegal and completely out of order. I should have you all arrested and charged with trying to pervert the course of justice. Indeed that is what I will do if I hear another word from you on the subject.'

They all just looked at him in utter amazement and one of them said: 'You Wacheera had better look out…' He didn't finish the sentence.

'Arrest these three,' he said to one of the constables on guard at his house.

There was a look of complete incomprehension on the faces of the three elders when they were taken away in a prison van an hour or so later.

'They will be charged with attempting to pervert the course of justice.' He told his wife when she asked.

'They are from your village; this means that whatever happens in the future we will not be able to return there ever.'

'Yes, I think that it is more important to stop people stealing than to pander to their illegal requests. They think that they can manipulate the system in their own favour just because I come from the same village. What do other people do if they don't have a minister or what they see as an important person from their village to do them all sorts of favours? This Kariuki has stolen a great deal of money from Government, most of it for his own use, something that the village people don't even think about. All they are worried about are their own precious little schemes. It's time they were all taught a lesson.'

His wife shook her head sorrowfully; she thought that there was no point in becoming an important person in the society if one was not able to help the people that originally helped to create the person that one had become. But she said nothing more.

Wacheera decided that it would be wise to mention the threats he had experienced to Rafiki, so he went to the Pumwani clinic in the hope that she would be there; he found her helping to teach Ziporah how to assess which patients should be referred to a nurse and which could be sent straight to a doctor. When she saw Wacheera she signalled to her head nurse to carry on and Wacheera was provided with a mug of tea in one of the back rooms that Rafiki used as an office.

After the usual greetings he said to Rafiki: 'I really came to warn you; the case against Kariuki is now watertight as far as we in the police are concerned but I am being put under a great deal of illegal pressure to abandon the case both from the village and from a telephone call I had in the middle of the night quite recently.'

'I heard from Wainaina that you had arrested three of the elders for trying to interfere in the case.'

'Yes and I am going to prosecute them; just because they think that I am an important person they think that I have the power to have the case abandoned, which is not the situation at all. They don't really understand the process and have no wish to understand it. I told them that it was now out of my hands in any event; they just thought that this was a ridiculous proposition and that I was lying. Anyway, to come back to the point, some people know that you and Munyu provided the original leads in this case and when their efforts to have it abandoned come to nothing they may seek to take it out on you. I would suggest that the clinics are a fairly soft target, so they may try something on here.'

'I have an armed security guard on here and in the other clinics all day and all night.'

'I wonder if that is enough? Also I am sure that most people are aware of that and any action against the clinic would take that into account.'

'Also Mwangi Mkubwa owns the premises here; he is delighted with the increase in business in his nearby shops since the clinic opened. I don't suppose that he will be very pleased if anyone tries to have it closed down,' said Rafiki.

'Would you like me to mention to Mwangi that I have some concerns?' asked Wacheera.

'Mmm, maybe not. I think that I can find a more roundabout way of dealing with the issue.'

Wacheera looked at her speculatively: 'Would you like me to post a police constable here at night, just until the Kariuki trial is over.'

'Yes, that would be a good idea. He needs to know about the security guard though and I will tell the guard about the police presence.'

Wacheera wondered what Rafiki had in mind. He was certain that she would not just leave things as they were.

'Before you go, there is one other very important thing that we need to deal with,' said Rafiki.

'Nyamita?'

'The 'not guilty' verdict on Kariuki is not acceptable to me; we both know that he is as guilty as hell. If we get Nyamita back here they will almost certainly incriminate each other and then they can rot in jail together.'

'I am in the process of trying the extradition process, but frankly I don't hold out much hope. There are certain forces at work who don't want Nyamita back here. Also my information from Dar is that Nyamita and his brother are well protected there and if an extradition order was granted, the Tanzanian police would find it very difficult to execute, so that might give Nyamita time to move on, if you see what I mean.'

'What is the answer then?'

'Well, I will say this to you once and once only. If we, the police, were directed to an address in Kenya where we were told we would find the ex-Superintendent of Police, then we would be able to take it from there.'

Rafiki nodded without saying anything. As Wacheera left he felt a charge of adrenalin: the look on his niece's face said it all; he knew that within months he would have Nyamita in custody in Kenya.

Over the next few days Rafiki made an excuse to get Ziporah alone on her own over what appeared to be a casual cup of tea during a break. She was almost certain that Ziporah had started an affair with Mwangi Mkubwa since he had started coming into the clinic at odd times of the day and Ziporah seemed to be paying an inordinate amount of attention to him during these visits.

'Do you think the security arrangements at night are sufficient?' Rafiki asked her.

'Maybe, but only from individuals.'

'The police have offered to post a constable here at night; they think that some people do not want the clinic here.'

'But everybody loves the clinic; it is quick, costs nothing, and is close to where they live.'

Rafiki shrugged. 'You must tell the security guards about the policeman, they may be worried otherwise.'

'OK, I will do that.' As far as Rafiki was concerned the fact that Ziporah did not even mention her own security meant that she was sleeping some-where else, almost certainly at Mwangi Mkubwa's compound. She smiled inwardly: 'Mwangi will know tonight, at the latest, that there is some threat against the clinic, and I'll bet that within two days he will know who, if anyone has plans to harm it.'

True to Rafiki's prediction two days later Mwangi wandered in to the clinic and with a nod of his head he indicated to Rafiki that he needed a private word. Ziporah was trying to concentrate on what she was doing but was like a cat on hot bricks while Mwangi was in the room.

Mwangi was offered a tin mug of tea which he took without comment, when they went into a back room. He said: 'This clinic idea of yours is very popular with the people here in Pumwani, they like coming here since they are treated kindly, maybe even like human beings.' He laughed.

'Yes of course, that is what we try to do, as well as helping to make people better. Most illnesses are cured naturally; we just provide a little help.'

'There are some people who want to burn the place down though, just to hurt you and Munyu. Something to do with a corruption case.'

'Yes, Uncle Wacheera came here few days ago and warned me. It's that minister Kariuki who also comes from our village; he has been stealing from the Government.'

'He and many others.'

'Yes!'

'Why are you and Munyu involved?'

'Information came to us and we passed it on to Wacheera. The case against Kariuki was one of the reasons that our son was kidnapped; they think that they can frighten us; as we have shown they are very much mistaken.'

'You need to understand that you are upsetting some very powerful interests; this is not a game, it would be safer if you left it all alone.'

'It would have been safer to stay quietly at home and let the British continue to run this country as a colony. This corruption is destroying this country as effectively as any colonial power. We will stop it.'

Mwangi shrugged. 'This clinic is good for Pumwani and also good for me and my businesses; if anyone tries to harm it they will pay and pay heavily. I am not a policeman though and will not go on some crusade like you seem to be doing; all that will do is to harm my wider interests. Munyu needs to be careful as well though; if they fail here they may try something elsewhere, maybe even your home in Karen.'

'What do you know about our home in Karen?'

'No more than most people in Pumwani; there were pictures all over the newspaper when you rescued your son.'

There was a brief silence.

'What should we do with security people here and of course the police constable?' asked Rafiki.

'Leave them in place; having them there will certainly help to deter people.'

Everything went on as normal for weeks. The day before Kariuki's trial began Ziporah came up to Rafiki and whispered excitedly: 'Mwangi Mkubwa needs to see you urgently, something about security.'

Rafiki had been expecting something to happen and had been surprised that there had been no further contact with anyone at the clinic or Peter or Wacheera, so she walked quickly to Mwangi's compound where she was let in without question. Mwangi waved her inside his office, when she opened the door; he was talking animatedly on the 'phone.

'Trouble, tonight, I have some people on the inside and they have plans to attack and burn down the Pumwani clinic.' He said as he put down the 'phone.

'Who?' asked Rafiki.

'It is better that you don't know,' responded Mwangi.

'Should we tell the police?'

Mwangi laughed: 'My policy is to tell the police nothing, nothing at all, so we will not be telling the police.'

'So whoever is planning this, what is their plan and what do you think we should do about it?'

'A number of people will try to burn down the clinic tonight; they obviously know that you have a security guard there and they know about the policeman since he stands around outside in his uniform. So they will have four or five people there. How many clinics do you have running at the moment?

'There are three, altogether, with two more planned.'

'Maybe they will try something on at those clinics as well, so I think that you should send the security guard and the policeman to those clinics and maybe you should try to increase security there as well for a few days.' Mwangi laughed. 'Ask your uncle Wacheera to provide some extra police at those places.' Then Mwangi's face darkened: 'but stay away from the Pumwani clinic, I will deal with that and I can tell you that anyone who comes near the place with bad intentions will regret it bitterly; I don't think that they will make the same mistake again.'

'What about Ziporah? She sleeps there,' asked Rafiki innocently.

Mwangi laughed: 'You are smarter than that; Ziporah will not be at the clinic tonight.'

'So what is your plan?'

'Don't worry about that, but I can assure you, the clinic will still be standing in the morning and there will be no damage. You will be able to open as normal at six tomorrow morning. If something happens I will come to the clinic sometime tomorrow. And look after that Munyu husband of yours; he may be in danger as well.'

Rafiki walked slowly back to the clinic wondering how she could persuade Wacheera to send a few more police to the other clinics without telling him what was really going on. She 'phoned Peter from the clinic and discussed the situation with him: 'There is definitely something going on,' he responded, 'I had some curious glances at cabinet this morning and one minister tried to raise the issue of Kariuki's upcoming trial in the meeting. He was quickly brushed aside. You obviously can't tell Wacheera that Mwangi Mkubwa is going to take the law into his own hands, but you can ask him for protection at the other clinics for a few days. Hopefully what Mwangi does will have a low profile and won't get into the papers. I will take his warning very seriously and so should you; we will both need one of Kahinga's men with us as sort of bodyguards all the time and I will make really certain that the security at Sattimma is watertight.'

'What about the school?' asked Rafiki.

'I don't think that there will be a problem there again; Kahinga has set up a surveillance regime there where the boys are monitored by the Kikuyu staff almost all the time. I will talk to the headmaster though.'

Wacheera had his hands full with the Kariuki trial but he was able to provide several more police for the clinics for the next week. Rafiki had managed to persuade him that she could best decide where they would be deployed from day to day. Wacheera had heard an unsubstantiated rumour the clinics and the Lawrences were under some sort of threat, but he decided that he couldn't deploy resources to every rumour that circulated and so far nothing had transpired from the personal threats against his own person, now after several weeks.

Mwangi briefed his own set of thugs very carefully: 'There will be six of them involved in the attack and they are going to try to burn the clinic down, they expect to have to deal with one security guard and one policeman. Those people have been sent to other places and three of you will be inside the clinic all night; it is important that you are not seen, so go in to the clinic as patients later in the afternoon, Rafiki will hide you in one of the back rooms. This is just a precaution; I don't think that any of the six will get near the clinic. I want all of the attackers taken prisoner and brought here; nobody is to be unnecessarily hurt, although if one person, carrying petrol, had an accident and burnt himself it might make others a bit more careful in future.' He laughed. 'Ten of you will be outside and I want you to capture all the people involved in this. You need to be in place by eleven o'clock.'

Rafiki arrived at the clinic in time to see it open at six the next morning. She had one of Kahinga's security guards with her. Everything appeared normal; the staff were on duty and as always there was already a substantial queue waiting patiently in the cool of the early dawn. The only exception was that as had been arranged the security guard was absent, which nobody commented on. Ziporah arrived about ten minutes later and pointedly went into the back room: 'There was a watch on all last night,' she said, 'no one came near the clinic, maybe you should go to see Mwangi, unless he comes here soon.'

Checks with the other clinics indicated that everything was normal. Later in the day Rafiki took the short walk to Mwangi Mkubwa's compound. She was given a cup of tea in a china cup.

'It seems that there has been a change of plan, my informant says that just before they were due to try to burn the clinic down they had a change of heart. They are now going to tell your nursing staff that they will be beaten up and their families attacked if they continue to work at the clinic.'

'What do you think that I should do now?'

'I'm really not sure; I still think that they will try to burn the place down.'

Rafiki was thinking aloud: 'I will ask the staff here to work in the other clinics and we will move the people from the other clinics to Pumwani, which will confuse the people who wish us harm, for a while anyway. But I need to do more, if I knew who was behind this maybe I could get Munyu to put some pressure on him politically.'

Mwangi ignored the comment: 'You will have to provide transport for the staff to be working at clinics that are far away.'

Rafiki nodded.

'I won't tell you who is involved, not yet and probably not ever. I will see what else I can do; they may try to burn the clinic down as well as intimidating your staff. The arrangements that were in place last night should remain for the next week at least.'

Rafiki went back to the clinic, closed it for thirty minutes and held d a quick meeting with the staff. None of them except Ziporah could look her in the eye. She came straight to the point: 'Do the people of Pumwani value the work that you are doing here in this place?' They all nodded uncertainly.

'Do you want to keep on working here and helping the people of Pumwani?' They all nodded vigorously. 'I know that you have been told that if you come here tomorrow you will be beaten up and your families attacked.' There were astonished looks all around; they had not exchanged any of this information between themselves as they had been told not to. They all nodded wordlessly. Rafiki went on: 'Tomorrow I want you to work at the other clinics; there will be a kombi to take you there at five thirty in the morning at the address I will give you.' She gave them the address of the senior nurse. Nobody will know where you are. This has nothing to do with anything that you people have done, they are trying to stop the trial of Minister Kariuki, and they blame me and Munyu for giving the police the information. This work here in Pumwani is really important we cannot allow them to stop it.'

There was an air of uncertainty in the room:

'Will there be anybody to run the clinic here?'

'Some of the people from the other clinics will come here tomorrow; Ziporah and I will be here to show them where everything is.'

'How long will this go on?'

'Not very long I hope, just a few days maybe two weeks.'

'These men will find us at the other clinics.'

'No, I want a description of the men who came to see you last night and I will write those descriptions down. We will stop them, if they continue they will be put in jail.'

The senior nurse took the lead: 'We all like working here and we are doing very useful work.' She looked each staff member in the eye. 'Do you all want to go back to the hospital with all those terrible bus journeys? No of course you don't. So we should try this. Rafiki has done many hard things, we trust her to stop this nonsense as well.'

There was a cheer from the rest of the staff and they all went back to work happily.

Rafiki dashed to the other clinics and told them of the new arrangements. In general there was a positive response.

Once all the arrangements for keeping the clinics open were in place, she went again to see Mwangi Mkubwa and gave him ten written descriptions of the people who had tried to intimidate the clinic staff, which Mwangi devoured in a few minutes:

'There are only two people described here,' he said having read all the descriptions. 'One of them I know and I will bring him here today,' he laughed, 'I expect we can persuade him to tell us who the other person is.' He made one brief 'phone call: 'Bring him here, as soon as you can, you know where to find him don't you?' he nodded into the 'phone and put it down. 'When they find out that the clinics are still open, they will be furious, so not tonight but tomorrow night they will try to burn the Pumwani clinic down, but we will be ready and most certainly they will regret that they ever tried. They think that they are just fighting with you and Munyu and maybe the police, they do not know that they are also fighting with Mwangi Mkubwa and I hope they never find out.'

'You are not prepared to tell me who 'they' are?' asked Rafiki.

'No, believe me, it is better that you do not know.' Rafiki went back to the Pumwani clinic and confirmed all the staff arrangements for the following day. She expected that one or two of her staff would be too nervous to continue to work in the clinics when they were under threat, so she contacted three people to come to the Pumwani clinic, who had said they would be prepared to work at the clinics even on a part time basis. She also 'phoned all the doctors who were giving their time free to the clinics and told them exactly what had transpired and what she had done about it. They were all angry and said that come what may they would be at their posts as they had all agreed. Rafiki went home after eight in the evening making sure that all the security arrangements were in place; wherever she now went she had one of Kahinga's security personnel with her.

Mwangi's people had eventually found one of the men responsible for the intimidation of Rafiki's staff and dragged him into Mwangi's compound, quite late that night. Mwangi was completely ruthless: Njogu was hauled out of sight around the back of one of the sheds in the compound. One of Mwangi's men lit a small fire, Njogu was stripped naked and tied to a post, and a panga was put into the fire. Mwangi went up to Njogu and slapped him hard in the face: 'I am not a patient man and I need some information very quickly or you will suffer great pain.' Njogu looked nervously around him. Mwangi continued: 'The clinic that is run by Rafiki is doing great work here in Pumwani; you went to the hard working staff who run those clinics and told them that they would be harmed if they continued to work there.'

Njogu started to struggle against his bonds. Mwangi pulled the now red hot panga from the fire and touched Njogu on the leg. This resulted in a terrifying shriek from Njogu and he voided his bowels. 'Who was the other person who also tried to tell the clinic staff not to work anymore?' Njogu remained silent. Mwangi touched him again with the red hot panga. Njogu shrieked again. 'Tell me now, who else was with you trying to destroy something that was helping the people here in Pumwani.' Njogu just looked at him. 'Tell me or I will really hurt you.'

Mwangi made a move to the pick the panga up again. 'No. No, I will tell you' shrieked Njogu.

'Who?' Mwangi raised the panga again. Njogu gave him a name. Mwangi nodded and two of his thugs disappeared into the night. Njogu was left tied up naked and shivering from fear and the now cold night. Mwangi went back to his office and waited. An hour later Waweru was brought into the compound. He was stripped naked and also tied up, but remained unharmed.

Mwangi then spent ten minutes on his own talking to the two. 'Take these two back to their houses,' he instructed, 'they will now work with us.' As Njogu and Waweru were hurriedly dressing, Mwangi said to them: 'One step out of line and I will have you thrown off the bridge at Garissa into the Tana; what the crocodiles don't eat will be washed into the sea. No person will ever know what happened to you. You do what I have asked you to do and you will be well paid.' He left them.

All went according to plan the next day at all the clinics. Rafiki was there from five-thirty in the morning until they closed at eight in the evening. Three of Mwangi's thugs had entered the clinic as patients towards the close and Rafiki left knowing that they were there and that the place was safe. She stopped briefly at Mwangi's compound but he was nowhere to be found, so she went home to the haven that was Sattimma.

Mwangi had made certain that all his people were in place by mid-night. Now he was only expecting four people to attack the clinic, because Njogu and Waweru had been neutralised. He waited with one of his thugs in the shadows near the shop and in sight of the clinic. Sure enough at two in the morning he saw four people gather in a nearby shadow and run towards the clinic, one had a four gallon can in his hand, which was obviously full because of the way he was carrying it. His ten men quickly converged on the potential arsonists who were all brutally taken to ground and beaten. The man carrying the can was made to stand up and pour the contents of the can all over himself: he was then made to run with the can in his hand and one of the thugs ran behind him and threw a lighted match on to him. He lit up like a beacon, shrieked and ran another hundred yards when he collapsed on the ground screaming. Ten minutes later all that remained was a charred corpse stinking of petrol. The thugs brought the remaining three men to where Mwangi was waiting. Mwangi told them to take them to three different addresses in Nairobi: 'Beat them very badly, break a few bones, but do not kill them. Put them right on the front step and make sure that the people in the houses will see them, but make certain that you are not seen by anyone and that the truck is not seen either. Come and tell me when all that is done.'

Rafiki was pleasantly surprised when all the arrangements of the previous day again worked like clockwork. The clinics all opened on time to the usual orderly queues. She was alerted to the fact that all was not entirely well when the police came to visit and asked if she knew anything about a badly burnt corpse that had been found in the vicinity. She was genuinely surprised: 'No, nobody has reported anything to me.'

Peter 'phoned just after seven in the morning: 'Kariuki's boss's house, the minister in his department, was burnt to the ground last night, luckily all the inhabitants were warned and they had all left just before the blaze started; it was clearly arson, there was a smell of petrol everywhere according to Wacheera.'

'So, why are you telling me this so urgently?' asked Rafiki.

'Are all your clinics OK? Have you had any trouble there?'

'No, everything is completely under control, the new arrangements seem to be working very well, although the police have found a corpse nearby, very badly burnt, I don't think that has anything to do with us here though. The security people that Mwangi has had in the clinic in than past two nights said nothing when they left this morning.'

'Mnn,' said Peter, 'I just wonder if all that has something to do with our friend Mwangi, it all sounds like his style somehow.'

'Maybe, but it is us who are under threat and Mwangi would not tell me who he thought was behind the threat. I will see him later today and see what I can get out of him.'

The usually garrulous Ziporah had said nothing when she arrived and kept her head down during the morning. The queues for the clinic were as busy as usual. In the early afternoon Rafiki walked around to Mwangi's compound. He looked a little tired but was his usual self otherwise. Rafiki was given a cup of tea in a china cup. 'There was a corpse, very badly burnt found not far from the clinic this morning; do you know anything about that?' She asked.

'I heard, suicide maybe, the man was in trouble I hear, he owed people some money.'

'You?' Rafiki looked at him enquiringly.

Mwangi laughed: 'No I don't lend money to shenzi's who can't pay it back.'

There was a newspaper on his desk with a picture of the Minister standing by his burnt out house. 'My husband mentioned that,' Rafiki indicated the newspaper, 'apparently it happened early this morning.'

'Careless, people are very careless with their nice fancy houses,' he clicked his tongue: 'maybe they should be looking after their own affairs better instead of running around interfering in other people's business.'

That told Rafiki all she needed to know, but she did ask: 'Was that something to do with you?'

'Me, of course not, I was busy here in Pumwani looking after my interests, and yours of course. The newspaper here says it was an accident.' Mwangi looked suspiciously innocent. Rafiki kept her mouth shut.

While she was in his office, there was a call from the gate and Mwangi fumbled in his drawer and pulled out a wad of cash and went out. He hurriedly gave the money to a rather unkempt looking pair who shuffled quickly out of the gate. Rafiki noticed that one of the men was limping badly 'I think that there will be no more trouble with people trying to burn down your clinics, I just need to check a few things, so the security arrangements should remain in place for tonight, but I think that your staff can return to their normal duties from tomorrow. I will visit the clinic later today.'

During the day a man came into the clinic, with two very unpleasant looking burns on his leg, which had become infected. One of the nurses alerted Rafiki who had a look at the burns. 'Where did you get these?' she asked.

The man just shook his head. When he walked away his profile reminded her of one of the men whom Mwangi had paid in his yard earlier that afternoon. A few days later she heard that the same man had attended one of the other clinics for treatment.

Mwangi sauntered in to the clinic towards closing time; he declined his mug of tea: 'For the time being anyway the clinics are safe, but they might try again sometime. Many people are very unhappy about the trial of Kariuki though.' He and Rafiki were in the back room as usual.

'Why are they unhappy, surely they can see that he has been stealing from the Government? This is their money we are talking about.'

'They don't really understand it like that. Anyway the people that are worried probably wonder whether it will be them who is next.'

'Was there an attack here last night?' asked Rafiki.

'Well, not really, as you can see,' Mwangi waved his hand around, 'a few people came around but they were taken care of very quickly. None of them will ever come back here again.'

'You still won't tell me who is behind all this?'

'No, it is better that you do not know, but if there are any other threats I will let you know.' Mwangi sauntered out and pinched Ziporah on the bottom on his way out of the door.

✳   ✳   ✳

Chapter 24

After one of his regular weekly cabinet meetings Peter said at dinner one night: 'I am suddenly being treated with enormous respect around the cabinet table. People have always been polite and considerate but now there is another dimension to the attention that I am getting. It seems related to the problems you were having at the clinics and the way that those problems have been sorted out. They know that we don't back off; I suppose that the message that they are now getting is that we are very ruthless as well.' He smiled: 'Not that I had anything to do with what went on; in fact I'm sure that neither of us really knows the whole story. I must say it is a little bit disconcerting to be beholden to a thug like that Mwangi Mkubwa. He hasn't made any demands or turned nasty has he?'

'Not yet; his businesses have benefitted greatly from the activity of the clinic in Pumwani and he was smart enough to acquire some land close to one of the other clinics where I think he is going to build another shop, so having the clinics in the vicinity of one of his shops benefits him considerably. At the moment at least he seems to be happy with the status-quo.'

Rafiki changed the subject: 'I told you about my conversation with Wacheera concerning Nyamita and somehow getting him back here.'

'Yes, I think that we should just get this Kariuki trial over with first and then deal with Nyamita; there are some Kikuyu in Dar-es-Salaam, who might be prepared to help. Nyamita is probably getting complacent, he almost certainly knows that any extradition proceedings will fail, which plays into our hands.'

'I will go and shoot the fat pig myself if this goes on much longer.'

'You won't need to, I'll get there first.' He smiled. They went to bed.

The corruption trial of Johanna Kariuki had now been going on for several weeks, with no interruptions, despite the turmoil surrounding the clinics in Pumwani. The evidence was clear that he had authorised invoices issued by his private companies, none of whom had any employees and whose physical addresses did not exist; Kariuki and his close family were the only shareholders. There was evidence presented regarding his lifestyle, with frequent trips to Europe, a large house in Nairobi with no mortgage, children at private schools; this was related to his salary as Deputy Minister and clearly he needed funds over and above his salary to sustain his lifestyle. The evidence provided by the police indicated that he had authorised invoices where no work had been done to the tune of several million shillings. The newspapers reported this all in a very sensational way with pictures of his wife in London on a shopping trip and his children dressed in their school uniforms outside his Nairobi mansion.

The Judge in the trial sitting with two assessors had found him guilty on all counts, with sentencing to be in two weeks.

All was eerily quiet during the period that the Judges were considering the appropriate sentence. Mwangi paid quite regular visits to the Pumwani clinic and often accepted a mug of tea with Rafiki. On one occasion he said to Rafiki: 'They are now planning on killing all the Judges in the Kariuki trial; you must understand that I will not do anything about this, I don't really like police or Judges, but I thought that you should know.'

Rafiki was outwardly quite calm but she couldn't wait to get rid of Mwangi and tell Peter and Wacheera.

'When will this happen?' she asked anxiously.

'The night before the sentences are due to be announced, the message will be quite clear: 'Do not interfere with things that do not concern you'. They will also try to do something about you and Munyu as well but much later, they have certainly been frightened by what has happened to them when they tried to burn down the clinic.' After a few minutes he left and Rafiki 'phoned both Wacheera and Peter.

During the call to Peter, Rafiki was cool and calm, but she said to Peter: 'We must not let this bastard get away with this, not under any circumstances, Kariuki has now been convicted in a court of law for the fraud, but he has got away with kidnapping our son, who might have been killed and there are some very strong forces at work to try to get him off the fraud charges as well. If he succeeds in getting away with this and the conviction is quashed or these people kill the Judges involved this country will not be worth living in. Also the two people who arranged the kidnapping our son have not been brought to justice and this means that the forces ranged against us will think that they have somehow won. So firstly we really must make sure that Kariuki gets his just deserts for the fraud, but more importantly we must get both Kariuki and that fat Jaluo pig Nyamita for kidnapping Kamau. You must understand that I am prepared to do anything, legal or illegal, to bring them both to justice and I need your help to do this.'

'I agree,' said Peter. 'Nyamita is in Dar, which makes it more difficult, but I have been thinking about what we should do; we can talk about it more later, but firstly I will make sure that Wacheera has all the help that he can get to stop this potential assassination of the Judges.'

'OK,' said Rafiki evenly, 'but there will be no compromise...'

'No, no compromise, just remember that both of us have successfully dealt with some pretty tricky issues in the past; this is no different.'

Rafiki's tone softened: 'I know, I owe everything to you and it could have been so different, we can't let this go now or all our battles will have been for nothing.'

'Come home early,' said Peter. 'I will phone Wacheera now and then we can discuss what else we might do.'

Peter also 'phoned Wacheera and after a warm greeting Peter asked him if he needed any help in dealing with the threat to the Judges.

'I am planning on having at least ten armed police on duty at each house twenty four hours a day until the sentence on Kariuki has been announced, maybe that is enough.'

'I know that this is entirely your business, but having raised the issue in the first place I feel some considerable responsibility.'

'Yees,' said Wacheera hesitatingly.

'The information we have is quite specific, that they are planning to attack the three Judges the night before the sentencing.'

'That is what Rafiki told me.'

'The source is very reliable,' said Peter.

'She would not disclose the source, but I am happy that you say it is reliable, I would not be planning on allocating such resources if I did not think the threat was real.'

'What I have to suggest is that as a back-up to your resources we should ask Kahinga to deploy some of his people just for the two nights before the sentencing. They will not be visible and they will be told to report to the police commander in charge of each location. This is just a back-up; they may not be needed and may only be needed if anything goes wrong.

Assuming that these attacks take place I presume that you want all the attackers captured and brought to justice.'

Wacheera hesitated, he thought: 'Here is this bloody M'zungu again interfering in police business.' Then he reconsidered; he had a low ego and all he was really interested in was maintaining the law in Kenya; he reflected that if anything went wrong the police would be blamed and if it all went right the police would get all the credit; Peter, Rafiki or Kahinga would not be mentioned, so the more help that was available the better. Also this case appeared to him to be the tip of the iceberg, he would need allies like the Lawrences to prosecute other cases, so he said: 'Thank you, maybe you could get Kahinga and the leaders of his groups to meet me at police headquarters sometime soon.'

'I will ask Kahinga to 'phone you. I will not be involved in any way.'

'OK, thank you again. We really just need to get this whole thing over and then start on the next case. I am determined to clean this whole business up.' Wacheera was relieved that Peter did not want to involve himself further.

Kahinga had been concentrating on his business and had stopped being Peter's driver some weeks before but he and his family were still living at Sattimma. Peter found him and told him about the planned attacks on the Judges and his conversation with Wacheera. After discussing the specifics of the situation and having 'phoned Wacheera to set up a meeting Kahinga then approached Peter for some advice: 'What do I do about payment? I will have to pay my people, but I am not certain that the police will pay me.'

'You should raise the issue directly with Wacheera, if he is uncomfortable about your usual rates then I suggest that you offer to just charge him cost, in other words what you actually pay your people. If this works maybe the police will use you on other occasions like this in future.'

Kahinga had several meetings with Wacheera together with N'guku and Macharia. Kahinga would lead one of the groups himself and the others would lead the other two groups. It was made very clear that the police were in charge and that Kahinga's men would be kept in reserve: 'Mainly to make sure that any attackers do not escape, we want them all captured,' insisted Wacheera.

'We just need to make quite certain that all our own security arrangements both here at Sattimma and at the clinics are not compromised in any way with all this other activity going on,' Rafiki said to Peter one night at dinner. 'If whoever is planning these attacks on the Judges gets wind of the reception committee that waits for them they might change their plans and attack us instead. I will see if our friend Mwangi has heard anything, maybe you could speak to Kahinga.'

'My information is that nothing is planned for any of the clinics or at your house in Karen at this stage, but that Wacheera may be in for a bit of a surprise,' said Mwangi when questioned.

'What do you mean by that?' asked Rafiki.

'It is very unspecific, but they know that Wacheera takes his own security rather lightly, there are only two policemen on duty there at his house. They see this as an opportunity. Something will probably happen on the same night that they attack the Judge's houses, but that is not confirmed.'

Rafiki 'phoned Wacheera and said to him: 'I don't want to worry you unduly but the same source of information tells me that an attack is probably planned on your house the same night that they are planning to attack the Judge's houses.'

'Mnn,' responded Wacheera, 'there are already two policemen there all the time, surely that is enough just for a rumour.'

'Maybe not, they already know of your security arrangements.' They went on arguing for a few minutes.

'Just during this difficult period, would you like auntie and the children to come and stay at Sattimma for a few days; you will be on duty and they will be safe here, whatever happens.'

Wacheera thought for a short minute. 'OK, that makes sense; then I don't have to worry. We have a maid, who will stay there and I can still have my meals there at home.'

'You will leave the police guard in place?' This was more of a statement from Rafiki than a question.

'Yes probably, one of the two anyway,' was the non-committal response.

Rafiki then 'phoned Peter and told him of the conversation: 'Typical of him,' said Peter, 'he is more concerned about everyone else than himself; unless we do something they will burn his house down and probably kill the maid as well. Just leave it with me and don't ask any questions; if anything happens Wacheera will never know anything of it.'

Peter then spoke to Kahinga and discussed the whole situation with him. Guarding the Judge's houses in conjunction with the police was quite above board, but this was something different. Kahinga just smiled: 'I have the very people, don't worry if anyone tries to burn down the house of the police chief they will never be heard of again.'

Mwangi continued to be a regular visitor to the clinic, Rafiki presumed so that he could keep an eye on Ziporah, but he sometimes took the opportunity to talk quietly to Rafiki: 'The plans to keep the Judges quiet are well in hand,' he told her a few days before Kariuki's sentence was due to be passed, 'and they are certainly going to try to burn down the house of your uncle Wacheera, hopefully with him inside it.'

'He has been warned,' answered Rafiki, 'I think that we can assume that the police will be able to look after themselves.' Mwangi looked at her speculatively and then looked away. He thought that Rafiki's attitude of trying to show that it was all out of her hands was too contrived. He smiled inwardly to himself; if indeed there was to be a raid on Wacheera's residence the raiders were likely to be in for a very rude shock.

Three days before the due date of Kariuki's sentencing Rafiki fetched her aunt from Westlands together with her two teenage children.

Kahinga had contacted Wanyoike and the four others who had all escaped to Tanzania after the debacle with the policemen and Hillsborough at Lake Naivasha. They had taken a bus from the Tanzanian capital, and had then walked round the border at Namanga and caught another bus to Nairobi and had lain low in Pumwani for a few days after Kahinga had briefed them: 'The attackers are only expecting to find one policemen at Wacheera's house, so you need to be sure that he is unharmed, but these attackers must disappear altogether, they must never be seen again and you people must all go back to Dar-es-Salaam; nobody knows that you are here. I don't want to hear the details, none of them, but make sure that you are not seen, then come back here and you will be paid, and don't let me down this time, otherwise it will be Hoteli-ya-Kingi Georgie for all of you for a very long time.'

The police guard had been in place for several nights before Kahinga and his cohorts reported for duty after ten, two nights before the scheduled raids were to take place. Wacheera himself took Kahinga around: the police were visible but not obtrusive.

'My people should shadow each one of your men, but they will stay right out of sight,' suggested Kahinga, 'and only get involved if any of your people get into trouble, maybe there should be some sort of signal, just a wave of the arm or something like that.'

'Yes, that makes sense, but no heroics please, there is a rumour of an attack, we don't know that it will happen but if it does our job is to stop them and capture the people involved, if possible. Most particularly we don't want any harm to come to the people in the houses.'

Kahinga thought that this approach might be too soft: he assumed that the attack if it came would be swift and ruthless, but he was not about to argue and he briefed his own men accordingly and he briefed the other groups similarly.

During the first night of the surveillance there were a several cars and a few pedestrians that as far as Kahinga was concerned appeared to have no business in the area, he assumed that people were just completing a final check on the disposition of the police guard. He was quite sure that all his men were invisible and would not have been seen.

The night before the sentencing of Kariuki was due was unusually quiet; Kahinga even wondered if anything was going to happen. Then there was the sound of a night jar, followed by nine other similar calls: he knew that his men would be familiar with the call, as they and used it in the forests to communicate with each other, so without Kahinga having to do anything they would have been alerted. It was possible that one or two of the police guard would be familiar with the call, but most of them would not and would just regard the calls as a non-threatening night noise, if they heard them at all. Kahinga knew that it would be most unusual for a solitary bird like the night jar to be in Nairobi, and there was no possibility that there were ten of them in one small area. He knew that he would not have to wait long, but he remained hidden and kept the policeman he was 'looking after' well in sight. Suddenly a man appeared with a club who silently tried to rush 'his' policeman. Kahinga instinctively raised the Patchett he was armed with and fired one shot. With a shriek, the assailant dropped his club and clutched his upper body; the policeman, in shock, jumped round and fired two shots into the writhing body which was just a few feet away. This started a flurry of shots and cries which went on for a good ten minutes. The neighbours had been told to stay in their houses and out of sight if there was any trouble, so quiet again descended on the area. The police contingent quietly gathered in front of the house; two had men they had captured, two police were slightly injured. Kahinga's men appeared with five captives and there was one dead body. 'I think that at least two attackers got away, but this lot need to be taken to police headquarters and charged,' said Wacheera. He sent the police contingent to scour the area and they returned with five four gallon cans of petrol. 'Use gloves,' he told the police, 'there will be finger prints all over these cans.'

The captives were driven off for interrogation. Wacheera briefly reported to the Judge who had emerged after all the shooting had stopped, the Judge was clearly shaken: ' I thought that you were all overreacting, I was sure that nothing like you were suggesting would ever happen.'

'This is how serious this issue is being taken,' responded Wacheera, 'these people think that if they can stop this case then they will be able to stop all of them.'

'There are going to be more cases like this?' the Judge was incredulous.

'Yes, probably,' answered Wacheera, who then changed the subject, 'We will leave a police guard on here for the rest of the night and the next few days. After that I hope that it will not be necessary and all will return to normal.'

Wacheera and Kahinga drove separately to the houses of the other two Judges; they were both as quiet as the grave and none of the police or Kahinga's people had seen or heard anything suspicious. 'Stay the rest of the night as usual,' Wacheera instructed the police guard. 'Maybe the same people were going to attack all three places,' he confided in Kahinga, 'I had better go and find out, from the people we have captured.' Kahinga's people were also left in place.

Kahinga then drove to Wacheera's house. All seemed quiet and all the lights were off. He noticed that there was a four gallon can in the middle of the garden. He leant down and sniffed it, without touching it: 'Petrol' he thought. He touched the can with his foot: 'Full,' he said to himself. There was absolutely no sign of anyone at all, the maid did not answer when he knocked and the house was firmly locked up. Strangest of all Wanyoike and his four men were nowhere to be seen and nor was there any sign of the police guard.

Wondering what to do Kahinga sat down in a deck chair on the small verandah at the front of the house, which was well in shadow. He had decided to spend the two hours before dawn there since everything else seemed to be in control: Wacheera's house seemed suspiciously quiet, and there was that unexplained can of petrol. Almost an hour into his sojourn just as there were faint streaks of light in the east Kahinga heard the sloshing sound of liquid being poured out of what sounded like a can. He quietly rose from his chair and peered out: there was a man now holding the can of petrol and pouring it out round the side of the house. Kahinga crept out from the verandah and watched for a second: the man was so intent on what he was doing he did not see Kahinga swiftly move behind him. As the man stood up and stretched Kahinga belted him on the back of the head with the barrel of the Patchett. He collapsed for a moment and then tried to get up and run. Kahinga tripped him and stuck the Patchett into the back of his head: 'Get up, with your hands up and turn around very slowly.' Kahinga thought that he would try to cart the man off to the police station, so roughly tore the man's belt off and was busy tying his hands behind his back with the belt. 'What do you think you are doing?' Kahinga asked in Kikuyu.

The man struggled: 'That Kariuki is s good man he must not go to jail,' he replied in the same language.

'I asked you what you thought you were doing?' Kahinga dragged the man roughly to his feet just as a pick-up truck came hurtling round the corner; much to Kahinga's surprise Wanyoike leapt out of the driver's seat and vaulted the little picket fence into the garden and asked Kahinga: 'What are you doing here?'

'I came here after an attempt was made to burn down the Judge's house, just to see if everything was alright and I found this can of petrol in the garden. I waited for almost two hours and your friend here came along and started to pour petrol all over the house, so as you can see I tied him up. What the hell are you doing? I thought that you would be gone from here a long time ago.'

'Well we have four people who tried to attack the house in the pick-up there. This one escaped but now we have found him again.' Wanyoike smiled.

Kahinga asked: 'Where are you going now?'

'The bridge at Garissa, what the crocodiles don't eat will be washed into the sea.' Wanyoike looked up and smiled. Kahinga let him take the man away and he was flung unceremoniously into the back of the pick-up. Wanyoike drove off.

Kahinga thought for a moment: 'None of this adds up.' So he dashed to his own vehicle and after a hair-raising five minutes managed to trace Wanyoike's pick-up in the almost non-existent traffic which he then followed into Pumwani. Wanyoike's pick-up stopped at a little house not far from the clinic and Kahinga saw him bang on the door, which opened. There was a furious conversation followed by what looked like a large bundle of notes being handed over, some of which fell on the ground. Wanyoike scrabbled around and managed to rescue all the notes. He then walked over to the truck and closely watched by a man standing in the door of the house, opened the back door and the five captives all emerged and ran off in different directions. Wanyoike then drove off to a house in nearby Shauri Moyo, followed at a distance by Kahinga, where his four compatriots jumped out and Wanyoike drove off, Kahinga presumed to dump what was probably a stolen vehicle. 'Ah, I see your little game,' thought Kahinga, 'the little shit thinks he is going to get a double pay off, and maybe part of the payoff was to let Wacheera's house burn down. Well, we will see about that.'

Kahinga returned to the Judge's house just as his men were due to pack-up as it was now truly light. 'Come, we just have one more little job, before you go home.' They all looked at him tiredly. 'This shouldn't take long,' he said. Kahinga explained: 'Wanyoike, who some of you know, was asked to prevent Wacheera's own house from being burnt down; people certainly came to burn the house down and he captured all the people involved, but instead of making them all disappear as we had agreed he let them all go after he was paid off. We will now see if we can make Wanyoike disappear instead.'

Kahinga picked up Macharia and N'guku plus another five men; they all crowded into his pick-up and returned to Shauri Moyo finding a vantage point overlooking the little house where Kahinga had seen Wanyoike drop off his four companions. He waited: one hour, then another hour; he was sure that Wanyoike would not have had the time to drop his stolen vehicle off and return, before Kahinga's arrival on the scene, even if he had taken a taxi, which Kahinga thought most unlikely, mainly because he wanted to remain anonymous and unseen. His men were all asleep in and around the vehicle. Then they saw a man walking unsteadily down the litter ridden road towards them: 'The stupid bugger,' thought Kahinga, 'he's been to a shebeen and had skin-full. Makes our job easier.' He quietly woke everyone up. It looked as if Wanyoike would have to pass very close to where they were parked, so they just waited. There were many other people at that time of day going hurriedly about their business, but they took no notice of Kahinga and his men, there were vehicles parked in all sorts of haphazard ways in the area. As Wanyoike stumbled unsteadily past the pick-up Kahinga opened the passenger door and two of his colleagues shoved Wanyoike into the front seat. There was a brief struggle and a few incoherent curses, and then Wanyoike found himself staring into Kahinga's furious eyes. He pissed himself.

'No, no, you don't understand, I can explain everything,' he said.

Kahinga said nothing but made a thorough job of searching the man. He pulled out almost two thousand shillings from his pockets: 'I saw you being paid off and then you let those murdering jackals go, I know that in a day or two you would be coming to me saying that you had made those men, who wanted to kill Wacheera, disappear. Yes they disappeared alright, in Pumwani, to do it all again. Anyway this is now my money' Kahinga waved the wad of banknotes in Wanyoike's face, ' and yes we will be making a journey to the bridge at Garissa—how did you put it, what the crocodiles don't eat will be washed into the sea or would you prefer it if I just handed you over to Wacheera. Anyway I will just go and fetch your colleagues. Tie this fool up and gag him and throw him in the back.' He waved at four of his men, leaving one on guard: 'Come with me.'

They walked confidently into the house that Kahinga had identified and kicked the door in. Before they knew what was happening the four sleeping forms in the main room had been overpowered and tied up. There was no one else in evidence in the house. Kahinga went outside and waved in the direction of the vehicle which was driven closer. The four men tied up like trussed chickens were heaved into the back with Wanyoike. Kahinga then said: 'I need three men to come with me; the rest of you should go home.'

Where are we going?' he was asked.

'Garissa,' was the answer. 'Blindfold the idiots as well please,' Kahinga instructed. Kahinga then went back to the house: he kicked over the Deitz lamp he found on the small table which fell to the floor, broke the glass and some of the paraffin leaked out on to the floor. He threw a lighted match on to the liquid, which burst into flames, he made sure that the flames would spread by putting a blanket he found in the bedroom on to the small amount of paraffin on the floor, making it look like the lamp had been knocked over by accident 'Two can play at that game, by the time anyone is aware that this house is on fire it will be too late,' he thought.

Before they went anywhere Kahinga thought that he had better get word to Wacheera that he would be out of town for a day or two. He thought that Rafiki would be at the clinic early making sure that everything was alright so he drove the vehicle the short distance to the clinic in Pumwani and to his relief he saw Rafiki's car parked nearby.

'What are you doing here?' she asked in surprise when Kahinga's head appeared uncertainly round the corner of the door just before the clinic opened. 'I need to tell you something,' he answered.

They went into the back room and Kahinga hastily explained all the goings on during the night. 'You have Wanyoike in the back of your vehicle here?'

Kahinga nodded: 'They will disappear very soon and will not be heard of again.'

'Stop, let me think?' said Rafiki. 'Do you want me to tell Wacheera anything?'

'Just tell him that I will be away for a few days, he doesn't need to know the details.'

Rafiki went out and made them both large tin mugs of hot sweet milky tea: 'Maybe we can do better than making Wanyoike just disappear. He now lives in Dar.'

'He will be in a crocodile's belly within a few hours, but yes, he was living in Dar; he will not be cheating anybody again.'

'Nyamita also lives in Dar.'

Kahinga nodded and started to see where Rafiki was coming from.

'We need to get that fat bastard back here; he was the mastermind behind the kidnapping of Kamau. Maybe instead of throwing Wanyoike into the Tana he could be persuaded to kidnap Nyamita and bring him back here for trial.'

Kahinga suddenly saw the possibility and he and Rafiki went on discussing the plan for another half an hour: 'Wanyoike needs money; we can let him go but to try to kidnap Nyamita he will need the promise of a reward.'

'If we promise him ten thousand shillings will that be enough.'

'Five thousand will be enough,' said Kahinga firmly.

'Just one other thing,' said Rafiki. 'I need to know the names of the five people that tried to burn down Wacheera's house and then were released by Wanyoike.'

'I don't know their names.'

'But Wanyoike does, if you are unable to get the names from him just bring him in here and it will take me less than five minutes.'

Kahinga came back with Wanyoike in tow, 'He won't tell me in front of the others, but in here by himself I think that he will.' Rafiki said nothing.

Wanyoike was clearly uncomfortable and tried to plead with Rafiki: 'W e worked together in the forests, please help me, we made a mistake but it will not happen again.'

'Names, just write down the names,' said Kahinga harshly. Wanyoike looked pleadingly at Rafiki who just nodded. He wrote down five names. Without another word Kahinga dragged Wanyoike out and dumped in the back of the pick-up.

'Is there anything you need,' asked Rafiki when Kahinga returned.

'Not really, I already have the money that Wanyoike was given to release the people who tried to burn down Wacheera's house, but I may have to give that back to him if he agrees on the Nyamita thing.' Rafiki gave him another one thousand shillings.

'Come back and tell me what is happening in a day or two and Kahinga just remember one thing: these people who are trying to get Kariuki released must not be allowed to succeed and that both those animals that planned the kidnapping of Kamau will either end up in jail or die, otherwise this corruption nonsense will continue and get worse. These people,' Rafiki waved the piece of paper on which Wanyoike had written the five names, 'will end up as crocodile food within a few days.'

Kahinga thoughtfully left the clinic and asked one of his colleagues to drive and two were on guard in the back: 'Namanga,' he whispered.

'I thought that we were going to Garissa,' said the driver. 'No,' I have a much better idea, take the road to Namanga, then we all need to sleep for a little while and then I will tell you what we are going to do.'

Chapter 25

Wacheera, Peter and Rafiki made certain that they found seats in the packed gallery of the courtroom where sentence was to be passed on Kariuki. Peter took particular notice of some of the other people in the gallery: there were three well dressed Kikuyu men in particular who looked very confident and were joking amongst themselves. Peter nudged Wacheera: 'Who are those three over there?'

'I'm not really sure, I have never seen them before.' was the response.

'All rise,' instructed the clerk of the court. Peter watched the three men's faces as the Judge and his two assessors walked into the court. From happy anticipation their expressions changed to consternation and then abject panic. 'Did you see that?' Peter whispered to Wacheera.

Wacheera nodded: 'I will find out who they are and have them watched, they obviously did not expect to see the Judges walk into the courtroom.'

The proceedings were thankfully very brief.

The Judge said: 'before I pronounce sentence firstly I should like to inform the court that last night a number of men made an attempt to burn down my house; most of those men were captured due to the very good intelligence and quick action from the police. The initial evidence from the first interrogations of the men captured indicates that this criminal action had everything to do with trying to influence the outcome of the case before us. I would like it to be known that as usual my wife and I plus our five children and a relative from up country were asleep in the house at the time of the attempted attack. Again because of the quick action of the police none of the occupants of the house were physically harmed and there was no damage to the house; we are all obviously very shaken though. The police have assured me that the attackers will be brought to justice and more importantly those people behind the attacks.'

'Will Mr. Kariuki please stand.'

Kariuki stood up with his head bowed.

'Do you wish to say anything?'

Kariuki just shook his head.

'If the answer is no, then I will pronounce sentence, but before I do I wish to say that Kenya is a new country and harbouring the limited resources we have is critical to the on-going development of our country. So this crime of which Mr Kariuki has been found guilty is very serious indeed, so I have no option but to pass the maximum sentence possible. Mr Johanna Kariuki I therefore sentence you to twelve years in prison.' There was a hush around the court and some deep breaths. 'There will be no parole period and no right of appeal. Mr. Kariuki you will therefore spend the full twelve years in jail.'

There was pandemonium in the press gallery with reporters all trying to rush out of the place to get their stories out first.

There was no sign of the three men who Peter had been watching in the visitors' gallery. Wacheera and the Lawrences stayed seated whilst the throng noisily made their exit.

'There was a very strong smell of petrol round one side of my house when I briefly returned there to get changed this morning,' volunteered Wacheera while they were waiting.

'Oh, was there anything else, a can or anything?' asked Peter.

'No, nothing, I asked the maid if she had seen anything but she said that she spent the night with a friend a few streets away and saw nothing. I asked her to heavily water the area, which I suppose she has done by now.'

Peter and Rafiki dropped Wacheera off at his house. 'Come in for a minute,' suggested the policeman. 'Maybe we can just have another look at the area where the petrol had been poured.' They all went into the garden. 'Just look at this,' invited Wacheera, 'I was in rather a hurry this morning and didn't have a chance to have a good look. It looks as if there was some kind of struggle here on the front lawn, look the lawn is all torn up. Maybe someone did try to burn the place down and they were somehow interrupted; surprising that this was not reported.'

'I thought that there was supposed to be a police guard on here all the time, what happened to him?' asked Rafiki.

Wacheera looked a little sheepish: 'I was short of resources so I assigned them both to other duties, they will be back here when auntie and the children come back here tonight.'

Rafiki just shook her head: 'Auntie can stay a few more days with us if you want.'

'I think with the Kariuki trial over, and the singular lack of success that the people who have been trying to sabotage the process are having, that the danger is probably over for the moment. Unless your source of information has any other ideas, it is probably safe for them all to return home.' Wacheera smiled: 'I don't want auntie to get any ideas about how modestly we live compared to some other people.'

Rafiki and Peter ignored the barb. 'I will ask my source, if he has any other information, after I bring auntie and the children back later today,' said Rafiki as they went back to Peter's car.

Rafiki popped in to see Mwangi on her way back to the clinic. As had now become usual tea was served on a tray with fine china cups. Rafiki smiled to herself: she was quite amused by Mwangi's slightly warped sense of humour, but she did not rise to the bait.

'Now that the Kariuki trial is over, what have you heard from your contacts?' She asked.

'Not much, but they are all in a funk about the people that are now in jail and they are wondering about what happened. They knew about the police presence at the Judge's house which they thought they had under control. There was some other interference though which upset their plans, and as I am sure you know whilst the Judge got a terrible fright he and his family are perfectly alright. Also, there were some other people who were going to burn down the house of your uncle Wacheera; they rescued them with some sort of a bribe for the group who stopped that happening. Now the people they bribed have disappeared altogether and the house they were resting in has been burnt to the ground. They don't understand what is happening to them-every one of their plans has been wrecked completely; I think that some people will now leave the country at least for a short while. They will probably stop and think about what to do next. I must say whatever you and the Munyu husband of yours did has really scared them all and they are wondering if others will now be prosecuted for similar crimes to the one's that Kariuki committed.'

Rafiki thought for a moment: 'Is your source completely safe and reliable?'

'Yes he is well paid, and if he lets me down he will go to the bridge at Garissa…'

'And what the crocodiles don't eat will be washed into the sea,' Rafiki finished the sentence for him.

Mwangi looked surprised but said nothing further.

Rafiki continued: 'Neither I nor Munyu had anything to do with what has happened; we just made two telephone calls that is all. We know nothing about who did what to whom. There was a very strong smell of petrol at Wacheera's house when we dropped him off this morning though. I do have some names though: these are the people that tried to burn down Wacheera's house and were let go because of the bribe that you just told me about, and on the bottom of the paper is the address of the people that paid the bribe.'

'My style exactly,' said Mwangi, referring to the two 'phone calls. He took the paper without saying anything. 'I will certainly let you know if there are any more developments. As far as I am personally concerned all this has fallen very well for me.'

'What do you mean by that,' asked Rafiki instinctively.

Mwangi smiled and shook his head: 'Nothing you need know about.' He put his cowboy boots on his desk indicating that that was all he was going to say.

Rafiki smiled to herself and quietly left; the association with Mwangi was certainly strange but it had paid both parties off immeasurably. She wondered how long it would continue in the same cooperative style.

The press made a sensation of the sentencing and wrote innumerable articles about corruption within Government. The police, and particularly Wacheera, came in for fulsome praise, firstly for bringing the case to trial and then for unearthing the plot to harm the Judges in the trial.

✳　✳　✳

<h1 style="text-align:center">Chapter 26</h1>

Kahinga asked the driver to stop in Athi River, which is s scruffy little town on the edge of the semi-arid area stretching some two hundred and fifty miles to within thirty miles of the lush Kenyan coastal strip. He stocked up with enough food for the whole party in a small Indian owned store on the outskirts. Driving a few miles down the road towards the Tanzanian border at Namanga, he directed the driver to take a poorly defined track and parked under a thorn tree well out of sight of the road. Wanyoike and his men were left lying in the back of the vehicle in the sweltering heat.

A small fire was lit and one of Kahinga's men cooked the mealie meal and meat. Wanyoike moaned: 'I need a crap.'

'Crocodiles won't mind if you stink a bit, maybe they will think that they have something special if it stinks,' joked one of Kahinga's men.

There was silence from the truck. Kahinga nodded to his men: 'One at a time, for a crap and then food, you will have to untie them, but if they try to run shoot them, always keep the blindfolds on.'

So one at a time the prisoners were allowed to relieve themselves and they were given a large plate of ogalie and meat. His own men looked at Kahinga curiously as if to say: 'What are we feeding these people for if we are to throw them to the crocodiles.' They could see that they weren't on the road to Garissa but were going in almost the opposite direction, so just waited to see what Kahinga had up his sleeve. Kahinga made sure that his prisoners bonds were again firmly tied and that they were all packed tightly into the back of the truck. One person was left on guard while the rest slept, with an hourly change of guard responsibilities. Just before dusk Kahinga woke everyone and they secured the prisoners and piled into the vehicle. They drove a little way and turned off the road to Kajiado where Kahinga knew there was a bridge over a river. The river was often dry but the situation would do for what he had in mind. The prisoners were still blindfolded and bound hand and foot and were hauled to the edge of the bridge.

His men had been told to make out that they were at the bridge over the Tana River near Garissa. 'I have just seen a very big crocodile on a sandbank waiting for his dinner,' said one.

'Oh, that one looks very hungry, maybe he has not eaten for days.'

The prisoners became noticeably more nervous; two of them voided their bowels. After about ten minutes of this, now that it was dark, Kahinga dragged a struggling Wanyoike away from the truck. He yanked his blindfold off: the look on Wanyoike's face indicated that he really thought his last moments had come. 'Now,' said Kahinga, 'will you ever try to cheat me again.'

Wanyoike shook his head. 'What will happen to you if you do?' Wanyoike looked his feet. 'You will be thrown off the bridge at Garissa and what the crocodiles don't eat will be washed into the sea.' Wanyoike looked at Kahinga uncomprehendingly. 'You are nowhere near Garissa,' Kahinga told him, 'we are not very far from Namanga.' There was a spark of interest from Wanyoike. 'You know where Nyamita now lives?' Kahinga changed the subject abruptly.

'I see him almost every day, but he does not know who I am,' Wanyoike could suddenly see where all this might be going.

'You will bring him back to Nairobi, you have three weeks. If that happens I will give you the money that I took from you as well as another five thousand shillings.'

Wanyoike tried to look doubtful, but at that point he would have agreed to anything: 'Yes, I think that I can do that,' he said.

'You will have to walk around the border post, and I will meet you all on the other side, so don't try anything clever. Now go and explain all that to your people, you have five minutes.'

Kahinga then had his people untie the bonds of all the prisoners and left them to themselves. The chances of anyone running away were remote since none of them really knew where they were and they would probably die of thirst or be killed by a wild animal before they reached any kind of help. Kahinga explained very carefully to his men the discussion that he had just had with Wanyoike: 'It is very important that that fat Jaluo pig Nyamita, be brought back to Nairobi-it is almost certain that he was personally involved in the kidnapping of Munyu's child, Nusu-Nusu, but he needs to face a court to prove that.'

'Why don't we just go to Dar-es-Salaam and kill him, it will be much easier than trying to bring him back to Nairobi and then all those people will try to burn Judges houses down again to stop the trial?' asked one.

Kahinga had some sympathy with that argument but he had been persuaded by Peter and Wacheera that if everyone behaved like that then the country would collapse into anarchy, so he said: 'No, we must bring him back for a proper trial which everyone will accept, even the Jaluo, and then there will be no more fighting.'

They went on discussing the issue until Kahinga saw that Wanyoike had completed his own briefings. Kahinga's men would follow wherever he led; they had been with him in the forests and had suffered the poverty and indifference of the Uhuru regime since independence. Now Kahinga had offered them a way where they could use the skills they had to make a legitimate living, so they would be happy to tramp their way through the bush escorting Wanyoike and his cohort back into Tanzania, if that was necessary.

They drove back to the main road and inside an hour Kahinga parked the vehicle and everyone scrambled out. Kahinga made certain that Wanyoike and his cohorts had food and water and that they knew the way.

'I will see you on the other side of the border in the morning, when I will give you some money. Walk about one mile directly away from the road, then about five miles almost due south and then walk back to the road; there may be a few patrols, so watch for them. There should be a moon, which will help you since you will be able to see Kilimanjaro, when you walk away from the road the mountain should be right in front of you, then when you walk past the border post it will be on your left and when you walk back towards the road on the Tanzanian side it will be behind you. Keep an eye on the mountain and you will never get lost. There will be some Masai herding cattle in the area; keep right away from them, they are be big trouble, but the cattle will be in one place while it is dark so that should not be a problem, the Masai will be busy concentrating on keeping the lions away from their cattle anyway. The walk will take you most of the night, so I will see you on the other side at about seven o'clock in the morning.'

'We know all this,' Wanyoike responded. 'We have made this journey before, but why do we have to walk. If you take us through in the truck and then bribe some of the officials it will be much quicker.'

'No, 'said Kahinga, 'I don't want any of you to be recognised or me for that matter, so go.'

There was another brief argument from Wanyoike and then Kahinga and his men watched them trudge off into the bush until they were out of sight; he drove to the border post, parked the vehicle under a suitable tree, and said, 'I was going to ask some of you to walk through the bush with them. If they don't turn up tomorrow on the other side of the border post then too bad, we will have to think again.' Amid relieved looks from his companions he locked himself in the cab and went to sleep, with his men in the back.

As the post opened Kahinga, on foot, ensured that he was first in the queue and he went through the formalities on both sides quickly.

Kahinga waited with the throng at the border until mid-morning when he saw a bedraggled and tired looking group walk towards him.

Kahinga handed Wanyoike all the money he had taken off him plus the one thousand shillings Rafiki had given him.

'I need guns,' Wanyoike whispered.

Kahinga shook his head, 'I could not bring guns through here, they are all on the other side; you will have to find anything you want in Dar.'

Kahinga watched as Wanyoike secured places for himself and his crew on a bus bound for the Tanzanian capital. He then went through the laborious process of returning the way he had come and joined his men in the pick-up They bought some bread and jam and drove back to Nairobi.

CHAPTER 27

Over the months in the hot and humid but very pleasant small city of Dar-es-Salaam, Nyamita had become careless. In the first weeks of his self-imposed exile he and been very cautious and had confined himself to his brother's mansion on the seashore. He had made sure that when he went into the main city he was always accompanied by his brother or one of his brothers 'helpers'. In time he found a way to access funds that he had carefully stashed away in a Swiss bank account, so he had cash to spend. His brother was quite happy to have Nyamita in the house; it helped with security and provided a drinking companion. Nyamita's strength gradually improved and with the help of some physiotherapy within six months he was almost back to normal.

He was very anxious to establish his status in Kenya; he was aware that an arrest warrant had been issued against him but had heard nothing more. 'Maybe they have decided to leave me alone and if I don't return to Kenya, nothing more will be done,' he thought.

Discreet enquiries were made through the Kenyan High Commission in Dar-es-Salaam but they had heard no word about possible extradition, so Nyamita thought he was safe.

As soon as Wanyoike had returned to the Tanzanian capital he set up a daily watch on Nyamita. He was surprised to see Nyamita drive into the city on his own, now on a regular basis. He saw him go to the bank and have lunch in a small rather seedy restaurant in a back street, then looking around he ducked into a door in the alley next to the restaurant. Wanyoike guessed that it was a brothel and kept watch for a few days. He made some discreet enquiries: he thought his luck was in when he discovered that it was run by a Kikuyu woman.

Wanyoike decided to pay the establishment a visit during the day, which he assumed would be a slow period for the business. There was a smart looking receptionist on a front desk and in Swahili Wanyoike said: 'I would like to see the manager please, this is a personal matter and I'm afraid it is rather urgent.' He was smartly dressed and the receptionist looked at him warily and dashed behind a curtain at the rear of the reception desk. She came out a few minutes later: 'Mrs Koinange is rather busy at present, can you come back later.'

'No,' responded Wanyoike, 'would you tell her it is rather urgent and that I will wait here until she is free.'

The receptionist hastily went out again and returned quite quickly: 'Can you tell me what this is all about...?'

'No,' responded Wanyoike sharply, 'this is a personal matter and I need to speak to Mrs Koinange herself, as I said I will wait until she is free.' The receptionist just glowered at him and then went out again. There was the sound of raised voices. She came back out and said nothing.

Forty minutes later a large, middle aged, well dressed Kikuyu woman emerged from behind the curtain. Wanyoike immediately stood up and greeted her politely in Kikuyu. She looked surprised and asked somewhat abruptly: 'Yes, what can I do for you?'

'I need a word in private,' answered Wanyoike, 'I assumed that you would not be very busy at this time of day, it will not take long.'

'Are you a policeman?'

'No,' Wanyoike smiled, 'certainly not.'

The woman looked at him suspiciously and then said: 'OK come with me.' She went through a door and they entered a well decorated bar area, which was deserted.

'Can I get you something to drink?' offered Mrs Koinange.

'If you are having something maybe a cup of tea please, otherwise don't worry.' Mrs Koinange noisily ordered the receptionist to bring them a tray of tea.

'If you are after money, you can forget it,' said Mrs Koinange.

'No, I am not after money, but I do need your help.'

'What help?'

'You will remember a few months ago in Nairobi, there was a child abducted from one of the better known boarding schools there.'

'Yes, of course I remember, the case had wide publicity here and elsewhere I suppose; what can that possibly have to do with me?' she said impatiently.

'Well they have not yet apprehended the people responsible.'

'Really, I thought that a number of people were jailed for the offence.'

'Yes, but just the small fry, the main culprits are still at large.'

'Mnn, I seem to remember that Johanna Kariuki managed to escape conviction, although he was as guilty as sin.'

'Yes, lack of evidence.'

'I still don't see what that has to do with me.'

'One of your customers was almost certainly involved; I need to take him back to Nairobi.'

Mrs Koinange looked startled. 'This is respectable establishment with a many high profile customers; discretion is part of what we offer. I really do not want any trouble. Surely if you know the man's habits then you can pick him up elsewhere; why bother me? Anyway who are we talking about?'

'Nyamita, the ex-police chief,' said Wanyoike quietly as he watched her expression.

There was then a look of real fear on Mrs Koinange's face; if Wanyoike had been a more cautious man he might have reconsidered his whole approach:

'I see: he is a very big man; what are you expecting me to do?'

'Does he ever have a drink here?'

'Yes, always.'

'All I want you to do is to put a small sedative in his drink; that is all. It will quieten him down; I will deal with him after that.'

'I'm not very happy about poisoning a good customer; our reputation is one of quality and discretion, our girls are all clean. I have never been asked to do anything like this in my life and if word got out the Government here might take action; they don't always like foreigners running businesses like this one here in Dar.'

'The man is a criminal and the child was threatened with death, he and that Kariuki both need to be brought to trial.'

'The Kenya police should do all this through the official channels; I really do not want to be involved in something illegal.'

'I will make it worth your while.'

'What do you mean by that?'

'One thousand shillings and one thousand when we have him back in Nairobi.'

'Double that and I will think about it?'

'Mnn, one thousand five hundred now and one thousand when he is back in Nairobi.'

They settled on one thousand five hundred now and one thousand five hundred when Nyamita was back in Nairobi.

Wanyoike handed Mrs Koinange a small packet of powder: 'All you have to do is to put that in his drink, it is only a sedative so it will make him want to go to sleep.'

Wanyoike paid her and left.

He went back to his colleagues and told them what he had done. There was an immediate objection from one of them: 'Surely she will warn him, and he will escape and then we will have wasted all that money.'

'If she does she will certainly have me to reckon with. Anyway we must plan for that as well.'

They kept watch over Nyamita's movements and sure enough one evening they saw him leave his brother's house and drive into town. Wanyoike then activated his plan; he had borrowed two vans from the Kikuyu 'mafia' in the city. One he parked in the main road as close as possible to the laneway leading to Mrs Koinange's premises and one near to the rear entrance. There were four men in each van. The idea was to subdue with the assistance of some chloroform the already sedated Nyamita when he emerged from the brothel at whatever time of night that was; it was assumed that if all went well he would emerge from the front door and would have been given the sedative. If he left by the back door it would mean that he had been warned and that he almost certainly would not have been sedated and that he would be very difficult to subdue. As a back-up Wanyoike had also placed four men at the entrance to Nyamita's brother's mansion on the beachfront.

To Wanyoike the wait seemed interminable; from his observations Nyamita normally left the brothel about ten thirty and then went home. They had seen him go into the place at about eight as usual but it was well into the early morning hours before there was any action at all. Then there was the sound of a powerful car racing down the main street bearing down on the alley-way where the brothel was housed. There was a screech of brakes and at the same time Nyamita and two others came bursting out of the front door of the brothel and rushed towards the car; Nyamita was bundled inside the car and it raced off. Several extensive bursts from sub-machine guns, raked the van from end to end with Wanyoike and his men inside. The two men who had accompanied Nyamita ran back inside the brothel.

Wanyoike's men guarding the rear entrance heard the shots and decided that discretion was the better part of valour and they drove off without investigating the disturbance. Within minutes several police cars were at the scene. There were no survivors in the van; Wanyoike and his four colleagues had been shot to pieces. The police eventually found their way upstairs and they were met by Mrs Koinange. She was all innocence: 'We heard some shots and I called the police, but we didn't see anything and nobody came in here; some of our customers were very frightened.' The police left.

The men hiding next to Nyamita's brother's house saw the car hurtling out of the driveway just after one in the morning and half an hour later it came racing back and smashed through the gates, without stopping, before they could do anything. The car had stopped abruptly in the front of the house and they glimpsed Nyamita scrambling out of the car and dashing into the house. Deciding that something had gone badly wrong they melted off into the night.

'FOUR KIKUYU KILLED IN GANG WARFARE.' Raged the local morning paper. The article went on to describe the influx of migrants from the north claiming that many of them were fleeing justice in their own country and were either working illegally in Tanzania or were engaged in drug dealing, prostitution and other illegal activities. It specifically mentioned Wanyoike's name.

The news eventually filtered through to the Nairobi papers and Wanjiru showed the article to Kahinga. He shrugged. He had not told Wanjiru anything about his discussions with Wanyoike although she knew that he had been involved in providing secret protection for Wacheera's house. She had been surprised that Kahinga had not asked her for any money to pay Wanyoike for his efforts. Wanjiru kept her own counsel: the business was going well and Kahinga was busier than ever.

Peter pushed the article in the paper under Rafiki's nose: 'Looks like the plan you hatched with Kahinga and Wanyoike didn't work, so maybe we will have to put another plan in place.'

Rafiki was silent for a moment. She sighed: 'I thought that my personal involvement in making sure that justice is done had stopped after Uhuru, but with the kidnapping we had to get involved and this is just the aftermath of that, so yes, reluctantly, we will have to do it ourselves; Wanyoike didn't really know what he was dealing with. He needed to remember that Nyamita is smart and he, after all, was the police chief here. I don't really know what went wrong but he must have made an obvious mistake and Nyamita ruthlessly nailed him.'

A few days later Kahinga went to see Peter. After the usual Kikuyu greetings Peter said: 'I think I have found a way of getting the boreholes in the newly settled areas working so that they will continue to be maintained and will not be vandalised. So if you have time maybe we can discuss that project.'

'Yes,' said Kahinga. 'Maybe, but what about Nyamita? Wanyoike made a mess of it again and Nyamita is still there in Tanzania.'

'Just leave it with me and Rafiki for a few days; we will certainly be doing something and will need help from you. Don't try to do anything yourself though or you may end up like Wanyoike.'

Kahinga nodded. He was quite happy with the money from his now burgeoning security business but he liked the excitement of the other activities such as preventing the judge's house being burnt down.

Peter did pay Wacheera a courtesy visit a few days later: they touched on the attempt at prejudicing the outcome of the Kariuki trial.

'I am going to have to continue my investigations into other fraudulent activities, you said that you had some other cases that needed some attention, can you give me a few leads please,' asked Wacheera.

Peter handed over a sheaf of documents: 'These are a little bit out of date, but they are still valid and if you need further assistance I can certainly help you as I did with the Kariuki trial.'

'I will have a look at these and come back to you.'

'Did you see all that stuff in the paper about some Kikuyu being shot up in what was described as gang warfare in Dar?' asked Peter suddenly.

Wacheera looked at him shrewdly: 'I wonder why he has raised that issue, it seems a long way from boreholes and corruption amongst the government employees in Nairobi,' he thought.

'Yes, I did,' said Wacheera.

'Is it as simple as that, or was there more to it,'

'I don't know, I have paid no attention to the incident,' said Wacheera nonchalantly.

'We are certain that it was an attempt to kidnap Nyamita.'

Wacheera shrugged.

'Are you going to extradite Nyamita from Tanzania?'

'No, the chances of success are almost non-existent for all sorts of reasons.'

'Rafiki and I are concerned that neither of the main perpetrators of the kidnapping have been successfully prosecuted. This means…'

'I know what it means, Munyu, give me some credit, it means that the corruption will continue because the senior people still think that they can get away with it.' He glared at Peter. 'Sorry,' said Peter, 'I didn't mean to be critical.' He looked at Wacheera, who somewhat mollified said: 'I had a conversation with my niece, Rafiki, a few weeks ago which she will have repeated to you.'

'Yes; If we deliver that fat pig to an address in Kenya, you will do the rest.'

Wacheera nodded.

'I would ask you for funding to do that, but I know that might be difficult. A contribution to the clinics would be appreciated if we are successful.'

Wacheera nodded and Peter left knowing that he had the tacit support of the police.

In the meanwhile Kahinga approached Peter and said: 'I can now help you with the boreholes.'

'OK, good. The plan is to repair individual boreholes and then leave a man there to run approximately six boreholes. We would have to install engines and pumps on each site and build a very secure pump house which can be locked. The man would be responsible for running and maintaining the boreholes for a few hours each week. The ministry would provide fuel and pay the man; he would also be responsible for laying pipes so the water can be directed to individual properties in the vicinity.'

'So I must build the pump house and then install the pump and engine in each place. This is a very big job. I will start at Naseby and then we can see how much work there is and who should do it,' observed Kahinga.

Kahinga was despatched with two three ton lorries, one with building materials sufficient to build two pump houses and one with the pumps and engines that he had already tested on the previous visit. He had four of his men with him.

Over several evenings Rafiki and Peter mapped out a scheme to return Nyamita to face trial in Nairobi.

'I had sort of oblique discussion with uncle Wacheera on this subject. The authorities here in Kenya will do nothing about extraditing Nyamita from Tanzania, partly because it is embarrassing and many high profile people don't want to be challenged; they think that the two people who arranged the kidnapping of Kamau have 'got away with it' because of their high profile positions and they think that this pattern will continue. Also and just as important they don't think an application for extradition will succeed because of Nyamita's contacts in the police in Dar. He more or less agreed with me, and this is what he told you, that if Nyamita was delivered to an address in Kenya he would do the rest,' said Peter.

'Yes, we will have to bring him here and I have put some thought into what we might do. We will need Kahinga and his men to help of course.

So this is the bare bones of a plan: we need to really understand Nyamita's habits, so we need to keep him under surveillance for two or three weeks, this will include his main contacts and places and times where he is most vulnerable. Neither you nor I will be able to do this, because we may be recognised, but Kahinga is ideal since he is probably unknown to Nyamita except possibly by name,' said Rafiki.

'OK.'

'Once we know all that, we can make a plan to kidnap him. The kidnappers must remain anonymous so that makes participation by either you or me quite difficult, for me it's because I am a woman and quite recognisable and you because you are an M'zungu and you also have a high profile. Both of us are well known to Nyamita and if he could claim that he was abducted, any case against him would fall apart.'

'Is there any chance that he could be persuaded to return to Kenya voluntarily,' asked Peter.

'Not a chance, apart from the kidnapping charge he would be up on all sorts of other charges: accessory to murder, growing a prohibited drug, running protection rackets and so on. He is clever; I don't think anything could persuade him to return here.'

'We should at least appear to be out of the country when the abduction takes place,' said Peter moving the discussion on.

'How would we do that?' asked a puzzled Rafiki.

'Purchase tickets for a flight to the UK, for example, check in for the flight, making certain that the ground staff recognise us and then give the boarding cards to John and Kamau; they don't match boarding cards with passports, at least they never have in my experience, if one has a boarding card one gets on the 'plane. Giles and Louise can look after them in London. We would have to book with an airline where they won't be recognised, probably BOAC, not Kenya Airways.'

'So any action would have to be during the school holidays, so they would not be missed at school,' said Rafiki thoughtfully.

'Yes.'

'What about passports, don't they stamp passports.'

'Mnn, I expect that your friend Mwangi Mkubwa could fix that at this end and I am certain that Giles could arrange appropriate stamps in the UK, especially if he was told what it was all about.'

'This means that we could not go to Tanzania ourselves, at least not officially, we would not want any Kenya or Tanzania border stamps in our passports coinciding with our supposed visit to England.'

'No, if we want to be in Tanzania and I think that we should be during any planned action, then we may have to do a bit of walking,' said Peter.

'Walking, you mean round a border post.'

'Yes, the border is very porous in many places; the Masai, for example, wander backwards and forwards with their cattle. There are several small border posts which we could walk around in two or three hours.'

'So we would be in Tanzania unofficially,' said Rafiki uncertainly. 'What happens if we are spotted?'

'We must make certain that we won't be. You have used disguises in the past and so have I. We would have to remain in the background.'

'This is exciting,' remarked Rafiki, 'something like the old days in the forests but we are more in control. Make love to me, let's go to bed.'

The plan was hatched over many nights and inevitably they left a trail of clothes from the sitting room to their bedroom.

Kahinga and his men went to Naseby, dug and laid a foundation for each pump house. They unloaded the appropriate amount of building material at each site. After having left the foundations to settle for a day they built the pump house and installed the pump and engine at the second site that Kahinga had previously repaired. The man who owned the property was delighted: his womenfolk would no longer have to trudge the five hundred yards downhill to the river for water, and then of course return uphill with full cans, and he was able to pump the water around his property, using the piping left there by Peter, when he left Naseby.

When they went to the other borehole Kahinga was horrified to see that all the building material left there had completely disappeared; not a scrap was left. Kahinga was furious: 'Maybe I should just leave this place and find other boreholes to fix,' he said to his colleagues. Eventually he went into the village and after having 'phoned Peter purchased some more material. By the end of two weeks both boreholes were operating and he had bought some more piping to service the small properties in the vicinity. He left N'guku there, who had managed to secure a room in Peter's old house. 'You must find some more boreholes near here,' Kahinga told N'guku as they left. 'When you have done that I will come and help you fix them.'

'Where do I get the diesel for the engines from,' asked N'guku.

'The duka wallah in the village will deliver it, he will be very happy to do that especially if you have six boreholes running.'

Kahinga was happy to be returning to Nairobi, he found the whole atmosphere of the new settlements too restricting and dull. With few exceptions nobody was really doing much with the land they had been given on very generous terms by the government and most people just expected more government handouts.

After a few days back with his family Kahinga sought Peter out to give his report: 'These people are thieves,' he said. 'They stole all the building material from the one borehole and I had to buy some more. They all want the Government to give them everything and they don't want to do anything.'

'Anyway, the scheme is working as far as you can see,' said Peter.

Kahinga nodded. 'The scheme will give them all the water they need but I don't think that they will do anything with it. They don't do anything when it rains, so this will not make a difference,'

'OK, well let's see. I have something else to discuss with you.'

Kahinga looked doubtful.

'The plan with Wanyoike failed but we still need to bring Nyamita back here for trial.'

'We should just go and shoot him, it will be easy…'

'No, it means that we will be seen as behaving just the same as all the robbers and gangsters.'

Kahinga didn't see what the problem was with that, most of the criminals that he knew were free and quite well off, but he held his tongue. He had learnt many things from Munyu and he could see that he was about to learn some more.

'We need to bring him here to face a trial; if Boniface and Otieno tell their stories in court then Nyamita will be put in jail for a very long time.'

Kahinga shrugged: 'In the days of my grandfather if someone had done wrong like Nyamita has, the elders would arrange for a warrior to kill him with a spear. If he is put in jail he will have to be fed for many years, and you can see how big he is. Now we have guns, so we can just shoot him and we will save all the food.'

'No; there are many people in high positions stealing like Kariuki did. If there is a big trial and if he is found guilty then all those people will worry that they will be the next on the list and that will help to stop all this nonsense.'

Kahinga shrugged. He partly understood: 'So what do you want me to do?'

'First I want you to go to Dar-es-Salaam and check all Nyamita's habits and movements. We will then make a plan to abduct him and bring him back here. But you must be very careful, we do not want any more mistakes like Wanyoike must have made; they knew what he was up to and shot him to pieces as I understand it. You may need two weeks in Dar, then come back here and you and Rafiki and I will make a plan. It all needs to be in place within four weeks because of school holidays.'

Kahinga became excited: 'I will need my people.'

'Yes, probably, but not this time, you need to be alone and really understand what Nyamita and that ghastly brother of his are up to.'

'How will you get there,' Peter asked.

'With my pick-up, I have all the right papers.'

'Why don't you fly?'

Kahinga looked quite frightened: 'Fly, you mean in one of those aeroplanes,' he made a sort of flying gesture with one of his hands.

'Yes, it will be quicker and maybe your friends can lend you a car in Dar, or you could even hire one.'

'You want me to fly,' Kahinga looked at Peter uncomprehendingly. 'I have never even been to the airport.'

'Why not, it's quicker, safer, and you won't have to drive all that way.'

'Safer? Don't these aeroplanes crash all the time?'

'It's much safer, when did you last hear of a plane crashing in this country?'

Suddenly Kahinga was excited. It would never have occurred to him to fly to Dar. Maybe it did make sense.

'I will give you the money for a ticket and where you should buy it. You must buy it, I don't want to be seen buying tickets for anyone going to Dar,' said Peter.

Kahinga told Wanjiru that he would be away for a few days without telling her where he was going. He had made one telephone call to a contact in Dar-es-Salaam and asked his contact to pick him up at the airport. Kinua dropped him off at Jomo Kenyatta Airport which is not far out of the city. Kinua was surprised but knew his friend well enough not to ask any questions and he kept his mouth shut on the subject. Kahinga was interested in all the paraphernalia surrounding the flight. They allowed him to carry on board the small briefcase with his few belongings; his passport and tickets were checked.

He was very surprised to be given breakfast for the one hour flight and reflected on the limited diet that he would have enjoyed had he chosen to drive.

His contact duly met him at the airport and as they drove into the city he asked about the demise of Wanyoike. The man laughed: 'He thought that the Kikuyu woman who runs the brothel would help him and that she owned the place. What he didn't find out was that Nyamita's brother owns the place and she would have told him exactly what Wanyoike was up to. He stood no chance. That man is completely ruthless, just like Nyamita. Nyamita is now helping him in all his criminal activities; he has many contacts in the police as you would expect and they will not touch him, I expect that he pays them all off quite handsomely.'

'So they won't listen to the Kenya police if they want to take him back to Nairobi to face a trial,' asked Kahinga.

'No chance, they will just pretend that they cannot find him.'

Kahinga borrowed his contact's vehicle and soon traced Nyamita's movements through the city.

It was clear that Nyamita and his brother thought that they had dealt with the threat from the Kikuyu and anyone else who might have a plan to take Nyamita back to Nairobi; so Kahinga saw him breezing around Dar-es-Salaam as if he owned the place. He was out and about most days with regular visits to his usual haunts, including Mrs. Koinange's establishment; he was obviously enjoying himself. After a week Kahinga had seen all he needed to see but he checked and re-checked all his observations. He returned to Kenya and saw Rafiki and Peter together at Sattimma.

Rafiki took the lead: 'Tell us all about Nyamita and his habits in Dar-es-Salaam.'

'He is very careless; the other Kikuyu in Dar says that he thinks that there will no attempt at extraditing him back to Kenya to face trial since that is what he has been told by the police there. Also having killed Wanyoike and his friends he thinks that there will be no more attempts to capture him and take him back to Nairobi. So he is really an easy target. He goes to the bank, some bars, small restaurants, but always on Thursdays he goes to this brothel run by a Mrs. Koinange.'

'Is she likely to be friend of ours? She must be a Kikuyu.'

Kahinga smiled: 'No that is the mistake that Wanyoike made, he thought that she would help, what he didn't find out was who owned the place.'

'Who owns the place?'

'Nyamita's brother.'

'Oh dear,' said Rafiki.

'He did not do a proper job, he could easily have found out who owned it; Wanyoike was just in too much of a hurry, as he always was. We will not make that mistake. Wanyoike was right in thinking that taking him at the brothel was a sensible thing to do. He leaves there late at night when he is perhaps a little drunk: there is very little traffic. We can take him easily and we will be across the border before they find out that he has gone,' Kahinga continued.

'Ok, said Rafiki. 'This is what we will do: we need two vehicles in Tanzania; one with a driver and three others will go through Namanga and go to Dar, the other one will be driven by you and only you and will go through Voi and the then the Taveta border post.' Kahinga was about to interrupt. Rafiki held up her hand. 'You will then drive towards Moshi and take the road to the Loitokitok border post where you will find Munyu and me.' She pulled out a map and showed him the various places that had been mentioned.

'You are coming to Dar, this is very dangerous. Many people know you. I think that this is not a good idea,' said Kahinga anxiously.

'Wait here,' said Rafiki. 'Just give me five minutes.'

About twenty minutes later the cook came in and said: 'There is a Masai woman out here who says that it is very urgent that she sees you, Munyu. I would send her away but I am still trying to remember that you want to see all these shenzies, whatever they may want.'

Peter said: 'Ok bring her in.'

Kahinga was about to leave but Peter held his arm and said: 'This will not take long just stay and we can continue with our discussion on the plans for our big fat friend.'

They went out on to the verandah and the cook brought round to the front garden, what appeared to be a youngish Masai woman dressed in a red blanket with a blue overwrap, a necklet ruff, many bangles worn as earrings and a beaded skull cap. Of course she was barefoot. Kahinga took no notice and was staring off into the distance thinking about how he would have to deal with his two well known mentors and friends in Dar. Peter started to talk to the new arrival in Swahili:

'Jambo, mama,' said Peter.

'Jambo-sana, bwana Munyu,' was the response. Kahinga suddenly looked up because of the familiar voice and he looked in amazement and looked again: it was of course Rafiki dressed up as a Masai woman. Peter started laughing and then Kahinga saw the funny side of it as well and they all laughed until tears ran down their faces. Only the cook could not see the funny side of the situation. He went off mumbling: 'Behaving like children, this beautiful Kikuyu woman dressing up like a bush Masai.'

'I see,' said Kahinga. 'You think that you will not be recognised. Having you in Tanzania makes life more difficult, but maybe we will be certain not to make any big mistakes if you are there.'

'Where were we? Oh yes, you will find Munyu and me on the Tanzanian side of the Loitokitok border post on a date that we will give you. We will know which vehicle you are driving so we will probably just find you. We will then all go to Dar.'

They went on discussing the plan for the next few hours and then they all had a very clear idea of who was to do what and when:

'It is very important that we only use your most trusted people,' said Rafiki, 'and even they will only be told what is necessary for them to do what we need them to do. Only we three will know the full plan.'

✳   ✳   ✳

Chapter 28

Between them they developed a very clear plan. Six of Kahinga's best and most trusted people including N'guku, back from borehole duty, and Macharia all met in a small house in Pumwani. In front of the house was parked an old, but very reliable, unmarked four wheel drive Landcruiser configured as a van having a row of seats behind the front seat and a small storage area behind those seats. The vehicle had been lent by a colleague on the understanding from Kahinga of future unspecified rewards.

N'guku on his own was instructed: 'You will take this gari (vehicle) to Sattimma in two days; Rafiki will tell what to do. Don't let me down, and don't play the fool, like you did with that policeman and his truck in the mutoni,'

N'guku looked downcast. 'Yes,' said Kahinga, 'I know about that and this is much more important.' He gave him enough money to buy fuel and food; he also gave him two Patchett sub-machine guns having already provided jerry cans for extra fuel and water. 'Keep the guns well hidden and make sure that you clean them regularly, you never know when you might need to use them: go now; I do not want you to listen to the rest of the plans, the fewer people that know what we are doing the better.' One of the remaining men was told to go with N'guku.

N'guku opened his mouth to ask something, but Kahinga put up his hand: 'You will find out soon enough, at this stage the less you know the better, and N'guku,' he said quietly, 'don't tell anybody anything, nobody, not even your assistant. You have trusted me in the past; you will just have to trust me now.'

Kahinga now called the others into the house, since they had been made to wait outside while Kahinga briefed N'guku. He indicated a new pick-up with a cage on the back parked outside, next to his own vehicle. It had taken all of Kahinga's persuasive powers to get Kinua to lend it to him. 'Macharia, I want you to drive that truck through Namanga to Dar-es-Salaam. These three people will accompany you.' He indicated the three others who had joined the briefing. 'You will meet me at an address that I will give you; you need to be there on this date,' he gave Macharia a note with the address and a date on it. At the border post, make sure that you are noticed, don't behave badly but maybe you could ask directions or something but make sure that the people at the post, on the Tanzanian side especially, notice you, enough to remember you.' Macharia smiled. 'And by the way I have already hidden guns and ammunition in the side panels; it will not be possible for anyone to find them except me, so don't worry about that.'

'What are we going to do in Dar?' asked Macharia. 'Why do we need guns?'

'I will tell you when we get there, all I can tell you is that it is very important. We will need the guns, but I do not expect that we will fire them.'

There was a lot of chatter. 'Now please make sure that you all have your travel documents in order, while you need to be noticed at the border, it would spoil all my plans if you were not allowed into Tanzania.'

'Is this something to do with the police again?' asked Macharia.

Kahinga nonchalantly shook his head.

'Is it legal?'

'You will remember when we were in the forests, many times we went on raids and I only told you what we were doing at the last minute.'

They all nodded.

'Was everything we did when we were together in the forests legal?'

They all laughed.

He gave Macharia money for fuel and food: 'It will take you three days to get to Dar; I will be at the address that I gave you.'

Rafiki picked John and Kamau up at the school and said to them: 'You will remember that I told you we had a secret surprise for you these holidays.'

They looked at her curiously: 'Well you are going to spend nearly three weeks in England with Giles and Louise and their children and of course Robert.'

'What? Aren't you coming?' asked a delighted Kamau.

'Not this time. We have some other quite important business which we are not able to put off. I can't tell you anything about it yet, so don't ask questions.'

They both knew when Rafiki was serious so they just looked at each other and shut up.

'You fly tomorrow, in case you wanted to know.' Rafiki smiled to herself, she could see their brains working overtime wondering what she was planning.

Rafiki had already taken her own and Peter's passports to Mwangi and they had departure stamps in them for the following days date.

'What is all this about?' asked Mwangi over the now usual cup of tea served in fine china cups in his office.

'It is better that you don't know,' answered Rafiki smiling.

Mwangi laughed. A dose of his own medicine, he thought. He would find out though, the whole situation intrigued him; information like this could always come in useful.

Peter had made one of his rare phone calls to Giles in London, who was ready to welcome John and Kamau. Peter then went on to explain precisely what they were going to do and why. 'Can't the police just deal with this, you could both get hurt or even killed,' Giles asked anxiously.

Peter tried to explain his reasons and then added: 'The tickets that the boys have are in our names, we are relying on the fact that the check-in people here will not compare the names on the tickets with the names in the passports. I'm not so sure that the people at your end will be quite so accommodating, so the tickets need to be changed into the boys names at your end.'

'I am sure that that will be easy to do,' answered Giles.

'There is one other thing.'

'Yees,' said Giles hesitatingly.

'We will give them a package with mine and Rafiki's passports in it. They both need a British exit stamp showing the date of their return flight.'

Giles drew a sharp breath: 'Jesus, you really are sailing close to the wind this time, but I will see what I can do. Please 'phone me when you have the fat bastard, as you so delightfully describe him, in custody in Kenya.'

'Certainly and thank you, please give my love to Louise.'

He put the phone down, took a deep breath and looked unseeingly at his hands. 'Yes, it is worth it,' he said to himself, 'we have come this far, we must see it through.'

Peter and Rafiki took the boys to the airport; leaving them in separate seating away from the counter and they checked in under their own names. There was as expected a brief glance at their passports and they were given boarding cards. They were well known and the people serving them tried to make sure that they made a bit of a fuss over them; there was absolutely no suspicion of anything underhand.

Rafiki put the passports in an envelope addressed to Giles which had a few other things in it, mainly so that it looked innocuous. She sealed it firmly and gave it to John together with the boarding cards:

'The luggage has gone through; you remember where to pick it up the other end, I expect. I have asked Louise to meet you at Heathrow; she will probably be in that ridiculous Bentley of theirs.' They hugged the boys and watched them walk through passport control and the boarding gate and then returned to Sattimma.

Both Kahinga and N'guku were waiting for them and they went out onto the verandah: 'N'guku, you will take Munyu and me to the Loitokitok border post and then you will come back to Nairobi and pick up your assistant. You will wait one week and then return to the Loitokitok border post to pick us up. We will find a place for you to wait where you won't be seen,' Rafiki instructed.

'How long should I wait at the border post, when I go back there?

'We will decide when we get there. Now the cook will feed you and we have things to discuss with Kahinga. We will go early tomorrow, maybe four o'clock in the morning, tonight, you can stay here at Sattimma, in Kinua's old place.'

Rafiki then went through everything again with Kahinga and gave him a map and suitcases containing changes of clothes for both Peter and herself: 'We will come through the border post at Loitokitok just after daybreak the day after tomorrow. The turn-off to the Loitokitok post is a right turn, not far from the Taveta post that you will come through. I don't expect that it is well marked but the mountain will be right in front of you, you have to turn before the mountain. Also please tell Macharia and his people to be at the Dar turnoff after Moshi in three days, we may need a backup in case something goes wrong,' Kahinga looked surprised for a moment, but then nodded in understanding and left in his own vehicle.

N'guku was outside the back door of the house at Sattimma just before four in the morning. He saw what he thought was a very tall Masai man and a young Masai boy emerge from the shadows of the back verandah, then to his amazement he saw that it was Peter and Rafiki, Peter was carrying his Rigby .416 as well as a traditional Masai spear, the gun gave the game away somewhat. They had two water bottles each strapped to their waists and Rafiki also had a revolver strapped to her waist, underneath the normal skimpy red piece of cloth knotted over one shoulder and only extending to just above her knees.

'Quite fancy you in that outfit,' joked Peter in English, knowing that N'guku would not be able to understand.

'Behave yourself,' replied Rafiki, 'anyway I am supposed to be a boy.' They were carrying an animal skin food bag each.

After the normal polite greetings Rafiki said to N'guku: 'Drive down the Mombasa road, we need to go beyond Sultan Hamud; the turnoff is between there and Makindu. It may not be very well marked.'

They drove through Athi River whilst it was still dark and then when the sun had been up over the horizon an hour they passed Sultan Hamud, which was just a railway station positioned away from the road. 'Another twenty miles,' said Rafiki, 'but maybe we should ask someone.'

N'guku stopped the truck and asked an old Wakamba man for directions to Loitokitok: 'If you can give me a lift I can show you the turnoff, it is not very well marked.'

N'guku hesitated. 'Ok,' Rafiki growled so only N'guku could hear.

Peter and Rafiki were sitting in the back seat so N'guku indicated to their guide to hop in the front. 'This will test our disguise,' muttered Peter.

The man never gave them a second glance and happily chatted to N'guku for the twenty minutes he was in the vehicle: 'These Masai, they stink like their ngombi's (cattle); how far are they going?' he said to N'guku.

'Amboseli,' said N'guku, 'they have ngombi's there.'

'Good, well I am glad that I am not going that far.' He asked N'guku to stop and indicated an unsignposted side road: 'Loitokitok.' He pointed.

Peter and Rafiki tried to contain their laughter when the old man stepped down from the truck: 'I think it must be you that stinks like an ngombi,' he said to Rafiki, 'I had a bath last night,' speaking in Swahili so that N'guku could share in the joke. The fifty five odd miles to the Loitokitok post took them an hour and a half, so they were close to the border by early afternoon. Rafiki told N'guku to stop and pull into the thorn scrub when they thought that they must be close to the post.

'Give me half an hour or so, 'said Peter, 'I just need to check the lie of the land. Maybe you could see if there is a more suitable place to park the vehicle.' Peter loped off into through the bush with his rifle and had returned within forty minutes. 'There are two small huts on each side of what looks like the border and there are Masai cattle all around; we told Kahinga that we would meet him in the morning, so I suggest that we find a place near here where we know that we will be able to find N'guku in a week's time. We should then spend the night here. N'guku can return to Nairobi when we head off at dawn tomorrow morning.'

'We have found a really good place about three hundred yards off the track here,' said Rafiki. 'There is a sort of small dip behind a large thorn tree. We can light a fire, have a meal and we can't be seen from the road. We are in more danger of being seen by the local Masai herdsmen than by the people at the border post, who I suspect don't wander very far.'

Peter collected firewood and Rafiki and N'guku prepared a simple meal. There was not much conversation and by seven in the evening they had all rolled up in their sleeping bags and were fast asleep. Peter made sure that he woke up every two hours or so to put another log on the fire. He didn't need to explain to others that just the faint whiff of woodsmoke was enough to keep the wild animals from getting too close. There were plenty of eyes out in the bush, shining in the dark: Peter loved it, it had been some years now since he had spent a night in the bush and he savoured every minute of it. A lion roared a few hundred yards away. Rafiki rolled over in her sleeping bag, but did not wake.

Peter was up before dawn: he boiled the kettle for tea and they ate some of the mealie meal cake that they had cooked the night before. What was left was packed into the food bags. They eliminated all the traces of their camp by burying the fire and sweeping the ground trying to eliminate their own and the vehicle tracks. It was impossible to erase all the tyre tracks but they made sure that there was no visibility of the vehicle having left the road. 'Anyway within a day the wind will have blown the fine longido dust over the tracks and obliterated them,' Peter told them.

Peter and Rafiki walked off into the bush after having seen N'guku off onto the track back to the main road and Nairobi. With the stick of greasepaint that she brought for the purpose Rafiki made certain that Peter's disguise was intact. Even from a few feet away he looked like a Masai herdsman, with his spear, thin red blanket over one shoulder and braided hair; the rifle was a bit out of character, although, since independence, it was becoming more usual for Africans to own and carry firearms. Both he and Rafiki each had a pair of leather sandals made by Masai years earlier. Rafiki was dressed as a young boy, also with the thin red blanket knotted over one shoulder, although for modesty's sake she wore a pair of brown pants that almost matched her skin colour. Peter said jokingly: 'Without those pants I may have become distracted.'

She slapped him playfully on the shoulder: 'One track mind.' They had water bottles and Rafiki had her revolver strapped to her waist under the skimpy outfit, but from more than twenty yards away they really looked like a Masai man and his son out herding cattle.

N'guku was intrigued with all the goings on; he had not been told any more than that he was to be back at the border post in a week's time. He had known Rafiki when she had organised food in the forests during the insurgency, he barely knew Munyu except by reputation. They were obviously up to something; he wondered how he might profit from the situation: he would in any event wait and see how things developed.

Keeping the majesty of Mount Kilimanjaro on their right Peter and Rafiki walked easily through the bush towards the border post. 'That is Mawenzi, the smaller peak on the left there and the big one with all the snow on the top is Kibo,' said Peter. Even with the seriousness if their quest and the undoubted danger that they had put themselves into Rafiki was able to admire the magnificence of the sight in the early morning. There was evidence of wild animals all around them: 'Fresh lion prints, not more than an hour or so old,' Peter said to an unconcerned Rafiki. Like many Africans, she did not share Peter's enthusiasm for the bush, it was really too close to what she had been brought up with and in a way had escaped from, but it held no fears and she was familiar with all the shapes a sizes of the animals so spotted them long before Peter had, although he kept pointing everything out. They came across a small group of cattle, which seemed to be unattended and drove them within a hundred yards of the border posts. Both sets of guards saw them but took no notice; clearly this was a regular occurrence. When they were well out of sight of the border posts they left the cattle to their own devices and continued to walk through the bush.

Two hours after they had left N'guku Rafiki said: 'We should now go to the road and walk along it, this is where we said we would meet Kahinga, but we should continue walking, it will save time in the end and we don't want Macharia to spend too long waiting in case he attracts attention. If a car comes along they will assume we are part of the local scenery, although we can always just go off into the bush if we hear a vehicle coming.' So they walked, moving off into the bush on the one occasion when they heard a car coming from the border post; making sure that it was not Kahinga.

At about midday Rafiki said anxiously: 'Something has gone wrong, Kahinga should have been here hours ago, but I think that we should keep walking, hopefully Macharia will be waiting for us, but we may have to spend another night in the bush, he will only arrive at the turnoff from Moshi tomorrow.' Peter shrugged and they walked on. They walked all day, although it was hot their attire made things cool and they were both fit. At about four in the afternoon Rafiki said: 'I think that we should stop before we get close to any settlements, we can start walking again an hour or so before the dawn since we have the road to guide us.'

They found a place off the track and Peter said: 'We have very little food, so I will go and shoot a small buck, maybe you could start collecting firewood; it is going to be cold tonight without those sleeping bags.' Peter disappeared into the bush with just his rifle; half an hour later Rafiki heard the crack of a high powered rifle and an hour after that Peter appeared with the haunches and fillets of a Thomson's gazelle. 'I skinned and butchered it where it was shot, which will keep the hyaenas and jackals occupied, the last thing we need is to have them running around here,' he explained. The roasted the venison over the fire and ate the remains of the ogalie (mealie meal cake) they had with them and then dug shallow indents into the sandy soil and cuddled up together for warmth: 'You had better get rid of those pants you have been wearing or I might do some damage to them and to myself,' said Peter laughing.

Rafiki giggled as she struggled out of her pants: 'You're dreadful, thank heaven, one track mind.'

They made love again in the morning before they snatched a few mouthfuls of the remaining tommy. They were on their way by four am. Before eight they had turned on to the main Moshi road and found the junction where Kahinga had arranged to meet Macharia. There were a few people about, since there was a bus stop a hundred yards down the road towards Dar-es-Salaam: 'I don't like this,' said Rafiki, 'if we are not careful people will see through our disguise and that may attract the wrong sort of attention.'

'Perhaps you would stay around here out of sight,' suggested Peter, just keep an eye out for Macharia and I will walk back towards the Taveta border post to see if there is any sign of Kahinga; I expect to be back here by lunchtime, whatever happens. Here you keep the rifle.'

Peter walked in the bush, just in sight of the main road. He kept well away from any people, knowing that his disguise would not stand up to much scrutiny. Within two hours he was in sight of the busy border post at Taveta and there much to his relief was Kahinga's vehicle with Kahinga's head buried underneath the raised bonnet.

Peter strode up to the vehicle and then said in a loud voice in Kikuyu: 'Wathieku.'

Kahinga jumped up in fright and banged his head on the raised bonnet; he looked round and did a double take when he saw Peter. 'Border was very slow,' he explained rubbing his head, 'and then they wanted to ask me many questions so the car overheated and now it won't start. I have been here since yesterday morning,' observed Kahinga.

Peter unobtrusively changed using clothes from the case in the back of the vehicle and he tried to wipe some of the grease paint off his face. He dumped his Masai spear and his disguise into the back of the pick-up. 'With two of us here we should be able to get this thing going within a couple of hours,' he said.

'How did you get here?' asked Kahinga?' Peter pointed to his feet:' Walked.'

'Where is Rafiki?'

'Back at the place where we arranged to meet Macharia; she is keeping out of sight though, we don't necessarily want Macharia and his crew to know that we are here, at least at the moment.' They cleaned and refilled the radiator, checked the sparkplugs and just went through all the obvious things one by one over a two hour period. Kahinga managed to obtain the help of a local who had a set of jump-leads with him, who gave Peter some curious looks. At the first attempt the engine started and seemed to be running smoothly.

Kahinga looked at his former boss and said: 'I did all that before you came and nothing happened, what did you do?'

Peter shrugged: 'Come, Rafiki is at the road junction. You can meet Macharia, Rafiki and I will stay out of the way. I am a little bit uncomfortable about N'guku by the way; we may need to keep an eye on him.'

Kahinga looked at him sharply: 'N'guku had better not get any ideas; he will be in big trouble if he does.'

Rafiki emerged from a hiding place in the bush as she recognised Kahinga's vehicle driving slowly past: 'Macharia is waiting just down the road; he does not know I am here. Kahinga parked his truck and walked the three hundred yards to where Macharia had stopped.

Macharia was looking anxious. There were only three of them instead of the expected four: 'Where is the other man?' asked Kahinga.

'The police on this side of the border wanted to question him; they were doing that to a lot of people, especially Kikuyu. The policeman in charge said that they were worried about something he was not quite sure what it was. I paid him some money so he let us all through but we did not have quite enough so they kept one of our people. I think that he will be able to catch a bus soon and will be in Dar tomorrow.'

'You don't know what they were looking for?'

'No, they talked about some trouble, but they couldn't or wouldn't say anything about it. Maybe they were just trying to see if there was any trouble, I don't know.'

'It was the same at Taveta,' said Kahinga, 'my truck overheated and broke down at the border post there so I have only just got here, so now you go on to Dar and I will see you there.'

'What are we going to do in Dar?'

'I will tell you when we get there, after tomorrow.'

Kahinga saw Macharia off and watched him out of sight.

Rafiki had arranged a small house in a quiet suburb of Dar through a friend whom she had dealt with in the forests. She made it sound like some sort of sexual tryst: 'We don't want to be disturbed, if you see what I mean,' she told her friend, who giggled understandingly. The friend had always disapproved of Rafiki's liaison with Peter and saw this as a sign that Rafiki had at last come to her senses. 'Come back here, tomorrow, when you have settled Macharia and his crew in properly,' Rafiki told Kahinga as he dropped them off. 'We can then finalise our plans.'

Kahinga settled everyone into a house that he had stayed in during his previous visit. The fourth man, travelling with Macharia, duly arrived the next day: 'They beat me, but only a little bit,' he said smiling.

'What did they want?' asked Kahinga.

'I really don't know, they talked about Kikuyu gangs in Dar, I know nothing of that. I gave them a wrong address as Macharia told me.' Kahinga silently applauded Macharia. 'I think they were just looking to see if people would tell them something that they did not already know.'

Kahinga let Macharia and his men run around Dar for a couple of days enjoying the sights and sounds and smells of a new city, while he and Rafiki and Peter went through all the plans. Neither Macharia nor any of the others had ever seen the sea before and they were encouraged to paddle on the beach: 'Don't go in too far,' advised Kahinga, knowing that none of them could swim, 'you might get eaten by sharks, very big samaki (fish),' he joked.

Peter rented a four wheel drive from a white owned safari company. He gave them a false name and hoped that he would not be recognised. He paid cash in advance for two weeks: 'Ngorongoro,' he answered when he was asked where he was going. 'American visitors,' he explained. This was all quite usual so apart from the normal pleasantries nothing much was said.

Kahinga showed Rafiki and Peter Nyamita's brothers' house and his various haunts around town. Peter and Rafiki, in the rented four wheel drive spent two nights in the street outside the brothel that Nyamita frequented; they saw him emerge as usual on the Thursday evening at about ten thirty, which is what they had been told would be the case.

On the evening of the third day in Dar Kahinga called Macharia and all the men together in the house they were staying in. In general the Kikuyu in Dar kept a low profile and just got on with their own business, some legal and some not so legal, so they were used to comings and goings from the northern neighbour and not asking or expecting to be given explanations of things that did not concern them. All they expected was reciprocity when they visited Nairobi.

'We are going to take Nyamita back to face trial in Nairobi.' There was a sharp intake of breath and then complete silence. He knew that he had everyone's undivided attention. 'As we all know he was almost certainly involved in the kidnap of Nusu-Nusu and probably many other illegal activities.'

'That is the big fat Jaluo we saw and then had a fight with in the mutoni,' Macharia said; it was more of a statement than a question.

'Yes, you will remember that he was wounded and then Wacheera took over as Police chief. After we found Nusu-Nusu, he ran away and now lives with his brother here in Dar. They run many illegal and some legal operations together. They also have developed good relations with the police here, maybe that activity at the Namanga and Taveta border posts had something to do with that.'

'OK, this is what we will do,' continued Kahinga: 'I have been watching him over many days now both this time and I was here for almost two weeks a little while ago. His habits have remained the same. He goes to the bank every Monday, and he visits one or two small restaurants on different days of the week, but every Thursday he goes to this brothel in a back street. He always arrives at eight in the evening and usually leaves at ten thirty, perhaps a little drunk. Most of the time he is alone, especially when he goes to the brothel. Tomorrow is Thursday. He parks his car in the main street right outside the lane where the brothel is located. The street is not busy, so hopefully we will be able to park near his car at about ten o'clock. I will drive since I know Dar quite well now. I have rented a four wheel drive from a M'zungu owned Safari Company, which will be parked about ten minutes drive away. You Macharia will knock Nyamita on the head with that rungu (club) that is in the back of Kinua's pick-up, when he is near his car; you will then put this cloth over his face which has some dawa (medicine) called chloroform on it which will make him sleep. Remember he is very big and strong, so he needs to be tied up and gagged very firmly when the rest of you have put him in the back of the truck. We will take him to the four wheel drive and transfer him to that and then I will tell you what to do.'

At ten o'clock in the evening the pick-up driven by Macharia with his three colleagues in the back, parked where they had been told. There was no sign of Nyamita's Mercedes. Kahinga beckoned from the shadows: 'I have been here since before eight,' he told Macharia, 'there is no sign of him, we will wait ten minutes and then leave and try again tomorrow; there must be something wrong, he has never missed a Thursday night since I have been watching him.' Unseen, Peter and Rafiki were sitting in the four wheel drive a little further down the street. Macharia and his crew left and Kahinga walked over to where Rafiki and Peter were parked and told them the same thing. 'We'll try again tomorrow,' said Rafiki.

The next day Rafiki kept watch on the Nyamita residence, but there was no sign of him. They went to the brothel at the appointed time again with no success. 'We just have to be patient, sooner or later he will turn up,' Kahinga told the rather despondent group after the third night of waiting outside the brothel.

During her watch on Nyamita's brother's house Rafiki had noticed the same car driving in every day. On the third day she followed the car back into the city, watched it park and then followed the lone driver into a building and stepped into the lift with him. The well dressed man looked at Rafiki and asked in English: 'Is there anything I can do for you?'

Rafiki thought quickly, she had noticed that there were a number of what appeared to be doctor's surgeries in the building so she replied: 'I was looking for a doctor; I see that there are several doctors in the building.'

'Yes,' said the man smiling, 'I am a doctor, I have to go out again now, but you can make an appointment with my receptionist maybe for this afternoon.'

As they got out of the lift and walked into the surgery there was Nyamita sitting in reception. Rafiki stopped dead and was about to dash back into the lift: 'Now we are in real trouble,' she thought, but there was no recognition on the man's face and with a gasp of relief she saw that it was Nyamita's brother. The doctor looked at her enquiringly, obviously not understanding Rafiki's concern: 'This lady wants an appointment,' the doctor told the receptionist in Swahili: 'maybe this afternoon.' The doctor said to Nyamita's brother also in Swahili: 'I won't be a moment, I just have to get something and then we can go, bullet wounds need…' he stopped and glanced at Rafiki who pretended to be focussed on the pretty receptionist and her appointment for the afternoon.

Quickly changing the subject, Nyamita's brother asked: 'How is Nyamita, by the way, I have not seen him for a couple of days with all this other business.'

'Oh, no problem really,' was the quick reply, 'he will be up today, he has had a very bad dose of 'flu, that's all.'

Rafiki gave a false name; made the appointment which she had no intention of keeping and quickly left. She had heard all he needed to hear. They would just have to maintain the watch on Nyamita and sooner or later she now had no doubt Nyamita would appear at Mrs Koinange's establishment. Rafiki went to a dirty little cafe nearby, ordered a soft drink and spent a few minutes thinking. She asked the cafe owner if she could make a quick telephone call. 'I will pay,' she said. She 'phoned the doctors surgery and cancelled the appointment. 'I'm sorry,' she told the receptionist, 'but I am in rather a hurry and I have found someone who can see me immediately.' She was hoping that they would just put her out of their minds. She raced back home and waited for Kahinga and Peter to tell them what had transpired. The surveillance outside the brothel was re-established. The first night they again drew a blank.

On the second night they hit the jackpot. When Macharia and the men arrived they immediately saw Nyamita's Mercedes parked in the expected place, so he parked a few feet behind it. Kahinga came out of the shadows: 'He is here alright, but there is one complication, his brother is with him. If he leaves the place by himself, all well and good, but if his brother is with him that makes it more difficult. I don't want to alert the brother too soon, he will have the whole Police force on to Nyamita's disappearance anyway, but I had planned on them only noticing that he had disappeared the morning after we had taken him and by that time we will be well on our way back to Nairobi.' Peter was parked down the street in the four wheel drive and Rafiki was driving Kahinga's pick-up.

A few minutes later Nyamita emerged and walked somewhat unsteadily towards his car. They collectively heaved a sigh of relief: he was alone. Then

Nyamita waited for a minute and looked over his shoulder to be joined by his brother. They had an animated conversation standing next to Nyamita's car for ten minutes. The brother walked off and Nyamita climbed into his own car and slowly drove away. Everyone was paralysed for a few moments, then Rafiki started Kahinga's vehicle and chased after Nyamita, not really knowing what she was going to do. She saw Nyamita's car stopped at a traffic light, so raced up and deliberately bumped Nyamita's precious Mercedes on the side door. There was no significant damage but as Rafiki had predicted, a furious Nyamita jumped out of his car and started swearing, but before he had really had a chance to say much, Kahinga and Macharia had arrived and Macharia swung his rungu and Nyamita collapsed in a heap in the road; they picked him up with the chloroform cloth on his face and flung him into the back of the pickup Macharia had been driving. Rafiki quickly drove off in the midst of the mayhem, followed by Peter in the four wheel drive.

While they were doing this Kahinga gave his instructions: 'Macharia, take the Mercedes and follow me.' He said to the others: 'just keep Nyamita quiet.' They drove through the deserted streets for ten minutes and found the four wheel drive that Peter had parked in a prearranged place. Rafiki had picked Peter up and they made themselves scarce by driving around the corner. Nyamita was lying on his back, out for the count: they dragged him out and dumped him none too gently into the rear of the four wheel drive on top of the mattress that Peter had taken from the house they had been staying in. Kahinga glanced at Nyamita: 'He will be out for a while,' he thought. 'Tie him up and gag him,' he said to the men now waiting instructions, 'legs, and arms, and make sure they are secure.'

'Very lucky he had that accident, otherwise he would have got away and we might have had to wait another week,' observed Macharia. Much to Kahinga's relief he made no mention that it was Kahinga's vehicle that had been involved in the accident.

'Macharia, could you park the Mercedes over there, under that tree.' Kahinga went over and checked Nyamita's bonds. 'Two in the back with Nyamita and one in the front with me,' he handed them all balaclavas which he had stored in the vehicle: 'Keep these on all the time and do not speak to Nyamita, not at all and not ever.' Macharia returned: 'You will take the pick-up and return to Nairobi,' instructed Kahinga, 'through Namanga, take it back to Kinua. The border will be very difficult, I expect they will search the vehicle very thoroughly but we have both cleaned it again and again, they will not find anything. You will be asked where the others are who came with you to Tanzania, tell them they will go home by rail in a few days. The border police may beat you. I will see you when we get back to Nairobi. Don't tell anyone where you have been, or what you have done.'

Macharia grinned: 'They can beat me all they like; nothing could be as bad as Hola camp.'

Kahinga then went to the four wheel drive and searched every pocket on Nyamita: 'Ah,' he said with satisfaction, 'His Kenya police identity documents and his warrant card, and passport.' He took the keys, detached the spare key, walked over to the Mercedes and made certain that the key fitted the door and the ignition. He left the documents on the front seat and the key in the ignition, which is what he had agreed with Rafiki.

They watched Macharia drive off, in Kinua's pick-up. 'What now?' asked one of the men. 'Moshi, and then I will tell you. You will have to give that animal in there, he indicated the supine form of Nyamita, water from time to time, but remember do not say anything. The next day or so will be very difficult, after that we will be back in Kenya, so it should be easier.'

'Which border post will we use, we can't use Namanga?'

Kahinga shook his head: 'No not Namanga, I will show you.'

Kahinga wiped the bunch of keys very carefully and then with the cloth he had used he told one of the men to put them in Nyamita's jacket pocket. 'Just don't touch the keys, the only fingerprints must be his,' said Kahinga.

When Rafiki and Peter saw Kahinga drive off in the rented four wheel drive they parked Kahinga's vehicle right behind Nyamita's Mercedes. Rafiki had a quick look in the car and started it with the key in the ignition: 'Everything is there, the car has been filled with petrol and all his identity documents, even his passport, are on the front seat, so I expect that if we get a move on you can be through the border pretending to be Nyamita before the balloon goes up in the morning. We just need to make sure that you look like a Jaluo policeman this time,' she said. Peter already had shaved his head and applied plenty of greasepaint; they now fitted a wig and Peter put two pillow cases into the front and back of his smart shirt. He was wearing a suit and tie and had polished his shoes. He was a bit taller than Nyamita, but he now really looked the part. 'OK,' she said, looking at him critically under a street light. 'I have never been on that road, but it looks like about two hundred miles to the coastal border at Lungalunga, so if you get a move on you will be there before the border opens in the morning. I will take Kahinga's pick-up to the border at Loitokitok. N'guku will have cleared off by now as it is more than two weeks since we came through there. One of the people who came into Tanzania legitimately will have to drive it through, back into Kenya, so Kahinga and company will have some means of getting the fat pig back to Nairobi; the others will just have to walk round the post, which should not be too difficult. I will bring the four wheel drive back here. Whew, have I forgotten anything?'

'The address where I rented the four wheel drive is in the cubby hole. You probably need to clean the vehicle properly; I think that it is important that they don't really remember us, so if you can dress up as a man that would be best, when you return it; we have paid in full, so there is nothing to worry about there. You can then catch the train; by then they will just be looking for Kikuyu at the various border posts, especially those that came through Namanga with Macharia, so I don't think that they will be worrying about a well dressed Tanzanian woman in a first class compartment. I need to get the dent knocked out of the car in Mombasa, which will take a day, but I will look for you at Voi on the way through,' said Peter.

'I may just dress as a nun,' said Rafiki, 'nobody bothers them and I can then hide my revolver under all those clothes they wear.'

It was now just midnight: 'We should be in Moshi by ten in the morning,' thought Kahinga, 'They will find that Nyamita and his car are missing by not later than eight o'clock, after that the police will be everywhere, but they will probably concentrate on Dar, the airport and the Namanga border post,' he thought. He took the road going due west to Morogoro and then took the turn, due north indicating Moshi; changing drivers every two hours while they stopped to relieve themselves. The second time they stopped while it was still dark: they pulled a still slightly groggy Nyamita out of the vehicle and made him relieve himself. 'Who are you and what do you want, you stupid fools, you won't get away with this you know, by now there will be police all over the place looking for me,' he shouted in Swahili. Nobody said anything; they just shoved him back into the vehicle. They gave him some water and drove on.

Although Kahinga had spare fuel in jerry cans on the roof of the vehicle, he wanted to keep that for an emergency so he decided to stop at the next service station that was open, which he thought would only be after seven in the morning. The question was how were they going to keep Nyamita quiet during the refuelling? The last thing they needed was to attract any attention. They saw a small village in the distance on the main road and Kahinga gave one of the men in the back a signal by waving his hand over his face. The man clamped the chloroform cloth over Nyamita's face, after a brief furious struggle Nyamita went quiet and they pulled up at the rather bedraggled service station just as it opened. A very sleepy attendant filled the vehicle up and asked disinterestedly: 'Where are you going?'

'Ngorongoro through Arusha,' answered Kahinga.

'Ah, yes, this is the best way,' was the answer. Kahinga paid and the journey continued. None of the others emerged from the vehicle. Just before ten in the morning they arrived at a major intersection: left towards Moshi and right towards the border at Taveta.

The scenery was now completely dominated by the majesty of Kilimanjaro, which Kahinga knew he would have to pass very close to.

Kahinga turned right to the surprise of his fellow passengers. He held his finger to his lips. A mile or two further there were very indistinct signs one of which seemed to read Loitokitok, turning left. The road was now quite rough and they made slow progress. After about thirty minutes they saw some men herding cattle on the side of the road. Kahinga stopped and took two packets of cigarettes from the cubby hole that he had stashed away for just such an occasion and walked over to them. Neither he nor any of his colleagues smoked; a habit they had dispensed with in the forests. Initially there was a frosty reception until Kahinga greeted them warmly and asked if they would like a cigarette. The atmosphere then changed when he handed over both packets. They got into a conversation about the way to Loitokitok, which he knew was only about twenty or so miles away. 'Hapana mbale, (not very far)' was the classic answer, which could mean anything from one mile to fifty. 'But the road is very bad, it will take you until two o'clock' said one man pointing to a position in the sky where the sun would be at that time.

'Is the border open?' asked Kahinga.

The man shrugged: 'Sometimes open, sometimes closed.'

'Are there many vehicles coming through?' asked Kahinga.

'Maybe one or two each day,' was the answer…

The very fine longido dust poured in through every crack and crevice in the vehicle. If they kept the windows closed it was stifling hot and if they left them open the dust just continued to waft in. Finally Kahinga decided that the only thing to do was to keep going as fast as he could in the very rough conditions and they kept all the windows open. The area was open scrub interspersed with tall flat topped acacia thorn trees. Kahinga tried to stop the first vehicle coming the other way but it cruised past ignoring them and depositing more choking dust all over them. Nyamita was coughing and spluttering in the back: 'What do you fools think you are up to,' he yelled, 'We are all going to die out here in this filthy place.' When he got no answer he continued in a panicky voice: 'Where the hell are you taking me, this is ridiculous, what do you want, just tell me what you want.' He got no response to that either. Kahinga saw the dust of another car some five minutes before they saw the vehicle. The man in the back looking after Nyamita was sensible enough to know that they had to keep Nyamita quiet if they stopped and spoke to the approaching vehicle, so he waved the chloroform cloth at Nyamita and held his finger up to his face in a gesture that Nyamita clearly understood to mean: 'Keep quiet or you will get another dose of this.'

The approaching vehicle stopped; it was full of safari going whites with an African driver. Kahinga had taken off his balaclava and gave the usual greeting in Swahili: 'Jambo, (hello)',

'Jambo sana', was the response,

'Habari (how are you).'

'Mzuri (good)'.

'How far to the border,' asked Kahinga.

'Two miles, but it is very rough, it has taken fifteen minutes from the border.'

'The border must be open then?' Kahinga asked as innocently as possible.

'Yes but you have to hoot, there is not much traffic here, sometimes they keep people waiting for a long time.' Then he added: 'If you get through soon there are some Lions on a Zebra kill just the other side of the border.'

'Oh, thank you, we will watch out for them,' said Kahinga. 'That's all we need: to bump into Lions while we are walking through the bush,' he thought.

Both parties waved and Kahinga moved on. He drove very slowly for a mile and a half and then pulled up on the side of what was now little more than a track.

Peter adjusted the seat and mirrors in the very grand Mercedes and drove carefully out of Dar. He had left his Masai disguise in Dar but had hidden his rifle and spear in the extensive boot. He followed Kahinga by taking the road to Morogoro and then the Moshi turnoff. There was little traffic and he drove like the wind, as fast as he possibly could reaching more than a hundred miles an hour in places; the road was inconsistent, tarred on some stretches, good dirt on others and heavily corrugated in some other parts, so he had to have all his wits about him. He passed Kahinga just before the turnoff to

Tanga and was at the border before six. He was greeted with deference on both sides of the border when he presented his papers; Nyamita's passport was duly stamped. Shortly after he had safely passed through the border he took a right turn on to a side road, found a deserted beach stripped off and spent thirty minutes washing off as much of the greasepaint as he could. He remained in his smart suit, minus the padding but now looked like a white businessman. He took the Likoni ferry into Mombasa, and found and checked into the Manor Hotel under a false name. The Manor was an old traditional hotel in the middle of town. He then had another wash and got rid of any last vestiges of his previous disguise. He found a suitable store and purchased a bush shirt and long khaki trousers more in keeping with the heat and humidity of Mombasa. Quietly asking one of the junior hotel employees to direct him to the Arab quarter, he found a small, rather dirty repair shop. Peter assumed that he would not be known in the Arab community. Peter approached the proprietor with what he thought was a polite Arab greeting and showed him the dent in the door of the Mercedes: 'One week,' he was told.

Peter shook his head. 'I am in rather a hurry, I need it in a day; I really don't want my wife to know about this dent, but I need to go to Nairobi tomorrow evening.' The man smiled knowingly and quoted an exorbitant price. Peter knocked it down by half.

'Midday tomorrow-cash,' said the man.

Rafiki drove Kahinga's' pick-up, following the same route that the others took. She prayed that it would not breakdown again. There were fewer stops and she knew the way to Loitokitok so arrived there only about an hour later than Kahinga. Parking just off the track she followed the four wheel drive tracks on foot into the thorn scrub. Spotting the four wheel drive, Rafiki made a night-jar call and returned to the pick-up. Kahinga appeared five minutes later.

'You or one of your men must drive this vehicle through the border post. I will take the four-wheel drive back to Dar. But I don't want to be seen, so you must drive it out here and transfer any of the things you need to your own vehicle and then I can take the four wheel drive.'

Kahinga had already taken one of the men aside and spoken to him quietly: 'We arranged for N'guku and one of the other colleagues to be on the other side of the border. We are much later than I thought we would be so if he is still there, he will have been waiting for more than a week. I think that he will have already left, but I need to be sure of that.'

'Why don't we just drive through?'

'They won't let us through with this vehicle; we don't have the right papers; if we try it will just attract the attention of the police.'

'Take the Patchett,' said Kahinga, ' but only use it in an emergency, you heard about the Lions, so stay clear of them , but don't worry too much: if they are on a kill they will not be interested in you unless you get too close. So go five hundred steps away from the road here and then one thousand steps back across the border and then five hundred steps back to the road. The mountain will always be on your left and slightly behind you. If N'guku is still there just tell him to wait and then you should return here.' Kahinga made him repeat his instructions. 'You must hurry,' Kahinga repeated as the man ran off.

They had already moved the four wheel drive to about two hundred yards off the track, into a natural dip making it invisible from the road. The area was dry, dusty and populated with small thorn trees. There was some evidence of cattle being grazed, but the tracks and dung seemed old to Kahinga. The majesty of Mount Kilimanjaro towered above them just to the west; not that they had the time or the inclination to marvel at one of Africa's most spectacular sights.

Kahinga made Nyamita sit down with his back against a thorn tree once he had been laboriously hauled out of the vehicle. Kahinga re-tied Nyamita's hands and feet with his hands behind him, and then he gagged and blindfolded him. With relief his captors removed their balaclavas; they built a small fire and cooked some posho and meat and sat down to eat. Kahinga thought that it would take an hour and a half to establish whether N'guku was still in place. Nyamita struggled mightily against his bonds and eventually fell sideways away from the tree with his face in the dust. One of the men got up to pick him up but Kahinga motioned him away and went to make sure that he was able to breathe and then left him there for ten minutes. When they had finished their meal the men put their balaclavas back on; they picked Nyamita up and put him back against the tree and removed his blindfold. One of the men then fed him by hand and gave him some water whilst the other stood a few feet away with his Patchett pointing straight at Nyamita. Nyamita glowered but ate hungrily and said nothing. His face and hair was covered in dust.

Kahinga left them to it and moved the vehicle back to where Rafiki had parked his pick-up. They transferred all the fuel and the mattress and all their belongings to the pick-up and Rafiki then drove off, back towards

Moshi and Dar-es-Salaam. She was exhausted so within a few minutes had driven off the track and hidden behind a large bush and had immediately gone to sleep.

Kahinga returned to his people and motioned one of them to come with him. The man was surprised to see Kahinga's pick-up and no sign of the four wheel drive. 'You will drive this car through the border post, here are all the correct papers and you have your papers showing how you entered Tanzania through Namanga. Meet us on the other side, we will walk through.'

'How did this gari get here and where is...'

'I'll tell you later, we must hurry now.'

Just as the man approached the border post they all heard the flat distinct sound of a long burst from a sub-machine gun. The people at the post rushed out and looked around. They signalled the pick-up to stop and then walked over towards 'no-man's land.'

Kahinga motioned his one remaining man to stay where he was and keep a very good eye on Nyamita. He took one of the Patchetts and walked through the bush towards the border post. When it came into sight he could discern no movement at all on the Tanzanian side, he then walked round and saw four men in border guard uniform talking and gesticulating in what Kahinga presumed was an area of no man's land between the two posts which were not more than one hundred yards apart. Two of the men then walked purposefully back to the Tanzanian side and two went towards the Kenyan side. All the men respectively went into their little border huts; his pick-up stood motionless at the barrier. Kahinga waited a few minutes and there was no further action. He supposed that both sides were going to report that they had heard the sound of gunfire and were awaiting further instructions. He thought that any action was most likely from the Tanzanian side first, since Moshi was not far away and was a reasonably large major centre. Any reinforcements from the Kenyan side would either have to come from Namanga and that would take several hours since they would have to drive through the Amboseli Game Reserve or from Sultan Hamud on the main Nairobi to Mombasa road which was even further.

When he returned to their little encampment, he found that the men had tidied the place up and there was little evidence that anyone one had been there. Nyamita was asleep against the tree. Kahinga had decided that all things considered he would be better off on the Kenyan side of the border so he quietly indicated out of Nyamita's hearing what they were going to do. He hauled Nyamita to his feet having untied the bonds round his legs and removed the gag and blindfold. The leg bond rope was attached to his belt, he handed the rope to his colleague and he then led the way across the border following the footprints of the man that he had sent to look for N'guku. It was now nearing four in the afternoon and he wanted to be safely in Kenya long before the short tropical dusk turned to dark before six.

After an hour's sleep Macharia drove the same route as his colleagues except that he turned left towards Moshi instead of right. He decided to by-pass Arusha altogether and went via Sanya-Juu in the foothills of the mighty Mount Kilimanjaro to the east and the smaller Mount Meru in the west. Anticipating trouble at the border post he had sewn most of his money into seams in his jacket; he was certain that only the most thorough search would uncover the money but to avoid suspicion, he was careful to leave some money in his trouser pocket. He arrived at the Namanga border post just before five in the evening. For a few brief moments it looked quite peaceful, but then all hell broke loose; the police swarmed towards his vehicle and he was roughly hauled out of the driver's seat to the amazement of the curious onlookers. He was dragged towards the rear of the main border post building and locked in a cell where he was left for nearly an hour.

Macharia was then dragged into what he thought was an interview room and beaten with vicious kiboko (hippo hide) whips for half an hour before he was asked a single question.

A bleeding and barely conscious Macharia was plonked on a wooden chair in front of a very angry police inspector. 'Where, where is he?' shouted the inspector in Swahili.

Macharia just looked blank: 'Where is who? And why are you doing all this to me?' He thought to himself: 'Just think of Hola, this is nothing compared to Hola.'

The inspector was beside himself with fury. He had assumed that when Macharia arrived at the border post as he, the inspector had predicted they would find Nyamita and his abductors in the vehicle. He would be lauded at police headquarters in Dar-es-Salaam and maybe that long awaited promotion would come his way. He had taken the truck to pieces himself and found absolutely nothing except the small bundle of Macharia's personal possessions. No evidence of Nyamita or anything linking the vehicle to Nyamita could be found; the vehicle was completely clean.

The inspector came to within an inch of Macharia's face and the spittle flew: 'Who?' he shouted, 'Who, you know perfectly well who, where is he, tell me where he is or you will be beaten again.'

Macharia succeeded in looking completely blank and said: 'I don't know what you are talking about.'

Macharia winced as several more blows descended on his back which was now bleeding profusely. He pretended that he was about to lose consciousness and fell off his chair.

He was picked up and put back on the chair. 'Superintendent Nyamita, you know perfectly well who we are talking about.'

'Who is this Superintendent Nyamita?' asked Macharia, 'I have never heard of such a person. I don't know any people in the Tanzanian police.'

'He is not in the Tanzanian police you Kikuyu moron, he is in the Kenyan police.'

'I don't know anyone in the Kenyan police either; I don't like the police and always stay away from them; I fought them for years, in the forests, when the British were in charge, they don't seem any different now so I stay away.'

Another policeman came into the room and there was an urgent whispered conversation: 'Lungalunga, he drove through Lungalunga this morning,' the inspector said in disbelief.

'Yes, the report has just come through.'

Macharia was unceremoniously thrown out of the police station and his possessions dumped on top of him. He assumed that he was free to go but it was now after midnight. He found a cold tap and managed to wash some of the blood off himself. He eventually found his vehicle in a yard at the back of the station. The keys were still in the ignition but the cage on the back had been removed and was lying next to the vehicle, it looked as if some of the panels had been damaged.

He decided to get some sleep and leaving the vehicle where it was he unsteadily climbed into the cab and went to sleep. At five in the morning, stiff and sore, Macharia crawled out if the vehicle and in the dim light saw that he would need help to put the vehicle together again. He went out of the police station precinct and looked around the queues that were already gathering waiting for the border to open; after drawing a blank with several people he found a young Kikuyu man and offered him a lift to Nairobi if the man was willing to help him make his vehicle roadworthy again. The man's name turned out to be Abraham and he had a good mechanical knowledge; it took them several hours to put the cage back on the vehicle and to make certain that all the panels were in place. There didn't seem to be any mechanical damage to the vehicle but it had been dented and scratched in several places; Macharia wondered how Kinua would react to the change from the pristine condition in which he had lent the vehicle to the now rather scruffy looking pick-up that Macharia would have to return to him.

As it got light Abraham looked at Macharia and saw that he had been badly beaten up and he looked at the truck and asked: 'What happened to you, what is all this about, it looks as if you should see a doctor.'

'It's nothing really, they thought that I had something to do with the disappearance of some policeman from Kenya, but they were wrong.'

'So they beat you up like this?'

Macharia shrugged: 'I will complain when we get back to Nairobi, if I complain here they will just beat me again.'

They managed to pass through the border posts without any further impediment although the man on the Tanzanian side had the grace to look embarrassed when he saw Macharia's condition. They found a service station in Namanga after the border post and Macharia, with Abrahams help succeeded in cleaning himself up. Macharia treated his young guest to a meal and they refuelled the vehicle and continued on to Nairobi.

When Macharia had unpicked the seam in his now torn jacket, after he had cleaned himself up, and pulled out what was a quite a large sum of money Abraham looked at him curiously but asked no further questions; he realised that there was more to the story than Macharia was willing to disclose. On the two hour drive to Nairobi they discussed Macharia's involvement with the Mau-Mau and his adventures in the forests, which avoided any awkward questions. Macharia dropped his young companion in the centre of Nairobi wondering what Kinua's reaction would be when he saw the condition of his vehicle. He was still looking much the worse for wear on arrival at Kinua's garage: Kinua looked at him in amazement and said: 'Good heavens man, what on earth has happened to you, come I will take you to Sarah and she can fix you up or maybe take you to a doctor.'

'Look, the pick-up is a bit of a mess, you won't be very pleased with what you see,' said Macharia.

'Kahinga will fix that up, but let us get you to the house and Sarah will treat those cuts, it looks worse than Hola.'

They walked over to the house that Kinua had built near the garage and Sarah spent the next two hours treating Macharia's wounds. She and Kinua knew better than to ask questions.

✳   ✳   ✳

Chapter 29

Kahinga was following the clear footprints left by the man that he had sent to look for N'guku. Nyamita's hands were still tied behind his back but the blindfold and gag had been removed, Kahinga's colleague held the rope now tied to Nyamita's waist. Kahinga was some fifty yards ahead of the others; he caught a glimpse of a man in a Tanzanian police uniform standing looking at something on the ground. Fortunately he was looking away from Kahinga who gestured to the others to lie down; he also made a gesture to indicate that Nyamita should be gagged again. Using his considerable bush craft Kahinga crept up behind the man who Kahinga could now see was following the same tracks that they were following; after two hundred yards the policeman stopped abruptly, Kahinga presumed at some imaginary line indicating the ill-defined border. Kahinga crept closer, but suddenly the man raised his rifle and shouted: 'Stand still or I will shoot.' While the policeman was distracted Kahinga, who was now closer that ten feet, rushed him and with a savage blow to the back of the head, using his Patchett, knocked him to the ground.

The man he had sent to find N'guku came up and said: 'I thought that I was going to have to shoot him,' and added: 'I have found the place where N'guku was waiting but he left at least two days ago. There were some lions; I fired shots to scare them away. This man must be investigating the shots.' They dragged the unconscious policeman away from the tracks, tied him up with his bootlaces and propped him up against a tree. Kahinga thought that the policeman would be unconscious for an hour but by the time the border police had worked out what had happened it would be dark and no further action would be taken until dawn.

Kahinga said: 'The other man and Nyamita are just two or three hundred yards away. We must go and fetch them, but I don't want Nyamita to know what happened here,' indicating the unconscious policeman. 'We will have to wait for the pick-up coming through the border.' They watched unobserved through the thorn scrub as the barrier was lifted on the Tanzanian side. The man looked at Kahinga in amazement: 'I thought that we would be stuck here, with N'guku having already left.'

They went and fetched the others and the continued on their way. 'What happened,' he was asked.

'Patrol, now back at the border post,' he said shortly. They removed Nyamita's gag: 'You fools, you won't get away with this you know,' he growled.

Nobody took the slightest notice; they could all feel that they would quite soon have Nyamita back in Nairobi facing a legitimate court. It was a bit later than Kahinga had hoped so they hurried on. Kahinga stopped suddenly and started to back away; there was a low growl and they saw a lioness not more than thirty yards away crouching. He signalled for the others to back off slowly and quietly all the while keeping a close watch on the predator. The low velocity slugs in the sub-machine gun in his hand would have been useless if the animal had charged. The policeman's rifle had been left with him. Over a twenty minute period they backed away some one hundred and fifty yards. Kahinga considered his options: once darkness fell the group would be very vulnerable to attack from the pride, it seemed that the lions were on the move again having eaten the Zebra they had killed: he was sure it would be the same pride that they had been told about and they were probably moving away from the border posts and the obvious presence of humans. Kahinga then led the group back towards the border posts and when he had them in sight he turned and found the track. Arriving at the track, which he was sure was on the Kenya side of the border the group turned away from what they could see, now through the gloom of the rapidly falling dusk, the little huts that made up the post.

A walk of a few hundred yards found a very relieved man in Kahinga's pick-up. 'The lions just came past here,' he announced, 'I thought that you might bump into them.'

'We did, but saw them in time,' answered Kahinga, 'Any trouble getting through?'

'No, they were all in a state about the shots we all heard and I gave them the money as you suggested, so they let me through after a short inspection of the gari.'

They bundled Nyamita into the back of the pick-up and tied up his legs again.

'We need to eat.' They were certain that there would be no traffic at this time of night since the border post was now closed. A small fire was lit on the side of the road and they cooked a meal of mainly posho and meat. Nyamita was made to sit up in the truck and was fed by one of the men. While they were anywhere near Nyamita all the men were meticulous in keeping their balaclavas on.

An hour later they noticed a large number of bright lights and vehicles on the Tanzanian side of the border.

'Mnn,' said Kahinga, 'we will have to go now, they must be responding to the shots that were fired. There will be a response from this, the Kenya side soon, but maybe they have to come from a bit further away.'

They packed everything up hurriedly and Kahinga took the turnoff towards the Amboseli Game Reserve; they drove two hundred yards down the track and then Kahinga handed the wheel over to one of the others to follow him as he walked fifty yards in the darkness, into the bush. When he was certain that they could not be seen, even in the light, from either the game reserve track or the track they intended to take to the main Nairobi to Mombasa road, they stopped and the vehicle lights were switched off. 'Try to sleep, just make sure that that animal Nyamita is properly tied up. One person on guard, change every hour. I will take the second shift.' With that Kahinga promptly went to sleep in the front passenger seat.

Into the third hour of the wait they heard the noise of vehicles coming down the main track; Kahinga was woken and he walked through the bush to get a better view. Two large army trucks bounced past heading for the border post: from what was visible there were at least a dozen soldiers in each vehicle. They waited thirty minutes, making sure that there were no follow-up vehicles and then retraced their steps heading for the main road south of Sultan Hamud. Kahinga drove to make the best speed he was able. Within two hours they turned left on to the main road to Nairobi.

Rafiki was woken by the noise of vehicles coming from the direction of Moshi. It was now dark and the post would have been closed at dusk. She had of course not heard the shots so had no idea what was happening. When the racket stopped she waited thirty minutes and then slowly drove back on to the main track just using parking lights. When there seemed to be no more vehicle movement from either direction she was able to use the headlights. Stopping once or twice to stretch and relieve herself she arrived back in Dar by daybreak. Her friend was already in the house and greeted her with much conspiratorial interest. They had breakfast and then Rafiki said: 'I need some help; as you know I came here unofficially, so I need to go back the same way, I also need to clean and return this vehicle.' The friend nodded happily. 'But I also need a big favour,' There was an anxious look from her friend. 'I need a nun's outfit, a train ticket to Voi for today and you must lend me your Tanzanian passport.'

The friend looked amazed but was excited by the new adventure: 'I can book a railway ticket in my name and there is no problem with the passport, you can just post it back to me from Nairobi. I will have to find a way to get you a nun's outfit.' She was dying to hear about what she had assumed was an assignation, but Rafiki said nothing on the subject. The friend left and Rafiki spent a couple of hours cleaning the vehicle. She decided just to be herself and not put on another disguise as Peter had suggested and returned the four wheel drive to its owners. They were somewhat curious that an African woman had returned the vehicle but it was very clean and there was no damage so nothing was said. When Rafiki returned to the house her friend was ironing a nun's habit in the kitchen: 'Good heavens, how did you manage that?' she asked.

'Don't ask,' was the smiling response, 'I will need to return it though. 'You must now hurry, the train leaves at five o'clock; I can take you there.'

Rafiki then carefully dressed in the nun's habit, strapped the revolver round her waist, underneath the habit, and packed her other possessions into a suitcase. They made the train with a few minutes to spare. 'Are you going back to Munyu?' asked the friend.

Rafiki nodded: 'I must look after Kamau, he is only fifteen.' They embraced at the station. Rafiki had determined that the friend was not particularly well of so had given her a large wad of cash as a present, which was well appreciated.

Rafiki was safely ensconced in a first class carriage which she found she was sharing with two other African women. An attendant provided her with bedding as the train eventually moved out of the station and Rafiki climbed on to the top bunk and did not wake until three in the morning when they had to clear immigration and customs. She had a very difficult time at the Kenyan passport control: 'This picture does not look like you, it is without that church outfit that you now have on, how do I know that it is you?' She was asked time and again. After about thirty minutes of argument Rafiki reluctantly slipped one hundred shillings to the man and suddenly there was no problem and the passport was stamped.

Shortly after the border a man joined the two women in the compartment. They pulled all the blinds down and then the women quickly got up and left. Rafiki was very suspicious and fingered her gun under the nun's habit.

Suddenly the man produced a knife: 'All your money,' he demanded.

Rafiki was quite calm: 'Wouldn't you like a bit more than money?' she asked coyly and started to lift her habit to expose a length of leg. The man was surprised and was off guard for a few seconds when he found that he had a Smith&Wesson .38 revolver stuck in his face.

'Drop the knife or I will blow your head off.' The knife clattered to the floor as a look of pure terror crossed the man's face. 'Out,' said Rafiki. 'Out there,' she slid open the compartment door and shoved the man into the corridor, which was deserted. 'Open it,' she pointed the revolver to the carriage door leading to the outside. The man did as he was told. 'Get down the steps,' the man reluctantly complied. The train was travelling quite slowly: 'Jump or I will shoot you.'

They were right in the heart of the Tsavo National Park at this stage of the journey. 'The lions will eat me,' wailed the man.

'No,' said Rafiki, 'they will not touch a shenzi like you, they will leave you to the hyaenas and jackals; off, go on, off.' She fired a shot over the man's head. He let go and she saw him fall off into the darkness.

She unsteadily returned to her compartment which was close by. There was no sign of any other passengers. She picked the knife off the floor and was struggling to open the carriage window when the door opened and one of the two women that had originally been in the compartment with her entered: 'That man that was in here, where is he?' she asked in a harsh voice. Rafiki was holding the knife hidden in the folds of her habit.

'That way,' she pointed back down the train. The woman left and then quickly returned just as Rafiki had managed to force open the window and was about to toss the knife out. The woman looked suspiciously at Rafiki, but it appeared that she had not seen the knife. Rafiki stared her down and she left leaving the compartment door open. This time Rafiki managed to get rid of the knife and she closed the window.

Within a few minutes both women returned and asked aggressively: 'Where is that man, he was here and now he is not here, you must know where he is.'

Rafiki shrugged: 'He left, he is not here.' Inside she was absolutely fuming; these three were clearly part of some sort of criminal gang and had targeted Rafiki assuming, very mistakenly, that she was a defenceless woman travelling alone. She kept her cool, it would spoil everything if she was to make a fuss and was correctly identified.

The guard then came in asking: 'People said they heard a gunshot.'

Rafiki just looked at him: 'Not here,' she replied, 'I did not hear anything, but then I have been asleep.' The guard left and the women dragged their belongings out into the passageway looking suspiciously at Rafiki and muttering as they went: it seemed that they thought that the man had double crossed them and had somehow disappeared. Rafiki locked the compartment door and left it that way until the train pulled into Voi two hours later, when she quietly disembarked. The two women were on the platform looking in vain for their male accomplice. Rafiki left the station and waited on the side of the road. There is not much to Voi except a railway junction and she hoped that Peter would find her on his way through. She waited hours and was about to try and book on the train going north to Nairobi when a very dusty black Mercedes pulled up beside her: it was Peter. She flung her suitcase into the boot and they drove off in a flurry of dust.

She kissed him and said: 'A great improvement on a fat Jaluo policeman,'

'Yes, I ditched him as soon as I was able to.' He smiled; it was a relief to be together again. Neither of them said much for the first twenty minutes of the trip. They then exchanged brief descriptions of their various adventures since they had parted three nights earlier in Dar: 'I just hope that Kahinga got through the border safely; if he manages that we are home and dry,' said Peter, who really put his foot down on what was most of the way a good tar road.

'Careful,' said Rafiki on one of the occasions when the road reverted to its original dirt and the car slewed and skidded until Peter had wrested control of it once again, 'an accident here would wreck everything.'

They eventually drove into Sattimma at four in the morning: 'I must 'phone Giles and get him to put the boys on the next 'plane,' said Peter.

'Hopefully Kahinga will 'phone soon as well,' said Rafiki.

Kahinga was anxious to 'phone Sattimma as soon as he could. As they approached Athi River, checking that they needed no fuel he stopped the vehicle away from the pumps at a rather shabby looking service station. 'I urgently need to make a call to Nairobi,' he said to the Wakamba attendant.

'You must buy petrol,' was the surly response.

'I don't need any fuel, but I will pay you double for the 'phone call.' The attendant saw an opportunity to pocket some change so he unwillingly unlocked an office door and indicated the 'phone. Rafiki picked it up in the first ring: 'Everything under control, you still have the fat pig?' she asked anxiously.

'Yes,' said Kahinga shortly. He did not want to say too much since the attendant was obviously trying to listen to his end of the conversation.

'OK, where are you?'

'Athi River.'

'Come into Nairobi and then call me again and I will tell you where to go.' The phone was put down and Kahinga left fifty shillings on the counter and returned to his pick-up.

Although it was still very early Rafiki immediately 'phoned Wacheera: 'Where do you want him?' she asked without any preliminaries.

There was a moment's hesitation as Wacheera quickly orientated himself: 'For some reason, the house that his mistress occupied is still vacant. I have had it cleaned and there is now food in the place. There are plenty of his clothes still there. I will have it under surveillance within thirty minutes.' He made sure that Rafiki had the correct address.

'You will have to collect Nyamita's car and his papers and passport,' said Rafiki.

'I will be with you within half an hour,' responded Wacheera

Kahinga 'phoned two hours later. Rafiki gave him the address: 'Nyamita needs to be washed and in a suit, the police will come and pick him up in three hours, so make yourself scarce before that, but don't worry they already have the place under surveillance.' With some difficulty they found the address and bundled Nyamita out of the vehicle without attracting any attention from the neighbours.

There was no sign of any police presence but Kahinga was sure they were there. 'Hey, this is my place,' yelled Nyamita. They took no notice and made him undress while one of the men ran a bath.

'Get in and wash,' ordered Kahinga pointing the Patchett at him, 'and get a move on. Just keep an eye on this moron and I will find him some clothes,' he said to one of his colleagues. Kahinga rooted round in the wardrobes in the main bedroom and laid out a very smart suit, shirt, tie, underpants socks and shoes which he dusted off on the curtains. He returned to the bathroom: 'Out and dry yourself properly and get into those clothes,' he prodded him with the gun into the bedroom. Kahinga had carefully removed Nyamita's old clothes and holding them with a cloth took the bunch of keys out of his pocket and placed them in one of the suit pockets. 'Make some tea, just for one,' he told one of the men, 'and put all these clothes in our vehicle.' Handing him Nyamita's dirty and dusty clothes and shoes. Nyamita dressed slowly but could delay no longer and Kahinga prodded him with the Patchett into the lounge and made him sit down. He poured him a cup of tea and added two spoons of sugar: 'Sorry, there is no milk.' Nyamita just glowered at him.

The others, still wearing their balaclavas did as they were told and left the premises. Kahinga looking around, making sure that there was no evidence of their presence also left. He thought that the police would anyway tramp through the place and obliterate any signs of him and his men.

Out of curiosity they waited round the corner just to see what happened. Less than two minutes after they had vacated the place there was a rush of police from all sorts of hiding places in the vicinity of the house and then there was a parade of police cars with sirens howling, charging down the street. They caught a glimpse of Nyamita being bundled into a prison van in handcuffs and being driven off at speed.

'Pumwani,' Kahinga said when he was asked where they were going. They went to the house where the original briefings had taken place and went inside. As soon as the sole occupant saw them he left. Kahinga held up both hands: 'Ten minutes,' he mouthed.

'That was very well done, you were all great,' said Kahinga, 'but no discussion, not with anybody. Nyamita will face the court as he deserves, but if there is any evidence that he was abducted then the case will be weaker. The police will say that all they had was a tip-off that Nyamita was back in Nairobi and they went to the address that was given and found him there; that is all. There will be some money; I will show you all exactly how much in one week from now and we will meet here. We will share it all equally after all the expenses have been paid. It will not make you rich, but since we have done so well with bringing that animal back to face justice, there will be more jobs like this one.'

'Who paid?' He was asked.

'It is better that you do not know,' answered Kahinga.

'Was it Munyu?'

Kahinga shook his head: 'It is better that you do not know.'

Kahinga then drove to Sattimma. Peter and Rafiki greeted him warmly: 'Wacheera has told me that they have the fat pig in custody, so well done and thank you,' she said. They swopped stories about their various escapades since they had abducted Nyamita from Dar. Rafiki then mentioned what had happened to Macharia: 'We have had Macharia in the clinic over the last few days, he was badly beaten up, but he would not say anything although it looked like cuts from a kiboko.'

Kahinga winced and asked: 'Where is Macharia?'

'He is with Kinua for a few days.'

'OK. I will find him there.'

Kahinga just slept for the next three days although he did have a chance to see Macharia who gave him a graphic description of his ordeal at the border. 'Not as bad as Hola though,' said Macharia when he had finished. Kahinga just shook his head: 'Maybe there will be some other jobs like this, Nyamita is now in jail with the police.' Macharia looked interested, but said: 'We will need to fix up Kinua's pick-up, the police at Namanga made a bit of a mess of it.' They went and had a look. 'I think that I can get that fixed, within the next few days,' he told Kinua later. Kinua just nodded and said nothing.

Peter took charge of Kinua's vehicle and made sure that it was returned in pristine condition a week or so later.

Wacheera silently thanked the Kikuyu god Ngai, who he knew lived on Mount Kenya, for his good fortune in having Nyamita returned to him without lifting a finger. The police and he personally had been given great accolades, through the press and more personally through contacts with Government, for at last bringing Nyamita to justice. The preparation for the trial was well in hand and Wacheera was hoping for a speedy trial and he was confident of a conviction. He had already lined up Boniface and Otieno; he had tried to get Kariuki to cooperate but Kariuki was scared that there would be another trial connecting him with the abduction of Kamau, which he wanted to avoid at all costs.

Rafiki eventually went to see Wacheera, but told him very little about the abduction: 'It is better that you don't know any detail, 'she said, 'it did cost though.'

Wacheera nodded: 'I have paid fifty thousand shillings into the account that you told me about, from a very private and untraceable source. Do with it what you will.' Rafiki recovered just the expenses that she and Peter had incurred and gave Kahinga fifteen thousand shillings. There was a considerable balance which was paid into the clinic bank account: Don Watson raised an eyebrow when his accountant pointed it out and said: 'Looks OK to me, it is a direct payment from Mrs Lawrence.'

'Was it Munyu who gave you the money?' asked Macharia, when they were each given three thousand shillings.

'I have told you before that it is better that none of you know any of these details, so I will not be telling you anything,' Kahinga responded.

They all relived certain aspects of the adventure, Macharia was made to tell everyone about his ordeal at the border again and then Kahinga wound up the meeting by saying: 'We can all go back to our normal jobs looking after security here in Nairobi, but because we did such a good job this time, we will be asked to do other similar jobs in the future, but there is one thing that may prevent that happening,' he paused for effect and they all looked at him expectantly: 'Nobody except us knows what we did and why we did it, and it must stay that way. If anyone talks, the police will come and then we will all be in trouble and go to jail; taking a person from another country against his will, and bringing him here is a criminal offence. I am sure that Nyamita did not see any of our faces, so he cannot identify us, but he will certainly claim that he was illegally abducted and if he can prove that, the case against him will fail so all our efforts will be no good. So keep your mouths shut, now and always if you want to stay out of jail and if you want to be included in another job like this one.'

'N'guku, where is N'guku,' Kahinga was asked.

He shrugged. There had been some rumours regarding his colleague but he was not in a position to discuss them with anyone at that moment.

The day before she and Peter were due to pick the boys up at Nairobi airport Rafiki had a call from Mwangi Mkubwa that made her blood run cold, after the usual preliminaries Mwangi said to her: 'There is a lot of excitement here among the people who desperately do not want Nyamita to be brought to trial. As you know he is claiming that he was abducted and they now say that they have a witness, a man called N'guku, who for a very large sum of money will tell the court that he took you and Munyu, dressed as Masai to one of the Tanzanian border posts. This may destroy your case and they may have to let Nyamita return to Tanzania, not to mention what might happen to you. You will have to fix this, I can do nothing.'

Rafiki went to see Kahinga: 'I will sort it, don't worry,' was all he said.

The conversation round the dinner table at Sattimma once they had picked the boys up from the airport was ribald and light-hearted:

'Giles wasn't really sure that ngweko was a suitable dinner table discussion for the family in London,' volunteered John one evening.

'Who raised it,' asked Rafiki looking accusingly at Kamau.

'Belinda, their daughter,' said Kamau defensively. 'Somehow I explained it to her and some of her friends one evening. She said that she thought that it should adopted by the British. It would make people less shy or some such argument.'

'They weren't exactly shy,' said John.' Couldn't keep them out of my bed, not that I wanted to.'

'Play any rugby?' asked Peter, trying to change the subject. 'Yes,' answered Kamau, 'They let me play for Robert's college team once with him in the team as well. Without any practice at all we easily developed an understanding. We absolutely ran rings around the opposition, I really enjoyed it and am determined that I should try to get into Oxford as well now.'

The boys had no knowledge at all of the Nyamita abduction and asked no questions. They happily returned to school.

Chapter 30

Nyamita's trial attracted wide attention both in Kenya and as it developed, overseas as well, especially in Britain, the former colonial power.

On the opening day counsel for the defence asked if he could make a statement which after he and the prosecution counsel had been allowed to approach the bench was granted. 'The Judge said: 'This is a most unusual request, but it is an unusual case so your request is granted.'

'The defendant claims that he was illegally abducted from his home in Tanzania, so therefore this trial is illegal and has no basis in law. He should be allowed to return to Tanzania and if the prosecution can provide sufficient evidence then a case can be made for his legitimate extradition to face a legitimate trial. The defence therefore requests that this trial be declared null and void and that my client be driven to the airport, right now, and be embarked on a flight to Dar-es-Salaam.'

'Does the prosecution have anything to say about this?' asked the Judge.

'There is no evidence to support the defendant's claims; this is just part of the web of lies that surrounds this case. The prosecution intends to prove its case that the defendant was instrumental in…'

'Objection, we are discussing the legitimacy of the case, not the case itself, which should be thrown out.'

'Sustained; does the prosecution have anything else to say in this matter.'

'Your honour, I repeat there is not a shred of evidence to support the defendants claims, if he would take the stand on this issue alone we can prove that the only possible conclusion one can arrive at is that he is here voluntarily.'

There was a whispered conversation at the defence table.

'The defendant is prepared to take the stand on this issue alone,' was the response from the defence.

Nyamita took the stand. He stood erect and appeared the epitome of success respect and self confidence in his well cut suit and clean shirt and tie and if they were visible his highly polished shoes. The public gallery looked surprised and if one had been able to read their collective thoughts it would have been: 'This man is an upright and honest citizen, he would never tell any lies.'

The counsel for the defence stood up: 'Mr Nyamita tell us in your own words the experience that you had when you were taken against your own will, late at night in a street in Dar-es-Salaam, thrown into the back of a pick-up truck and then brought here to Nairobi.'

Nyamita started confidently: 'My brother and I were in a late night meeting and came out into the street where we had a short conversation, he then went off to his own car and I got into my car, which was just outside the meeting place, and I intended to drive home. On the way home this pick-up truck banged into me, deliberately I now realise, as I was waiting at a traffic light, so I got out to see what the damage was and I was then hit on the head with a rungu. The next thing that I knew was that I was being transferred to another four wheel drive safari vehicle. They put this cloth on my face with some sort of dawa that made me lose consciousness, but also I was tied up very tightly and gagged and blindfolded most of the time. I was then driven for a very long time. There were stops for toilet breaks and food and fuel.' He hesitated.

'Please continue,' said the defence counsel.

'I then noticed that progress was much slower and that the road was very rough. We stopped once to talk to the driver of another vehicle, there was a short conversation in Swahili just asking how much further to the border post. The dust was terrible, very fine choking dust which covered everything. Then we drove off the track so that we could not be seen and one of the men was sent away, to do what I do not know. I was given food and we waited. I heard shots, quite a long way away, probably from a sub-machine gun and then in a hurry my legs were untied and the blindfold was taken off and we walked first away from the road and then parallel with the road. I think that we were walking round a small border post somewhere. We then stopped for a while; I thought that I caught a glimpse of a man in uniform. We waited for quite a long time and then walked on. We nearly walked into some lions, but the leader of the group seemed to know what he was doing and we managed to back away without being attacked. We then found another track and after a short walk we found another pick-up.

We stopped to cook food but then there were lights and the noise of vehicles on what I think was the Tanzanian side of the border, so we left quickly. We were by this time on the Kenya side of the border. We then went a little way and drove off into the bush for quite some time. I thought that I heard the noise of trucks on the main track and shortly after that we left and then we were on a main road, which must have been the Mombasa to Nairobi road; we stopped for a short time, presumably to make a telephone call. I was blindfolded and gagged all this time so I could only guess where we were. We continued on our way but again stopped again, probably to make another telephone call and shortly afterwards we came to my house in Nairobi. I was made to get in the bath at gunpoint and then they made me dress in one of my suits and they gave me a cup of tea and left. Five minutes later the police arrived and arrested me. The people that had kidnapped me must have told the police, otherwise how would they know I was there.'

'Anything else to add, that was very comprehensive and detailed description of your ordeal, it should be enough to convince the court that you were indeed kidnapped and that you should be released immediately,' said the defence counsel.

The chief prosecutor stood up: 'Your honour I have some questions of the defendant.'

'Objection, your honour,' from the defence. 'Surely the case has been made, the man should be released.

'Overruled,' the Judge indicated the prosecution bench: 'please proceed with your questions.'

'Mr Nyamita, do you live in the same house as your brother in Dar-es Salaam.'

'Yes,' said Nyamita confidently.

'Mr Nyamita, this business meeting that you had with your brother very late at night, sometime after ten pm. What was the nature of the meeting?'

'It was just a business meeting at the premises of a business that is owned by my brother.'

'If you live in the same house as your brother in Dar why did you need to go to the premises to have this meeting, so late at night? Also it must be a very unusual business if it was still operating that late at night.'

'Yes it is a night club, so it operates at night, we went to talk to the manager,' answered Nyamita confidently amid sympathetic titters from the public gallery.

'Can you give the court the address, please?'

Unthinkingly Nyamita gave the address of Mrs Koinange's establishment.

'What sort of night club, are you sure that it isn't just a brothel and that you were there as a client.'

Nyamita hesitated: 'Please remember that you are here under oath,' intoned the Judge.

'It is just a night club, there is a bar...'

'And girls,' interrupted the prosecution. 'I can produce a witness, who has seen you in that place, that very address, it is just a brothel isn't it, just tell the court the truth for once in your life.'

There was a titter from the gallery and Nyamita said quietly: 'It is just an ordinary night club.'

'It is not, it is a brothel, now let us continue please.' And before Nyamita could say anything more the chief prosecutor asked: 'These people you say abducted you, did you see any of them?'

'No, they wore balaclavas all the time.'

'Did you hear them speak?'

'Very little, the leader spoke Swahili the few times that I heard him speak.'

'How many days were you held captive?'

'Three or Four, I think.'

'Three or four, you think, don't you know?'

'I was unconscious some of the time, I have told you that.'

'And you are trying to tell me that during the three or four days, you think, that you were held captive not one person uttered a word that you could hear.'

'They must have been told not to speak to me, I tried talking to them but I was ignored.'

'They must have been very disciplined.'

'Maybe.'

'Can you describe any of them, short, fat, thin, tall.'

'They were all quite short, like the Kikuyu or Kamba, not big like the Luo.'

'Anything else?'

'They obviously knew about guns, they all had guns and were careful with them.'

'Guns, what guns?'

'I saw some of them with Patchett sub-machine guns and the some of them with revolvers.'

'How many of them were there?'

Nyamita thought hard: 'At the beginning there were five including the leader, then there were only four. There were only two when we waited in the bush because two were sent off on different errands. Then when we had walked through the bush there were three again and then on the road there were four; maybe one of the people had driven a pick-up through the border post quite legitimately.'

'Which border post did you walk around?'

'I don't know, I was blindfolded much of the time. It was a very small one, though. The only border post that I have been through is Namanga, it was definitely not Namanga.'

'Can you tell me the registration numbers of the vehicles that you say that you were abducted in.'

'No, I tried to read them when I had the opportunity but they were always obscured by dust and mud.'

There was a titter from the gallery.

The defence was handed a note then excitedly asked for permission to approach the bench again: 'Yes, what is it this time?'

'Could we have an adjournment until tomorrow, please your honour, we have a critical witness who will be here in the morning. I am certain that this witness will convince the court that the defendant was abducted.'

'Are you certain of this, we have already wasted enough time on this nonsense.'

'Yes, your honour.'

'The court is adjourned until the morning,' said the judge, he banged the gavel.

On the resumption the prosecution said confidently: 'I call upon Mr N'guku to take the stand.'

Wacheera, Peter, Rafiki and Kahinga had all decided to attend the trial that day. The three men who had taken a very close interest in the Kariuki trial were behaving as if they expected some major turning point in the current proceedings.

There was a hushed silence in the court. Everyone waited and waited and waited.

'Could we have a brief adjournment?' asked a very troubled defence lawyer.

'Five minutes,' agreed the judge.

Ten minutes later an extremely flustered defence lawyer returned to the court: 'Mr N'guku has disappeared, he is no longer available.'

'May I resume my cross-examination of the defendant now please,' asked the prosecution.

Kahinga left the gallery and whispered in Rafiki's ear: 'What the crocodiles don't eat will be washed into the sea.' Her eyes widened and then she nodded. The three excited spectators were very still and they had all gone ashen.

'Do you know what these are?' a bunch of keys were held up, together with his passport and Kenya police warrant card, by the prosecution.

'They are my car keys and my house keys for the house in Dar, as well as my passport and warrant card,' responded Nyamita now back in the witness stand.

'They were found in your jacket pocket.'

'So, someone must have put them there.'

'The only fingerprints on the keys and documents are yours.'

Nyamita shrugged: 'I told you that I was abducted and I have given you a detailed description of the abduction. The suit I was wearing when the police came and arrested me I have not seen for months. The keys and documents must have been placed in the pocket of the suit.'

'What happened to the clothes that you say you were abducted in?'

'I saw them being taken away.'

'Changing the subject, why were you in Dar-es-Salaam at all?'

'I was shot in a drug raid and I was recuperating in hospital; my brother lives in Dar and I thought it might help my recovery if I spent some time at the seaside.'

'What, more than a year?'

Nyamita was silent.

'I will bring evidence that you left the hospital in which you were recovering, in the middle of the night and before the doctors were ready to discharge you. You will recall that this was during the time that the young boy was…'

'Objection, this is not the trial. We are in the process of establishing that Mr Nyamita was abducted against his will.'

'Sustained.'

'Where did you hide your Mercedes when you drove back here?'

Nyamita looked at the prosecutor in disbelief: 'The car should still be in Dar, I have told you in detail how I was abducted against my will. Ask the people who abducted me.'

'The police found it three streets from the house where you were arrested. What do you have to say about that?'

Nyamita was genuinely shocked: 'That is impossible,' he started to shake,

'I told you I was abducted and brought here against my will. The car has a dent in the left rear door where I was deliberately bumped into.'

'We have a record of you coming through the border at Lungalunga, and here are the stamps from both the Tanzanian and Kenyan side of that border post on the day before you were arrested.' The prosecutor waved the keys and handed them and the documents to the judge. 'There is no doubt about it. Also there is no dent in the door of the car. The Tanzanian police have confirmed the record independently.' The prosecutor shoved a document under Nyamita's nose. Nyamita refused to look at it; he pushed the prosecutors hand away and stood up to his full height of six foot two and said to the court:

'This whole thing is a set up; I was genuinely abducted and brought here against my will. If my car is here as you say, then it was driven here under false pretences and I have never been anywhere near the border post you mention.'

The defence just looked utterly baffled and had nothing to say. Nyamita was asked to step down from the stand.

There was a deathly silence in the courtroom and the chief prosecutor said: 'To summarise, your honour, this claim of abduction is pure make-believe. The defendant lied about his so called business meeting. He is unable to describe any of his captors; he was apparently unable to get a single word out of even one of them. He could not tell us the registration numbers of the vehicles he was supposedly abducted in and to cap it all there is incontrovertible evidence that he drove his big black Mercedes motor car into this country a few days before he was arrested by the good work of the police acting on a tip-off. I submit that the case proceeds as designated and that there should be no further discussion of abduction.'

The Judge looked at the defence, who nodded and then said: 'The court will resume in the morning as scheduled.'

Nyamita was led away without looking at his defence team.

That evening while Peter and Rafiki were quietly celebrating there was another call from Mwangi: 'They are going to get Boniface.'

'But he is in jail, how can they get him there?' said Rafiki. There was no answer and the 'phone was put down.

Rafiki immediately 'phoned Wacheera: 'I have it on good authority that they are going to kill Boniface, in jail,' she told him.

There was a brief silence at the other end: 'Your information is correct, but I am afraid that we are too late, I have just been told that he was killed in the showers at six o'clock this evening.'

'That blows that case for the prosecution, completely. All you have now is Otieno, unless we can persuade Kariuki to cooperate.'

'We have Otieno in protective custody,' said Wacheera tiredly. 'I am not sure that we can do anything more about Kariuki though.'

'You are going to have to see Kariuki and see if you can persuade him,' said Peter to Rafiki after the phone had been put down. 'We can't let it go now, we are so close.'

※　※　※

CHAPTER 31

When Nyamita was brought back before the court a few days later, he was still well dressed and he had an air of someone who still thought he had a chance of an acquittal. He knew that the case against him had been severely affected by the death of Boniface. The fact that he had not been able to prove that he had been abducted was a severe blow, but he still had hope. He knew that Otieno was an unreliable witness and that was the best hope of the defence.

The charges all related to the kidnap of Kamau Lawrence and as they were read out Nyamita pleaded 'not guilty' to each and every charge.

Peter and Rafiki had decided against further attendance at any part of the trial, unless they were called as witnesses. Kahinga had found a sudden interest in repairing boreholes and he had told his colleagues that they should stay right away from the trial: 'Our job is done, nothing will be served by attending the trial and we should let the police and the people in the courts do their job. I am sure that Nyamita will be jailed for a long time.'

Otieno's testimony was jumbled and inconclusive. The defence were cockahoop and they advised Nyamita that they thought he would get an acquittal.

Then the prosecution said: 'I have one more witness to call who has just agreed to testify, I call Mr. Johanna Kariuki to the stand.'

Nyamita collapsed in his box and had to be removed from the proceedings for a few hours.

Kariuki proceeded to give the court chapter and verse about his dealings with Nyamita. He told them in a quiet voice about all his visits to the hospital and how they had planned the kidnapping of Kamau together. He told them about his call to Peter and repeated the words of the call precisely and where he had made it from.

Hi testimony tied in with the rather jumbled testimony of Otieno.

The only positive testimony from Nyamita's point of view was a written reference from his old mentor Chief Inspector McLoughlin, long since retired and living in England which said:

'Mr Nyamita was a recruit in my charge from the day he left the police training centre until he was promoted to another command some ten years later. He was always the most diligent of the local recruits and at all times behaved in a most exemplary manner, his honesty was always beyond question. The idea that he has been involved in corruption and possibly child kidnapping is beyond my comprehension. There is no possibility that I believe he has been involved in any of these schemes. If indeed he is found guilty then I would ask that the sentence be as lenient as is permissible.'

Throughout the short trial Nyamita maintained that he had been abducted and that the trial therefore had no basis in law.

In his summing up the Judge said: 'Mr Nyamita, the evidence of your involvement and indeed masterminding the abduction of Kamau Lawrence is overwhelming. The fact that a man in who had been put in a position of trust in the community even contemplated such activity is difficult to believe. I therefore have no hesitation in finding you guilty on all charges. The minimum sentence that I can impose is twenty years in jail. There will be no appeal and there are no grounds for any kind of leniency or parole.'

The court was hushed as the once mighty powerful police chief was led away. There was no sense of triumph, just sadness that a man with Nyamita's obvious abilities had chosen to use his position to further his own interests and not those of the wider community. Among the Jaluo there was a sense of disbelief and the mistaken sentiment that somehow they as a community had been wronged.

Afterward Peter asked Rafiki what she had done to persuade Kariuki to cooperate with the prosecution:

Rafiki had gone to the jail not even sure that Kariuki would agree to see her. 'I am from his age group in the village where we were both brought up,' she said to the authorities.' Kariuki was looking his absolute worst; he was grey and had lost weight. There were some polite greetings to start the conversation and Rafiki said to him:

'I know that the kidnapping of my son was all Nyamita's idea but we need your testimony to make sure he is convicted. If you turn state witness they will not prosecute you for the abduction. I can get that in writing from Wacheera and the prosecution.'

'Why should I help you, you have not done anything for me,' he responded belligerently.

'Maybe there are some things that I can help you with,' said Rafiki firmly, 'how are your children, for example?'

'What do you know about my children?'

Rafiki shrugged: 'Maybe they are OK, but that is not what I hear from Wainaina.'

Kariuki looked away and despite himself he wiped away a tear.

He asked to be returned to his cell.

After another unsatisfactory visit Rafiki returned on the third occasion, this time with the written guarantees that he would not be prosecuted for the Kamau kidnapping if he turned state witness.

'How are you children?' asked Rafiki as Kariuki read through the documents.

Kariuki burst into tears: 'That bitch of a wife of mine has taken up with another man, I think that he is a gangster from Pumwani, she never comes here anymore. The children are forgotten, they are running wild all over the place and I think they will get no education at all. They will die soon unless something is done.'

Rafiki tried to look sympathetic: 'If you turn state witness I promise you that I will look after your children. I know that they are good kids, they will be properly brought up and go to the right schools.'

Kariuki had immediately perked up: 'You would do that, after all that has happened?'

Rafiki nodded: unbeknown to Kariuki she had already rounded the kids up, a girl of twelve and a boy of ten and had taken them back to Sattimma and then the village, where currently her mother was looking after them.

'I have no argument with your children and wish them no harm; you have already been punished. It is my duty to make certain that Nyamita is also punished.'

'Boniface was killed so he could not be a witness; will the same thing happen to me?'

'No, you will have noticed that some other people in this jail have suddenly started to look after you.'

'Yees,' said Kariuki hesitantly.

'That is your protection until after the trial, after that the police will take over.'

'Those are Mwangi Mkubwa's people.' He said.

Rafiki nodded as she left.
Peter hugged her: 'Unbelievable,' he said.

✳   ✳   ✳

ABOUT THE AUTHOR

Guy Hallowes was born and brought up on a farm in the so called 'White Highlands' of Kenya (described The first book of the 'Winds of Change' trilogy—'No Happy Valley'), and attended school in Nairobi.

He lived for many years in South Africa and Botswana as well as the UK

He now lives in Sydney, Australia.